Pra

"This f   s
and in   a
fascina   had ch   n
life yet   , and he owns a
dog that will steal readers' hearts."   —*RT Book Reviews*

"A well-written novel that spills over with description, both
in terms of character backgrounds and rich settings. Its
characters spring from the pages with vitality, emotion,
and reality."   —*Bookreporter*

Please Don't Tell

"Brawn, bravado, and romance . . . Adler is in top form
in her latest thriller. She delivers fascinating characters
[and] twists that shock and surprise."   —*Mystery Scene*

"A page-turner . . . [These] are among the most appealing
figures in a thriller."   —*Publishers Weekly*

"Told with Elizabeth Adler's knack for terrific female
characters and breathtaking twists, *Please Don't Tell* will
keep you guessing, right up to the end."
—*Night Owl Reviews*

"Elizabeth Adler, veteran author of twenty-eight novels, is
in top form in her latest romantic thriller."
—*Mystery Scene*

"A wonderful, romantic thriller."   —*RT Book Reviews*

Also by Elizabeth Adler

One Way or Another

ELIZABETH ADLER

St. Martin's Paperbacks

This is a work of fiction, All of the characters, organizations, and events portrayed in this novel are either products of the author's imagination or are used fictitiously.

ONE WAY OR ANOTHER

Copyright © 2015 by Elizabeth Adler.
Excerpt from *The Charmers* copyright © 2016 by Elizabeth Adler.

For information address St. Martin's Press, 175 Fifth Avenue, New York, NY 10010.

ISBN: 978-1-250-05820-1

Our books may be purchased in bulk for promotional, educational, or business use. Please contact your local bookseller or the Macmillan Corporate and Premium Sales Department at 1-800-221-7945, ext. 5442, or by e-mail at MacmillanSpecialMarkets@macmillan.com.

Printed in the United States of America

St. Martin's Press hardcover edition / July 2015
St. Martin's Paperbacks edition / July 2016

St. Martin's Paperbacks are published by St. Martin's Press, 175 Fifth Avenue, New York, NY 10010.

10 9 8 7 6 5 4 3 2 1

PROLOGUE

~

ANGIE

Fethiye, Turkey

The sea is aquamarine. Azure, now, as I sink deeper into it, the color and texture of bridesmaid's velvet. Translucent, though. Even with my water-pressed eyes I can see the two of them up on deck, champagne bottle held aggressively in the woman's hand, which a moment ago she'd swung at me, striking my temple where my hair grows in a soft coppery-red wave. Now bloody.

I'm surprised no one noticed my fall. I'm also surprised how little sound a body makes hitting the ocean. I slid in silently, with scarcely a bubble to mark my entrance. I did not even leave a wake behind the boat as it sped on.

A watery grave was never my intention; somehow, I always felt I should pass gently in the night, safe in my own soft bed, to some other warm and welcoming place not too different from the one I already inhabited, where everything went on much as before, only more smoothly.

It seems I was wrong. I was going down again, for the last time, I knew it now. Swept along by a swift current, my lungs filled with water, the salt taste filled my mouth, stung my still-open eyes that I seemed unable to shut.

I didn't see anyone, though I did hear the faint shrug of the boat.

Heard an unknown male voice say, "She is dead." Then, "No, she may live."

I hoped he was right.

The woman who had wielded the deadly champagne bottle, and who stood in the stern of a fast-departing black yacht watching as Angie disappeared into the sea, was known only as Mehitabel. No need for a last name in her way of life where most people knew each other only by their first; some invented, as was her own, some real, as was Ahmet Ghulbian's, the billionaire owner of the fast yacht who saw no reason to falsify a name so world renowned, like Onassis, for its success story and his wealth.

Mehitabel was not Ahmet's mistress, not even a some-time lover; she was his long-term cohort, keeper of his secrets, of which there were many, and carry-outer of his commands, whatever they might be.

Mehitabel never refused to do anything Ahmet asked of her. Their deal was unspoken, noncontractual, but perfectly understood by both for the simple reason that they were essentially alike: both were immoral to the *nth* degree; both driven by needs unknown to most people; and both incapable of deep emotion.

Mehitabel cared for no one other than herself; she would never have *given* her life for Ahmet, but she would *take* other people's lives for him. That was what he liked about her and he compensated her well for her services. Personally, Ahmet was not a man who liked to get his hands "dirty." There were people like Mehitabel for that.

Watching the red-haired girl struggle in the wake of the fast-moving boat, Mehitabel did not so much as crack a smile. A shrug was the most she could summon in response, as she walked away, barefoot, since Ahmet allowed no shoes on his immaculate teak deck, her black dress blending into the blackness of the boat, of her surroundings.

All she was thinking was, So, another one bites the dust, or this time, "swallows up the sea." She almost allowed herself to enjoy the thought.

1

Marco Polo Mahoney sprawled happily in a listing sun-lounger whose webbing straps would certainly not last much longer. Still, it was a comfortable spot to rest and sip every now and again from a bottle of arak, a bit acrid but it gave him a peaceful buzz. Pleasant for the time of the evening. Sixish? It had to be sixish, didn't it? A man certainly could not be found drinking earlier; people might think badly of him.

He reached out to stroke his dog's ears. What the hell, he was on holiday and he liked a drink or two. Maybe more. Sometimes. But drinking alone was not supposed to be good for you; he should stir himself, go out and find some company in the village. He got to his feet and stood surveying his own small part of the southern Turkish coast: a strip of white beach, a turquoise sea turning azure where it met the deeper blue of the sky now darkening with storm clouds, all set against a green, foresty background.

Marco was a well-known portrait artist. He was thirty-five, attractively craggy, currently bearded because he never shaved on holiday; brown hair brushed straight back and salty-stiff from swimming in the sea; dark blue eyes narrowed against the sun, eyes which seemed to see everything. At least that's what his sitters said, and it was true. He saw all their flaws, something they also said made them uncomfortable. But of course he was worth it.

Marco was in good shape though he never worked out. He'd played basketball in his youth; tennis too, but more often he was the one on the sidelines, charcoal in hand, sketching the action. The girls had been flattered, the boys called him a wuss. He'd laughed, but that passion was what made him who he was today, sought out by the rich, the famous; a man who knew how to play the social game but, when on his own, wore old shorts and went barefoot, like now. He was also a man who enjoyed solitude.

He was taking a short vacation, alone but for his dog, renting a cabin and sailing a small wooden boat known as a gulet out of the Turkish port of Fethiye. He was sun-brown and naked but for his bathing shorts—surfers' shorts, baggy-legged, hanging low on his lean hips—a scuffed pair of ancient flip-flops dangling from his toes.

He lifted his face to catch the last of the sun, welcoming its warm caress. He knew he should have remembered about the sunblock; had his girlfriend been with him it would not have been forgotten. The daughter of an English lord, the Honorable Martha Patron was consistent, persistent, and insistent. You knew exactly what you were getting with Martha; slightly severe beauty of the straight nose, high cheekbones, tightly pulled-back blond hair variety. It would have been worn in a ponytail on vacation, but in what Martha would surely have termed "real life" she would have worn it in a neat bun sitting low on her long neck. In bed though, it hung loose and soft over her shoulders.

On vacation too, Martha would have worn a designer bikini with a designer cover-up, which Marco knew from experience would probably be of some chiffonish material in a gentle green or blue, with rope-sole wedge heels, the real thing, made of canvas in Spain or somewhere like that. Martha was the kind of woman who always knew where they made things and where to get them, how to be first with them. With everything, actually.

Which was why Marco was still surprised she would go for a guy like him, a bit of a scruff really, his light streaky brown hair too long, always in shorts or jeans; he didn't own a real shirt other than the ones she bought him, and which were mostly still in their plastic wrappers. He did own a pair of shoes, though. They had belonged to his grandfather, handmade by Berluti in Paris many moons ago. Marco kept them polished to a rich gleam in respect for that grandfather who had raised him, and also in case he might one day have to wear them to a stylish event in some international city where shoes were the expected norm, though in any case he usually got away with sneakers.

In "real life," which this vacation most certainly was not, Marco was "an artist" as Martha kept on reminding him. "A *portrait artist,* in fact," she would add, pleased because Marco's clients included some of the top international CEOs, men whose likenesses Marco painted to keep the wolf from his door, enabling him, financially, to slip away from that reality into the glorious reality of this vacation, where he could be alone. Apart, that is, from his dog, Em, who went everywhere with him.

Long story short, he'd reply when strangers were curious about the grizzled mutt always at his heels, always at his side in cafés, always tucked under his arm when he traveled. Small and unbeauteous, Em lived in a part of Marco's heart that understood the loneliness from which he had rescued her.

When he'd found her, a few years ago, he'd been alone

on a terrace café in Marseilles. The place did not even have
a view and he'd stopped there solely for the purpose of a
quick caffeine fix, served in one of those short, dark green
cups with the gold rim all French cafés seem to use; plus,
of course, a glass of wine made from vines grown up on a
hill near St. Emilion *and* an almond croissant made with
enough butter to die from. That's when he saw the animal-
catcher van with its wire cage drive slowly by. The dog
sat, small, grayish/brownish, youngish, a street survivor.
Until now. The van stopped. A man got out on the passenger side, strode across, reached for the dog. Marco got
there first.

"Oh no you don't," he said, or words to that effect,
quickly scooping the mutt from under the man's hands.
"This dog is mine." And so of course, from then on
it was.

He named the dog Em, for the St. Emilion he'd been
drinking when he saw her. It seemed to fit and she responded to the name from first go. Now, of course, that's
who she was. Em. Marco's dog. She ate anything, which
was useful since he took her everywhere. He would not
visit a country that would not accept his dog, not fly an
airline where she would be made to fly in the hold, would
not stay at a hotel that did not welcome her as well as him.
He was, Martha told him, more in love with that bloody
dog than with her. Marco did not admit it but it could be
true. And that was why the dog was with him now, on this
beautiful southern Turkish coast, sharing the small, white-
washed plain slab of a one-room house with the bright
blue wooden doors and shutters he'd painted himself, and
the even smaller boat, the old wooden gulet, as well as the
orange inflatable from which he fished every day.

If he was lucky and caught something bigger than six
inches, big enough not to throw back in, that evening
Marco would grill it over hot coals on an improvised bar-

becue made with stones and a piece of wire mesh. He'd share it with the dog, sitting outside under the stars, moving on from the arak to that odd Turkish wine with the slight fizz that caught in his throat but which he enjoyed. Other evenings, they'd walk to the village café/bar where they'd sit under the spreading shade of the ancient olive tree and devour roast goat and couscous flavored with lemon, or a sandwich on thick crusty bread with sweet tomatoes picked that very moment from the garden, with sliced onion and crumbly feta cheese.

The proprietor, Costas, a lean, haunted-looking man in his forties with a springy mustache, very white teeth, and deep blue eyes, knew them by now, and there was always something special for Em: a bone that might have come from a dinosaur it was so big and which made Marco pause to think twice about what he might be eating; or a bowl of fishy stew complete with heads and tails, of which Em seemed particularly fond.

Anyhow, of an evening and sometimes deep into the warm night, Costas's café/bar became their place, where they were known and there was always company and conversation, and where there was always somebody who spoke enough English to make sense of it all. It was a good, simple life, quite separate from Marco's life in Paris, and the cities where he painted rich men's portraits and their wives in pearls and diamonds and small, superior smiles. Still, he made a good living at that, and despite the drawbacks he enjoyed it. And it paid for all this. *This* kind of life, this village, this coast. *This,* he loved.

Sprawled in his sagging lounger, he swapped back to the arak, took another swig, pulling a face. He told himself he really should go a bit more upmarket, spring for the extra couple of bucks and drink something that did not make his eyes water. He turned to watch as a yacht chugged slowly out of the harbor, its black hull cutting smoothly through the waves. The sky had darkened, the air was tense with the threat of thunder, and lightning flickered quick as a blink. A storm was approaching and pretty fast too, as Marco knew from experience they did in this area. The storms could be severe and in his opinion the boat would have been better off waiting it out in the harbor, or at least moored close to shore.

The boat was a hundred yards away by now, and picking up speed. Marco got to his feet, hitched up his baggy shorts, and picked up his binoculars. It was a modern yacht. This one, though, was bigger, smarter, faster.

As he watched, a woman emerged from the cabin and ran along the deck. Her long red hair caught in the wind that was coming with the storm, clouding around her in a coppery halo where the sun's final gleam lit it momentarily. She was wearing a blue dress that, as she balanced at the very stern, whipped back from her slender body. She put a hand up to her head, her neck drooped in a gesture of what seemed to Marco to be pain. Shocked, he caught a glimpse of a gaping, bloody wound, her white skull. And that's when he saw her fall.

Marco stared at the place where she had gone under, waiting for her to come back up. The yacht chugged on. There was no sign of her in its wake. No one had come running to help, no one on the yacht seemed to know she had gone. It had been maybe thirty seconds too long and Marco knew she was in trouble. He ran for the old orange inflatable, dropped it into the waves. The outboard started at first go. In a few minutes he was where he'd seen her go in. He circled, staring deep into the sea, but the water was less clear here, disturbed now by his boat. He stilled the engine and jumped over the side.

It was like falling off a cliff. He went so deep his lungs were bursting when he finally popped back up next to the dinghy. The sea was kicking up, the sky dark, the storm was getting closer. And then he saw her hair, long, copper hair floating upward toward him. He was there in a second.

But he could not find her. He dived, and dived again, but the storm had moved in and turbulence shifted the waves, shifted him. He had lost her.

And now the past came back at him, bringing memories he never wanted to relive.

2

The dog cowered in the dinghy, ears flattened by the rain coming down in a single sheet as Marco clambered back onboard. He could not see so much as a foot ahead. Cell phone reception, never good in this remote area, was impossible; he could not even call the coast guard station or the harbor. Thanking God he always put a life jacket on Em, he snapped on her lead and wrapped the end around his wrist. If the boat capsized he would be able to hang on to her.

Green waves sloshed them upward into a froth of foam, then slid them steeply back down again. The outboard sputtered then died. Marco scanned all around, searching for the horizon, for land, for anything but the sea that had already claimed one victim. He wondered if he and Em were going to be next. If so, nobody would ever know about the red-haired girl in the blue dress with the bloody wound on the side of her head. If they ever found her, that is. Nobody would know that wound had been made before she fell, that someone on that big black-hulled gulet had struck that blow. It was something only Marco knew. Now, though, was not the time to think of that; he just prayed he could get himself and his dog out of there.

With a final quick flick of lightning and a diminishing boom of thunder the sky began dramatically to change. In minutes a blade of sunlight shone through and the sea fell back into a blue-green swell, lifting them smoothly toward land.

Marco unwrapped the dog leash from his fingers. Water dripped off the points of Em's ears, dripped off Marco's head, ran down his chest. He put a hand over his eyes, searching all around, but did not see the girl.

Other boats appeared, heading fast for the harbor. Marco flagged down a small fishing boat and hitched a lift, hunkering down amongst the scaly catch as they towed his disabled dinghy to the wharf. Both he and Em smelled strongly of fish when they finally walked along the harbor to the coast guard office, something which pleased the dog more than it did Marco.

The office was a square room with two desks, each with a large leather chair, one of which was occupied by a self-important man in a gray uniform and heavy dark glasses which he did not remove as he inspected the still-dripping Marco, up, then down, then back up to his stubble-bearded face. The man's glance swiveled to take in the wet dog, who proceeded to give a great rolling shake, sending drops of water flying all over him.

"Sorry," Marco apologized. "It's a bit wet out there."

Giving him a disdainful look, the officer brushed off his uniform with a large, well-manicured hand and asked abruptly what he wanted. Marco got the impression he didn't much care. He'd probably interrupted him on his way to the café for a glass of wine and a chat; soaking-wet vacationers and their even worse dogs who came in messing up his office and his outfit were unwelcome.

He smoothed back his hair and tried to arrange himself

so he looked more presentable, difficult when you were that wet and wearing only bathing shorts, but he had more on his mind than mere appearance. "I came to report a drowning."

The officer gave him a quick glance from behind the dark glasses. "Who?"

"I don't know. A woman. Young. She fell off a large yacht."

"How do you know she fell?"

Marco resisted the temptation to roll his eyes. "I saw her."

The officer took off his glasses and stared at Marco. He obviously distrusted him. "So? Why did you not save her from this drowning?"

"Sir," Marco knew politeness was the only way to success with bureaucracy, "I tried. I dived many times but the sea was in turmoil. I could not find her. All I know is she fell from a large yacht, black, and very fast. It took off, she was left in its wake. . . ."

The officer sat back in the leather chair. He narrowed his eyes suspiciously at Marco. "What was the name of this yacht?"

Marco said he didn't know, he had not had time to look.

"And what were you doing out there in the storm? What boat were you on?"

Marco explained he was a vacationer, about his dinghy, that a fishing boat had towed his small boat back to shore. "She was young, though," he said, then stopped himself. He had spoken in the past tense. "She had on a blue dress, not exactly what you would wear if you meant to go for a swim off a boat."

The man eyed him coldly, waiting.

"She had—*has* red hair," he remembered. "A great cloud of coppery hair, kind of wavy, if you know what I mean. . . ."

The officer said nothing. He turned away and flicked on his computer. He clicked around silently for a few minutes. "Nobody is reported going overboard. Nobody missing," he said. "The storm is over. She probably went for a dip." He shrugged dismissively. "Foreigners on vacation think everything is safe everywhere. On vacation, they become immortal."

Marco watched him write a message on a yellow Post-it, then walk over to the empty desk next to his own and stick it on the counter. "My assistant will keep an eye on it," the man said, buttoning his jacket, already heading for the door, which he opened for Marco and the dog.

And that was that, Marco thought, as he squelched toward the café, where Costas greeted him with raised brows and a quick demitasse of boiling hot espresso from his fancy new Gaggia machine, his pride and joy.

Costas did not ask what had happened, that was not his way. Costas listened. He knew everything about everybody and mostly he kept it to himself. And to his wife, of course, the lovely Artemis, ten years younger and second only to the new Gaggia as his pride and joy. So what if Artemis gossiped with her friends, holding back her long dark hair with one hand while the other held her coffee cup, or in the evening a glass of the pink Cinzano and soda she preferred. She also always came back with more news for Costas to keep to himself, unless circumstances dictated otherwise. Which perhaps today, with what Marco Polo Mahoney told him, might well be that kind of occasion.

"Red hair?" he asked, casually. He had been told too many stories over his years behind the counter to take them all too seriously. He took a glass from the row stacked over the bar, poured a good shot of brandy into it, pushed it toward Marco. "Looks like you need that," he said.

He yelled for Artemis to bring a towel for the dog, dripping onto his white-tiled floor, already awash in a litter of the small greasy papers in which snacks were served. Every now and again a helper, usually a young boy, would come out with a broom and sweep them into a pile in the corner, to be removed later by someone else.

Marco downed the shot. It hit his stomach like a time bomb, exploding a minute later to swirl through his veins. "*Jesus*," he exclaimed. "What *is* that, Costas?"

"My own special brew. I don't give to everybody."

Marco bet he didn't or there wouldn't be many people able to walk out of there. He signaled for coffee, and a ham sandwich, which he gave to the dog. He took his cell phone from his wet bathing shorts pocket. It was ruined, of course. There was no phone at his cottage and he eyed Costas's landline instrument and asked if he might use it. Costas pushed it toward him, then watched, alarmed, as Marco dialed many numbers.

"*Where* you call?"

"Oh, just New York." Marco smiled at him. "My girl-friend is there."

"New York? *U-S of A*?" Costas was stunned.

Marco nodded then heaved a sigh of relief as Martha picked up.

"*Sweetie*," she said in that soft husky Brit accent he so enjoyed, "I was just thinking about you."

"I'm glad to hear it," he said, his mind still on the red-haired girl who had drowned, and his memories. "I'm in trouble," he said, and then explained what had happened. "And I think it's murder," he finished.

There was a long silence while she thought about it. Then, "I'll be right there," she said, as though she was just next door and not thousands of miles away.

3

When Marco called her from Turkey, Martha Patron was in her pajamas in New York. She thanked God he couldn't see her. The pajamas were flannel because she was always cold when alone in bed; blue and white stripes like a prison uniform, and she wore red bed socks. Added to which, taking advantage of a night alone, she had lathered her face in Vaseline, something she did once or twice a month and which she believed gave her skin a soft glow. In fact she often used it all over her body, of course only when there was no one to see her. She had just washed her hair and was letting it dry, skipping a comb through it and giving her head an upside-down shake every now and then. Martha's hair was quite beautiful, a natural light honey blond, dead straight and blunt cut to just below her shoulders, something she maintained every three weeks. Expensive, but worth it, and anyhow she offset the cost against the pricey face creams she did not buy. It worked for her.

If you analyzed her looks, something Martha did critically every night before bed and in the morning when she first got up, she was definitely not beautiful: her jaw was too square and her chin too determined; her cheekbones were good though, for which she was grateful because, after all, that's what held up the rest of her face. Her eyes were her best feature, rounded and endearingly childlike, a beautiful pale blue color that in some lights looked almost transparent.

In fact Martha was far from childlike; she was practical, competent, and determined. She was good at her job, which you might have expected to be something in fashion and, in a way, it was. Martha was an interior designer, not of the plush sofa, fluffy pillow variety, more of the clean, spare, industrial type—what Marco called her "concrete bunker look." Needless to say she'd had a go at doing over Marco's Paris studio, a one-room place, large though, and with a gallery sleeping loft where the mattress still rested on the floor, as it had since the day Marco moved in, and the chairs were threadbare green Eames worn practically to the frame. He had allowed Martha to do over his bathroom, though, which he described as cool—all steel and white tile, not a hint of granite in sight because Marco hated granite. The kitchen had rubbed concrete counters and gray slate floors.

The work part of the studio itself remained as it was when Marco had bought it with money earned from his first decent commission, a portrait of a French fashion icon that made him famous and sought after. Then he'd bought the tiny slab of a one-room house on the Turkish coast, with the small wooden boat, the gulet, with its pointed prow and wide painted eyes, which Marco said always seemed to be showing him the way, and which he had not allowed Martha to touch.

One look at that small boat and Martha knew there was nothing she could do with it. No cushions were ever going to turn it into the yacht she'd been expecting when

Marco invited her to stay with him in Turkey. It had not mattered, they were so enamored of each other they hardly noticed their surroundings, until they came up for air and gazed, glasses of cool white wine in hand, at the beauty all around them.

Love, Martha decided, was what made her world go round. She had been content with her work, enjoyed what she did, had a busy social life, friends, a big family who mostly lived together, sharing the ancient country home in England, somewhat ramshackle now, but still beautiful, all mellow golden Cotswold stone and dark beams, as well as her own small and very charming New York apartment. Of course she had been in love before, madly, horribly, but he'd been too attractive, too smooth, too popular with women. He'd flirted and he'd cheated and he'd cast her into despair. She met Marco on the rebound in an antique store, both of them examining a strange brass ram's-head lamp which she said was Egyptian and which he told her was certainly French.

They'd checked it out on Google over cups of coffee and bacon-and-egg sandwiches on kaiser rolls in the café around the corner. Martha could still remember clearly what she was wearing that day. It was a Saturday and under her coat she had on retro flared jeans and a skinny black cashmere sweater with pearl buttons. Her hair was held back with an elastic and she wore no makeup. She liked makeup-free weekends, when she had the time to herself; it gave her skin, and her, time to breathe, not to have to think about appearance, not to be "on," or to be charming to please her clients. With only herself to please that afternoon she was not charming to Marco.

"Excuse me, but I saw that lamp first," she'd said frostily. Marco already held it in his hands and was examining it.

He glanced up at her, taking her quickly in, the painter

in him finding her bone structure interesting, the man in him finding her coldness irritating.

"Is that so? Then I wonder how I managed to pick it up and contemplate purchasing it. If it was already taken, if you see what I mean."

"I do not see what you mean." Martha reached out for the lamp.

Marco hefted it teasingly from one hand to the other, pretending to drop it.

"Jesus," she exclaimed, snatching it from him. "You might have broken it."

"But I didn't."

They stopped looking at the lamp and took a long look at each other.

"I was thinking of getting a coffee," she said, making the first move.

And that was the beginning of that.

4

Through her job, Martha knew everybody. She had worked with many of them on their various homes, and now she was able to make a few calls and hitch a lift on a private Learjet to Paris. From there she accompanied a fashion shoot on their plane to Istanbul, then on to the small local airfield where Marco was waiting to meet her.

It was very hot and dark clouds pushed the blue from the sky, portending another storm. Marco knew the long journey must have been rough and Martha must be tired, yet she walked down the steps off the small plane immaculate as ever, in a white shirt, sleeves rolled, black skinny jeans, and red canvas espadrilles. An oversized white tote hung from her shoulder, stuffed with magazines and the goodies she knew Marco liked, including four Snickers bars; two slightly stale New York bagels that would be okay toasted; six giant sticks of red licorice, which she liked too; and a bottle of the Jim Beam she thought would make a change from the arak or whatever they drank in places like Turkey and Greece. She also carried the dog-eared trade paperback of *War and Peace* which for twenty years she had been promising herself to read. It was that or *Pride and Prejudice,* but she found Jane Austen incredibly slow and anyhow much preferred finding her way through all those Russian names. She was still on page thirty-five, but had hope.

She looked wonderful, Marco thought, dazzled anew by her wide blue eyes and swinging blond hair and the curvy body he knew so well. Martha was exactly the right height to fit under his arm when they walked along together, as they did now, out of the airport to Marco's battered Jeep Safari with its rattling canvas top. He carried the heavy tote, demanding to know what was in there, then shoved Em from the passenger seat into the back, while Martha took the dog's place.

"I feel badly," she said, turning to caress Em's snout, hanging over her shoulder. "Throwing her out of her rightful place."

"Em's good at sharing."

Their eyes linked and there was a long silence. "I'm glad you came," he said finally.

"Me too."

Nothing more was said as Marco made his way through the suburban sprawl and out onto the sea road where the colors of the water changed in stripes of pale turquoise to greenish blue to cobalt. The sun sparked off the tiny wavelets in diamond points of light. Small pastel houses clung to rocky hillsides and white villas overlooked the sea, half hidden under swathes of fuchsia bougainvillea. The road narrowed and the countryside became more rural. They drove through a couple of seaside villages where fishing boats rested until they would sail into the moonlight and not be back until dawn.

Martha said suddenly, "Nothing bad could happen here, it's too simple, too peaceful. I feel it in my heart."

Marco glanced sideways at her. "That's why I came

here," he said. "And why I didn't want to believe what I saw with my own eyes."

Em rested her head on Martha's shoulder, drooling all over her pristine white shirt. Martha stroked the dog absently. "But you have no proof," she said.

He shook his head. "Not even a body."

"Marco, did you ever think she might simply have gone in for a swim? I know you said the storm was coming, but girls can be impulsive, a spur-of-the-moment thing, perhaps she'd had a row with her boyfriend. . . ."

"Perhaps she had, and maybe he was the one that bashed her head in. *Martha!* That girl's head was covered in blood. I could see the white of her skull! Someone hit her. And hit her with something hard." He shrugged. "Anyhow, I believe she was murdered. And I want to find her, and who did it."

Martha was silent. She wondered what she was doing here. Marco seemed set on this idea; he did not seem to want to escape from it and simply enjoy a vacation.

They drove through the village, past the harbor crammed with holiday rental boats and the happy sound of English voices having a good time. At the end of the long, cobbled street an illuminated red sign blinked on and off. *COSTAS BAR AND GRILL.* Marco pulled up and Em immediately leapt out and headed, tail waving, through the beaded curtain.

"Come on in," a man called from inside, as a shy maiden swept back the jangling curtain and stood, frowning uncertainly at them. The young woman's brown eyes widened as she took in Martha's appearance, then she stepped back and said, coolly, "Welcome, Marco's fiancée. We know all about you."

Martha threw a questioning glance at Marco, who lifted a shoulder. "I said you were my girl and you were coming to stay."

Martha followed the dog into the cool, dark bar. She stood for a minute, adjusting to the dim interior after the sunlight, hearing a distant peal of thunder.

Costas, haggard and mustached, eyes blazing a welcome, took her hand and dropped a whiskery kiss on it. Suddenly exhausted—after all, she had been traveling forever, what with the connections and the delays—Martha sank into a woven leather chair and accepted a pink drink, clinking with ice, brought to her by the shy maiden with the curtain of black hair and the sexy body.

"My wife, Artemis," Costas introduced her proudly.

Artemis kissed Martha three times on her cheeks and said something in Turkish. "She says you smell good," Costas told Martha, who dove into her huge white bag and found amongst the accumulated junk, buried beneath *War and Peace,* the small freebie vial of Chanel, which she presented to the girl. "So she will smell good too," she told Costas.

But Marco was looking at the gold chain Artemis was wearing: a thin rope linked with a tiny gold panther. Also dangling from the chain were the initials AM. He wondered, out loud, where Costas had found such a charming piece.

"The police had it," Costas explained.

Martha recognized the signature panther and said, surprised, "But it's Cartier. How lovely."

Artemis lifted the initialed chain and inspected it. "Cartier?" she said doubtfully. "I found it on the beach, washed up by the waves. I thought it simply some pretty trinket lost by a tourist while swimming. It happens all the time."

"Once," Costas added, "someone found a diamond ring. Three stones in gold. Of course he gave it to the police and it was claimed by an engaged couple; they'd had a fight and she threw it in the sea, but they reconciled. It's the only thing of value ever found on our beach."

"Well, now there's something else." Marco remembered the girl in the blue dress whose body had not been found, and had the sudden gut feeling it belonged to her. He asked Artemis if he might take a look. She lifted her heavy black hair and unfastened the lobster clasp, sliding the chain reluctantly through her fingers as she handed it to Marco.

"Martha was right," he said, pointing out the tiny Cartier signature, making Artemis sigh because she realized she could not keep it if it was expensive.

"Then we must hand it back to the police," Costas said. He felt sorry for Artemis, losing her chain. "I'll buy you a new one," he promised.

Marco paid for their drinks and he and Martha held hands as they walked back to his cabin, with Em darting ahead, seeking out interesting scents.

"You're thinking it belonged to the girl who fell off the boat," Martha said, tripping on the stony path so Marco had to grab her. He put an arm around her waist. It felt good and they smiled at each other, pausing to kiss.

"Like teenagers," Martha whispered, burying her face in his neck. It smelled of clean air and sea salt and fresh sweat and faintly of the citrusy cologne he used, a combination that was uniquely his. But Marco had other things on his mind, and he looked away, staring out to sea, obviously thinking about what had been said, about the gold chain and the initials.

"I can e-mail someone I know at Cartier, if you like," Martha suggested. "Explain how we came by the chain, tell them we would like to find who it belonged to so we can return it. I'll ask if they have a record of it, perhaps they can identify it from the initials."

"I don't know why but I feel it must have belonged to the girl I saw drown," Marco said. "What I'm asking myself is how it got off her neck into the water. You saw how difficult that lobster clasp was to unfasten. It could not have simply slipped off."

"You mean you think someone took it off then threw it into the sea?"

"Perhaps it was the only item that could have identified her."

"Apart from finding her body," Martha reminded him. "Marco," she protested, "you are simply pursuing an idea. There is no girl, there is no murder. Nothing happened, just someone diving off a boat for a swim. . . ."

Marco threw her a cold glance. "I may not be a detective," he said, "but I know what I saw and I know she didn't come back up. Somebody hit her, somebody wanted her dead."

Marco recalled the girl running to the stern of the big black boat, turning with a hand held to her bloody skull to look behind her . . . and then her fall. He replayed it in his head, seeing her again and again, falling, her long copper hair a cloud floating above her. And him staring, waiting for her to come back up . . . diving in after her when she did not. And never finding her. He was beginning to think perhaps Martha was right, except now he had the chain with its initials. *AM.*

5

It was a week later, and Martha had already left for New York. Marco was sitting alone under Costas's ancient olive tree, stripped of its fruit, which Costas was now serving to his customers on thin wooden toothpicks, warning them to take care, the olives were so juicy they might squirt. And they did, as Marco knew from experience. Em too. She was fond of an olive every now and then, rolling it on her tongue, never quite sure what to make of it until she finally swallowed it whole and sat with imploring eyes asking for more. Two were the max for any dog, Marco decided; Em was better off with the mastodon bones. And he was better off with the braised goat which smelled delicious wafting past in a steaming dish straight out of the oven to a lucky couple on the terrace. They scarcely seemed even to notice, they were so busy looking into each other's eyes. *The eyes of love,* Marco thought jealously.

Martha's visit had been quick; she had left for New York the day before and he was bereft. Not only did he miss her physically, he missed talking to her; she was the only person who would ever understand that he was speaking the truth when he said he had seen a young woman murdered. Well, not actually *seen* the act, merely the end result. No one understood because apparently no such young woman ever existed.

Artemis served the couple and walked briskly back. Her long black hair was pulled into a ponytail and she wore an embroidered white cotton peasant blouse that slid sexily off her shoulders, with a full red cotton skirt that swished sexily around her knees. On her feet were un-sexy flip-flops. Her toenails were painted a pale pink and her full mouth a glossier shade. Marco thought there was no doubt she was a lovely woman. He had already made many sketches and one day he meant to paint her portrait. Now, though, he had the red-haired girl on his mind.

"Artemis." He caught her hand as she passed by. She turned, questioningly. "Do you have a minute? I need to ask you something."

Intrigued, Artemis pulled up a chair. "Only a minute," she said. "As you can see we are very busy."

Café life swirled around them. The usual row of weathered old men were lined up against the wall as they were every day, with their caps and canes, elbows on tables, chairs facing out onto the street so they could see everyone that passed, and make comments in low tones. The day's heat still lingered, the single streetlamp lent a dim glow and candles flickered in red and green glass holders left over from the previous Christmas.

"Marco?" Artemis's eyes were wide, waiting for what he had to say.

"I'm looking for a red-haired young woman."

"Martha has been gone only one day and already you are looking for another woman?"

"It's not like that. This woman is dead."

"Dear mother of God." Artemis quickly crossed her-

self. "I don't know any dead young women. We are all still alive."

"This one had red hair. I need to know if you ever saw her here in the café, or on a boat, at the jetty."

Artemis's eyes rolled back; she was thinking. "I saw that girl." She remembered her now. "Clouds of long red wavy hair. She passed by once or twice but never came in here."

Marco heard his own sigh of relief. He wasn't imagining it; the girl did exist.

"You think the gold necklace belonged to her," Artemis said, and Marco nodded.

"All I have to do now is find out her name."

It was not easy; in fact it proved impossible. Nobody knew her. People came in and out on boats all the time: vacationers, backpackers, college kids on the loose. She could have been anybody.

Well, there it was, Marco thought, moodily, back in Costas's bar, sipping a sweet wine that made him long for a glass of cool, clean, French sauvignon blanc. He eyed Em, lying with her head on his flip-flopped brown feet, ignoring the nightly bone. Even Em seemed to have lost her taste for this place. It was time to go. Leave the girl and the mystery of her death that maybe wasn't such a mystery anyway; it was just him and his faulty memory. He needed to move on.

He went back to the simple white cottage, packed his old T-shirts and bathing shorts in his canvas duffel, fed Em the last of the chicken he'd bought the day before, threw out the jasmine blossoms he'd picked from the tree outside his door and which still smelled fragrant and sweet. He stood for a moment looking around his small home away from home. He loved this place, loved his solitude. This was the first time he had ever felt disturbed here. He did not like that feeling. Worried, he went and sat on the terrace. Em hunkered nervously next to him, paws neatly arranged.

He stretched out to stroke her head, such a small skull, so fragile . . . it brought him back again to the way the girl's head had looked, smashed to the bone. There was no escaping the memory. He knew what he had seen. There was simply nothing he could do about it. It was time to go home.

Lightning lit the sky, another storm coming. It was that time of year. In the flickering light he caught sight of a boat making its way to the harbor. A large, black-hulled yacht. Of course there were other black-hulled yachts but somehow he knew this was the boat. Same cabin door from which she had emerged in her blue dress, the rail over which she had fallen as though dead. Which Marco believed she now was.

6

ANGIE

Am I dead? It's a supposed fact that when you are dead you feel nothing. Then I must be. Yet I was aware of the wound to my head, I'd felt the sea licking at it, perhaps the salt water was medicinal. Or perhaps the wound was too deep for that. And if I'm dead, then it makes no difference anyway.

All I'd been aware of was the current pulling me, so fast I was helpless against it. Not that I could have saved myself, it was too late for that. I must be far from the spot where I'd fallen off the yacht, far from those people whose invited guest I was. Well, sort of a guest. Supposed to be anyhow, but it turned into something else. I was the dumb innocent who thought she was going to be a star in a hair commercial with her mane of long red wavy hair!

I am trying frantically to remember everything before it's too late. I'm twenty-one years old, I remember that. I also remember my name. Angie. Raised by a single mom. I remember her too. In fact, I can see her in my mind's eye, right now, her thin, always-worried face, her sweet expression when her glance lingered on me, which was not often enough since she had to work three jobs to keep us afloat. Afloat. Ironic, now that I am drowning. Drowning without you, Mom. Perhaps it's my own fault.

Here's how it began.

A month ago I was working as a hostess, a greeter at a well-known restaurant in Manhattan. Raised in Queens, I had traveled no farther than New York State in my life, never had the money, or perhaps even the ambition. Manhattan was it all, for me, and as an attractive young woman with my mane of red hair, always worn tied back when working, of course; a faintly freckled nose which I tried to cover with concealer; hazel eyes—greenish in some lights—and a slim, well-toned body from working out at the gym five mornings a week, I knew I looked good. No beauty, but certainly attractive enough to generate interest from diners at the expensive place that was really nothing but a glorified steak house faking out the menu with exotic French- and Italian-sounding dishes. Naturally, most people ordered the steak anyway, and the chunky fries. I could have written out their orders before they opened their mouths.

Not that I was the one taking their orders. I merely showed them to their tables, handed out menus, indicated the specials and the better bottles on the wine list, made sure the candle was lit so the women looked younger, smiled my professional smile and was gone in minutes. Except when an interesting man showed up, especially if he showed up alone. Which is how I met Ahmet Ghulbian and sealed my fate.

I was not the one actually to greet him; a coworker had that privilege, but I could tell right off he was important just from the way he strode into the place then stood silently taking in the softly lit room, the white linen table-cloths, the huge urn of flowers at the desk whose scent mingled with that of good food and excellent wine. He wore a dark suit I recognized was of European cut, narrow and fitted perfectly to his body, and he had the kind of thick dark hair I'd heard described as "luxuriant," though it was conservatively cut; olive tan skin; clean shaven. Oddly, since this was a dark room, he wore tinted glasses which he kept on the entire time he was there.

There was just something about him that attracted me immediately and when my coworker hurried off to place his drink order, I moved in. Smoothing my short black pencil skirt over my thighs, adjusting the collar of my white shirt, I drifted casually past, throwing him a smile as I went.

"Everything okay?" I asked, hesitating for a moment, giving him an opportunity to eye me up and down, which of course he did.

"Better now you are here" was his reply, making me laugh.

"Corny," I replied. "Hackneyed, if you want the truth. I can't tell you how many times I've heard that."

He was silent, though still looking at me. I felt uncomfortable and made to move on, but he said, "Wait."

I waited.

"Is your hair naturally that color?"

He could not have said anything that would have surprised me more. My hair was pulled straight back and firmly anchored with a clip, as per the rules of the house. No hairs in our food, no mane sweeping sexily over one shoulder, enticing men when you should have been selling them more wine. I said yes, cautiously, but with a professional smile, it was real. He was looking intently at me and I was uncomfortable. I wanted to leave but he said, again, to wait. He felt in the inside breast pocket of his jacket and took out a thin leather wallet from which he removed a card. He handed this to me.

"I have connections in advertising," he said. "I know there's a shoot coming up in Turkey and Greece. The model has to have red hair, your color hair. Unfortunately today, the girl they wanted fell and broke her ribs and has had to back out. What they are looking for is that great mane, not that they can't add to it with extensions, but this is an outdoor, sea and sand, wind-blowing deal. The hair must be right."

He paused, still looking at me. Out of the corner of my eye I caught my supervisor lifting a hand to call me back to my job. I palmed the card quickly and agreed to call him. Double-sealing my fate. Which is why I am now drowning in the cool, clear azure waters off the coast of Turkey.

7

It was Apollo Zacharias who saw her. He was the owner and proud captain of the fast black-hulled trading boat, the *Zeus,* a modified version of the Turkish twin-masted wooden gulet. He happened to be on the bridge, binoculars held to his eyes, scanning the sea and the storm clouds, when he spotted what looked to be seaweed, kelp or something like that, spiraling upward. Except the seaweed was attached to a woman's body. *It was her hair he was looking at, floating above her.*

Yelling for help, he ran to the deck and leaned over the rail. His crew, three bare-chested men, arrived at a gallop.

"Turn the boat," Apollo screamed. He was always at full throttle when excited. "There's a woman in the water. Take care now, look out for her."

He pushed back the gold-braided captain's hat he always wore to ensure people knew his status, leaning anxiously over the side as the boat made its maneuver. He was a stocky man, Greek, a sailor all his life, but this was the first time he'd seen a woman's body floating past his ship. Fifty years old, experienced, married with three children, owner of a retirement home north of Athens, he would rather not have seen her. It could only mean trouble. Now he had to do something about it.

"Throw down the net," Zacharias ordered, worried because he could no longer see the hair. She might have gone too deep; the currents were treacherous, causing riptides that could suck you under in minutes. But no. There! He could see her now.

"Get in the water," he yelled to his crew. "Catch her." It was as though he was after a marlin.

The net was lowered, as well as an inflatable dinghy. Two of his men jumped after it, hitting the water with a thud. The engine was shut down. The only sound was the slap of waves against the black hull and the cry of seabirds overhead searching for prey. The gulet heaved silently on the swell.

Zacharias pushed his captain's hat from his sunburned brow, leaning anxiously over the side. He had seen her, hadn't he? That was red hair and not seaweed? The heat penetrated his shirt, layering his skin with sweat. Maybe he should have left well enough alone, not gotten himself into this situation. Finding bodies at sea meant a lot of explaining to police, a lot of paperwork, more angst when he should have been looking forward to a peaceful retirement. But that was a woman he had seen down there. Or a woman's body. Who knew which? He would soon find out.

ANGIE

Am I now a "body"? A mere creature? A person from whom all emotion has been stilled? It's strange but I can see myself, a smaller image of me, somewhere above my broken head, floating in a deep blue sky crisscrossed with meshes that tangle with my hair, pulling at my head, pulling me upward. Please, I want to say, please leave me. I am calm and peaceful here. I do not want to feel again, to have to remember my own vulnerability, my "innocence," or at least the kind of innocence I thought I had, where I knew who I was. I knew how to deal with men, how to take care of myself; I was no silly girl ready to be duped by the next smooth talker. After all, I worked in the smart restaurant where men always gave the eye to an attractive girl. We expected it, knew how to fend off the pushy ones, how to smile at the guys out for the night from under the wife and kids. Girls like me "understood" them. And if sometimes, we had a "fling," well why not, though the truth was we were always hoping to find Mr. Right. Or at least be "discovered." And that is what happened to me. I was suddenly, amazingly, discovered, and all because of my red hair.

Mom would have been surprised. She had always wondered where the red came from. She herself had been blond as long as I could remember, covering up the gray as she grew older, only to depart this world, my world, too young. It was the saddest day of my life, the saddest year before it when she was sick, the saddest after, when she was gone. It had been two years now and I still could not think of her without tearing up. Which was another reason I was ready for an adventure, a change; a radical change.

It was a fairly quiet night when Ahmet Ghulbian first came into the restaurant and made himself known to me. Well, made a pass, to be frank. I was used to it but this time I was also attracted. Still, I was wary. He was different, foreign looking. "Exotic" was the word I used to myself. Of course I did not call the number on the card he gave me, I figured that was that, just another guy wanting to hook up for the night. I thought of my mother and what she would think of me, her daughter, who by now should have been on her way to being married. Sometimes, standing in five-inch heels and a narrow skirt, white shirt strategically buttoned so as not to reveal what should not be revealed to the restaurant's customers, believe me, I wished I was that girl my mom had hoped I would be.

That night, disappointment filled my mouth like bile; I had achieved nothing, not even my "potential," as Mom called it. I had done well in school, good enough to be accepted by a college, though of course I could not go. I had to work, bring in some money; pay the rent on the third-floor, two-room apartment in Queens, the grocery bills; vodka; cigarettes. It was the latter which killed her, though to her credit she had stopped. Too late. It's because of her I never so much as put a cigarette between my lips, just to try; neither that, nor marijuana, because I was afraid of that too. Drugs were sold on the streets where I lived, I'd seen the results and wanted no part of it. I was, I guess, what was known as "a good girl." The truth is I had never wanted to be "bad."

I did not go in for one-night stands. My first relationship was head-over-heels passionate. We were so madly in love nobody else mattered. His name was Henry, always known as Hank, and for a year we were all we knew; all we saw was each other. Then one day, it was over. Thanks for everything, hon, he said, as he left for a Southern college where he would stand out like an onion in a field of tulip bulbs. And I went to work the cash register at the local supermarket, where I blended into the background as though I belonged. Which I did. Apart from the red hair of course, but in a tearful downbeat moment after watching an old DVD of Audrey Hepburn in the movie *Roman Holiday,* like her I had it all cut off, shorn like a sacrificial lamb. Which, looking horrified at the result, I knew I might well have been. I had sacrificed myself to the ego of Hank, the new college boy, and now look at me. It took ages to grow in again.

And now. At the moment of my demise I had this cloud of coppery red hair standing out from my head as though electrified, spiraling in tendrils around my face, curving in the glossy waves that attracted Mr. Ghulbian and were to be the cause of my death.

"I'll rest in peace with you now, Mom" was my final thought when the blow had vibrated through my head, sending me spinning, tumbling over myself, my hand to the bloody spot. I'd staggered forward, caught from the corner of my eye a glimpse of them, watching me. Him and the woman who had struck me with the champagne bottle. Watching me about to die.

8

Zacharias trawled Angie in like a fish from the ocean. Her red hair tangled in the meshes of the net; her skull gleamed white in the sun; her open eyes stared into his.

"She is a dead woman," he said, peering closer. And then she blinked. He jumped back. "How can she be still alive? She must have drowned. No woman could survive that, and that broken head."

But I am alive, she wanted to say. And you are right to call on God, because I need all the help I can get. You saved me from drowning but you might not save me from what happened that made me run from them, to fall—or did I jump?—into the sea to escape.

They brought towels, wrapped her in them, carried her into Zacharias's cabin, laid her down in the shade. Zacharias himself bathed her face with clean freshwater. He himself lifted her long red hair out of the way. He saw the gaping wound, the broken skull, and drew in his breath sharply, asking who could have done this to her? And why?

Because I knew too much, she wanted to tell him. I was a fool, an innocent, or more probably merely dumb. I be-

lieved what they said. I did as they asked. I thought it was
the adventure I had been looking for. I did not understand
that I was perfect for their plans, a young woman alone
in the world, no family, only the usual friendships that
could be dismissed with talk of plans to move to the
West Coast. No one really to care or come looking for
me. What a sad state of affairs, that I could reach the age
of twenty-one and have no one who cared enough to find
out what happened, or where I was.

It began on a cold night in a luxury hotel in New York.

I had known Ahmet Ghulbian for exactly one month.
He was lying in bed next to me, propped on one elbow,
gazing into my eyes. A half-empty bottle of champagne
and two glasses waited on the table. He sat up, leaned over
to refill them, offered me one. I shuffled upright, tossing
back my hair, allowing it to fall forward again over my
breasts because I suddenly felt very naked in front of this
man who had just made love to me and had already seen
it all.

"You'll have a private plane, of course," he said.

"A private plane," I repeated, wondering what he was
talking about. I seemed to be having memory lapses these
days, sometimes forgetting what day it was and whether I
was supposed to be at work, or what. Ahmet had been giving me some pills. He said he suffered from the same
thing and they would help.

"Think of it," he'd said, smiling, popping another pill
into my champagne. "A private plane, all to yourself. Just
you and the pilots. Then a yacht where my friends will
look after you. Oh, you can trust me, dear little red-haired
Angie, they will certainly look after you. Anything you
want will be yours. Caviar, foie gras, breakfast in bed, sunset drinks on deck. It will be champagne all the way."

"All the way to where?" I'd asked, puzzled. I really did not understand what he was talking about.

He laughed at that. "Private yachts do not have to go anywhere. They float free as birds in the air, letting whim take them where they might at that very moment they choose. You can be part of that, my dear little Angie."

Through the champagne blur and my foggy brain it sounded great, though somewhere the person still in my head, the rational young woman I used to be before I met this man and took his pills and drank too much, asked the question, Why me?

"Why me?" I vocalized the query that so puzzled me.

"Because, my dear little Angie, I care for you, I am falling in love with you, I want you to meet my friends, and then my family. I am serious about you, you must know that by now."

His eyes, dark without his glasses, melted into mine, he wrapped his arms around me, held me to his naked chest. I could feel his heart beating, beating for me, I thought happily. At last I had found a man who loved me. My mother would have been thrilled, as I myself was. At least I thought I was, at that moment, anyhow. Yet I hardly knew this man, I did not even know where he came from, or anything about his family; I had never, in the few weeks I had known him, met so much as a friend of his.

"It's our lives, our private lives," he'd reassured me, when I'd questioned this. "I want to keep you to myself while I can. In the beginning, anyhow."

Now, though, in the hotel room, he stretched behind him and opened the drawer on the nightstand, took out a slender red leather box and offered it to me.

"For my lovely girl," he said.

I had seen the ads in magazines, knew a red Cartier box when I saw one. I'd never held one in my hands, though, never expected to. I took it, smiling questioningly into his eyes. He touched me lightly, two fingers on my lips, like a kiss. "Go on, open it."

I almost did not want to, didn't want to end the surprise, the pleasure, like holding back when making love, delaying the final moment. I opened it.

Inside was a slender gold chain with a small animal ornament, a panther, and my initials also in gold. The initials sat exactly in the hollow of my throat as I held it up. Ahmet turned me around so he might fasten it, then turned me back again, and looked expectantly at me.

"You like it?"

"*Like?* Why, I *love* it. I *adore* it. It's the best present anyone ever gave me." I didn't need to say it was the most expensive present anyone had given me, he obviously knew hostesses in restaurants were not millionaires.

"Well, then." He stroked my hair back, gently fingering the tendrils around my ears, smoothing my eyebrows, the two fingers again, like a kiss, on my mouth. "Well, then, now maybe you can give me a present in return."

I laughed. "Anything you want," I promised recklessly.

It was that promise that left me drowning in the beautiful azure and green Aegean Sea. The blow with the champagne bottle had been carefully aimed, I knew it now. In fact I had seen it coming. He was standing there with the woman I had not even seen earlier. I was to be gotten rid of, that was clear. I knew too much, knew what they were selling, and I was the only witness to the transaction.

As I sank into that blueness, blood drifting upward with my long hair, with what might be my last conscious thought, I vowed I would be back. I would get them. One way or another. It wasn't revenge I wanted. It was justice.

9

Martha Patron had a younger sister named Lucy. She lived in London and seemed to Martha to base her philosophy on life and how to live it to the full on a song called "It Can't Be Bad If It Makes You Feel Good." Unfortunately this also led to that Janis Joplin winner that went, *Take another little piece of my heart, now, baby*, which is precisely what happened, in what seemed to Martha to be the space of a few days.

Lucy first encountered a man Martha eventually find out was Ahmet Ghulbian a month previously—sexy, dark, exotic—in the lobby of the Ritz Hotel in London. It was a Thursday evening and she was awaiting the arrival of a girlfriend with whom she was supposed to have a drink. Both girls were "actresses" who so far had acted only in drama school, but they were hoping. "Being seen" was, they believed, the best way to get "discovered," and the Ritz was where they hoped they might meet someone important in showbiz and be asked to audition, or maybe even do a TV commercial. Anyhow it beat sitting home waiting for a phone call from some elusive director that never came.

Lucy was too well brought up to perch at the bar; she sat discreetly alone at a table, making her champagne last because she could not afford a second glass. She heard her stomach rumble and longed for a sandwich, to say nothing of a good meal. A chicken sandwich, she thought, closing her eyes, visualizing the chicken on sliced white bread, her favorite. Even if sliced white was supposed to be rubbish, to her it still made the best sandwich and the slices were all the same size, which they were not if she was the one doing the slicing. Tomato, lettuce, mayo, no ketchup, perhaps just a hint of mustard. Her mouth watered at the thought and she took a sip of champagne. Over the rim of her glass, her eyes caught those of the man at the adjacent table. Well, not exactly his eyes because he was, oddly, since they were indoors, wearing glasses with tinted lenses. Still she could tell he was looking at her.

Her phone played its little tune. A text from her friend to say she couldn't make it. Lucy, dismayed, stared at her half-drunk glass of champagne. She had trusted her friend would pay because she had no money, well, barely enough. They always did this, took care of each other when one was broke. Now what?

"Excuse me, but I can see you are troubled. Is there some way I could help?"

It was the man in the dark glasses from the next table. Lucy thought quickly of her overdrawn credit cards, any one of which might be rejected. She thought of the small amount of cash in her purse, of her overused checkbook. She *might* just be able to swing it, it would have been okay sharing with her friend, but right now she was kind of stuck. Accepting money from a stranger was against all her principles and she gave the man a searching stare, a small frown between her lovely eyebrows, a look that definitely questioned his intentions.

"I only seek to help a damsel in distress," he said, and then his face lit up with amusement. "Sorry, I sound like a bad poet, but I saw you were concerned about the bill. I'm guessing your boyfriend, fiancé . . . ? did not arrive and now you are compromised. Please, allow me. It will be my good deed for the day."

Lucy thought quickly: she was either going to be deeply embarrassed—at the Ritz of all places—or in debt to some man, who, though he was good-looking, she did not know from Adam. "*Well*," she said, drawing out the word to show her reluctance. "Well, perhaps, maybe, if you would be so good as to . . ."

"Offer my help? Of course." He took out a black AmEx card, placed it on top of the bill, and signaled the waiter. "I think under the circumstances, I should introduce myself. Ahmet Ghulbian. And I must tell you right away, that lovely as you are, I have no evil intentions. Seriously, I saw you were in trouble, that's all."

"Well, thank you." Lucy found she was blushing. "But you must give me your address so I'll know where to send a check. Return your money, I mean."

He shrugged. His eyes behind the tinted glasses were very dark.

"Please, it is so little, there is no need." He looked at her for a long, silent moment, then said, "I was going on to dinner at the Italian place I'm fond of, on the Kings Road. I'm wondering if you might also be hungry? Perhaps you would join me? All cards on the table, though." He laid his big square hands in front of him, smiling at her. "No evil intent, simply companionship and a nice meal. For two instead of one. A man traveling can get lonely. I feel the need for some conversation with my wine, a little company, no obligations beyond that."

Lucy thought she might quite like a glass of red wine and some conversation with this stranger, who already seemed more interesting than most men she knew. Besides, she was broke and starving. "Why not?" she asked with a wide smile that enchanted.

And that's how she first met Ahmet Ghulbian. A month ago.

10

ANGIE

I was lying on my back, looking at something round, greenish, encircled in tarnished brass. The green undulated against glass. A porthole! I was on a boat, but not the grand yacht from before. Then how did I come to be here?

My mind struggled to find the memory, my head ached with a kind of violent throb that would not stop. I lifted a hand to my head, an act that seemed to have its own momentum, with no connection to my brain. My hand did not find the expected hair. I felt only a wrapping which I realized must be bandages. Panic lit through me, my hand shook as it fell back onto the sheet that covered me from neck to toes.

I heard a rasping sound, realized it came from my chest, my own lungs, seeking air the way a drowning person might. Oh God, I had drowned. I saw myself again, sinking deeper, from azure to green, to darkness. Had I not died? Had there been a savior?

"She's coming round," I heard a man say. A deep voice with an accent. Greek, perhaps? I could not tell. Afraid,

I kept my eyes firmly shut. I did not want to see him, knew he would not want me to be able to recognize him. Not a killer like that.

Then, "She's young, same age as one of my own daughters. How could this happen to her?"

My brain clicked in. This man had a daughter. He was concerned about me. He was not the one who'd tried to kill me. I kept my eyes shut though, just in case I was wrong. I wondered why someone would want to kill me. I was unimportant, a nonentity, simply a young woman trying to earn a living that matched her expectations and, like most, barely succeeding.

My throat was parched, my lips dry. I put out my tongue and licked.

"See!" the man crowed triumphantly. "She is not drowned."

Suddenly, remembering, I wished I was.

The man looking at her, Apollo Zacharias, realized he was stuck with a severely wounded, half-drowned woman. His three shirtless crew members stood staring down at her, wrapped like a mummy in blue towels, red hair clogged with blood. Zacharias observed that it had stopped flowing. He knew this happened when a person died. No more heartbeat to push the blood through the veins, keep the arteries working. He had never longed for anyone to bleed before.

Theos. He was tempted to throw her back in. Get rid of her—*the body* he meant, because he was certain now she was dead and there was no way he was going to be responsible for a dead body. But then she blinked again.

Zacharias thought of his wife, of his children, the eldest only eighteen. Young, like this girl. *Too young to die.*

"Carry her to my cabin," he ordered, then he got on the

radio and called for help. Another ship might be close, there might by some stroke of luck even be a doctor. To his surprise, he got an immediate answer.

"I am in your vicinity. My boat is fast. I can get her medical attention. Stand by, we will be approaching from southwest."

Zacharias summoned his men back, told them to return the girl, or the body, to the deck, whichever, he did not care, she would no longer be his responsibility. He instructed them to prepare the rope ladder to lower her over the side. He was stunned when a few minutes later, a large yacht appeared on the horizon, steaming fast toward him. She must be 250 feet, he thought, impressed. Sleek as a dolphin, all coal-black and steel. A rich man's boat, it gleamed with care. The crew were immaculate in white shorts and shirts—no bare chests here.

The black yacht looked, Zacharias thought, stunned, like a ship from the gates of hell, ready to take you over the River Styx into the flames guarded by the fierce three-headed dog Cerberus.

But the man who hailed him from its deck was clearly not from hell. He was red-faced, self-important, and gave orders like he was used to being obeyed. Zacharias noticed he did not wear a captain's cap, yet the crew members obeyed him immediately, throwing out fenders to guard their craft from Zacharias's lowly boat, sending two men across a rope which they attached, then slinging the cage over.

Two of the men picked up the girl in her blue blanket. They did not so much as look at her, simply laid her inside the cage, closed it up, and propelled it back to their ship. Then they went back by rope to their own smart craft, signaled Zacharias to release the rope, which he did. The grand black yacht took off, churning up a swell that lifted

Zacharias's boat to the peak of a twenty-foot wave and back down again, taking on water, half drowning them all.

Cursing, Zacharias shook a fist. The boat was already almost out of sight. He did take a silent moment, though, to think about the girl, and what might happen to her. Dead or alive, he assumed she was in good hands. Rich men's hands anyhow.

11

Yet another week had passed and Marco was still in Turkey, unwilling to leave the peace and sunshine, and the mystery of the girl, behind. Relaxed, at Costas's bar in the shade of the giant olive tree, he looked the very picture of a man content with his lot in life. After all, what could be bad about sipping a decent wine in a shady spot with the cheerful chatter of voices in a mix of languages around you, the clink of ice in glasses, the smell of roasting meat in the air, the dish of green olives on the table, and of course, the small dog's soft head resting on his foot, as always. Three things spoiled this image. The mystery girl. Martha's absence. And a memory. A slice of his past that, try as he might, he was unable to shake off.

It was strange, Marco thought, the way the past had of creeping up on you, just when you thought you had finally dismissed it. He never talked about what happened. Not even to Martha. Nary a word. It was locked in his heart, in his brain, forever.

He had been so young, eighteen, ingenuous, curious, eager for life, and for love. He thought he'd found the love part right away, his first week in college where he was studying, of all things, economics. This was, of course, at the insistence of his father, who viewed his son's artistic talent and style—the long hair, the faded jeans, the ubiquitous T-shirt—as a personal offense.

"Ours is a family of bankers and businessmen," he declared when Marco presented his case for art school. "There'll be no messing around with artsy shit here."

So Marco had had no choice but to strike out on his own, work three jobs to put himself through Rhode Island School of Design, living in a shared dump optimistically called an apartment in a bad neighborhood where you'd better have eyes in the back of your head if you wanted to keep your money in your pocket, whatever small amount that was. On those streets you could buy heroin for three bucks a packet, and addicts were desperate people.

It was a long way from his upbringing in the spacious gray clapboard house overlooking the Atlantic Ocean, where a sea mist hung everlastingly in the air and the cushions smelled of damp, and roaring fires were lit every evening; where you stood, warming your backside while the front of you still felt the chill, an experience he and Martha found they had in common. Apparently vast old houses in England suffered from the same dampness, the chill that could never be quite excluded unless, in the Brits' case, one put a small fortune into updating the central heating system, and which Martha told him only the newly very rich ever did.

"The rest of us," she'd said, "just put on another woolly."

Marco remembered thinking "woolly" an intriguing word, so much more descriptive and charming than "sweater," implying softness and warmth rather than overheated sweat. It had been the basis of their first conversation, in fact. In that coffee shop he'd watched Martha un-stripping layers of scarves and jackets, an outer quilted green one, then a black gilet, worn over the black pearl-buttoned cardigan, that she'd called her "woolly."

It was that seemingly perpetual Atlantic mist that had drawn Marco to the warmer ends of the earth. To the south of France, the shores of Italy, the beaches of Greece and Turkey. He loved the smell of sun-warmed rocks, the salt tang of the sea, and most of all the color palette. The first time he experienced it, he was on a trip alone trying to salve his conscience, eking out a couple hundred dollars over as many months as possible, sleeping where he could, in some long-dead grandparents' small white-washed room in a village not unlike the village where he now found himself, only perhaps even more remote; or on a fishing vessel where the rough seas made him ill. The sea had been his blessing and his tragedy. That he had now overcome the memory and loved his small place with its water view was the best, and hardest, decision he had made in his life.

Back then, though, he had slept rough, grown a beard by necessity, carried his few belongings in a canvas knap-sack, taken a job here, a job there, anything he could get where they paid him in cash, enough for the next meal, the next bus ticket to the next place. Wherever that might be.

A year passed. Thirteen, fourteen months, before the memory of his sister faded, just enough that she was not the first thing in his mind the moment he woke. She was nine years old when it happened. He was sixteen, old enough to be left in charge, his father had said. There was no mother, had not been since the sister, whose name was Elinor, always shortened to Ellie, was born. "Mom went to a better place," Ellie would inform people solemnly. "She left me for my father and my brother to take care of."

Marco could remember her voice as clearly as if she were speaking now. He remembered her running through the spiky sea grass that nicked your legs in little smarting cuts, berry-brown from a summer at the beach, long dark hair swinging in a ponytail, slipping and sliding, jumping over the rocks, shrieking as the waves rolled in at her. And then she was out of sight.

He had gone after her in minutes, seconds maybe. Seconds too late.

Ellie disappeared from that beach in those moments he'd taken his eyes off her. He could still hear her now though, laughing as she jumped, shrieking when she slid into a rock pool, making him smile. "Hope a clam bites your toe," he remembered yelling after her as he scanned the horizon to see if the whales were spouting that day. She never answered.

When she did not return he went to look for her but the bit of beach where she had been was empty. Holding a hand to his eyes he'd looked around; he checked the rocks, then with a lurch of his heart ran to the water's edge, stood scanning the ocean hurling itself almost gently that day onto the pebbles, then slurping back, only to rush in again in a froth of white foam.

Ellie was not in the water. She was no longer on the beach. In the space of minutes she had been taken. A sexual predator, the police told him. He was known to be in the area. A repeat offender.

"No way," Marco remembered himself saying as the horror of what might have happened to Ellie took hold of him. *"I'll kill him if he's hurt her!"* he'd yelled. He'd even, later, found out where and how to buy a gun. It was tucked in his belt when the police called his father to say they had found Ellie's body, and Marco immediately went in search of the man.

The cops got there first, shot the predator before Marco even knew where he was. But never in his life would he forget the primitive urge for revenge; an eye for an eye, a life for a life. And he would never forget Ellie, whose childish sweet voice he could still hear in his head, even though he was sitting under the old olive tree in Costas's bar, smelling the sweetness of jasmine and the aroma of roasting meat and the salt lick of the sea, viewing its blueness that was so unlike the gray Atlantic where her abused body had been found.

It was the reason, he supposed now, that he was so concerned about the red-haired girl in the blue dress. What had happened to her was not so far from what had happened to his sister. It made it that much more urgent to find out.

From his seat in the bar, he saw a boat approaching. It was the *Zeus*. He'd heard a rumor that its captain had rescued a half-drowned girl. He was in the Jeep in a flash.

The tires screeched as Marco swung to a stop on the jetty. He was out and running toward the black gulet, Em yapping alongside him, casting a wary eye at the water. As the boat edged to the mooring Marco saw the man in a gold-braided captain's hat throwing a fender over the side. A young T-shirted man was at the helm.

He hailed the captain, said he needed to speak with him. "About a young woman," he called as the gangplank was lowered, "a half-drowned woman you rescued."

Zacharias rolled his eyes; he'd known she would be trouble. He surely was not letting this guy on board, spying around, asking questions. "What is she to you?" he demanded.

"I saw her. I saw someone strike her, hit her head so hard it sent her reeling, bleeding . . ."

"This was not on my boat," Zacharias said. "No woman got killed on my boat."

Marco eyed him from the foot of the gangplank. The captain stood at the top, barring the way.

"Then she *is* dead," Marco said quietly.

Zacharias's expression turned to shock. "She is *not*

dead," he said, deciding quickly he had better tell what happened. "Only *almost*. I think not much longer and she will be. She drowned," he added, to further clarify the position. "My crew found her, got her out of the water. She must have fallen off some tourist boat, smashed her head open. It was not good," he added with a deep sigh because he saw no way out of this with the authorities.

"Then if she's not on your boat, where is she?"

"On another boat. Big. Expensive. They came to pick her up."

"The name of the boat?" Marco demanded, impatiently.

Zacharias shrugged. He had not taken notice, in fact he did not remember even seeing a name, he'd been too involved with getting rid of the girl.

Marco knew he had to get to the girl first if there was any chance at all of her being able to speak. If she was even, please God, still alive. He was witness to what was probably going to turn into murder, not simply a violent attack. Somebody had to protect this young woman's rights. Somebody had to help her and it looked like he was the only one who could do it. But first he had to find that boat.

12

In New York, Martha was lingering over her usual morning macchiato and sesame bagel in the deli near her apartment, prior to meeting a client to go over the revamped designs. This was the third set and Martha suspected the total might rise to four. Or even five. Some of these women were too rich even to *know* their own minds, let alone *make up* their minds. One day it was this, the next that; in fact the grass was always greener. It paid, in Martha's opinion, to have less and enjoy what you had, but ever the diplomat, she was always concerned for her clients' well-being, striving to make sure they were, in the end, happy. That was her job, and despite its frustrations she loved it and found it creative.

Anyhow, for once her mind was not on her job; it was back in Turkey with Marco. *Marco and Martha*. It sounded like a cartoon, an animated movie that would make people laugh. Marco had called her again about the girl he supposedly had seen fall off a boat and drown, and since then she'd been worried about him. This was a girl, Marco also said, who had been beaten around the head. She was bleeding as she fell; a girl he had searched the sea for—and not found.

Spooning up the froth on her macchiato Martha wondered if there had been such an incident. Since no missing person had been reported she had questioned Marco as to exactly what he thought he had seen.

"Not *thought*," he'd said, sounding angry, something she had never heard in his voice before. "*I saw* a girl fall from a boat. A black yacht. Her head was bloody. She had red hair. I got in the dinghy and went to look for her."

And never found her, Martha thought. And that was the problem. She sighed as she took a sip of the coffee. It was too hot and she burnt her lips. She slicked on her cherry Blistex to take the sting away, which of course made the coffee taste awful. She sighed again. She had never known Marco like this, so concerned, so adamant as to what had happened. About the large black boat from which the girl had fallen. About her red hair floating in the sea. And the extent of his despair when he was unable to find her. It was as though Marco felt guilty, that somehow it was his fault that an unknown woman had "disappeared." Yet no one had been reported as "disappeared." No one was lost. No one found. No one drowned.

Martha's phone rang. She checked it quickly. It was her youngest sister, Lucy. "Hi," she said, answering. "What's up?"

"I met a guy." Lucy's voice was high-pitched with excitement.

There was a lull while Martha took in this news. Then, "Who, exactly?" she asked, wearily, because this was not Lucy's first foray into love, and when Martha had seen her a few weeks ago she was not even attached. Nor, as far as she had known, was she seeing anyone in particular.

"His name is Ahmet." Lucy told her quickly all about him. He was not an Englishman, he was "foreign." When

Martha asked exactly what kind of "foreign," Lucy told her he was probably Croatian, and a millionaire. "And good-looking," she added, sounding more thoughtful. "And sexy."

Oh God, Martha thought, she's done it again. Lucy fell in love at the drop of a hat. And besides, no Croatians were called "Ahmet."

"Maybe I'll bring him over to New York to meet you," Lucy told her in that rapid-fire way of speaking she had. "And I want to meet your Marco."

"He's not exactly *my* Marco." Martha wished he was though.

"Anyhow, this guy owns a yacht. He asked me out on it."

"*What?* You didn't go, did you?"

"Of course I didn't, I'm not that daft." Lucy was laughing. "Not yet, anyhow. But you'll get to meet him. We'll have dinner or something. Talk to you later." And Lucy rang off.

Just what I need, Martha thought, switching off her cell phone. Lucy was the youngest, just seventeen, and most irresponsible of the three sisters. The eldest, Sarah, was a pediatrician in England. Lucy was supposed to be at drama school, auditioning for acting jobs, but was perpetually out of work "seeing how the real world lives." A typical Lucy remark if there ever was one.

In Martha's opinion their parents had indulged Lucy shamefully. The family lived at Patrons Hall, "the Ancestral Home," as Marco had called it, amused, when Martha had taken him for a quick visit. They'd been en route to Paris with a stopover in London, when she'd rented a small car and driven them there, whizzing fast down the motorway with Marco flinching next to her while she laughed at his fears and told him she had been doing this route for years, knew it like the back of her hand. She did, but he'd still heaved a sigh of relief when they arrived without incident.

Martha remembered turning to look at Marco sitting silently in the seat next to her. He was staring intently at the rambling, creamy-stone house with what she recognized as his "painter's eyes," a special look where he seemed to absorb a place, or a person, somewhere deep within his brain, in his soul perhaps. That was one of the reasons he was such a good artist. A great artist, it had often been said, though Marco would only describe himself, simply, as "a painter."

"I'm looking at history," he'd said quietly. "I'm looking at masons and woodworkers, at slate that must have been mined locally, for nothing came from far away, not when this place was first built. Elizabethan chimneys, Queen Anne tiles, Victorian gothic architraves . . ."

"And antique boilers that barely keep the place warm," Martha said, laughing because it had always been that way. She remembered men standing by the fire after a dinner, lifting their coattails to warm their backsides while the women, gorgeous in their sleeveless silk and jewels, fanned themselves as if too hot because to admit they were not would have been rude to their hostess, who was, in this memory of Martha's, her grandmother.

Still, whatever its defects, Patrons Hall was home and always would be, and nothing, not the small flat in London's Chelsea, nor her charming, cozy-in-winter-cooled-by-air-conditioning-in-summer Manhattan apartment would ever replace it in Martha's heart.

Now she sighed: there was a new man on the scene who Martha would have to deal with. She'd probably have to extricate her sister from his clutches, at a time when she had so much personal stuff on her mind. Lucy was small, she was blond, she had Martha's clear blue eyes inherited from their mother, and as far as men were concerned, absolutely no bloody sense. "Love" was what ruled Lucy, and she was about to become Martha's responsibility. She guessed she had better call Marco and warn him.

First, though, she would get onto her friend at the jewelers about the chain with the initials, see if they might find to whom it had belonged. Like Marco, she had the feeling it might actually have belonged to the girl he claimed to have seen fall off the boat, never to be found. A shiver ran through her. *She might be searching for someone dead.*

13

Sometimes, Martha felt a long way from home, which, of course, she was. Even though she now officially called New York "home," nothing could replace Patrons Hall, where she and her two sisters had been raised, like wild kids, she remembered with a reminiscent smile, allowed to roam on their ponies through fields and woods, jumping fences and falling off; somebody always seemed to have a broken limb with a grubby white plaster cast scrawled with silly messages written by friends.

Patrons Hall was built four hundred years ago. Though Marco referred to it laughingly as her "ancestral home," it was the truth. The ancestor in question, one Horatio Patron, had started out as a stonecutter working the local quarry, graduating to building small cottages, eventually helping restore larger houses, learning his trade until finally he'd built his own home to his own design, which if truth were told, was decidedly eccentric.

Martha remembered winters there, the roaring fire in the nursery grate and old-fashioned Nanny, who, though she had a proper electric dryer in the laundry room, still liked to dry their clothes on the brass fender in front of the fire, causing it to smoke, as a result of which the children always smelled of applewood.

In fact, now, as she thought about the past, sitting in busy, bustling, towering Manhattan, its bumpy, cracked streets teeming with people intent on their lives, oblivious to those around them, Martha remembered her childhood home as full of friends, her parents' friends and their own. She remembered the butler, who nowadays would have been called "the houseman." Then, though, "butler" was a prestigious job to which a man might aspire. Besides, he had been with the family for forty years and was so much a part of it, they could never have done without him. His wife, known only as "the Mrs.," was shorter than her husband, who was a very tall, very thin man with silver hair and a beak of a nose, and who Martha remembered as never smiling, though he was kind enough to the children, when he acknowledged their presence in "his" house, that is. The Mrs. barely made the five-foot-tall mark on the kitchen wall where the three children were measured annually, their height marked with a Biro. Of course, the butler himself was never measured, he kept his dignity at all times. They were an odd-looking couple, she in charge of housekeeping, overseeing the cook and the maids, always in her dark blue daytime dress, which was changed to black at five P.M. and never with an apron. The Mrs. was above all that. The fact was they were "family."

They lived in a cottage near the gates, down a mile-long avenue bordered once upon a time with magnificent elms, later decimated by disease and felled to make way for hardier chestnuts, which now cast shade where needed and protected the old house from wind and storms. Martha loved the trees best when their branches were limned with the first winter snow, an event that often coincided with her and her sisters' return from boarding school for the

Christmas holiday. She remembered those trees at another time too, at a party, hung with scarlet Chinese lanterns for their parents' wedding anniversary, throwing their glow across white linen cloths on the two dozen tables, when miracle of miracles and with what some called Patron luck, the English night was balmy, no rain fell, and all was calm and full of happiness.

How, Martha wondered now, sitting alone sipping her macchiato on a New York morning, could she ever find that again. It was part of her life, her background, her family. But times had changed; her parents were long gone, hopefully to what was called "a better place." And with them went that way of life. Patrons Hall was still there, but there was no butler to ensure its upkeep, its "soul" as Martha liked to think of it.

The sisters often returned to their old home but there were no more times like the wedding anniversary dinner, at which the girls had been allowed to mingle with the grown-ups, and to choose what to wear, which resulted in the eldest sister in jeans and a Rolling Stones tongue T-shirt; the youngest in her mother's strapless long red silk dress, hitched up with safety pins, and Martha in a short black velvet dress with a puffy skirt. Nobody warned her that a puffy skirt flipped up when you sat down and she still recalled the hot embarrassment of dropping onto a chair only to reveal her girly white cotton knickers to the entire room. She blushed even now, at the memory. She'd kept that dress, her first grown-up party dress; still had it sheathed in a plastic cover, though when she looked at its tiny waistline she marveled at how she ever fit into it.

That night had been the most magical of her childhood, both parents so good-looking; James Edward Patron, tall, dark, and handsome in the classic style, elegant in a dark blue dinner jacket, with tiny sapphire studs, a gift from his wife, in his shirtfront. The shirt, though, was not buttoned

to the neck and bow-tied in the conventional way, because
he was not "conventional." He wore it open at the neck and
removed his jacket halfway through dinner, with apologies
to the ladies, getting up to prowl the tables, pour more
wine, stopping everywhere to chat, making everyone feel
welcome. Her mother was the best at that, though. Mary
Jane Patron had the happy knack of making each person
feel they were the most important guest, the most vital to
the spirit of the party, the most interesting of all. Her wide
pale blue eyes, which Martha inherited, sparkled with
amusement, her laughter rang out across the dark night
from where they sat beneath those red Chinese lanterns.
It was, in Martha's memory, as though they were touched
by magic. And she was sure, even now, that they were.

Sadly, that magic had deserted them some years ago
now, and life without them at Patrons Hall was simply not
the same. Even when the girls got together, sitting on the
red Turkey rug in front of the drawing room fire, toasting
crumpets on a long fork, "like Jane Austen women," they
said, laughing at themselves, they did it from *nostalgie,* a
wish to bring back that past, where they were all so happy.
And so loved.

"Old-fashioned" was how Martha's mother had described Patrons Hall when she first stepped through the
door, brought there as a bride by the too-gorgeously good-
looking husband, seven years younger than herself. She
was twenty-eight, practically "on the shelf," her already
married friends warned, urging her to get a move on before it was too late.

"Too late? For what?" had been Mary Jane's noncha-
lant reply.

And she'd turned out to be right. After all, look what
she ended up with just by waiting a bit—a lovely husband;
two lovely homes—there was one in London as well as the
country house. And, best of all, three beautiful children,

all girls. Mary Jane wasn't sure how she would have dealt with boys—sending them off to school in that British way at seven years old would have broken her heart, a heart which, before she met her lovely husband, had been broken several times, once quite severely. But that was in the past.

Making up for lost time, Mary Jane entertained lavishly in both her houses. She enjoyed her daughters, saying they kept her young, which they probably did if they were not driving her crazy—well Lucy, anyhow—and she really enjoyed her husband: his company, his smile, his caring demeanor. How lovely her life was.

Until, quite suddenly, on a small twisting mountain road driving over the Pyrenees back from Spain to France, it wasn't. One mistake, on her part, one tiny turn too wide. And it was all over.

Martha was fourteen at the time, and she made herself believe her mother was still with her, always there, invisible but protective. It was years before she could bring herself to face the truth and simply get on with her own life, something she found she was, quite suddenly, enjoying again. It was correct, the old saying, life must go on.

The girls continued to live at Patrons. Her father's sister moved in, along with her husband and a positive tribe of children, aged four to sixteen. They took over the orphaned girls' lives; saw them through schools, first dates, arguments, and illnesses, and somehow they all muddled through, successfully, as it turned out.

Sarah, Martha's eldest sister, was studious. From playing childhood doctors and nurses she'd gone on to become a well-respected pediatrician, putting her love and knowledge into helping other people's children while having none of her own. She claimed to be too busy for marriage, and perhaps she was right.

Martha was puzzled about what to do when she left

school. The university degree didn't seem to help much in the arts, to which she was inclined, so she got a job in an interior design store catering to wealthy clients, where she was the coffee girl/errand runner/folder of bolts of fabric and dropper-off of stuff in taxis, learning on the job.

Three years and three different boyfriends later, she was asked by a friend's mother to redesign her bathroom, make it larger, grander. She was able to do that and she did it well. "So now let's do over the kitchen," the friend said. It had taken off from there with recommendations from friends, until she made the time for a proper design course and became a professional. Martha wanted to call her company Patrons Pleasure but was warned it sounded like a sex shop. She thought about Martha Designs but realized there was already a famous Martha in the same field. Finally she ended up, simply, as Patrons.

She was young, connected, attractive, and in demand. Life was good to her. And eventually, she met Marco in the antique store. It was the old hook, line, and sinker.

Martha was no one-night-stand woman but the sexual attraction was mutual, and high octane. When Marco sat next to her in that coffee shop, Martha had to stop herself from reaching out to touch him, to run her fingers over his sexy mouth, to put her arms round his neck, to be close to him.

Half an hour later they left together. Forty minutes later they were in bed—well, that is, lying together on the mattress on the floor of his messy studio, naked, skin on skin, body on body, mouth on mouth. She wished it would never end. And it had not. For which both she, and he, thanked God.

Now, back in New York, she wanted to get the next flight out back to Turkey, to be with Marco anywhere in the world. She knew he wouldn't be coming home any time soon. He was too obsessed with the girl he believed he had seen drown. She hoped he was wrong.

Her phone beeped. It was her friend at Cartier in Paris. He told her the necklace with the initials had been bought by an Argentinian oil company. It had been picked up from the store by a documented messenger and delivered to a suite at the Plaza Athenée hotel, and signed for by a young woman employed as an assistant by that company.

The company's records were brief: headquarters a PO address in Cairo, a second in Buenos Aires. But there were no company records filed and no one knew who the directors or owners of the company might be. It was a mystery, as was the necklace.

14

When he wasn't at his English house, Ahmet Ghulbian lived mostly on his yacht, the MV *Lady Marina,* sailing from port to port, country to country, the way other well-known kings of shipping and tankers had done before him. Ahmet had added the extra-lucrative business of illegal money laundering to his CV, yet he still maintained a low profile. He had seen the way to disaster in a flashy lifestyle, in expensive women who must be paid to be on his arm or in his bed, and to keep their silence.

The yacht was 250 feet of black splendor, built five years previously to Ahmet's own design, modified, obviously, by shipbuilding professionals, but the result was exactly what he wanted. A showpiece of a craft, sleek, elegant, with luxurious accommodations for as many as thirty guests and vast social areas, complete with two swimming pools, one indoor, one out. It was decorated by the yachting world's top designer, with the permanent crew of sixteen housed carefully belowdecks.

The "social deck," as Ghulbian liked to call the main deck, had seen its fair share of wild parties over the years.

It was an expansive space whose length gave it the feel of a large hotel, with careful groupings of sofas and comfortable chairs in pale linens around glass coffee tables. Antique lamps topped with pleated bronze silk shades cast a discreet light over the "goings-on," whatever that might mean, but there was certainly plenty of it. Ahmet was not a man who liked women, he merely enjoyed them. Which is not to say, either, that he was a sexual expert, or even proficient, simply that he needed to be thought so. Image was all. Actually, that was not quite true. *Money* was all. Image came second, though if you had them both, then you were really in business. Which Ahmet believed he was.

He had no need for multiple properties to be maintained in countries which would demand taxes be paid. Of course, Ahmet was also an expert in the art of the payoff; he or his minions always knew the right man in the right place. So far, it had worked well. Nevertheless he worried about that unknown "tomorrow." And, in a way, that tomorrow might have arrived in the form of the red-haired Angie, who was surely not the "angel" her name might imply.

Oddly, it was his own mother, a woman Ahmet hated, who had pointed the route to his future. "Get rid of people that stand in your way," she'd advised at the end of a long night of drinking her part. Ahmet had rarely imbibed then, and never more than was good for him, and he never did any form of drugs, though he wasn't averse to using them on others, which was quite another matter. He despised people who used drugs, people "who leaned on them," he'd say, smiling ruefully, "for moral support." In Ahmet's opinion they did drugs because they were unsure of themselves, had no confidence in what they were doing or their chosen path of life. Or death.

The first person Ahmet killed was a woman. Her name was Fleur de Roc. It sounded like a perfume to him but she was no flowery-scented lovely young girl: Fleur was middle-aged, fat, and well-off. Not rich, Ahmet was not then in a position to meet rich women; they lived in a different world, but to him, then, Fleur was wealthy, with three or four small shops in the Cairo bazaar, a weekend sailboat kept in Alexandria, and an overstuffed apartment with its own bathroom. Ahmet had never had a bathroom of his own until he met Fleur; he'd been lucky to have a bathroom at all.

Poverty, he recalled now, sitting at his desk on the luxurious MV *Lady Marina,* was made up of memories like that: the odors never left you.

Anyhow, one way or another, when he and Fleur were out on her sailboat, somehow she slipped, fell, drowned in a storm. He'd cried when he told the authorities the story. He ended up owning that sailboat, and Fleur's savings. And he'd found out something new about himself. He enjoyed killing women. It was better even than sex, at which he'd always suspected he wasn't quite good enough. In fact, if it were not for the money, the gifts, the flowers, the trinkets . . . who knew if those women would even so much as consider him. Sexually.

His mother found out about his affair with Fleur and her sudden mysterious death. She knew what her son was capable of and threatened to expose him unless he gave her a share of the money. The mother was as ruthless as the son, only far simpler.

It had been so easy with Fleur that drowning was to become Ahmet's favorite method of disposal. His mother was his second victim, after, of course, he had taken out an insurance policy on her life, not a vast amount because he did not yet have the funds to pay for anything like that, but sufficient to get him to his next goal in life. Which was away from Egypt, away from home, away from his own identity. Ahmet needed to become a new man. So he reinvented himself.

Ahmet was intelligent and now he claimed to have attended good schools, a fact no one ever seemed to check, and certainly never challenged, taking him at his confident word. He'd become an attractive man, middle height, stockily built with olive-toned skin and eyes so deeply set and so dark they looked almost black behind the tinted lenses he always wore. Those glasses were to become a part of his "look," along with the Savile Row suits, the floral silk pocket handkerchiefs, and the faint aroma of Violettes de Parme, a perfume made only for him in Paris.

But it was Ahmet's charm that brought him success. He worked hard at losing his accent and his deep soft voice acquired an almost British tone, though he was careful not to overdo it, which might have meant one of those upper-class Brits asking what school he had attended. He would have had to lie, and he knew lies had a way of coming back at you, leaving you more entangled than when you started out. He'd also learned that the hard way. Life's experiences accounted for a lot of the way Ahmet had turned out, the man he finally became: rich, successful, admired by many, sought after by women, who mostly, he suspected, would like to get their hands on his money, but he had Greek billionaire examples to show him that was not the way to go.

Besides, he did not like women. He used them for sex, always charming them first, of course, then later for the other, deeper pleasures. There was no longer anything rough at the edges about Ahmet. He did not want cheap hookers; he wanted women who responded to his wealth and his billionaire aura, yet somehow he still could not get along with aristocratic, wealthy women. With his hidden background and the mental issues that remained from his poverty-stricken youth and his slut of a mother, as well as the father he had never known, Ahmet needed to keep himself strictly private. Upper-class Brits knew everything about everybody else. That was how you counted in their world.

Which is why he had so often ended up with girls like Angie. Nice, simple young women, attractive of course, that was a given, and with no background to speak of, no one to look out for them, no one to come looking for them when they disappeared. He believed no one would miss the Angies of the world, and so far they never had. Angie was the perfect target. He enjoyed her so much, enjoyed best of all seeing her long red hair floating in the wake of the *Lady Marina* as he'd taken off, full-speed ahead. None of the crew so much as knew she was missing, since it was none of their business where she was at any time or, in fact, who their boss was with or even if she was on the ship. Only his longtime assistant, Mehitabel, who had been with him forever and was utterly devoted, knew anything about Ahmet's sexual proclivities, his need for violence, his ultimate fascination in death.

Pleased, Ahmet had decided it was time to move on. And that's when the call came through from the gulet, *Zeus,* that they had taken on board a badly injured young woman, an almost drowned young woman. Ahmet did not have to ask if she had red hair. There could only be one half-dead young woman in the Aegean right then. He gave orders to turn the *Lady Marina* around, asked the master of *Zeus* his exact nautical location, and set off to get Angie back. To "rescue her," he thought with a sardonic smile. Now he would have to start all over again. And now there were witnesses.

Of course he had not pushed Angie off the deck of his boat. There had been no need. Enough pills in her champagne, the kind of pills roving guys out for an easy hookup slyly slip into women's drinks at a bar, worked like a charm. Once Angie was sufficiently doped, all he had to do was threaten her, let her escape onto the deck, where

Mehitabel was waiting with the bottle of champagne. He watched Angie take the blow, watched her slip to one side, fall overboard. Then they had taken off smoothly across the green waters, leaving her to her fate.

She'd had to be gotten rid of. The lonely, isolated young women he employed to "help" in his business, secretly delivering parcels of cash, or documents, when he bought and sold armaments, always had to go. In fact Ahmet was surprised none of them ever *understood* that was part of his game; that he was hardly likely to keep them around after they had done what he'd asked, done their job, so to speak, so afterward they could sell their tale to the tabloids, or go to the international police. Murder *him,* in a way. Did that make him a serial killer? Though he enjoyed killing them, it was, after all, part of the sexual thrill, Ahmet thought not. He was simply a man doing what he had to do in order to survive. *Survival of the fittest,* wasn't that what it was called? In fact, more likely it was survival of the cleverest.

The MV *Lady Marina* was named, he always told guests, for the goddess of the sea. He was not too sure of his facts about the sea goddess but it gave him an air of intellectual authority he needed, coming from his background. In fact, though Ahmet claimed to be Greek, he was of mixed Egyptian and Armenian-gypsy heritage, something he would never have admitted. There was no need with his fabricated story of an upbringing in a wealthy Greek family forced to roam the world, as he did himself now, when the rich were replaced by a socialist regime and no longer ruled their own world of autocrats and playboys and demimondaines, of which Ahmet claimed his mother was one.

Ahmet acknowledged secretly, and only ever to himself, that his mother was a slut. However, he also acknowledged it was her very sluttiness which had paid for his upbringing in the small apartment in Cairo, in a urine-smelling alley teeming with shady men in white caftans and women in black burkas, their faces hidden, something which excited him. He'd longed to see what lay behind those veils. That urge had never left him. A voyeur he was and would forever be.

Angie's great tumbling mass of flame-colored hair had the same effect as that of a garment hiding her nakedness: it had turned him on so completely he had contemplated allowing her to stay. But of course he could not. He'd given her a job to do, a package to be delivered to a man who would meet her in a café he specified in the port of Fethiye in Turkey, where afterward Ahmet would pick her up. Angie did not know that the package contained several million dollars in various currencies, part of a drug deal Ahmet had made for a client.

He'd kept the promise he'd made to Angie, in bed in that expensive hotel room. She was flown to the destination by private plane—not his own, because he did not want any connection made between the two of them. It was rented from a commercial airline and paid for from an Argentinian company account that would be impossible to trace back to him. But Angie had been allowed to go shopping before she left. Thrilled, she'd bought a load of things, undergarments from La Perla, dresses from Prada and Dior, shoes from Louboutin and Manolo.

"After all, a young woman on such an important journey will need clothes," Ahmet had said to her, teeth gleaming in a white-porcelain-bonded smile. It was an expensive smile, and very well done by one of the best cosmetic dentists in Paris, as Ahmet's natural teeth had barely survived his poverty-stricken upbringing.

Poverty was the one thing Ahmet was afraid of. The memory of it clung to him like the sweat-stained clothing of his youth, the odor returning every now and then to remind him, to urge him onward. Whatever it took, he was determined to do it. He had run from that room on the stinking alley, putting all thoughts of the woman he called Mother behind him, taking any job, however mean, however corrupt, however evil, Ahmet was your boy. Success had come easily after that.

Now, he wondered what to do with Angie. Should he simply allow her to die, alone in that cabin belowdecks where only Mehitabel knew she was? Or simply slide her, helpless, over the side again, where she would finally be swallowed up by the sea. The sea that had given her back to him. The sea that did not seem to want her.

Yet there was something about Angie that stuck in his mind. She was different from the other girls, a rare type, ballsy, funny, and courageous. He even liked her. He decided he would take her home.

15

Trust played no part in Ahmet Ghulbian's life. The word itself had no meaning. He had emerged unwanted from his mother's womb with all his self-protective instincts intact. He could only trust himself. His mother ceased to exist, disappeared. He had no other family, he was a child of the rough Cairo streets, and babyhood was a non-memory, for which, had he believed in God, he would have thanked Him. Poverty of the lowest, most humiliating kind, begging in the streets, a child offering small packets of chewing gum for a coin, rapacious men with hungry eyes wanting to buy him instead. It took a lot of fear and a lot more desire for him to begin to believe there was a way out, and that way led with himself.

He was nine or ten when he bought out the old man who sold the chewing gum to resell on the street, using the small amount of money saved so bitterly at the cost of going hungry. It was something he would never forget. At twelve he controlled his own area, three streets, each of which led into a major artery, which in turn led to a better neighborhood where families lived in apartments, and not like him, in a shed flung together from tarpaper and wooden debris with corrugated tin for a roof that broiled in the heat of summer and flooded in the rains. For a bed, he made himself a kind of bunk using two old oil drums and a couple of the planks. It didn't occur to him, fixing up his oil drum bed, that one day he might be selling oil in drums larger than that, and sleeping in a bed bought with money made from that, and with a proper roof over his head from which no rain gained admittance. That was a long way ahead. After all, he was only a boy.

Of course there was no such thing as boyhood where he lived. "Lived" was too good a word. Existence was all it was and there were times, days on end, weeks, in fact, when young Ahmet asked himself was it worth going on. Small for his age, thin with the popped belly of malnutrition, eyes too big in his sunken face, teeth broken or lost. He was a nothing child. Disposable. He was only like all the other boys around him. One of hundreds, thousands.

In a single day he became different, a business owner with his packs of chewing gum, selling them on to other boys, making a bit here, more there, moving inexorably upward. To drugs. A ready market if ever there was one, and who would ever suspect the skinny kid in the ragged shirt with the dirty face and frightened eyes. He was, he realized, a natural. With his looks, the way he could turn on the big-eyed wonder, the helplessness, he was a success.

Of course he soon lost the need for the big-eyed wonder. Tough was what he needed to be. In his first encounter with a real street tough, of the kind that brandished a knife and threatened to cut his guts out if he didn't hand it over, he'd had to gather his wits together and strike back. He grabbed the knife and he used it. He'd stood for a moment after he'd done it, staring at the knife sticking out between the young thug's third and fourth ribs, right above his heart, at the blood seeping out. He had been disappointed it had not actually poured.

He'd thought enough to snatch the knife from the boy's gut, surprised it was so difficult. Then he'd turned to face the small crowd of youngsters who'd been watching, only to find they'd all disappeared. That was the way it was—when trouble came, your friends disappeared. These were only street friends, of course. After that he would never allow anyone to be his friend.

The drug dealers were different, older, meaner, dangerous. His life depended on how quickly he could deliver the "goods" as they all called it, the packets, the parcels, the plastic bags of white powders that he never once experimented with. He knew it would be the death of him and he was only just starting to live. He made enough over a couple of years to go into business for himself, after all, he already knew all the dealers, the customers, the financial workings of the drug trade. It soon became known that he could be trusted. He was an immediate success.

He acquired an apartment, the first place of any substance he had ever lived in. It was on the third floor, at the top of the building because the ground floor was dangerous; a gun could be poked through your window, a machete could break down your door, a fire could be set to smoke you out and rob you. All anyone wanted from him was his money, hard-earned, by the skin of his teeth—now better thanks to a cut-rate dentist he had done a drug favor for. And all he wanted was to earn more. To get it. To keep it. To be a rich man.

It didn't happen overnight.

He was eighteen, thick dark hair, burning dark eyes, olive-skinned, a lure for women on the loose and men on the prowl. Whatever, it was always his choice. But the women paid better. As he found out when he met Fleur.

And that was the real beginning of everything.

First, he opened a small café as a front for money laundering, did well at that. He found an old tanker for sale, a rust bucket but still usable if you could find men desperate enough to sail it, filled with cut-price oil that threatened to explode at the drop of a careless cigarette. It was a risk that paid off. He bought more tankers, losing only one, and that went right to the bottom along with its men but without any evidence of exactly why. Insurance paid mightily on that one, gave him his first real push upward, in the right direction.

He bought an apartment in Cairo, custom-tailored suits, ventured into the smarter cafés for a drink in the evening.

Insurance was where he'd really taken off, small, private insurance. He found shady men only too willing to be protected, found also the chink in their armor was that they needed the security he offered. He was better than they were, cleverer, a sharper businessman.

And so it went. And here he was now. Ahmet Ghulbian, reputed billionaire, which, if you counted his real estate assets, his oil business, his banking, might not amount to that, but throw in the loan-sharking and the gambling game and he was surely it.

He was a king amongst men, a god women aspired to know and the world envied. To himself he was still Ahmet Ghulbian, whose real name had been buried along with his mother—a kid in the Cairo bazaar, looking for a life.

16

The gray wooden house on the Romney marshland in England was Ahmet's hideout, his special place where he could be completely alone. Its previous owner was a newspaper tycoon who'd met a sad end in a fight with his lover involving a knife with which he was about to carve the Sunday roast, an ample side of beef, locals remembered admiringly; enough to feed twenty, yet they were only the two. The place had remained empty for many years with stories of haunting and unexplained mists surrounding it on moonlit nights.

When he first inspected it Ahmet's comment was that at least there were no hounds baying at that moon. Still, he liked the location on the edge of the marshes where the grass was greener than normal grass, a vibrant, dazzling, wet green that changed abruptly to deep dark brown mud which sucked in any wild creature unfortunate enough to make the mistake of alighting on it. The house was remote yet accessible from London, a secret kind of place with no locals loitering curiously. In fact

they kept away, put off by the legendary murder and ru-
mored haunting.

And that was the reason Ahmet was able to purchase
the house for a minimal sum, the estate being only too glad
to finally unload it. And, since local men were reluctant to
set foot in the place, Ahmet brought in his own workforce,
Italians and Croats mostly, whom he housed in temporary
prefabricated buildings with the minimum amenities, but
who were anyway glad of the job.

The gray wood was strengthened with stone, the roof
retiled in a darker gray, windows double-sealed against the
prevailing wind and winter storms. The inside was made
luxurious with paneling taken from older houses, with
probably better histories and reputations. In the grand hall
there was a crystal chandelier, musically and permanently
aflutter in the also prevailing draft, no matter how his ex-
perts tried to find its source and seal it. Silk rugs covered
the gray stone floors, which were heated electrically, and
the heavy-looking furnishings came from the most expensive antique stores in Paris and London. A complete
restaurant-size kitchen with stainless equipment, black
granite counters, and six ovens awaited a chef, a man
Ghulbian imported on the rare occasions he occupied the
house. Or sometimes not, when he needed to be completely
alone. As he did now.

He sat in front of the fire in what used to be called the
drawing room, sipping red wine, a Pétrus of noble vintage,
from a glass so fine it seemed the mere touch of his teeth
might shatter it. The log fire smelled of pine, the grate was
aglow, flames edged with blue licked gently. The cushioned red leather chair was soft, there was the sound of
the wind outside, the shift of logs in the grate, the aroma
of the wine in his nose. Its exquisite flavor on his palate
gave Ahmet no pleasure. He was consumed with the image,

not of the redheaded girl, who was already his, but of the small blonde, of her delicate features, the wide forehead from which she pulled back her hair severely, of her almost blue eyes. Were they blue, were they gray? He could not decide. And the image of her lips as she'd pouted, wondering beneath a flutter of lashes whether to join him for that drink at the Ritz bar. Lucy.

He knew he must be patient. He had learned how to make a woman his own. He would groom her. "Groom" was the phrase he used when he thought about how to make a woman his, readying her with small gifts along with handwritten notes saying how much he had enjoyed her company. Then flowers, of course, always long-stemmed white roses, even in the depths of winter. He would suggest she might enjoy dinner again sometime. He always left the ball in the woman's court, knowing she would be intrigued and would agree. He was so confident she would accept, he'd even make a reservation at a top restaurant in anticipation.

The young women he showered with this attention were not used to such a high-flying lifestyle. They were ordinary, not necessarily small-town but certainly with provincial mentalities. He knew how to pick them out. Angie was perfect, but she had beaten him. Temporarily, of course. Now, he was "taking care of" Angie. He'd bring her to the house on the marshes, a treacherous land where you were safe to walk only if you knew the correct path. People had disappeared in those marshes, sucked deep in the glutinous brown mire, unable to extricate themselves as the swamp closed over their heads. When he was ready, Angie would no longer trouble him.

Restless, he got up and paced the room. He needed light, space. *Air!* He was choking, and suddenly for the first time since he was a boy, he felt a thrill of what he recognized as fear.

He picked up the phone and summoned his plane. He would leave at once for the yacht. He would take care of business, return the same day. There were advantages to being rich, after all.

17

ANGIE

I knew I was still on the yacht and that it was moored, not because I could see out but because all movement had stopped. I heard excited shouting, the harsh run of rope, the rattle of chain, then the stillness with just the sound of men's voices, the cry of a curlew, the groan of the ship against the fenders as it heaved into place.

My hands were bound. There was a gag in my mouth. I did not know how long I had lain on this bed, and now the fact that it was a bed and not a bunk registered. I reached out my hands, bound at the wrists, rolled over a little so I could touch either side of me: cotton sheets, a soft blanket. I did not need to touch my body to know that I was naked. Had I been raped? I felt nothing, no pain, no trickle of blood, no headache. I felt almost normal. Except for one thing.

Lifting my bound hands I touched my face. Higher until I managed to touch my forehead. Back a little. Enough to know. *They had cut off all my hair. My beautiful, long red hair.* The only thing under my fingers was a faint, harsh stubble and a long line of stitches holding together my broken scalp.

Tears coursed down my cheeks, ran into my mouth. I was bald as any baby and I was crying for the hair that had been my only claim to beauty. It occurred to me, through my tears, that I might well be crying for my life too, because I was sure as hell about to lose it. I was trapped on Ghulbian's boat. I knew it must be him.

The pillow was wet with my tears. I rolled my head to one side in an attempt to escape the cold dampness but now it was under my cheek and still the tears kept on flowing, adding to the soggy mess.

Tears. What good were they? What had tears ever done for mankind other than express grief? Could I really be lying here bound and gagged, a prisoner not knowing my fate, only that it was likely to end in my death, crying like any vain woman for my lost hair? Had it not grown in again when I'd had the cropped Audrey Hepburn look all those years ago? But that was by choice. This was abuse of a kind the perpetrator understood very well. Sadistic. That was the correct word for the man who had done this to me; Ahmet Ghulbian was a sadist.

Eyes closed under the bandage, I thought of Ghulbian telling me to go shopping, buy whatever I liked; after all, he'd said, a girl would need pretty things on a yacht trip. And oh how I had enjoyed that, starting from bare skin up with the prettiest, softest, sexiest little underthings that felt like a second skin on my own, and which also looked, I had to admit, sensational on the body I had toned at the gym at five every morning, five days a week.

The only shadow over my enjoyment had been the thought that I was going to have to show myself in these flimsy outfits to Ghulbian who, while not uninterested in sex, was a man who preferred to devour with his eyes.

A voyeur mostly, which left a girl unsatisfied and wondering what she had done wrong that she could not stimulate him sufficiently to make him want to devour her with his mouth, to penetrate her, hard and fast the way I liked. With Ahmet—I cannot go on calling him by his last name, I know him too intimately for that—with Ahmet what you got in a fast few minutes was all you got. Then it was back to business: his phone, his iPad, his inner thoughts, which left a woman very much alone.

If only he had left me alone in the end. Simply sent me on my way with my small suitcase of new clothes, tottering a bit on my new Louboutins, a cheery goodbye and thanks it was lovely maybe we'll see each other again . . .

But that was not to be. I remember opening my eyes when I'd felt Ahmet on top of my naked body. I felt his excitement as he pressed himself between my open legs. The next thing I'd felt was the edge of the knife against my throat. I glanced quickly down, saw the gleam of sharp steel, moaned out loud in fear, felt the blade press harder, nicking my skin, felt the thin stripe of blood that now lay over the small wound. He'd yelled out, pushing the knife deeper with one hand. I'd been too afraid even to scream as he raped me.

It was over. He climbed off me. I was still alive. I was still afraid I was going to die but with what had just happened, also fighting the horror, the pain, the man I had not really known, I silently wished I could die right now, this minute.

There were sounds. A door opening. Ahmet was now standing by the bed. He was talking to someone. A woman, who answered in a low voice. Neither of them addressed me and I lay like a frozen slab of meat in the very center of that luxurious bed, stained now with my blood and the excesses of gratified masculine sex.

I heard the woman's footsteps coming toward me, heard

the door close behind Ghulbian, did not dare open my eyes and look upon my fate. I felt her breath on my cheek. She was bent over me, staring directly into my face. Then the sudden vicious prick of a needle in my arm made me whimper. And I knew nothing more.

When I came around I had no idea of how much time had passed. I raised a hand, touched my naked head, held back the moan, told myself at least I was alive. Or was I dreaming again, hovering somewhere between reality and memory? Unable to bring myself even to try to open my eyes, I listened. The soft slap of water against the hull of the boat was all I heard. Not even the cry of gulls. Did that mean I was somewhere out at sea, too far for the greedy gulls to follow, kept at the harbor by the promise of easy food?

I listened again: the slap of the water was rhythmic, quiet, a tiny swell that barely rocked the boat. If we were anchored out at sea surely there would have been more movement. More sound. We had to be in a harbor. And if we were, there must be other boats, other people.

I was suddenly aware that someone was in the room with me. I heard the soft rasp of breath, the quiet subtle movement a leg made swinging gently back and forth. Whoever it was sat opposite, watching me.

Eyes tight shut, still as any mouse, I wished my own breath to be silent so whoever it was might think me already dead. I wished I were dead, oh how I wished. No! I did not. I did not want to die, here at the mercy of the silent watcher. Why had he not already killed me? Was he another pervert, a sadist, wanting to watch me die slowly, painfully? Yet I was not in pain. What's more, my hands were no longer bound. Nor were my feet. I was free to stand, to move if I wished.

I lay for a moment longer, asking myself if I was really ready for what I might see, who I might see, what might happen if I opened my eyes, came face-to-face with my potential killer? I thought of my mother, of her courage in the face of her own death, and knew I must.

Putting my hands on either side, I levered myself upright, opened my eyes, and looked directly into the gaze of the woman watching me. Stunned, I said not a word and neither did she.

Her black hair spiraled from her scalp with a life of its own in sharp Medusa-like twists. Instinctively, I put up a hand to feel for my own soft locks, only to experience the shock of the loss all over again. Somehow I knew this woman had done it. She had cut off my natural glory and she had enjoyed every second. What, I wondered, would she do next?

She spoke.

"Do you know your name?"

I nodded.

"Tell me your name."

"Angie."

She nodded.

I watched carefully, wondering when she would make her move against me.

"My name is Mehitabel. You will never forget it."

I knew that name, it came back to me now, something charming, gentle, a cat in a poem, wasn't it? There was nothing sweetly catlike about this Mehitabel unless it was in the slant of the dark, watchful eyes and the long, claw-like nails, though hers were painted a flawless crimson. She was wearing a gray dress, sleeveless. I could see the muscles in her golden-tan arms ripple as she leaned toward me, smoothing her skirt, still staring intently into my own frightened eyes.

"I have instructions you are not to be bound," she said.

"You will do as you are told, move only when I say you might. We are to take a helicopter ride. You will be strapped in the seat next to me. You will act as if we are friends. The pilot is not to know anything different. I have your small suitcase with your new things. You chose well, particularly the undergarments." She gave me the smile that lifted only the pointed corners of her scarlet-painted mouth, mean and spiteful. "They will look good on you."

I became suddenly aware again of my nakedness and hung my head, shamed in front of her. Was she another part of this strange, terrible game I found myself in? Was I to be subjected to a different kind of sexual humiliation? She leaned closer and I felt her fingers on my nipples, shrank from her in shock.

"What a beautiful body you have, Angie," she whispered, using my name for the first time.

Then suddenly she got to her feet, thrust a bundle of clothes at me, told me briskly to put them on. "You may take a shower first," she said, already on her way to the door. "I will come back for you in ten minutes."

I scrambled painfully to my feet. The bathroom was small but it had a window I could see out of.

The boat was moored at a middling-size dock. Yellowish lights beamed from high above and I realized it was night though I had no idea of the time. I saw people coming toward the boat, pushing trolleys piled with baskets of fresh fruit and vegetables. Live chickens squawked in cages. Fish leaped in water-filled glass containers. Crates full of bottles: Evian, Pellegrino, Badoit. Ghulbian and Mehitabel lived well on this grand yacht but there could be no escape for me from this small window.

I turned and looked around the cabin: cream colors and a pale leafy green, a delicate antique gold-rimmed mirror over an old-fashioned organdy-skirted vanity complete with a silver brush set and an embroidered little stool where some old movie diva might have sat to put on her lipstick and fix her hair. It was a room from another era.

I could stand the sweat on my body no longer. I went quickly into the shower, soaped myself, let the cool water slide off me, off my bald head. I wrapped myself in a luxurious towel, soft enough to feel pleasant, crisp enough to dry properly. I even rubbed lotion into my newly clean limbs; the scent was the old Guerlain, L'Heure Bleue. I wondered, did they even make it these days? It was delicious though and gave me a small respite from the horror of my situation, until I remembered the perfume's name alluded to the hour between the end of the workday and the start of the proper evening: the "blue dusk" hour when men met their mistresses to make love. Oh, God, how strange was this? Was this Mehitabel's perverse sense of humor?

I got to my feet, went and looked in the spacious closet. It was empty. Wait, though, at the very back a garment swung on a padded satin hanger. I stared at it. The temptation was too much; I had to look, maybe I would find to whom it belonged, to whom this stateroom belonged.

It was a pale blue-green chiffon, draping softly from thin straps, swirling gently at the hem. I held it to me. Looked in the mirror. Saw my naked head, the bold new woman I was, and almost fainted from shock. Then my self-respect, my body awareness, and my selfishness struck me like a blow. There were women around the world who had lost their hair under terrible circumstances, whose bodies were mutilated by cancer, who stood up for themselves, for their integrity, their inner self and the beauty they knew they still owned. I was nothing compared with them. I was not devastated by sickness. What I was, was a victim.

In that moment I knew that if I were about to die, then

I was going to do it in this dress. It wasn't a matter of courage, of defiance, of self-esteem. It was simply that I finally understood who I was. After all these years of being Angie the greeter at the pseudo-posh eatery in Manhattan, if I was to die, I wanted to be someone when I met my maker.

"Put it on," I heard Mehitabel say.

I swung around, the dress clutched against my nakedness. I had not heard her come in.

"Get dressed, and quickly."

Her voice snapped at me.

"The underthings are there. Hurry, now. You no longer have ten minutes. You have one."

I scrambled into the undies, threw the dress over my head, got my arms stuck, struggled with it. She did not come to my aid. Finally, I had it on, smoothed it along my flanks, patted it over my breasts. Automatically, I put up my hands to fix my hair, felt the tears sting as I realized again the truth.

"The helicopter is waiting."

Mehitabel took my arm, led me out the door along the ship's deck to the stern. Hers was the long stride of an athlete, a woman who made her body into steel, a weapon to be used against you if necessary.

The helicopter was white, its rotor blades already turning. I could see the pilot at the helm. No one sitting next to him, no one behind him in the passenger area. Mehitabel pushed me up in front of her. There were six seats. She indicated one at the end and I went and sat there, obedient as a child. And as though I were a child, she strapped me in, clicked the seat belt, took the seat opposite me, and before I knew it we were airborne.

The ride must have been forty minutes, an hour maybe. I had no idea of time, it was all simply a sequence of events. I was flying into the dark and did not know where I was going or even where I was. I struggled to find the spirit to care anymore.

Then we were landing, soft as a bird on a grassy meadow, blindingly green under the helicopter's down-lights. A golf cart with a merrily tasseled striped canopy was waiting as we stepped out. Mehitabel grasped my arm and we took our seats in the cart and were off again.

We drove for several minutes. The lights on the cart were very low, all I could see was what looked like meadowland with here and there the brownish glint of water. And then a house loomed out of the darkness. Large, impressive, and with only a single light over the entrance.

The cart stopped, Mehitabel got out. She came around to my side, took my arm roughly, jerked me out, walked me to the big double wooden doors studded with bronze nail heads. She opened the door then turned and looked at me.

"Go on inside," she said.

I did not dare to disobey her.

I walked into that house, and once again, into my fate.

18

ANGIE

Mehitabel had gone. I was alone in that great dark house.

A faint light came from a half-open door leading into a room at the very end of the hall. Afraid almost to breathe, I heard the crackle of a fire, smelled the crisp sweet scent of the wood, heard the complete silence of the rest of the house. My pretty blue-green chiffon dress moved slightly in a draft coming from above. Goose bumps rose on my arms and instinctively I clasped them across my chest, a hand on each shoulder as though to warm myself. I turned to look at the door, thinking of escape, but again, to where? The question seemed to hover over my head in bright lights like on a theater awning, only this was no play and I was the victim, not the actress.

Courage. The word flashed through my mind and again I remembered my mother. She would expect me to be courageous, to take whatever was coming at me on the chin, to fight back. But I was broken. I had been raped by Ahmet and molested by that vicious woman. I shuddered, remembering her smile, her scent. . . . Another memory stirred and I remembered the bottle of Guerlain's L'Heure

Bleue and my need to perfume myself, the foolish need to feel like a normal woman.

Courage. The word still hovered. I wondered how to find what it meant to be courageous, what I should do now, what I could possibly do to help myself.

Then I heard Ahmet say, "Angie, come on in, why don't you? It's so much more comfortable in here, warmer too. I have a nice fire going and a very good bottle of red opened long enough for it to breathe."

I was not shocked that it was Ahmet, I had almost expected it. And it wasn't a suggestion, it was a command. Again I obeyed. I walked to the door, pushed it wider, saw Ahmet comfortable in a red leather chair, the bottle of wine on a small table beside him, his feet in monogrammed black velvet slippers propped on a dark ottoman.

He rose from his chair and stood in front of the blazing fire, smiling at me. Sparks from the fire flew all around him and I couldn't help thinking it was as though they were from the flames of hell itself, because he was my fate. Whatever he wanted to do with me he had the power to do it.

Courage. My mother's word rang again in my ear. I knew I must face him on his own terms, after all, the only thing left that he could do was actually kill me and it suddenly struck me that Ahmet was not the man to do that. He might employ a killer but I knew instinctively he would not do the deed himself. The soft chiffon folds of the dress flowed around my bare legs as I walked toward him.

His eyes lit with a mocking smile. "Bravo, Angie," he said. "I like women who do not show their fear."

"I am no longer afraid of you," I said, because there was, after all, nothing left to fear.

"Come, sit here, why don't you?"

He indicated the ottoman on which his feet had rested. I did as he asked, clamping my knees together, smoothing the dress down in the ladylike fashion my mother had taught me. He poured the wine and offered me a glass. I didn't want it but, since I had no choice, I took it. His fingers brushed mine and he gave me that smile again that told me he knew me well, knew everything there was to know about me, the way I had felt under his probing hands, the faint aromatic tang of my body under his lips. And I knew he knew what I was thinking, that I was also remembering the way his body had felt on mine, and I blushed.

"You are quite beautiful tonight, Angie," he said, going back to his red leather chair. "Like a pretty feline, a smooth little pussycat in that dress."

His eyes still mocked me and I glanced away.

"No," he said loudly. "Look up." He was giving me an order. "Look at me! I want you to remember this night, and all the nights that went before. I want your body to remember me as well as your mind. Fair's fair, Angie. I remember you perfectly. I remember that first time when you couldn't wait for me to put my hands on you, to put my cock in you, and I remember how much you liked it."

"You enjoyed it," I said and wished I had not because it showed that of course I remembered. Then despite myself I added, "More than me."

Ahmet shook his head, tut-tutting. "Angie, Angie, you must learn. It's 'more than I.' Not more than me." He laughed and took a gulp of his wine. "Perhaps I will have to get you a tutor, teach you the proper use of the English language."

"You mean the way you had to be taught?" I don't know how I knew, but I was right. I'd struck a sore spot and the color rose from his neck up his face, an angry red that made me know he was on the verge of hitting me. Courage, I told myself again and raised my chin, staring contemptuously at him.

"You are only up from the streets yourself," I went on,

unable to stop now I had started. "You are just a poor boy made good, a boy who didn't learn the niceties of life at his mother's knee. This good wine you are drinking you had to learn about, just like the rest of us poor folk did. Your own mother didn't teach you, that's for sure."

His fist flew toward me, smacking back my head. I suddenly knew what was meant by seeing stars. They danced before my eyes like mini space rockets while the pain seared through my jaw and wine spilled from my dropped glass all over my pretty chiffon dress and the carpet.

"Mehitabel!" Ahmet's voice roared through the room, sending more mini rockets through my head. "Mehitabel," he roared again and, as if by magic, there she was standing next to me. I caught her looking at me, taking in the spilled wine, Ahmet's furious red face, my own strange calmness.

"Take her away!" Ahmet roared. "Get her out of my sight. I will deal with her later."

As Mehitabel took my arm and led me away I heard Ahmet's beautiful wineglass crash against the limestone fireplace, and then I thought I heard what sounded like a sob, a deep, terrible sob that came from unknown depths. Of course I knew I must be wrong and it was only the sound of my own sobs I was hearing. Wasn't it?

19

ANGIE

I did not know how much later it was when I woke. It was dark, I had no idea where I was. I cried out for help, knowing it was foolish, ridiculous, nobody would help me ever again. If I was ever to escape from this dark place I must be cleverer than them, smarter, more resourceful, I'd need to be friggin' biophysicist material, a nuclear specialist. In that case I didn't stand a chance! Brains and ingenuity were not in my makeup. I only got through high school by cramming for exams the night before. I had a good memory and did well enough to pass, but did I learn anything? If I had would I have been a greeter in a glorified steakhouse with other women's husbands giving me the hopeful eye, simply because I was there and they could? I guess they thought I was worth a try, and who could blame them. And then the one time I succumbed—well, that's not quite true, it wasn't the only time, but my first time with a "really rich" man—look what happened to me.

I choked back the sob in my throat. I was definitely not going to cry. I was going to get out of here, that's what I was gonna do.

I touched my jaw gingerly. It was sore as hell where Ahmet had punched me, probably black and blue and purple by now. Rage rose in my throat instead of sobs. The bastard. I would get him, I surely would. And that witch Mehitabel. One way or another.

I was lying back on a sofa; I had no recollection of how I had gotten there. Somebody had put my feet up, straightened out my dress. I knew it must have been her; that woman radiated evil even when she was smiling at you. It was there, in the back of her eyes, a subplot lying in wait for you.

In real life, which is what my own life used to be, I wondered whether Mehitabel would have been considered normal. Did she live in a regular apartment like a normal woman, maybe even in a grand apartment seeing how she was working for a billionaire? Did she have a family? It was hard even to believe some woman had given birth to her. Evil is born, it says so in the Bible. At least I think it does. And to me, Mehitabel personifies evil. I know that she will stop at nothing.

I swung my legs off the sofa, saw I was wearing shoes. Chanel, black with cream-color toes and kitten heels. I would never have bought those shoes, not in a million years; I wore stilettos for work and biker boots off duty, and my old pink fluffy slippers all the time at home. It was the memory of those slippers that finally reduced me to silent tears.

They had to be silent because I was afraid if Mehitabel heard me she would come swooping through that door, maybe this time with a knife in her hand or a gun, ready to finish me off. I told myself to stop the crying. I told myself to get up, go look out the window, find a way out. I was afraid to check the door and see if it was unlocked because she—or someone else—might be on guard, waiting for me.

It was so dark outside all I could see was myself reflected in the window, the new me because I certainly no longer resembled who I used to be. Bald, with bruised eyes and jaw, emaciated in the too-big silk dress and the Chanel shoes, I was so stunned by my appearance I no longer wanted to cry. I wanted to kill someone. I wanted revenge. I wanted to get my own life back. But I was helpless, trapped in this lavish room with a door I dared not step through and a window that led only into the blackest night ever known to man.

The window was the old-fashioned type that lifted upward. I tried the latch and found it unlocked. Could my abductors have forgotten something this important? Or was it a trap? Were they allowing me to escape only to come after me, enjoying the chase again, with me as the prey and their hounds baying at my heels? I stared for several minutes at that latch. It was all that lay between me and freedom.

I took a deep breath, slid it back. The window moved easily under my hands. Again I stared suspiciously at it, then beyond, at that overwhelming blackness. There was no sound, not even of a small creature rustling through the grass. The night air slid into the room, so humid it brought drops of sweat onto my skin. I was on the ground floor. A small paved terrace lay immediately outside. Still, I hesitated, torn between the known and the unknown.

Of course I had no choice. If I was going to live, escape was my only chance.

It was easier than I'd thought and a moment later I was on that terrace, breathing the magical air of freedom. I pulled myself together, glanced right, then left. There was only the paved area fronting the house, which was in complete darkness. Before me I could just make out a flight of stone steps. I knew this must be the only way. Yet still I hesitated.

20

ANGIE

I had so wanted my freedom that now I was giddy with it. Unable to put one foot in front of the other, I stood frozen on that narrow terrace, surveying the night until gradually shapes began to form from it: a balustrade with stone urns balanced at each end; thin spears of weed poking between the pavers; a wavering path just a step or two down that led who knew where, only that it was away from here and could be my salvation.

I was suddenly filled with excited anticipation, I could already taste that freedom, almost see myself back with people again, real people who would listen to the story of my abduction, of attempted murder, of molestation and drugs; people who would look at my shorn scalp and the scar and wonder, as I did, that I was still alive to tell my tale.

Yet, "But why?" was what I knew they would, so rightly, ask. And would they believe me when I told them it was a sick man's fantasy, a sociopath with power and money and a famous name they would all know, who had done this to me for his own enjoyment? I could never tell the true story because, after all, I would be seen as just another young woman on the make, out for a quick buck, and with no way to back up her silly lie.

I was on my own then. I shrugged, or was it a shiver that ran through me? Here I was, facing life or death on my own. Same as always. We lonely girls are like that; all smiles and sleek hair and high heels, except when we are alone, which is almost always how we end up anyway.

It was then, I swear, I heard my mother's voice coming at me out of that blackness, saying she had not raised me to talk like that, to think like that, act like that. I was a fine young woman, working for a living, keeping hope alive for that fairy-tale ending. My mother had been so sure of that ending. I wished I was and that I had not been so foolish.

The empty grass meadow lay in front of me. My eyes had become more used to the dark and I could see here and there, the dips where water trickled endlessly. So, okay, I would avoid those areas, keep to the grassy bits.

With one hand over my heart, the other clutching the shoes, I took that first step forward. I held my breath, expecting my bare foot to sink into water, but no, there was a firmness there. I put my other foot forward, rested my weight on both feet, on the tuft of grass. It held. It was safe. It was not marsh after all, just a long meadow with here and there those strange tiny flickering lights.

A breeze sprang up out of nowhere. More of a rough wind, cold with a sighing edge to it, as though the earth itself was moaning. Or some person. I froze again. I told myself it could only be the wind, there was no one out there, no killer waiting with a knife, no Mehitabel.

I stood for minutes more, Chanel shoes in hand, dress blowing against me, my naked scalp prickling uneasily: I felt eyes on me, watching my every move, waiting for what I might do next. Panic fueled a scream that I strangled immediately; I must be silent, not make a sound. They couldn't see me. Could they?

Suddenly, though I didn't want to cry, tears sprang from under my closed lids, bringing the memory of the azure Aegean Sea pressing on my eyes as I was drowning, making me ask myself what I was doing here, how had I got here? I was just a simple girl from nowhere who wanted nothing from anybody. Until I was picked out by a psychopath looking for girls exactly like me to deliver his drug money.

I could bear it no longer. I ran into that marsh, splashed barefoot through the grassy mounds, up the muddy slopes, staggered heedless along the side of a brown river so silent and dark I hardly noticed it until I was ankle deep. It brought me to my knees, slipping on the mud. I got myself up again, started off again, heading only in front of me, not knowing where. I heard a roaring noise and came to a stop, almost falling over my own feet. Something was approaching, fast . . . could it be the sound of a car's engine?

Filled with hope, I ran forward. "Please!" I yelled into the darkness. "Help me, please, I'm lost, I'm so lost."

The darkness seemed to lift a little, a mere iota, just enough for me to make out the surging wall of water coming at me. I stopped dead. I knew what it was. This was a tidal river and the tide was turning with a great swirl into a wall of water whose pressure swept everything in front of it. Into it. And under it.

As it would me.

I could take no more. I flung wide my hands and shouted into the dark night.

"Welcome," I called. "Thank you. And welcome."

Watching through binoculars from the safety of the bank, Ahmet had to admire the way Angie awaited her end. She stood, arms flung wide, facing that wall of water, "As though she welcomes it," he said to Mehitabel, who was by his side, also watching.

"By now, I believe she does," Mehitabel said. "What's left for her anyhow?"

Ahmet turned to look at Angie.

"Go get her back," he told Mehitabel.

He watched again through the binoculars. Mehitabel got there, grabbed Angie's arms, pinned them behind her, dragged her out of the way.

Just in time, Ahmet thought, satisfied, as Mehitabel hauled the girl back to the house and her imprisonment. He was not done with her yet.

21

It was a few days later and Marco still had no luck tracing the black yacht he'd seen sailing fast out of Fethiye harbor; in fact, his inquiries were met with shrugs and sardonic smiles. Didn't he know how many boats sailed this area? Was he a crazy man? Anyway, what was he doing looking for a particular boat? Marco did not tell why but found himself at a dead end.

Literally, he thought, gloomily awaiting his flight from Istanbul to Paris, with Em tucked inside his jacket next to his heart where only she and Martha belonged. He hated leaving his idyllic getaway cottage, hated leaving the glorious countryside strewn with boulders and alive with the sound of bumblebees in the hibiscus and oleander, with the faint ripple of the freshwater stream, silver and brown, trickling its way to meet the sea. His painter's eye caught it all, kept it in his mind, and also in the many photographs he took for reference which he later plastered on his studio walls so he always had a part of the place with him.

He picked up a tiny cup of coffee from a stall, forgoing the sticky-looking pastries they also sold. Downing the coffee in one gulp, he gritted his teeth at the sandy texture. God, he couldn't wait for a cup of good French coffee. But he would miss this place, and so would Em. As did Martha. He knew that because she'd called him and told him so. She'd also said she was missing him. She'd also asked if he had finally given up on the ridiculous quest to find a missing girl who nobody else seemed to know about.

She was wrong there. Zacharias knew about her. Artemis had seen her. The girl was no myth of his imagination and neither was the scene where she had fallen into the water and he'd trolled in the orange inflatable searching for her, seeing her coppery hair floating, only to lose sight of her altogether. He decided it was ridiculous even to give the matter any more thought, yet the similarity to his sister's disappearance kept her in his mind.

Meanwhile, an announcement crackled over the public-address system, in Turkish, then in English: the flight was delayed, engine trouble; there was no guarantee what time it might be fixed and ready to depart. When Marco inquired at the desk along with a flurry of other outraged passengers he was turned away with an indifferent shrug of the shoulders and a what-do-we-know raise of the eyebrows. Shit. He was well and truly stuck.

He repaired to the bar along with most everyone else and ordered a beer. It was not cold enough. Sighing, he took out his phone, wondering who he might call and with what purpose; nobody was going to get him out of here and back to Paris. Not today anyhow.

He felt a tap on his shoulder and turned to see a young man smartly dressed in a dark suit, in which Marco thought he must surely be sweating. A conservatively striped tie was knotted firmly at the neck of his pristine white shirt. Marco glanced down at his own creased khaki shorts, at his blue T-shirt that even though it was clean was still only an old T-shirt, and at the beat-up suede loafers he'd been wearing for years on trips like this because they were comfortable and he never had to think about them. Though Martha did. She had even offered, with a small concerned frown, to buy him a new pair. With Em's bright eyes peeking out from under his black Windbreaker, Marco had to smile. He certainly did not present the image of the successful, well-connected first-class passenger, a position to which he had been upgraded by an observant member of the staff who'd recognized his name.

"Sir. Mr. Mahoney . . ."

The young man stammered in his eagerness, making Marco wonder if he wanted an autograph. "Yes?" He looked expectantly at him.

"Sir. Mr. Ahmet Ghulbian presents his compliments and wonders whether you would do him the honor of joining him in the private lounge. Mr. Ghulbian understands the Paris flight is canceled and he wishes to discuss the situation with you."

"Does he, now?" Marco knew the name, there would be few who would not. Ghulbian ranked up there with Getty and Onassis, wealth and reputation-wise. As he followed the young man to a private lounge he wondered whether Ahmet wanted his portrait painted. If so, he was not sure he wanted to do it. He'd learned from experience that commissions from men that wealthy and demanding could be a demoralizing experience, and their self-image invariably turned out to be different from that which Marco saw and painted.

Still, when he met him, he thought Ghulbian an arresting figure: compact, impeccably clad in a pale suit, though unlike his minion he wore no tie. What Marco did notice were his shoes, lovingly polished to a discreet low gleam. They reminded him of his grandfather's.

Ghulbian followed his glance. "Berluti," he said. "Paris."

Marco nodded. "They are well cared for."

"As all fine things should be." Ghulbian waved an arm for Marco to take a seat. "I heard of the trouble with the flight and since I'm on my way to Paris myself," he paused to glance at the thin gold Patek Philippe watch worn on his right wrist, "leaving in fact in ten minutes, I'm wondering if I might offer you a lift?"

Marco almost felt his jaw drop; it was as if he had been transported from the simplicity of his village life to outer space. Em poked her head out of his jacket and Ghulbian's brows rose.

"I'm sorry, but I never travel without my dog," Marco said. "But thank you for your offer anyway."

"No. No. Please. The dog is welcome, I'm sure there will be food for it on board, I only hope it does not mind eating from Limoges plates."

Remembering Costas's café/bar and the dinosaur bones, Marco laughed. "You know what they say, a change is as good as a rest. And thank you for your offer. It would have been hell trying to find a room here for the night and I'm getting too old to sleep on airport floors."

Ghulbian smiled, showing his perfect teeth. "As I am myself. Which is not to say it was not something I had to do in my youth, but then most of us have been through that in our time."

Ten minutes later Marco was shepherded on board a Cessna 520 painted a pleasing silver-blue. The seats were cream leather, wide and comfortable. A pair of young stewards in blue uniforms and wearing ties made sure they were strapped in, and within minutes they were airborne.

Ghulbian took some papers from his briefcase and commenced to study them. Marco stared out the window at the vivid blueness of the sea disappearing under a downy quilt of white cloud. Ghulbian was the kind of man who managed even to have the weather match his color scheme. Feeling the man's eyes on him, he turned to look.

Ghulbian had taken off his tinted glasses. It was the first time Marco had seen his eyes: dark, heavy-lidded, they seemed to hold a world of secrets. He guessed a man like that, with his money, his power, would certainly be the keeper of many secrets.

Ghulbian said, "Tell me something, Mr. Mahoney. Are you a happy man?"

Marco was astounded by such a personal question. He stalled and said, "Please, it's only right that you call me Marco. After all, you just saved my life."

"I did nothing as important as that. Only the situation."

Marco thought Ghulbian was sharp. And sure of himself.

Ghulbian said, "I have a favor to ask you."

"Of course, if it's something I can help with."

Ghulbian extracted a photograph from the papers on the table in front of him. He did not show it to Marco immediately but held it to his chest.

"I wonder," he said, speaking quietly, "if you would paint a portrait for me. I know this is not the way you usually work, but this young woman was . . . *is* very dear to me. I would like . . . no, I *need* a memento, a living record of her in my home. I'm asking if you would do me the honor of attempting this for me. Naturally, I will pay whatever fee you ask."

Still looking at Marco, he handed over the picture.

The first thing Marco saw was the cloud of red hair, that great, lovely wavy coppery mass. It was the girl he had seen fall off the yacht.

"She's a friend of yours?"

"I knew her slightly. Sadly, she is no longer with us. She drowned, Mr. Mahoney." Seemingly overcome, Ghulbian turned to look out the window, dabbing his eyes beneath the dark glasses with his silk pocket handkerchief.

He said to Marco, "Forgive me, but sometimes memories can be difficult to deal with. But yes, Angie was a friend and I should like to remember her. Immortalize her, you might say, through the beauty of your artistry."

Marco handed back the photo. He was concerned about the way the red-haired girl had died; he wanted no part of Ghulbian's emotions. "I'll have to think about it, sir, I have a lot on at the moment."

Ghulbian laid a heavy hand on Marco's arm, as though exerting his authority. "Whenever the time is right, of course. Meanwhile, I would also like you to paint my own portrait, an image I can leave for future generations so they will never forget who Ahmet Ghulbian is."

"That'll be who you *were*," Marco said. "Since obviously by then you too will be dead."

Ahmet's thick brows rose again in surprise. "Trust me, Mr. Mahoney, *Marco,* I will be around for a long time to remind them. Still, I would very much like to have you as my guest at Marshmallows." He gave a small barking laugh. " 'Marshmallows' is a pun on the fact that the house stands in the middle of some marshland. Very beautiful, as you shall see."

Despite his initial antipathy, Marco found himself intrigued, as well as curious. There was something almost *beguiling* in Ghulbian's self-deprecating demeanor, an eager friendliness, a charm about him which Marco found himself liking. To his surprise he heard himself agreeing to make the visit to Marshmallows. In fact he thought he would enjoy the experience, life with a billionaire in his secluded paradise did not sound half bad, though in fact he doubted Ghulbian would make good on his offer.

22

Back in London the following night, sitting opposite Lucy Patron in the small, intimate Italian restaurant, watching her devour a plate of spaghetti Bolognese as rapidly as any starving animal, Ahmet Ghulbian realized that in fact she probably was starving.

"Is it part of the tradition?" he asked. "That actors must starve for love of their profession?"

He saw Lucy frown and he marveled that she was actually considering what he had said. A sense of humor was definitely absent.

"Only if they have no job," Lucy explained, twisting more pasta strands around her fork. "No job, no money. That's the way it goes in my profession."

In any profession, Ahmet remembered, as his own penniless past suddenly reared in the back of his mind. He had to remind himself that he was now a rich man, that he could buy everyone in this restaurant, buy the whole place in fact without so much as making a dent in his wealth.

Lucy put her knife and fork neatly in the proper five-o'clock position on her still-half-full plate. Obviously, after what Ahmet had said, she had remembered her manners, her upbringing, and that you never finished everything. Her wide blue eyes looked up at him from across the table.

"Thank you very much," she said primly. "That was delicious."

"Please," Ahmet said, suddenly concerned because she was so thin and so obviously hungry. "Please, I'll order something else. Chicken parmigiana perhaps?" He could practically see her brain ticking over as she contemplated the chicken.

In fact Lucy was wondering how she might be able to taste only a little, then ask for the rest to be boxed so she might take it home for the following night's supper. She knew she could always ask Martha to help her out financially, and that no doubt her sister would do so immediately, but Martha would also ask questions. Martha would tell Lucy to get a proper job, she couldn't simply do nothing and starve while hoping for a role on TV. And what's more, Lucy knew she was right. What she really needed, she thought, attacking the spaghetti hungrily again, was a rich boyfriend.

The last two words clashed together in her mind. She stole another look at the mysterious man sitting opposite, the man in fact paying for her dinner and also right now probably saving her from starving to death. Or at least from running to New York, tail between her legs, hoping for some of her sister's famous apple crumble, even a potato baked in its jacket, which she'd bet anything if it were Ahmet he would probably serve topped with caviar.

She smiled at the thought and Ahmet smiled back. He had very good teeth. She just wished he would take off the tinted glasses.

Always one to speak whatever was on her mind, she said, "Why do you always wear those glasses?"

Ahmet automatically put up a hand to adjust them, contemplating what to say. Certainly not the truth, which was that he rarely allowed anyone to look directly into his eyes because he was afraid they might see who he really was. This charming young woman had no idea, sitting in this civilized restaurant amid civilized people enjoying a civilized dinner, that he would kill her as easily as pouring her another glass of wine. Not yet, of course, but in due time. He contemplated how much he would enjoy that act, how he would enjoy seeing the fear in her eyes as she realized her fate, how much pleasure he would derive from seeing her naked dead body, when she would finally, completely belong to him, and only him, forever more. He had not yet answered her question.

"Why?" Lucy asked again, taking a sip of the wine he had just poured.

"My eyesight has been bad since childhood. My family was poor, and by that I mean deprived." Ahmet waved a hand over the table, indicating the lavish food, the chicken parmigiana, the spaghetti, the delicately dressed green salad with anchovies and capers, the warm bread and the saucer of rich olive oil; the second bottle of expensive wine. "We were fortunate to eat at all. And what we ate," he shrugged, "it's better not to remember."

Lucy's shocked blue eyes stared into his. She reached out to touch his hand, full of sympathy. "How awful for you, I feel so badly now, with all my complaints. I mean, I was hungry but that's my own fault. My sister says I should get a job, but eventually, she always comes through, helps me out. Financially, you know."

"Tell me about your sister." Ahmet crumbled a piece of bread in his fingers and dipped it in the olive oil. He was not hungry, he never was nowadays, that longing had dispersed over the years of being rich. When you could have anything you wanted you suddenly found you wanted nothing. It was the way of the very rich, and in another way, he almost envied Lucy, who could still feel that longing, that urge, the pleasure of a good meal. When she came to his country house he would make sure to feed her well before he sent her out alone into the marshes.

"More wine?" he asked pleasantly.

"My sister is beautiful," Lucy said, copying him and mopping up the olive oil with a piece of the very good bread. "Her name is Martha. Such an old-fashioned name, don't you think? Actually, she was named for my great-grandmother Patron. The thing is, though, Martha doesn't even realize she's beautiful, she's so modest, so un-vain, if you see what I mean." She looked earnestly at Ahmet across the table. "She's tall, willowy, has these lovely blue eyes and blond hair. And she's talented. And, damn it, successful."

"Is she an actress, then?" Ahmet found himself intrigued with the idea of a second beauty in the family. Well, actually, truth be told, Lucy was no beauty. She was attractive and sexy and very young, a winning combination in his eyes, and just what he'd been looking for. In fact, it was what he always looked for in a woman, though usually not as classy or "upmarket" as little Lucy.

In fact he already knew all there was to know about the Patron family; he'd investigated every bit of Lucy's life, knew about Martha and her work as a designer, and the other sister, the pediatrician, and the way the parents had died. It might be useful to suggest using Martha to redecorate some rooms at his country place.

Lucy was, he thought, a long way from Little Miss Angie, that cheap troll who'd first managed to disappear into the Aegean, leaving him to wonder whether she might turn up, alive, what she might say about him, what she might try to do to him. Then, of course, he had gotten her back, safe and sound in the safest, most secret place he knew, his country house on the marshes, where the wonderful, the one and only, Mehitabel had taken care of her for him. Angie was the past, Lucy was the future.

He contemplated Lucy, innocently stuffing herself with chicken parmigiana, making little sighing noises of pleasure. She was such a child, really, a fact that made him sigh with pleasure too, so that she looked up, smiling, and asked, "What?"

"*What* what?" he answered with a smile. "I really have to take you to my country place," he said. "We grow our own vegetables, have our own sheep. Our lamb is delicious."

"Oh, God." Lucy stared, horrified, at him. "I couldn't possibly eat anything I'd seen grazing in a field."

"May I point out you are eating chicken that surely grazed somewhere."

Lucy took another sip of wine, suddenly uncertain about him, he was so self-assured, so smooth, so kind-of *old*. "And may I point out," she said, getting her wits back, after all, she was no dummy even if she was an actress who all men thought were dumb. "May I point out that chickens do not graze. They are not animals. They are birds."

Ahmet laughed. He liked her. "I have to admit I never thought of it that way," he said. "And I will make sure no lamb is served when you come to visit me."

"Who said I was coming to visit you?" Lucy sat back. She did not like to be taken for granted, and anyhow no young woman should go alone to a man's country house unless she was his lover or fiancée. Or wanted to be.

Ahmet was still laughing. "Certainly not you, Miss Lucy Patron. And nor, if you think about it, have I asked you. But should I ask, then I would also include your beautiful sister in the invitation."

"Then you would have to ask Marco too."

Ahmet raised a brow, took a sip of the wine. It was good but not top level; he should have ordered differently. "Marco Polo Mahoney?"

Of course he already knew Marco. "I know his work," he said. "A brilliant portrait artist."

"Painter," Lucy said, glugging the rest of her wine and sighing deeply. "That's what Marco calls himself." Her stomach was full, the wine was good, and she was unexpectedly enjoying herself. A drop spilled onto her dress as she put the glass back on the table. "Oh, bugger," she said crossly. "I love this dress and now it's ruined."

Ahmet called the waiter to bring a wet cloth. "It will probably come out," he said. "I'm sorry, Lucy, it was my fault, I distracted you."

Lucy sighed again. "No, you didn't," she said. "I'm just clumsy, that's all, everybody says so. Tell me," she said, gazing earnestly at him, "how can anyone this clumsy ever hope to be an actress?"

Ahmet thought it really didn't matter, but what he said was, "I think I have a way to make that hope of yours come true. I was considering investing in a movie, just a small affair, no star names, but an interesting script and a wonderful location, a house on the marshes. In fact," he added, thoughtfully, "part of the reason I was attracted was that I have a house on the Romney marshes." He leaned across the table, reached for her hand. It was smooth, warm. Her fingers curled against his palm. "And now, I might have an actress to star in it."

It was, Lucy thought, beaming, all too good to be true.

Ahmet smiled back at her. He knew what she was thinking, and she was right.

"We might also get your sister to come along and take a look at my country place. The drawing room could surely use some refurbishing, fabrics and such."

"Well," Lucy said, pleased, "of course Martha's really good at all that. I'll ask her for you."

Ahmet gave a satisfied smile. Two birds with one stone.

23

In Paris, the next day, Marco was surprised, more, he was *astounded,* to receive a call from Ghulbian's assistant, the thin young man he'd encountered sweating in the suit and tie at Istanbul's Ataturk Airport, now presumably cooler and enjoying the benefits of air-conditioning, which was reflected in his cool, calm voice as he relayed his employer's invitation, though Marco thought it more a command than an invitation.

"Mr. Ghulbian would be pleased to see Mr. Mahoney at three P.M. in his suite at the Four Seasons George Cinq." A car would be sent to pick him up.

No question as to whether Marco might be available, simply the astonishing arrogance of a wealthy man that, of course, he would. Why would he not, when it could mean an important commission?

Smiling at the irony, Marco thought Ghulbian probably believed all artists were starving. At some point in their careers, most had, as he remembered only too well from his own solitary beginning. Now, though, he had options and he wasn't too sure he wanted to take up this one, though Martha had urged him to meet Ghulbian, saying how important the financier was, and how as far as she knew he had never had his portrait painted.

"Yours would be the first," Martha had said. "Maybe it will be the only one."

It was certainly something to think about. Marco picked up the phone, called back, and got a woman who said her name was Mehitabel, and that she was Ghulbian's "personal" assistant. She told him to be waiting outside at the appointed time.

The car was an expensive silver Mercedes, chauffeur-driven, which came as no surprise, but when they arrived at the hotel, Marco was surprised by Mehitabel's appearance: wafer-thin, around forty, with coils of Medusa-like dark hair that gave the impression she'd had an electric shock. She wore a gray linen shift dress, black heels, and an armful of silver bracelets, which he thought looked antique and expensive.

She caught his look. "Galleries Lafayette," she said, unsmiling. "They do good copies."

Embarrassed, Marco felt he should have blushed. She told him her name, and showed him in.

Ghulbian was standing by the French windows, holding back the silk draperies with one hand and staring out at the street below, though Marco sensed he was not really seeing it. He was lost in his thoughts and Marco wondered what the high-powered man was contemplating. A takeover bid, perhaps? Or the purchase of a new aircraft? Or simply a date for dinner with a woman he was pursuing. It turned out to be none of them.

When he heard him come in Ghulbian turned immediately from the window and offered his hand. "Good to see you again. I was just thinking about where I would like my portrait to be painted. Not here, I think. Paris is not my 'home' in that sense of the word."

Marco understood, though he was a little surprised. "We could still do it on your yacht, sir," he suggested, though Ghulbian had dismissed the idea previously.

"Please, please, you must never call me 'sir.' I'd like to think we are—or at least shall become—friends. After all, having one's portrait painted is an intimate business, almost equivalent to baring one's soul."

"None of my sitters have yet bared their souls to me." Marco took the seat on the sofa Ghulbian indicated. The man sat opposite, hunched forward, hands between his thighs, listening intently to what the artist had to say.

"Painting a portrait is more *about me*," Marco said. "About what *I* see in the subject's inner being that I transmit to the canvas. Which, I suppose," he gave a deprecating little shrug, "does not always please the sitter who commissioned my work."

Ghulbian nodded, interested. He said, "I recall a story about Winston Churchill. His wife, Clementine, commissioned the world-renowned artist Graham Sutherland to paint Winston's portrait. She was so incensed with the result she simply tore it up, right there and then, in front of him."

They both laughed and Marco said so far nobody had ripped up any of his paintings. "Though there's always a first time," he added, taking a deeper look at the man opposite.

Ghulbian looked steadfastly back. He kept his face implacable, without any emotion, yet in reality he was unexpectedly nervous, wondering if it was true that some people could see into your soul, into your inner being, know your thoughts, what made you tick, what your darker urges were, and how you carried them out. Could this artist, with his all-seeing painterly eyes, possibly know who he really was? About his urge to kill. Could Marco know, looking at him now, that he would go to the ends of the earth to satisfy that urge, that he would let nothing stand in his way? Ghulbian had never loved a woman and never would. They were prey, that's all. A sudden image of Angie flickered through his mind. Instinctively he half closed his eyes, shutting her out.

Wondering what he was thinking, Marco studied Ghulbian's impassive face, noting the wide planes of the cheekbones, the narrowed very dark eyes, the low brow, and the thick hair with no sign of gray though he'd guess Ghulbian to be in his early fifties. He was not a big man, yet there was a hint of latent physical power about him that was intimidating. It was in the force of his gaze, the tension that seemed to hold him together, kept him fixed in his seat when Marco sensed he wanted to be up and pacing the room. It was almost as though Ghulbian's thoughts were elsewhere yet he was still talking about the portrait.

"I had considered my yacht," Ghulbian said, quite suddenly smiling and relaxed. "But a movable location for something as permanent as a portrait somehow does not seem appropriate. I'd prefer, after all, if you could paint me at my country house."

Marco agreed that wherever was most comfortable for the sitter was always best.

"It's a place of atmosphere," Ghulbian said. "It stands quite alone amid the marshes. There are just the cries of the waterfowl and the rush of the tidal river, the 'bore,' as it's called when it turns and begins to flow inland again. I love to watch the deep brown water surging toward the house, the powerful undercurrents that swirl beneath the surface."

He finally got up and began to pace the room, as Marco had suspected he'd wanted to do.

"No grass ever looks greener than marsh grass." Ghulbian stopped and looked out the window again as though he could see the marsh before his eyes right that minute.

"It's more inviting than any well-tended country house lawn with its simpering young women and afternoon tea beneath the trees. There are no trees in marshland, no young women pouring tea, only that inviting green grass that will swallow you up faster than you can even think about taking that final step forward."

He turned with a sudden smile, holding out both hands, palms up. "Of course, I'm only joking. Nobody drowns in my marshes."

"I imagine it's the silence that attracts you," Marco said. "For me, it would be the color. That perfect green."

"Then you must come and see it. Paint it."

They made an appointment for a few days later.

Marco saw the enthusiasm on Ghulbian's face; the man obviously loved his silent, lonely home in the marshes.

"I'll come," Marco said, surprising himself. "I'll paint you there. It's your place."

For the first time Ghulbian smiled a genuine smile, not forced or polite.

"Then you will make my dream come true," he said.

24

Of course, Ghulbian sent his helicopter for Marco. It was evening, and already getting dark, when he arrived. He had expected the house to be typical Ghulbian over-the-top ostentatious, and he was not disappointed. The front door, opened by a manservant, led onto a long paneled hall where an immense crystal chandelier, surely bought from some Venetian palace, tinkled in the draft. Stained-glass windows in reds and greens lent a dim shimmer, while soaring above everything, an opaque domed ceiling gave a cathedral-like air.

An upper landing ran across the back of the house, branching off on either side into corridors which faced over the central hall. There were many paintings on the walls, not crammed together but properly hung and lit with sufficient space to give each its own area, so they might be better viewed. Ghulbian was, after all, a man who appreciated the arts.

The subdued gray of the walls, the dark earth tones of the furnishings matching the mansion's exterior, seemed forbidding, a touch of the movie *House of Horrors,* Marco thought. Except, that is, for the pair of red leather chairs, set in front of a blazing fire in the drawing room where the servant left him. Between the chairs was a black leather ottoman on which rested an ornate silver tray that Marco felt surely must be by Paul de Lamerie, the famous eighteenth-century silversmith. On that tray stood a bottle of Patron Silver tequila. Not your usual supermarket bottle either; this one looked as though it might have been made by Lalique. There was certainly nothing understated about Ahmet Ghulbian's possessions. He had the money and he bought only the best.

Marco walked toward the fire. The rug under his feet was soft, a symphony of pale corals and greens, not silk though, and he guessed it was probably Turkish and certainly of the finest hand-knotted wool.

The curtains were of a dark green heavy corded fabric held back with thick gold tasseled cords. There were no lights outside and the night looked very black. Marco thought "secluded" was not the correct word for this place. It was "*remote.*"

He wondered why a man who could buy anything he wanted, any house he wanted, in any part of the world, would choose this godforsaken place. There was not a sound outside, not even of a dog leaping and barking a welcome. But there was Mehitabel.

Marco did not hear her come in, then there she was, standing beside him.

She smiled. "I startled you. I'm sorry. I came to see what I might offer you to drink. Mr. Ghulbian always keeps excellent champagne chilled if you wish for a glass? Of course, if there is anything else you might like, from wine to . . . well, I suppose beer."

"A beer would be good, thank you. Dos Equis, if you have it." He put her to the test by ordering a Mexican beer but she was unfazed.

"Of course." She gave him a smile that upturned only the corners of her lips. "I shall get it for you myself."

It occurred to Marco that except for the helper at the door, he had seen no other servants. Surely, with a place this size and an owner as demanding and discriminating as Ahmet, there must be at least a personal valet, a housekeeper, a cook or chef, even a butler. Yet there was only this woman, who placed the chilled bottle of beer on the priceless silver Lamerie tray and set a glass straight from the freezer, white with cold, next to it. She noticed Marco flinch as he saw what she had done and this time she laughed.

"Mr. Ghulbian wants his things to be used the way they were when they were first designed and made. Antiques are only antiques because we have made them that way, is what he believes. He uses them, makes them his own. Their original owners would surely be grateful to him for doing so."

Marco had to admit he had never thought about it that way but Ghulbian had a point, though an iced beer bottle on the three-hundred-year-old silver was a bit much.

Thinking of Em, he said, "Mr. Ghulbian does not keep a dog, out here in the country?"

Mehitabel had walked back to the door. She turned and looked at him, brows arched in surprise. "Why should he?"

"This is a lonely place. Remote. A safety factor perhaps? Or companionship?"

"There are dangerous marshes all around this house, Mr. Mahoney. It's safer here than any place with a dozen armed guards. Mr. Ghulbian cannot have a dog, because it would get lost out there in the marshlands. Everything that looks like grass is in reality water or mud. That's why there are no trees; there is nowhere for their roots to take hold."

"So it would be cruel of Ahmet to have a dog companion because it could drown in the marshes?"

"It has been known," Mehitabel acknowledged. "There are no wild creatures around, no foxes, no raccoons, even very few wildfowl. The house overlooks a tidal river. Twice a day, that tide turns. One minute you are looking at a placid stretch of water, the next it's rising up and surging toward you. It's best to stay out of the way of our river, Mr. Mahoney. Even the wildfowl have learned not to build their nests there; too many of their young were lost in that surge of water, so brown, so deep, so . . . strong." She said the last word almost in a whisper, then quickly made her exit, closing the door softly behind her.

As she did, Marco heard a cry. High-pitched, like a creature in pain.

He leapt across the room and yanked open the door, almost falling over Mehitabel, who was standing immediately outside.

"What the fuck was that? It sounded like someone being tortured."

"*Tut, tut, tut.*" Mehitabel shook her head at his language, sending her tight Medusa curls dancing. She even laughed, a sound Marco had never expected to hear from her, yet she seemed to find something amusing in what he had said.

"Good heavens, no, Mr. Mahoney. It's only a wild bird, of course. The herons nest in our roof and they make the strangest cries. Mr. Ghulbian would like to be rid of them but they have been nesting here for centuries and I'm afraid the locals would not approve."

"And where exactly *is* Mr. Ghulbian?" Marco was fed up with being left standing in the strange drawing room in this strange house on these strange green marshlands with birds screeching like Emily Brontë's Mrs. Rochester locked in the attic. He wanted out of Wuthering Heights or Marshmallows or whatever, with its wailing birds and antique silver salvers and a woman who somehow made his skin crawl.

"Please send for the golf cart. I can't wait any longer."

Mehitabel put a shocked hand to her mouth. Her fingernails were long and painted crimson, her hand strong, her bare brown arms muscular. It crossed Marco's mind that if it came to a fight she could probably take him on; this woman had more tricks up her sleeve than any pro fighter, he'd bet on that. He also wondered what kind of hold she had over Ghulbian that he kept her close to him. She probably knew all his secrets, and that man certainly had more and deeper secrets than normal people.

"But you cannot leave yet," Mehitabel protested. "Mr. Ghulbian will be here any minute." A helicopter clattered in the distance. "There, you see, here he is," she said. Her dark greenish eyes met his again and Marco thought he caught a glint of triumph in them. He wondered uneasily what she was up to, and what exactly that cry was that he'd heard.

Minutes later Ahmet walked into the room, both hands outstretched, that welcoming smile on his face.

"So sorry to keep you waiting. A bit foggy out there. Often is when the tide turns; got stuck for ten minutes the other side of the river, had to wait 'til it cleared a bit." He eyed the bottle of beer on the silver tray and added, "I'm glad to see Mehitabel took good care of you. She's a treasure, you know. I don't know what I'd do without her. She keeps me on track, knows where I have to be and when, and makes sure I get there. I suppose we all have someone like that, we busy men, to help us out, you know."

Actually, Marco usually knew exactly where he was going and got there under his own steam, but he nodded and said he was glad Ghulbian was finally here. "I didn't realize this place was so remote," he said. "Out on the marshes."

"But that's exactly what I love about it." Ghulbian went over to the sofa. "Come, sit down, why don't you. Let's talk about my portrait. Remember, I asked for it to be painted here? Now you see why. This is my territory. I am the only person within miles, no one else even nearby. Welcome to my world, Marco."

He leaned forward and slapped Marco's knee jovially, smiling as if they were two boys at a school reunion. "Now, d'you think you can see what I mean? *This* is where I belong, in real life as well as in my portrait."

To his surprise, Marco did see what Ahmet meant. This strange place could only be home to a man like this. Only a house like this could contain his volatile personality, his ability to become whomever he wanted you to think he was at that moment. And right now, Ghulbian wanted Marco to believe he was a simple, honest country lover, a man who enjoyed the peace and quiet of these dangerous marshes.

"What kind of wildfowl are there around here?" he asked, taking a sip of the beer, which was perfectly chilled.

"Almost none, only the occasional heron that likes to nest on my rooftop, but I've pretty much put a stop to that. Nobody needs those great birds swooping around, messing all over everything. No, I like to keep my house clean, Marco. No birds, no dogs, no cats."

"Only Mehitabel," Marco said, and Ahmet roared with sudden laughter.

"You're right. Mehitabel surely belongs to some strange animal world of her own making. Still, she's efficient, she's clever, and she's loyal. What more can a man want in a woman?"

"Love," Marco suggested, surprised when Ahmet sank, shocked, back in his chair.

Ahmet said, "I believe I asked you, on the plane from Istanbul, whether you were in love. You did not answer me, though I already knew of course that you were. I have not been so fortunate. But enough of that. Let us decide where you would like me to pose for the portrait. At first, I thought on the landing where the light is so beautiful from the Rossetti stained-glass windows. But now I think it's far too romantic. You know I'm a practical man, a businessman, though I love all the arts." He threw his arms wide, indicating the paintings, mostly very modern, that lined the corridor. "I have every artist here you've ever heard of, and I paid more for most of them than any man ever paid before, and maybe ever will. I'm a fool when it comes to something I really want, Marco. I don't care what it costs, I must have it."

Marco thought it a strangely childish philosophy for a grown man but guessed that kind of money gave you reason to believe you could have anything you wanted, all you had to do was pay for it. He remembered with sudden misgiving Ahmet saying he could name any fee he liked. Now he said quickly, "You know I never charge any sitter more than another, however rich he is. I put a price on my talent, that's all."

"That's the way it goes with you artists. It's your children and grandchildren that'll reap the benefit. But you will paint my portrait, won't you?"

The tough billionaire had disappeared. It was as though Ahmet had two personalities: one hard and indomitable; the other insecure and vulnerable and which usually he kept carefully hidden. Marco wondered which he would be allowed to see for the portrait, that of course he agreed to paint, though he did not like the location.

In Marco's view, there was a darkness about the house that had nothing to do with the limited light coming from the stained-glass windows. It was more the sense that all was not right here. Yet Ghulbian was beaming at him, had welcomed him to his home, and Marco was instantly ashamed of his thought. Sure, the house was dark and its remote location off-putting, but his host was dismissing the beer and breaking out a perfect bottle of Pétrus, already opened in anticipation of his arrival, pouring it into glasses so fine Marco wondered who dared wash them.

He felt Ahmet's anxious eyes on him as he took the first sip; knew the man wanted him to love it and liked him for that. He might be rich but he enjoyed the pleasure of giving. And when he tasted the wine, he found it smooth yet not overwhelming. "It's so good it takes my breath away," he told Ahmet.

"I knew you would understand it. You have good taste, my friend. Now, with it you must try this pâté. It's made for me by a woman in Aix-en-Provence, not what you might think of as pâté country, that's more to the north-west of France, but she has her own small goose farm. Ducks too. And oddly, bison, though of course they don't end up as pâté. I believe I keep her in business, which is good because she's in her eighties and alone. I like to think I'm helping her, and with reason, because she is excellent at what she does."

Marco found himself liking Ahmet more as he told the story; he was generous with his time, with his money, and with his compassion. Rare, in a rich man, many of whom had no time for anyone but themselves and the very public charities their PR people involved them in. Besides, the pâté was excellent, served on thin triangles of crisp toast.

"Perfect with the wine," Marco agreed. "Which, by the way, may be one of the best I ever tasted. Martha and I don't get much beyond the usual market buys, except when we're in France, and then it almost doesn't matter where you get it, even in the mini-market like Casino, you always seem to end up with something good." He rethought that. "Well, let's say, drinkable."

"I shall send you a case." Ghulbian raised a hand to dismiss Marco's polite protest. "Please, it will be my pleasure. And let's not forget I am trying to bribe you to make the time to paint my portrait."

"You're making it very hard for me to say no."

"Then, while you are considering it, why don't you join me on my yacht, the *Lady Marina*. Take a few days, bring your lovely fiancée, let us all get to know each other better. I promise you the wine will be good, and I might even persuade Martha to take me on as a client."

Softened by the good wine, the delicious pâté, the generous hospitality, and the man's charm, Marco agreed and a date was tentatively set for a few weeks later. They would fly in Ahmet's Cessna 520 to Antibes, and be helicoptered onto the yacht anchored off the coast since it was too large for any of the local harbors. From there they would take a few days' "stroll" as Ahmet called it, along the coast, where he said the sea was the bluest Marco would ever see, dark and deep, cool and inviting even on the hottest of days.

"I promise we shall have a good time," he said as he saw Marco off in the helicopter. And Marco believed his promise.

25

The house on the marsh had become Mehitabel's home and was the place she liked most in the world. She had seen most of "the world" via her excursions with Ahmet either on the *Lady Marina*, with its many ports of call in Europe and the Far East, or via the Cessna 520, which, though it was a few years old, remained Ahmet's favorite plane and which he refused to change for the latest model. Ahmet could get pretty stuck in his ways and Mehitabel considered it part of her job to keep him abreast of the latest and most expensive toys available to a man like him. The "toys," of course, included women, of which she was chief procurer.

Mehitabel had not set out in life with that job in mind, though the seamy side had always attracted her by its very nature, with its secrecy, its insider status, its readiness for violence.

She had started out the usual way any attractive woman from her lowly station in life might, by posing nude for magazines, moving easily on to porn, though she preferred selling other women than selling herself. If the truth were known, which it most certainly was not, Mehitabel did not enjoy sex. In fact, she despised it. No matter how she looked at it, sex gave a man control, he was the one who entered, the woman merely received. Even in play-games of sadomasochism, dressing up in fishnet tights and heels and wielding a whip, it was all only playacting, until the one time it wasn't and she had brought that whip down too hard, though he'd begged for mercy, a quality she found she did not possess. She had killed him. He was her first and she'd enjoyed it.

The act had taken place on a private island off the coast of Greece, a place where the rich and sometimes famous played games for high stakes, sometimes even life or death. Mehitabel had seen a lot but had kept her own counsel, not because she was afraid of what might happen, but because of what *would* happen—if she talked, went to the media or the police. Which was how she became a woman these men knew they could trust. And how she happened to become Ahmet Ghulbian's right-hand woman. Keeper of his secrets. Executioner supreme.

She had no fear about getting caught, or of Ahmet betraying her. How could he? He was up to his eyes in the whole business. Ahmet was as much a deviate and a killer as she herself. They were both evil and they suited each other. If she had cared, Mehitabel could have tallied up the count on how many young women—some so young they were still "girls" in the real sense of the word—had passed through the Ghulbian portals, departing, as he'd say with a laugh, for "the other side." Mehitabel wasn't sure if there was another side but if so she hoped she would never meet them there, and if she did that they would not recognize her.

Looking in the mirror, she contemplated cutting off her signature Medusa hair, maybe trying a long, sleek black wig, or even a short blond bob, a chic fashionista approach that would match her style. But when she pulled back her hair, held it away from her sharp-boned face, her narrow green eyes stared back as though they hated her.

She was in top shape, of course, thanks to the gym and the jogging track that encircled the *Lady Marina*'s deck, and which she used several times a day. Eight miles total. Plus the weights that gave her the long, sleek muscles and the strength of a man twice her size. And of course she had perfect control over what she ate; every morsel, every sip, was logged in her memory every day and she never, ever, went beyond the calorie count stipulated by her London trainer. Champagne, though, was her downfall. She wasn't quite sure why she was addicted to it and would not even admit she was, but she wanted it, craved it, and, thank God, with Ghulbian, could always have it. Sometimes that turned out to be convenient when you happened to have a bottle in hand with which to take out a red-haired woman who, God knows how, had managed to return from the dead. Not once, but twice.

But no more. Angie would soon take her final walk, and Mehitabel needed to celebrate with another bottle of that excellent French champagne; no particular brand, but it must always be French. She had visited Rheims several times, in the very heart of Champagne country, where she had sampled every vintage, down to the smallest vineyard that produced a mere couple hundred bottles, mostly kept for special customers. Of which, of course, by dropping the name Ghulbian, she had immediately become an honored member. This particular champagne was now exclusively served by the billionaire and the vintner felt fortunate to be so honored, and to get such a good and steady price for his wine.

Mehitabel didn't really give a shit about the vineyard or the winemaker. To her he was just another of the men who served her, kowtowed to her, did their best to please her. In her view, men should always be in that position.

Of course she had learned this the hard way. Sometimes, after a bottle of the bubbly, alone in her room, Mehitabel wondered if all women didn't learn about life the hard way. Even that poor little bitch Angie. God, if any woman needed to learn, it was surely Angie, too dumb to even know what was going on and try to take advantage instead of becoming the victim.

Mehitabel had never been the victim. She had never sold herself, only sold others. She sometimes wondered if "evil" began with those transactions, the first time she had led a girl from school into the woods, delivered her to the man waiting there, watched what happened, hands over her ears so she would not hear the screams, then run off with a few dollars in her pocket, money to buy drugs that she would not use herself, but sell at a profit, after which she would scrape up the poor idiot girl she had sold the dope to from the floor and deliver her to any man who wanted her.

This happened three times, each in a different town, a different county. Mehitabel was a foster child with no family of her own. When these events took place she would complain to the authorities of abuse and, tears streaming, would be moved on to a fresh family, a new area, a new start. When she was eighteen, she moved on, and out, for good, the possessor of a minimal and mediocre wardrobe and a couple hundred dollars.

Now, she glanced round her spacious room with its walls of gold French brocade, its canopy bed draped with the finest silk and the gilded finials depicting lions' heads; at the rich antique carpets flung casually one across the other like her own personal magic carpet ride. Her closet was full of designer clothes made especially for her, fitted to her body so there was never even a crease. Her shoes were not handmade, because she loved shoe shopping and preferred to buy the best in Rome, in Florence, in Paris. A special closet held her handbags, predictably Hermès, the very symbol of the nouveau-riche woman. Only Hermès, in every color and type of skin, from python to alligator to calf. Her jewelry was minimal but expensive, her large diamond studs and her platinum Rolex Oyster her favorites.

All that remained now, Mehitabel thought, staring round her luxurious room, was for her to become the sole proprietor of the business she was involved in. She had become close to Ahmet and he was now so used to her he trusted her implicitly, something Mehitabel knew no one should ever do. Not only did she know all Ahmet's personal secrets, now she knew all his business secrets, who he dealt with and when and where. And she intended to use them.

26

Martha had just finished an important and complicated job designing, of all things, an English country kitchen in the middle of London for a Russian woman who wanted every possible newfangled American invention, including three refrigerators with glass doors so that everything inside would be on display. Martha warned her she'd have to change the fruits and vegetables every day to keep the image perfect but her client was not fazed. "We eat out most nights anyhow" was her answer.

Like the flowers with which the house was also overstuffed, the refrigerators were meant only for display. It was disheartening to put so much work, so much thought and effort, into a place that ultimately would never really be lived in. Martha was simply not that kind of decorator, yet she could not afford to turn down the job, and she had to admit that when it was finished, with every vegetable polished, every floral arrangement glowing perfectly in exactly the right enormous crystal vase in exactly the right spot, it looked pretty darn good. And her client was thrilled, which made Martha feel good too.

Now there was a lull. She was free and thinking perhaps she could take a holiday with Marco, who needed a break from dealing with Ahmet Ghulbian. He'd told her Ahmet had invited them on his yacht, the *Lady Marina*. She had not been too keen, preferring to be alone, but then, out of the blue, though later she suspected Marco had something to do with it, she got a call.

"My name is Mehitabel," the caller said. "I am Ahmet Ghulbian's personal assistant. Mr. Ghulbian has heard good things about your work, from Mr. Mahoney."

Mehitabel's voice was low and she was so soft-spoken Martha had to strain to hear her.

"I'm always glad to know that," she replied, cautious because you never knew when somebody was going to ask you to work for free or at a big discount simply because they were somebody's cousin or had been at school with somebody who knew you.

"Mr. Ghulbian would appreciate it if you could take a look at his country place," Mehitabel said.

Martha thought quickly about whether it would be correct for her to do over the mogul's country house; what with Marco painting his portrait and all, things seemed to be getting a little too close for comfort, yet there was no doubt it would be a lucrative and prestigious commission. Presumably Marco wouldn't mind her working for the mogul. Yet somehow it made *her* uncomfortable. She couldn't get Marco on the phone or via text, so she decided to take a leap of faith, visit Marshmallows, meet Ghulbian, and see what it was all about.

Getting to Marshmallows was not easy; it was way out in the southeast in the English marshlands, but Martha had turned down Ghulbian's offer to helicopter her there. She'd wanted to see the lay of the land, the neighboring homes, the gardens and landscaping, only to be stunned by the place's complete remoteness and lack of any of what she termed "lovable" features.

There were no trees and, to Martha, a big house in a landscape without trees was like a well-dressed woman without jewels, or one who had forgotten her perfume. All she saw as she drove up was a flat gray house that looked rooted to the earth on which it stood. Its small-paned windows reflected back the gray clouds, its gray-tiled roof pressed on top of it. She got the impression the house was trying to hide itself away. "No one lives here," is what it seemed to tell her. The only thing of life, of beauty, was the herons' nest atop a chimney from which a slender white bird poked its beak, protecting its young. Anyway, it lifted Martha's heart, as she sped up the graveled drive and stopped at the flight of four shallow stone steps leading to the front door, where Ahmet stood waiting for her, a smile on his face, both arms extended in welcome.

"My dear Martha, you cannot know how happy it makes me to see you here. Welcome to my home, or at least the house I'm hoping that you, with all your miraculous talent as a designer, will turn into a real home for me."

Getting out of the car, Martha found herself in Ahmet's embrace. It was quick but he held her a tiny bit too tight and a touch too long, so her breasts pressed against his chest. It was only a fleeting moment but enough to make her uncomfortable. She told herself she was being foolish and of course Ahmet had meant nothing by the hug, that he was a nice man, a well-known figure in the charity world, a man who only did good for humanity, for the world's sufferers, and a man for whom she would now do her best to create the "home" he seemed so badly to want.

Throwing open the big front door, and not merely the smaller inner section, so Martha might get the full effect of the baronial hall and the wide staircase with the Art Nouveau stained-glass windows, Ahmet ushered her inside. Of course Martha had heard details of the house from Marco. "Strangely bleak" he had called it—and now she saw what he meant. Everything was there: the expensive brocade sofas; the immense limestone fireplace, obviously brought from a French mansion; the glittering Venetian chandelier; the enormous grandfather clock in an ugly yellowish oak, ticking away too loudly; the black-and-white-tiled floors that, in a different house, would have been elegant but in this solid old structure were out of place. Everything she saw was expensive, with heavy-looking antiques that had once belonged somewhere, and none of which, she decided immediately, belonged here.

"Well?" Ahmet was standing beside her, arms folded over his chest, watching her, an amused smile on his lips.

"Well, indeed!" Martha repeated, shaking her head.

"It's worse than you thought, then?"

She had to laugh at his earnestness. "It's terrible," she said. "I don't want to hurt your feelings, Mr. Ghulbian."

"Ahmet, please."

"Ahmet, sir." She suddenly did not quite know what to call her client. "But whoever did this spent a lot of money and very little time, and had absolutely no taste."

Ahmet roared with sudden laughter and she swung round to look at him. Instead of being pissed off that she had dismissed his entire home as rubbish, he seemed to think it the funniest thing he'd ever heard.

"Bloody hell," he exclaimed through his laughter, "as you English would say, you do not mince words, woman."

"I have found that a waste of time. A client hires me for my experience and my reputation, and my good taste. Whomever you took on to do this cheated you and I'm sorry because it obviously cost a lot of money. Far more," she added, looking more carefully, taking in with her experienced eye the proportions, the ceiling height, the depth of the windows, "far more than I will charge you." She turned to look at him again. "That is, *if* you hire me. I warn you, though it won't be what you paid before, it still won't be cheap."

"*Cheap* is not what I'm after, Miss Patron." Ahmet threw out his hands. "Oh, hell, I'm going to call you Martha. I think we are going to get to know each other very well, and I can't keep up this formal business, calling you Miss Patron every time I get you on the phone. But anyhow, sometimes you get 'cheap' when you've paid a lot for it. That's unfortunately what I got."

"I'll clear it all out, send it to the auction house, see you get fair value, though I'm not guaranteeing you'll get what you paid." She knew Ahmet had been overcharged, that was what happened to very rich people who somehow never seemed to know the true value of anything much, other than in a business deal, buying and selling property, shares, boats, Caribbean islands . . . then, they were on top. She did wonder, though, about the beautiful, creepy Mehitabel. Surely it was one of her jobs to keep checks on her employer's purchases, see that he was billed what had been agreed, make sure he got receipts for the taxman.

"What I'm going to do is come back here with my assistant and measure every room in the house, every passageway and corridor and kitchen alcove. We may end up doing quite a bit of restructuring, Ahmet." She threw in his name with a smile. He gave her that too-intimate smile back and, embarrassed, Martha turned away, adjusting her scarf so it floated over her breasts, over the sweater. Her jeans were tucked into flat black boots and she carried her coat, the waxed green English three-quarter-length jacket known as a Barbour, always seen at country events, or now even on London's Knightsbridge. It had become ubiquitous, fitted all occasions, rain or shine, and that's what a trip to the countryside always involved. Rain or shine.

Today she was lucky and had gotten the shine, something she thanked God for because in this low-slung land, under the looming clouds, this house needed all the help it could get.

"Tell me, Ahmet," she said as he walked her back to the car. "What made you choose this part of the world? Was it simply the house? Or . . ." she flung out her arms, "do you like all this marsh?"

Ahmet was silent for a moment, thinking about it.

"Well," he said finally, "since the house was already here, I obviously was not the first to find the place interesting. Exciting too, in a way. All this beautiful flat green meadowland—*marshland* really—it looks like one long, giant front lawn leading to the river, which you can just see from here, that glittering brown stripe across the horizon. To me, it has a unique beauty. I doubt you can find terrain like this anywhere else in the world, well, perhaps the Camargue in southeastern France, but still, not quite like this. Not with this . . . vividness . . . this remarkable greenness. Your Marco saw it so well, with his painter's eyes, he understood why I'd fallen for the place. It's the silence too, Marco said to me. And yes, he is right. Tell me, what do you hear, Martha? Only the sigh of the wind, the idle ripple of the water, the occasional flutter of wings, a heron in flight. There's no roar of suburban trains in the distance, no flights low overhead, no autoroutes spewing fumes. No, oh no. All we have here is pure nature. And that is why I love it."

His heartfelt speech took Martha's breath away. "You did what you had to," she agreed. "And now I shall do my best to make it even more perfect for you."

Ahmet took her hand, bowing over it as she stepped into her car. "I am honored," he told her. And it was true, he was.

He called after her as she took off. "Will you have an assistant then?"

"My sister, Lucy," she flung over her shoulder with a goodbye wave.

Ahmet was smiling as he went back inside his house and shut the door.

Martha knew exactly what to do with Marshmallows: she would do a Syrie Maugham. Syrie was not only the wife of the famous author, Somerset Maugham, she was also a renowned interior designer of her era, one who'd created a new, modern look, away from the heavy old pieces and the dark beams, the red wallpapers that still reflected Victorian times. Syrie transformed houses with pale walls, infused them with white and light, with soft silken drapes and linen sofas, pale rugs and white-stained wooden floors, pleated lamp shades lined with gold that cast a special glow, everything geared to make a woman look more beautiful in gentle light and soft colors.

Ahmet's house was like a feudal throwback, almost horror-movie style. It needed lightening up and that's exactly what Martha intended to do. It crossed her mind that he might not like being "lightened up" but hey, he'd hired her, that's what she did, and that's what he would get. And, in her book, it would be a hell of a lot better than what he had now. *More!* It would be bloody wonderful, she would make sure of that. It would also consolidate her reputation. She was well aware you didn't do a billionaire's house without attracting notice, that was for sure.

She had dinner that night with Lucy at Scott's in Mayfair, indulging in oysters which they ate straight, no fancy sauces, only a brief squeeze of lemon so the brininess slid sumptuously down their throats.

"I'm going to have the halibut next," Lucy said, already attacking the breadbasket.

"And I suppose you'll have that with fries." Martha was

not asking a question, she knew her sister well, knew that she was perpetually hungry. For a creature who looked more like a waif than any ballerina, Lucy could certainly pack it away, when she had the opportunity, that is. Martha was concerned over Lucy's perpetual joblessness and fixation on a life on the stage or on TV or in movies, probably even pantomime if she ever got the chance: Dick Whittington and his Cat; Robin Hood and his Merry Men . . .

"Lucy, it's time you stopped playing Snow White," she said. It was not anger she felt for her sister, it was fear for her well-being. "People don't starve to death for their art these days."

"They do if they have no money," Lucy said, buttering yet another chunk of baguette. "You should try this," she added. "The butter's really good."

"Since you've already eaten most of it, it's hardly worth the effort."

Lucy threw her sister a calculating upward glance. Sighing, she put down the piece of bread. "Okay. So what's up? Tell me what I've done wrong this time."

Martha eyed her sister, skinny in her blue jeans and the Rolling Stones T-shirt she could swear she remembered from their youth; no hint of makeup—probably because Lucy could not afford any—no polish on her nails either, probably for the same reason. In fact, the only way Lucy had a roof over her head was because, thankfully, the Patron family still owned the house in Chelsea, now divided into flats. Lucy had two basement rooms reached from a small area down a flight of cement steps, and where the door was practically in your face as you turned to open it. There was a cupboard for a kitchen, used, it seemed, only for fixing endless cups of coffee, of which, by some miracle of financial dexterity, they never seemed to run out. Nor did they seem to run out of booze, which Martha suspected was mostly provided by the guys who came to visit the three fun girls who lived there.

Just look at her, Martha thought, watching her sister devour her dinner while throwing Martha a smile and managing at the same time to tell her about the acting job that had gotten away. As they all seemed to.

"So far, that is," Lucy said, assessing her sister as Martha had just assessed her. "You look terrific, Marthie," she said, slipping into the old childhood nickname. "All blond and fair, the perfect woman. So?" Her brows rose, fork poised halfway to her mouth. "When are you gonna marry him, anyway?"

"You mean Marco?"

Lucy rolled her eyes with pleasure as she took a taste of Martha's Dover sole. "Mmmm, I should have had that."

"You can have all of it if you want." Martha pushed the plate toward her sister, who smiled and shoved it back.

"I'm not that hard up that I have to eat your food as well as my own."

"Yes you are. And that's why we have to do something about it." Martha leaned in closer. "I have a proposal for you."

Lucy rolled her eyes again. "Probably the only one I'll ever get."

"Be serious. This is your life we are planning."

"You mean *you* are planning." Lucy could be stubborn when she felt like it. Besides, she didn't want to hear about a job unless it was on a stage of some kind. Even behind stage would do, painting scenery, pushing cameras around, sweeping the bloody floor.

"I want you to come and work for me." Martha saw Lucy's face turn to stone. She put up her hand to stop her from saying immediately, you've got to be kidding. . . . "No, I'm *not* kidding, Lucy, and yes, I do need help, and so do you. I'm not saying it's forever, but it would get you out of the hole—the *funk*—you're in, and at the same time it would help me out when I need it. I've been offered the biggest job of my career so far, redoing an important country house for a businessman." She thought for a moment. "Well, actually, *mogul* is the only word to describe him. I'm talking about Ahmet Ghulbian."

"You've got to be kidding." Lucy said it anyway. She slumped back in her chair, stunned.

Martha stared at her. "No, I'm not. Why?"

"Because that's the Ahmet I told you about, remember? He paid for my drink one night when I was stuck. I didn't have enough money and he was at the next table." Lucy explained what had happened. "Actually, I was going to ask you for the thirty quid so I could pay him back. I don't like being beholden to a man, especially one I don't even know, even if he is a mogul and can afford it anyway."

Martha thought her sister would never learn; she would just go through life as ingenuous as she was now, believing a man took pity on her and paid for her dinner without any thought of any kind of repayment, which would certainly not be in money.

"Sometimes, Lucy," she said coldly, "I have to think you are a silly bitch."

"It was only a glass of champagne. Martha, I was at the Ritz! What else could I do?"

"You could have called me, I would have given them my credit card."

"Ohh, well, he got there first with his." Lucy grinned. She was bewitching when she grinned, her tousled blond hair falling into her eyes, her unmade-up face all shiny and clean. She looked about fifteen years old at that moment and Martha sighed and took pity.

"So, are you going to take the job as my assistant on this project, or not?"

"You betcha," Lucy said, grinning again.

27

The next day, Martha flew to Paris to be with Marco. Later she fixed dinner at his apartment and since each liked different foods it was a varied assortment. For her: salad greens, braised tomatoes with Parmesan, and fresh shrimp with a good garlicky mayonnaise. For him: grilled sirloin and a baked potato with butter on the side. Nothing she could do could turn Marco away from the food of his youth. It was okay, though she did wish he would go easier on the butter. But she had other things to talk about tonight, more important than butter, something she had caught, by chance, earlier that evening in the newspaper:

MISSING BROOKLYN WOMAN it said in large black letters above the photo of an attractive girl whose hair clouded round her head in a fizz of energy. As though she could fly away with that hair, Martha thought. She remembered Marco's description of the red-haired girl who had "gone missing." Now here that girl was, officially missing—in print—in the newspaper. There could not be two women of that description, with that hair, who had suddenly disappeared. Marco was right after all.

Marco was leaning against the kitchen sink watching the preparations, a glass of chilled rosé in hand, his mind on other matters.

"So?" he said finally.

Martha threw him a glance. "So—what?" she asked, tearless, even though she was chopping onions.

Marco thought it was amazing that Martha never cried when she chopped onions. Just another of her special talents.

Marco's kitchen had been done over by Martha. The polished concrete counters were her only concession to his aesthetics. Personally, she would have preferred a silvery granite. The view beyond the counter, though, was unmatchable: the classic Paris skyline of rooftops and chimneys. Below, paulownia trees were budding in the square while tiny cars in bright colors skidded round corners, brakes squealing, in a never-ending search for parking spots, of which there were none.

"So? Whaddya think?" Marco said.

"Think about what?"

"About who?"

"*Whom.*"

He sighed. "Martha! You know what I mean. *Who* and what I mean is the red-haired girl."

Martha stopped cutting. She wiped her hands on her blue-and-white-striped butcher's apron and took the newspaper clipping from the pocket. "I saw this in today's *Herald Tribune*. I was saving it to give to you after dinner, hoping to have some time to ourselves first, but I can tell you're not totally into it. Into *me*. You have another woman on your mind." She handed it to Marco. "Read that, why don't you."

Wineglass in one hand, the clipping in the other, Marco glanced casually at it, then read it.

"Shit." He slammed his glass onto the concrete countertop. "Martha! Do you realize what this is?"

"Of course I do." It was Martha's turn to lean nonchalantly against the counter. First, though, she turned off the heat under his steak. She was wearing a white short-sleeved tee and white jeans under her apron. She was barefoot and her blond hair was tied back with a green wire twist from the supermarket bag that had held the vegetables.

"It's a picture of the girl you said you saw. It says she's missing, that she never showed up for her job at the restaurant where she worked as a greeter. Her landlady reported to the police that she had not seen her around and got no response when she knocked on her door, nor from her telephone."

Marco read the clipping again. "No one seems to have a cell number for her. Don't you think that unusual, these days? Everybody communicates by cell phone."

"What's her name?"

"Angela Morse. Age twenty-one. 'Home' is a two-room apartment in an old building in Brooklyn." He checked the address again. "Not a very good part of Brooklyn, I'd say. A young woman who looks like that, she'd have to keep her wits about her, coming home late at night, have street smarts and eyes in the back of her head."

"So what was a Brooklyn girl doing all alone in a small Turkish seaside town?"

"More important, what was a Brooklyn girl doing on a yacht in the Aegean?"

"Falling off it," Martha said, with a sudden lurch of her heart as she contemplated the thought that it was probably true and the red-haired girl had drowned, right before Marco's eyes.

"I'm so sorry." She put out a hand, touched Marco tenderly, leaning her head against his shoulder. She had no doubt now, and neither did Marco, that Angie Morse was the girl Marco had seen drown.

And Marco had no doubt that he would have to do something about it.

28

Ahmet was sitting by the fire, reduced now to a few embers. He checked his watch. Three A.M. He had been there, alone, five, maybe six hours. He'd finished the red wine, drinking it right from the bottle since he'd smashed the glass and it wasn't worth getting up to go find another when all he wanted was to get drunk. The wine wasn't enough to achieve that and he'd moved on to scotch and then tequila, his favorite liquor of the moment. He enjoyed the brashness of it compared with the honeyed malt of the scotch, though no doubt he'd switch back again before too long. He had also found tequila useful for getting women drunk, not falling-off-their-chairs pissed but enough to loosen up their "values" as they invariably called their modest stand against sex on a first date. Well, okay, he had his values too: didn't the white roses he sent and the occasional trinket count as a form of wooing? Enough at least for them to think he was falling for them?

How many had it been now? How many women in how many countries? He wondered sometimes how it was that girls could simply disappear without any fuss being made, though of course he chose his girls very carefully. They all had to meet the same criteria: must live alone; must have no family, or at least none close enough to come looking for them; must work in the kind of job that was interchangeable, where no one would care if they moved elsewhere; and must belong to that floating population of young women on the make.

Of course almost every woman had friends, but not every woman had close friends she saw all the time. There were, he'd found, a lot of lonely girls out there, those who showed up at temporary jobs, Starbucks in hand, good-morning smiles on their faces. They went and sat in small enclosed cubicles and made cold calls selling whatever they were attempting to sell, usually without much success. A break for lunch, a sandwich or a burger, off at five or six, picking up a slice of pizza and a Coke or a bottle of cheap wine on the way "home" to a rented room with a shared bath down the hall.

His technique was simple enough. These days via his laptop he could find out almost anything about anybody. It saved a lot of time. It was easy to choose someone, manipulate a casual meeting at the pizza joint, or the coffee shop she frequented, a fancy-seeing-you-here-again kind of setup or else, like with Angie, in a restaurant. No need for Match.com or Christian Mingle; a man like him did not need to pick up a woman online, and especially one who was "looking for love." He was rich and successful and because of that he was famous. Women wanted him. And he wanted to kill women. He'd thought about why he wanted this, thought of his hated mother, his life with veiled women, something that made him, as a male, feel exposed, vulnerable, with nowhere to hide. But that was a secret part of him and never now even acknowledged by himself. He was who he was. He did what he did. And he enjoyed the power it gave him.

It still irked Ahmet that he was not accepted by the British upper classes. Of course he mingled with them, at Ascot where he sometimes had a horse running, and at Henley for the boat races where he would hold a Pimm's Cup party of his own. Pimm's was the traditional gin-based Henley drink, served in tall glasses brimming with fruit. It sank like gentle rain into the stomach and before you knew it you were tipsy, in the very nicest possible way. To prevent the tipsiness he served regular grilled sausages, American-style, in hot dog buns, which his amazed English guests said "went down a treat."

He was well-known for his generosity: he gave to all the important charities that would be reported in the media, but he also contributed to a smaller charity whose aim was to rehabilitate young vagrants found huddled in cardboard boxes under railway arches and in shop doorways. It never failed to cross his mind that there—not "but for the grace of God," but for the murder of Fleur de Roc—was he. Fleur had unknowingly set him on the path to greatness.

What he could not forget, though, was Angie's open eyes, staring at him from the blue Aegean. And the anger in them.

Now Angie was here, sedated and shut in a room, watched over by the amazing Mehitabel, whose icy blood sometimes chilled even Ahmet's own. He was an evil man. Evil was born in him. It was what he was, and it was the path he had taken despite his success and all its accoutrements. As it was in Mehitabel, yet even he never failed to marvel at her chilling lack of emotion. She was the perfect partner.

They had met ten years ago when she'd attended a cocktail party he was giving to raise funds for the survivors of some global disaster, a party which would give him plenty of media coverage, praising his work for charity and his generosity. Mehitabel arrived arm in arm with another woman, a blond *Playboy*-page-three-in-the-sun type who she unloaded quickly onto him, saying she thought he might enjoy meeting her.

They both understood what she meant by "meeting." Unfortunately Mehitabel had got it wrong; the blonde was not the type Ahmet liked at all. He wanted a classy woman on his arm, not someone who looked as though he'd paid for her, and who anyhow would no doubt expect him to pay. He'd offloaded her quickly and left his own party to walk the streets. For the first time in years he'd found himself wondering what was to become of him, where he was headed, even who he was. In fact all he was, was who he had invented. Nobody really knew Ahmet Ghulbian. Including himself.

Mehitabel followed him out onto the street. He heard her heels click-clacking on the sidewalk behind him but he did not slow his pace and allow her to catch up. What he did was walk for miles through the darkened streets of London, a city where he did not even own a home. He felt as homeless as the young men his charity rescued from their cardboard boxes under railway embankments; he was no better. He knew the life they lived intimately. He was still one of them. Only cleverer.

He turned the corner and stepped quickly into a shop doorway. Mehitabel came clacking round the corner. He threw his arm round her throat, dragged her backward, held her tight against him. He growled the question at her: what did she want?

"You" was Mehitabel's answer.

He let her go. They'd stood looking at each other. There was only a faint light coming from where the archway ended.

He put both hands around her throat this time. Her skin was silky under his thumbs; all he had to do was push down, right there where the pulse beat. He stared, hypnotized, at the beating pulse, at the living flesh under his hands, then up at her unfrightened face.

"I can kill for you," she whispered.

Her throat moved under his fingers as she spoke and Ahmet was suddenly drenched in sweat. His knees shook, he wanted her yet he did not want her. She was too like him.

"I can find the women you want, I know what you are looking for."

He let his hands drop to his sides. "How do you know?"

"Because I am like you. I knew it before we even met, before that cocktail party for the homeless boys. You were helping them because you had been one of them. Good can only come from an evil heart when it is touched by personal memory."

It was true, Ahmet thought, sitting restless in front of the dying embers, the bottle of tequila in his hand, acknowledging the suddenly terrifying loneliness in his heart. He had no friend, no man who really knew him. Those boys he'd helped along with his charitable foundation showed up for the reunions, the presentations, the public thank-yous, and many of them wrote to express their gratitude and say how their lives had changed because of him. But none wanted to be his friend. He was the famous billionaire and they were sure he would want nothing to do with their ordinary small lives.

And the rich men he knew? Perhaps it was because they sensed something different beneath the jolly bonhomie façade, the pleasant well-dressed man, flaunting his riches, his Bentleys, his helicopters, his yacht. He must be the only yacht owner who had a hard time finding friends to fill it on vacation, though God knows he issued enough invitations, often refused politely, even warmly, thanking him for his offer but the timing was wrong, there was an important family wedding, a prior trip arranged.

Marshmallows might have been a house on the moon for all the visitors it got. Now he was hoping that by involving Martha Patron, he might also gain access to people she knew. When it was finished he would throw a party, ask her to invite them all. He would floodlight the house, the marshes would glimmer, beautifully green and seductive under all that light. He would have a band, a singer, whoever Martha said would be the best, the most famous. He would serve Veuve Clicquot champagne and five-pound tins of the best caviar; he'd even have chefs carving sides of roast beef the way the man who had once owned the house had done, before being knifed by his lover.

Martha would lay a parquet floor in the hall for dancing; he would have tumblers and acrobats and magicians. He would invite dukes and movie stars and tell them to wear only black or white, like Truman Capote's famous ball in New York. He would present Lucy, bring her out in couture, a black gown from Dior or Valentino. And a mask. Of course everyone must be masked, that's what made it so much fun, not knowing exactly who you were holding in your arms as you danced, or who felt safe confessing secrets in your ear not really meant for you.

It was all there. His plans were perfected. Tomorrow he would put them into action. Meanwhile, what was he going to do about Angie? He couldn't keep her locked up. And he wanted her. Not the way he wanted Lucy, his lovely young Lucy, so well brought up she wouldn't even finish her dinner because it was bad manners; so innocent she probably didn't know what real sex felt like; and so sweet she recoiled with horror at the thought of a lamb becoming meat on her dinner plate.

For once in his life he had some interesting women, one he might hope to marry and one he meant to kill. He had already thought of an attractive way to accomplish the latter, since the first attempt had gone so dramatically wrong. Not this time. This would be final. He'd let Mehitabel take care of that.

He put a bottle of the very rare tequila to his lips, drained it, then threw it into the fireplace where it joined the shards of the three-hundred-dollar glass he had pitched in there earlier.

He felt pretty good.

29

Lucy got the e-mail from Ahmet the following day.

> Dear Lucy, now you are to be working on reinventing my house into a "home," along with your sister, Martha, I think I am safe in inviting you to come look at it, and perhaps have dinner? Lunch? So we can discuss your own views on its new look, as well as Martha's. Do tell me you think this a satisfactory idea and of course I will send a car and the helicopter for you. Remember, I told you, all square and above board! No funny business! Ha ha! May I look forward to your visit?

Lucy sighed. Ahmet was persistent, she'd give him that. It was probably why he'd gotten where he was: persistence; cunning; smarts; and—she had to admit with a smile—charm. She didn't fancy him exactly, but he was kind of creeping into her life despite that. Was he attractive? According to the gossip columns and girlie reports, he was. Sexy, too. That was also on the gossip rounds: well endowed; fast but knows how to use it; always sent flowers and gave small, pretty, expensive gifts. Ahmet knew his way into a woman's heart, that was for sure; Lucy would bet there were half a dozen right now willing to step into the role of Mrs. Ahmet Ghulbian. Thankfully, she was not one.

She was lying amid the tangled sheets of her bed, which truth to tell could have used a wash, only her flat had no washing machine and she was too broke to buy a second set of sheets and too lazy to rush over to her sister's place and ask to use her washer, so for now she just avoided thinking about them. *"Buggie-wuggie,"* she whispered to herself, which was her code for the curse word "bugger," which she tried never to say. Martha would have hated it and Lucy respected Martha, who anyhow she guessed was right. Curse words coming out of the mouth of a young woman were even less attractive than her grubby sheets. So? What was she going to do? Call Martha, of course, and ask about the job and how much she would be paid, when she could start, what would she do, where to even think about beginning. You had only to look at her scruffy bed sit to know interior design had never so much as entered her thoughts. The futon, saved from her school days, had an old kelim rug flung across it, that was actually quite good and had come from the family home where it had once graced the drawing room. The scuffed dark wood floors had claw marks from some previous owner's dog, with a blue and cream dhurrie rug donated by her sister to cover the worst and stop her feet from freezing when she stepped out of bed—well, off the futon—in the morning. And plenty of afternoons and evenings too. Not that she was the kind of girl—"woman" as she liked to think of herself now—that went to bed with every guy she met. Truth be told again, not with any of them, really. Sometimes, she'd been tempted in the heat of the moment, when she was in the latest boy/man's arms and that flushed feeling ran through her, heating her blood, tingling in her veins and other places she had rarely previously even thought about, but she'd been too busy playing lacrosse and winning the spelling bee and trying on other girls' clothes to think much about "the end result," which is what all the girls at school called it. "It" being sex, of course.

Martha had tackled her about "it" some time ago.

"I think we should have a talk, Lucy," she'd said with a meaningful look in her eyes so Lucy knew immediately what she was up to.

"Ohh," she'd dismissed her loftily. "If you're talking about sex, I know all about that."

She'd never forget Martha's stunned look; her round pale blue eyes had grown even rounder with shock, making Lucy laugh.

"Well, not firsthand experience," she'd added, for which Martha said thank God and began to breathe again. Lucy was only fifteen at the time, and completely inexperienced. The fact was you didn't get much of a shot at boys when you went to an all-girl boarding school, as Lucy had for what seemed forever. And all those years, all she had wanted was to get out; she'd felt she was wasting her time, missing out on life. And then, when she graduated and was free at seventeen, she'd immediately wanted back in the safety of knowing where she belonged, somebody to tell her what she was doing every day, where to go, her friends, her support system. Now, the school friends were scattered far and wide, taking a year out in Australia; crewing a yacht in the Bahamas; helping with starving children in Africa; or like Lucy, attempting to be actresses.

The annoying thing about Ahmet was he'd mentioned a movie script that might just be perfect for her, but since then she had heard nothing. Not a word about it after that night at the Italian restaurant; not about the possible movie; not about another date; not even until now about helping

Martha do over his house, which was, ridiculously in Lucy's eyes, called Marshmallows. I mean, didn't you have to be some kind of jerk to name your house *that,* simply because it was built on marshland, which anyhow seemed like a dumb place to her. Creepy, in fact.

Her phone gave its little tune and she sat up against her in-need-of-a-wash pillows and checked it. Martha. Hah!

"I was just thinking about you," she said.

"And I you, which is why I called. And which, I have to say, Lucy, is more than you have done recently."

"Sorry." Lucy heaved a sigh that ricocheted off the dank bedroom walls. How she hated this flat. She must get her act together, find somewhere better.

"I need to live somewhere more suitable," she said to Martha.

"If you mean more suited to your circumstances then I think you're in the right place."

Martha could be tart when she wanted.

Lucy sighed again.

"What the fuck—"

"Lucy!"

"Aw, I mean, what the hell, oh *buggie-wuggie!*"

Lucy really, normally, was not into cursing. She respected the English language and knew perfectly well how to use it. Even the bad words.

"Lucy, what are we going to do with you?" Martha was picturing her, accurately, amid her scruffy chaos. "At least open the window, get some air into that filthy den of yours."

"It is not filthy, merely in need of a cleaning lady, which since you know I am not working and have no money, I cannot afford."

"And I suppose it's beneath your elevated status in the world as an out-of-work actress to pick up a vacuum and a mop, give the place a good going over."

"I don't have a vacuum, something else I can't afford,

and truth is, Marthie, I don't really give a shit about 'clean.' I'd really rather eat."

Martha was silent, thinking about that. "It is possible to do both, as you will find now you are coming to work for me."

"Oh, yeah? And when is that event to take place?" It seemed to Lucy at least a month must have gone by since she'd heard about Ahmet's house makeover, though in fact it was only a week.

"Tomorrow. I'll come by and get you. Be ready nine fifteen latest."

Lucy sat up, perked up, became interested. She twirled a blond lock round a finger. "I'm not sure I have anything to wear."

Martha groaned. "It's not a cocktail party. We are going to work. Put on jeans, sweatpants, a woolly jumper; it's bound to be cold. And sneakers, it'll be damp too, around there, marshy."

Lucy shuddered. "I don't like the sound of it."

In fact, neither did Martha, but a job was a job and this was a big one. Important.

"I'm calling Pizza Express," she said. "They'll deliver a sausage and pepper thin crust along with a salad and a Coke, in half an hour. At least eat something. Then take a shower, for God's sake, and I'm calling Peter Jones and buying you some sheets. Jesus, Lucy! What would Mum say if she could see the state you're in?"

Lucy fell silent as she thought about her mum. "I'm just hoping she doesn't know," she said quietly. Then, "I'll be ready. Thanks, Marthie."

30

Of course, it was that very same night that Lucy fell in love.

She'd fiddled with the TV channels while awaiting the pizza delivery, finding nothing but the usual grim news and game shows; she'd cleaned up the flat, something she was to be thankful for later when she asked "him" home. Well, by home she meant "the flat"; obviously her real home was Patrons, though she rarely went there anymore, not since Mum had gone.

A short while later, she found herself eyeing the gorgeous blond young man on her doorstep. Parked behind him was a small car with a pizza delivery sign on top. Despite his good looks and his smile Lucy couldn't help wondering who would go out with a guy with a pizza sign atop his car for everybody to see. She wondered what the parking valet might think, or her friends. Except he was so good-looking her heart was making little jumps in her chest, and not her stomach, because she had suddenly lost all hunger.

"Are you really a pizza delivery guy?" she asked as he

held out the flat box, still smiling that white smile. "I mean, like *in 'real life'*?"

"This is 'real life,' baby," he said, sounding like an American movie star.

"You mean you can't get a better job than this? With your looks, and all?"

"*And all* is where it's at. I need two more college credits before I can graduate."

"Where from?" She took the box, still looking into his eyes.

"Oxford."

"Ohh." Lucy thought quickly of her own shamefully misused education. "How wonderful," she said brightly. "Would you like to come in, have a Coke or something?"

"Well . . ." He hovered uncertainly on the top step, faded jeans propped on his hip bones, ancient T-shirt clinging to his abs. "I really should get back."

"Just a Coke," she persuaded. "It's diet, so it's okay, like, y'know what I mean?"

"I guess I do."

Lucy knew for certain she was getting into uncharted waters and was absolutely loving it. This, she thought as he finally stepped over the threshold and she closed the door behind him, was what true love felt like.

Standing close, he made her shabby basement room look even smaller, with his wide shoulders, his over-six-foot height, his shock of blond hair falling so sexily over eyes that might be blue but she hadn't had time to check before he put his arms round her and kissed her with a kind of hunger she had never felt before, tongue and all, then he licked her face, her eyebrows, kissed her closed eyes.

"You are beautiful," he said, and for the first time Lucy thought it might even be true.

Tempted though she was, after ten minutes of passionate kissing and fondling she sent him on his way, knees atremble, heart thumping, with a promise to call the next day since he was working late that night, but maybe he could call her later. . . .

He did not call later, and then the next morning Lucy had to go with Martha and so she didn't know what had happened. She tried to put him out of her mind, temporarily at least, so she could become a proper working girl, Martha's helper, helping Ahmet Ghulbian change his bloody awful house, which could only be for the better. She would call him tomorrow.

You know what? she told herself, shocked. You don't even have his number. You don't even know his name. And that was the truth.

She wished her mum were here to ask what to do.

Lucy often wondered exactly where her mum and her dad had "gone." Death baffled her and she'd even gone to church to contemplate it, something she had not done since attending school chapel every morning for all those years, when the girls' straw boaters with the striped-school-colors hatbands fell off with a clatter every time they bent their heads to pray. But, oh God, how she missed her. Why oh why, Mum and Dad, she asked herself as she had so many times since the accident, did you have to take that road, on that day, at that hour, at that moment? Martha had done her best to console her, though she herself was distraught, taking emotional responsibility for her young sister, promising she would never leave her, never be in an accident, never get killed or something awful like that, like what had just happened to their parents.

In all her life, however long, however short—and Lucy recognized now there was a time limit, a sort of sell-by date on mortality, each different, each unknown—anyhow, in all her life, she would never forget how Martha had consoled her, helped her, held her in her arms, told her she would take care of her. Forever, Martha had said, though even then Lucy recognized that forever was a meaningless word, that there was no "forever." There was only what you had, what you were given at birth, absolutely no longer and no shorter than destiny allowed. Unless somebody killed you first, of course. That could happen to almost anybody, given the right circumstances, though not to people like her; other sorts of people who got involved in bad stuff or with men or drugs and suchlike.

Speaking of drugs, she had tried a joint or two, found it didn't do much for her except make her giggle and she didn't need drugs for that; then the odd sniff of cocaine, smuggled into some party by one of those types you really should avoid who only wanted to get you interested, then hooked, then take you for as much money as he could get, or, in fact, "she" could get: it wasn't only men who were evil; women counted in that department too. Lucy had known a girl like that at school, well, she had only been there a few weeks and that was because no other school would take her, her reputation was so bad, but her father was so filthy rich he thought he could buy everything, until one day she bopped him on the head with a hammer and that was that. Jail for life, no more grass, no more hammers, no more dad. The shock had reverberated through Lucy's chain of school friends, causing them to pause for a moment and think about their own families and be grateful for what they'd got. Especially in Lucy's case, grateful for Martha, who right now was expecting her to be clean and presentable, or, at least in jeans and a sweat-shirt and decent sneakers, at nine fifteen, which was in exactly five minutes.

She was a whiz at the quick shower, learned necessarily at boarding school, and was waiting, hair still wet, cleanish sneakers properly tied, ripped jeans and all, when Martha honked the horn outside her door. Lucy galloped up the cement steps from the basement flat, forgetting as always to lock the door behind her, waved a jolly hand, beaming a good-morning smile as she climbed in beside Martha and they edged off into the traffic.

"So, what's it like, this house?" Lucy asked, taking the Danish pastry Martha offered because she had known Lucy would not have had breakfast.

"Heavy."

"Jesus!" Lucy took a bite of the Danish. "Sounds terrible."

"Which is exactly why we—by that I mean you and I, Lucy—are about to turn things around, make it light, summery, gorgeous, filled with atmosphere and beauty."

"I expect you mean 'good taste.' " Lucy had already finished the Danish and was riffling through the paper bag on the console between her and Martha for a second. "Oh," she said, disappointed. "Apple."

"Get your own next time." Lucy always had the ability to rattle Martha. "Selfish bitch," she added.

"Marthie! Really!" Lucy grinned at her. "Selfish, maybe, but certainly not a bitch."

"Okay, I'll allow you that."

"Buggie-wuggie, I hate apple." Lucy rejected the pastry with a sigh. "We could always stop at McDonald's for breakfast; eggs, chips, y'know."

"I'm sure there'll be coffee waiting at Marshmallows."

"And buns, I hope."

"And antiques, which, my dear sister, you and I must as tactfully as possible get rid of and replace with a whole new look. My idea is white and light and touches of bright, a twenties kind of vibe . . ."

"Like that Maugham woman, you mean."

Martha threw Lucy a surprised glance. "I shouldn't have thought you knew about Syrie Maugham, other than maybe as the author Somerset's wife."

"Oh, everybody knows about her, she was quite a girl,

wasn't she? I mean, the rumor is she got around a bit as well as tarting up people's houses. Not that we know it's true, of course, since she's been dead forever and it seems nobody cares anymore after you're dead, or not for much longer anyway. I mean, Marthie, who do you ever think of that's dead, legends in their lifetime, actors and actresses, like oh, well, Rita Hayworth, I suppose, and Frank Sinatra? Before my time of course, so I would never think of *them*. Maybe I only think of Mum and Dad like that anyway," she added in a suddenly small voice.

Martha threw her a quick glance again and reached out and squeezed her hand.

"It's okay, Lucy, we'll always remember them."

They sat in silence for a long time after that, Lucy with her eyes shut, feigning sleep, opening them only when Martha told her they were there.

They passed through a pair of ornate iron gates set between stone pillars with recumbent oversized lions, which Martha decided she would need to get rid of immediately. They drove slowly between an avenue of stunted trees, loose gravel spitting from the tires, until they came to the house. Martha stopped, switched off the engine, and the two sat and looked silently at it: gray, pressed into the ground by a lowering gray tile roof, marshland a disturbingly bright green behind it; on top a spiky bird's nest over which a white heron hovered as though daring them to come near. The bird was, thought Martha, her heart sinking, the only thing that brought the place to life.

"Buggie-wuggie," Lucy whispered, staring, horrified. "It's the Hammer House of Horror."

Martha pulled herself together, opened the door, stepped out of the car. "That's why we're here," she said briskly, grabbing her bag and the batches of samples from the backseat. "Come on, Lucy, give me some help here."

"If you insist, but I don't like it. I mean, look at those

windows, little panes gleaming at us like eyes or something. Don't you feel it, Marthie, like it's watching us?"

"You're being ridiculous," Martha said, but she knew exactly what Lucy meant. To say the house did not have a welcoming feel was an understatement. It seemed to give off waves of animosity, something she had never previously encountered in any home she had been in.

"Just look at those beautiful birds," she said brightly as she walked up the front steps, followed reluctantly by Lucy clutching swatches of sample fabrics to her chest. "Now, Lucy, think what you and I can do with this, bring it to life, fill it with love. . . ."

"You need the right people to fill a place with love," Lucy said. Since she had been brought up in a place of love she knew about such things, and so did Martha, though now she was working, she had to look at things differently, think about what she could bring to a place, like this, that might give it "love."

"Love" was what Ahmet believed he felt when he opened the door and stood at the top of the wide flight of four worn stone steps leading into the hallway of his house, which soon was to be made into "a home," and saw Lucy again. He had already thought out a code of behavior for himself that would be suitable for the occasion, which was to be the perfect gentleman, allow Martha access only to the downstairs of his house, with Mehitabel to keep an eye on her, and Lucy as well, and to make sure they did not venture upstairs, where Angie was.

"That's for next time," he told Martha when she admired the heavy mahogany balustrade while frowning at the red-patterned stair carpet with the huge brass clips holding it in place. "Today, I would like you to start on the main downstairs rooms. Mehitabel will show you round, give you any information you need. And please remember, Martha, you have free rein. *Mi casa es su casa.* And Lucy, dear little Lucy, welcome."

But Lucy's absent mind was on the pizza guy. She was wondering when she'd get a chance to call the pizza place and ask to speak to him, though not knowing his name was a problem. She grinned, thinking about him. She'd had worse problems.

The huge house seemed deserted, no maids bustling, no smiling help welcoming them. Lucy remembered Patrons and the butler and the Mrs. who were part of the family all those years. Patrons could not have existed without them, and was the reason it barely did now they were gone.

"But how do you manage this big place?" she asked Ahmet.

"Well, of course, I have Mehitabel, she takes care of everything for me, hires the help and all that sort of thing. I assure you, Lucy, Marshmallows runs perfectly. I wouldn't have it any other way."

Lucy could see he would not. Ahmet was fastidious to the point of persnickety; always immaculately turned out, always with the silk handkerchief in his breast pocket. She couldn't imagine Ahmet in a T-shirt, hair ruffled by the wind, in jeans and the sort of thing her friends wore, but of course he was an "older" man and being a billionaire she supposed he had to present a certain image. Not knowing any other billionaires, or even anyone who had millions, which she guessed might seem like small change to him, she wasn't too sure of her facts. But what she did know about, because everybody had heard about it, seen pictures of it in newspapers and magazines, was his yacht, the *Lady Marina,* which had cost a fortune. Ahmet himself had told her so.

Two hundred million was the price of that luxury, he'd said, adding that the boat was 250 feet long.

"Expensive," Lucy said, shocked by such numbers, but she had read somewhere that Ahmet's worth was reputed to be more than six billion, and to him the cost of the boat was probably small change, and certainly a long way from wondering if you could afford to order the spaghetti in the local Italian. Someone had told her Ahmet had made his money in metal trading; Lucy wasn't sure what that was but it was certainly lucrative. And the boat supposedly was spectacular; they said the dance floor had a swimming pool above it so you almost felt you were floating, and the cabins had quilted silk walls, or beautiful wood paneling, with the softest terry bathrobes, and every possible lotion and cream and powder from Paris. But his house was intimidating.

She sank into a too-deep burgundy brocade sofa which made her legs stick out in front of her like a child's, still clutching the batches of fabric samples to her chest. She glanced round under her lashes, checking it out, hoping Ahmet would not notice, but of course he did. He also noticed the stunned expression that flitted briefly across her face as she took in the heavy wood furniture, the oversized cushions, the crystal chandelier—three, actually, all in one room—and the Tiffany lamps that did not go with anything else. And those bloody awful weighty dark green curtains looped back with gold tassels.

Shit. Lucy thought this place looked like a bordello, or anyway, her idea of what bordellos looked like.

She felt Ahmet's eyes on her, forced herself to look back at him, smiling.

"You don't like it," he said.

She had been taught always to be honest. "Not much," she admitted carefully. To her surprise, he laughed.

"Men who live alone do not have much taste. The place needs a woman's touch, don't you think? Soften it up a little?"

"Get rid of all the red," Lucy advised, suddenly finding her way into the interior design world. Not that she knew much, but she did know when it was wrong. "And all those chandeliers."

"I should take you to see my boat," Ahmet said, coming to sit next to her on the sofa.

Uncomfortable with his nearness, Lucy edged slightly away, hoping he would not notice, though of course he did and immediately moved to the other end.

"I'm sure you would find that beautiful, more to your taste, all very simple."

"Martha will take care of this for you," she said, hoping her sister could see her way through all this "stuff," all this heavy darkness, because she surely could not.

"Of course I will." Martha strode into the room, iPad in one hand, memo pad and pen in the other, phone tucked under her chin as she waited for a call to the fabric place to go through. When it did she told them exactly what she needed, and asked if they would get back to her right away. The job was urgent. Priority was everything.

Ahmet had gotten to his feet when she walked in and now he smiled his approval. "I do like efficiency, especially in a woman," he said. "Rarer, you see, in women than men."

"I don't believe I agree with that," Martha said in what Lucy recognized as her "acid" voice. "Women have come a long way in every facet of business. Surely you have met many of them. Your own Mehitabel is one of the most efficient women I've ever encountered."

"Mehitabel is a gem. I appreciate her more every day," Ahmet agreed, making a quick decision to keep Mehitabel away from Martha. "Well, now, what do you think of my little palace?"

"It definitely needs to be less 'palacey,' more 'homey,'" Martha said. "I told you I needed to rip it all out, and

I wasn't joking. Ahmet, you'll simply have to trust me on this. I promise you'll be happy with the result."

He shrugged in agreement. He said, "Now, what do you say we all have some tea?"

He was, Martha thought, amazed again by him, always the perfect English gentleman.

Driving back in the car she said to Lucy, "So? What d'you think?"

"Of him, or that house?"

"Both."

Lucy thought a minute, then, "He's oddly fascinating. The house gives me the creeps. And all that green swampy stuff and that scary river. Why would anybody want to live there?"

"The previous owner was killed by his lover in the dining room. Using the knife with which he was about to carve the roast beef."

"Jesus." Lucy's eyes were on stalks. "No wonder it's creepy. What happened to him?"

"Well, he was killed, of course, with the roast beef knife."

"No! What happened to the killer?"

"Nobody knows. It seems he just wandered off into the marshes, and nobody cared to take the risk and follow him. Never seen again."

"OMG," Lucy said this time. This was a long way from the cute pizza delivery guy and suddenly she wanted to get back to him, and that "normality." "Are you sure about this, Marthie? Doing this house over? It's so far from anywhere, it seems almost uncivilized, with the river and the marshes and the red brocade sofas."

"We'll change all that, you and I," Martha said, just as

her phone rang. It was Marco. She pressed Answer and kept her hands on the wheel.

"Am I glad to hear your voice," she said, astonished by the sudden feeling of relief that swept through her. Today had been exhausting in a different way; challenging, in fact.

"You hadn't even heard my voice yet," Marco said, and she heard the smile in his voice. "Are you alone in the car?"

"Lucy's here."

"That's okay then. Besides wanting to hear your voice, and tell you I'm missing you, I wanted to tell you I'm on the track of Angie Morse. I've found out where she lived and I'm going there to see if anybody knows what happened. And it's my belief she is the girl I saw murdered."

"Jesus." Martha said it this time.

31

Ahmet was alone again. The place he seemed always to be. Even Mehitabel was gone, off to check on the yacht, make sure supplies had arrived, make sure the crew was not roistering round ports at all hours of the night, causing trouble. It wasn't easy keeping a crew, even with the generous wages Ahmet paid. Men got bored and bored men got into trouble. Mehitabel knew that from experience and Ahmet appreciated her concern, but he missed having her to share his thoughts with, to plot with, to prowl those ports with in search of the next young woman. It was surprising how easy Mehitabel made those searches; she knew what those young women on the make wanted and she told them she could give them their dreams. And they believed her.

It was rarely Ahmet who made the first move. It was usually she who found them.

"It's so easy," she'd told Ahmet once, sitting and drinking very good brandy with him after a long night in the port of Piraeus, Greece, where they had dined and danced and even thrown plates around, though Ahmet had no girl on his arm. There'd been none he'd fancied. That, or he simply had lost the desire. The urge. It worried him, and Mehitabel of course noticed that.

They sat on deck, gazing at the lights twinkling on shore, the flickering red and blue bar signs, the yellow streetlights, the darkness above picked out with a few stars and no moon. Both were comfortable with the dark, comfortable with each other, neither had any secrets the other did not know. At least that's what Ahmet thought. Mehitabel knew differently.

She recognized that Ahmet had the ability to overcome his circumstances, to become whatever any new situation asked of him. Ahmet was mercurial, a personality jack-of-all-trades: humble when needed, authoritative when he wanted; and always, underneath, the one in charge. Except with her. She was the only person Ahmet needed. She believed that without her, Ahmet could not exist. He'd asked her the other night what they should do about Angie.

She kept her eyes straight ahead. "Nothing," she said. "For now, anyway."

"She bothers me," he said. "Her very presence bothers me."

"Is that why you want Marco to paint her portrait?"

He sipped his brandy silently for a while, thinking about it, then he said, "I want that portrait so I can forget the look in her eyes when she was drowning. I have to change that. Remove it from my mind permanently."

"I can do that for you." Mehitabel thought of how much pleasure she would derive from that.

Ahmet thought about it too. "Later," he said finally.

32

Rather than do battle with Brooklyn's motor traffic, Marco rented a bicycle. The fact that it was bright orange and had racing wheels made him feel ready for the Tour de France, though Brooklyn's downtrodden streets seemed light-years from the cobblestones and small cafés, the cups of coffee under yellow umbrellas with the wind blowing your hair and Em tucking into the croissant Marco always shared with her. So, all right, it wasn't good to feed a dog a croissant, but it made a change from the mastodon bones and Em loved it. She would eye him guiltily, as though she knew it was wrong, always licking off the strawberry jam first, like a child with a treat. Marco knew of no other dog that liked strawberry jam, and of course he gave it to Em infrequently, and never, ever gave her chocolate, even when she asked for it. Dogs and chocolate were a no-no.

But Em was not with him today. His trip to Brooklyn promised the unexpected and he would never subject his dog to any possibility of danger. What that danger might be, as yet he had no clear idea. Just that something was not right.

The apartment building Angela Morse had lived in was brick, faced with peeling limestone of a color that Marco thought might be described as dung. Dingy too; definitely not a place any parent would want their daughter to live, with its unwashed windows, dirty front steps, and the swing door propped open with a pile of bricks that looked permanent.

He climbed off the bike, wondering what to do with it. On this street, even chained up, it would be gone in minutes. Finally he hefted it under his arm, negotiated his way past the pile of bricks into a foyer—it was a hallway; "foyer" was too grand a word for the long, narrow area overlit with fluorescent tubes so every crack and crevice, every dust ball and pile of unswept litter showed up in fine detail. He felt very sorry for Angie Morse.

A handwritten sign on a flimsy wooden door to the left of the hall said this was the manager's office, and gave a phone number in case he was out. Which, after ringing the bell and standing waiting, then hammering on the door and waiting, Marco decided he was, when he showed up. Right behind him. A big man with the overstuffed body of a weight lifter, muscles bulging, neck straining, wife-beater shirt sweat-stained.

"Wha' the fuck ya wan?" he asked, fixing Marco with a glare from behind black sunglasses.

Marco quickly decided he'd better play it nice. "Sorry to disturb you, but I'm looking for Angie's place."

"Angie Morse, y'mean? That woman owes two months' rent, I've been after her for days. You wastin' yo' time, bro, I'm bettin' Angie's not comin' back."

"In fact, sir," Marco remained polite, "that is true. Poor Angie will not be coming back. I know you'll be sorry to hear this, but Angie is dead."

The man took a fast step back. He eyed Marco up and

down, stiff with tension, ready to strike. "Wadd' ya do to her?"

"Angie had an accident. She drowned."

"Y'mean, like here? In the river?" He took off the dark glasses and stared hard at Marco. "She wouldn't've gone swimming, not the type. . . ."

"Not here," Marco said. "It was off the coast of Turkey. She fell off a yacht."

The tension left the man and he flung back his head, throat rippling in a laugh. "You got the wrong girl, there, bro. Angie never went on no yachts. She worked as a hostess at that steakhouse, uptown, smart place. All the guys hit on her. She told me so. I kinda like Angie, she's okay, y'know, just got a raw deal in life, way some of us do. . . ."

"She fell off a boat. A fancy yacht. I was there. I saw her fall. I tried to save her." If he was to get any information at all Marco knew he had to convince the guy he was on the up-and-up. "Look, I'll level with you, I know Angie was murdered."

Shocked, the guy held up his hands, palms out. "Whoa-ho-ho, feller, don't tell me no more, I don't wanna know about no murders, I don't give a shit who, what, where, when. Let Angie RIP, and that's it for me." Turning, he strode quickly away.

Marco flung a leg over the bike and wondered what to do next. But then the guy turned round. He walked quickly back, stood in front of Marco, put his face in his.

"Listen, prick," he said in a low, menacing voice, dark glasses off again, eyes boring into Marco's. "Angie was decent. All right? She helped my girlfriend one night after we'd had a bit of a . . . well, a fight. Angie took her to the ER, got her patched up. Listen, I ain't proud of that and I'm on probation with my girl not to do it again, but I'll tell you, Angie missed a night at her job, lost wages to take care of my girl. Anything I could do to repay that, y'know I would. But I don't know nuthin' about Angie being on yachts. Only thing I know is she'd met a rich guy and he'd come a' courtin', flowers, expensive gifts, pretty things like a gold chain necklace I knew musta cost . . . maybe that's the guy you need to question. Not me."

He turned quickly again and made to walk away. "Hey," Marco called after him. He looked back over his shoulder.

"Y'know the rich guy's name?"

He shrugged. "Only ever heard the first name, foreign sounding. Angie was discreet about her men, trust me on that. She was a good girl," he added, sounding so sincerely saddened Marco felt for him.

He got back on his orange bike and pedaled swiftly through the mass of traffic, honked at on every side by irate drivers who barely missed him as they swerved lanes. He was glad he was wearing the crash helmet, though he felt a bit like Darth Vader. He stopped outside Houlihan's Steak and Crab House. The neon sign flickered up and down, red and blue, blue and red, then across in a sparkle of white light. "Houlihan's Famous."

Well, famous it might be, but he had never heard of it and, what's more, it was not a place he would have frequented. Inspecting it from outside, Marco got the impression it was the kind of expensive joint that would have a very low-lit interior, even at noon, with red, fake leather booths in the bar and stiff white tablecloths in the restaurant, and enough flowers to asphyxiate a man. Quite turned him off his glass of vodka tonic with a wedge of lime, which is what he ordered when he went in there.

He leaned up against the bar, helmet on the counter in front of him, checking out the clientele, in suits, ties unknotted after work, propped on their elbows, half turned so they could check out the girls who clustered at the other end and who were gossiping in girl-speak about the men while giving them the eye. The place was a pickup joint all right, though the menu was predictably expensive. Two male bartenders were keeping busy shaking cosmos and margaritas while a couple of girls in white shirts, black pencil skirts, and heels trotted around, trays aloft, looking for customers.

The greeter at the door, though, was a man. Marco sipped his vodka tonic, making it last since he was not there for the booze but on a mission and besides, he was "driving." He watched the door, waiting to see if anyone had taken over Angie's role, but there was only the guy: black, smartly dressed, well-spoken, and very much in charge.

Finally, Marco went over. "I can see you're busy but I need to ask about Angie Morse."

The guy threw him a sideways glance as he handed menus to a waiting couple. "Don't ask," he said shortly.

"So, okay, I'm not asking," Marco said. "I'm just hoping you're telling, because Angie might have been murdered."

The guy, whose name tag said he was Phil, took a white handkerchief from his breast pocket and mopped his suddenly sweaty brow. "Listen, Angie is a nice girl, works hard, does her job well. I'm real sorry but I don't know much more than that about her. She keeps to herself. A very private kinda young woman. Very nice. And if she's really . . . I'm sorry . . . about all that, what happened . . . Now, if you'll excuse me . . ." He went back to his customers and Marco went back to his vodka tonic.

He was getting nowhere fast. Nobody knew anything personal about Angie. Or if they did, they were not telling.

33

Lucy was thinking that if she was going to have to mess about helping Martha work out how to restructure Ahmet's awful house, she might as well nail him on the elusive movie script he'd mentioned. More than mentioned—promised, in fact, though she did have the uneasy feeling that something might be expected in exchange for that promise. Well, shoot, he'd soon find out she wasn't that kind of girl, even if she did accept a glass of champagne, dinner even, from a complete stranger. That was a one-off. A deal made out of necessity. Now, all she could think of was the pizza guy. She had dialed the pizza place, described him to the girl who answered with a knowing laugh and said of course that would be Phillip Kurtiz the Third.

"The third of what?" Lucy asked.

"In line of succession." The girl paused, then added, "To Kurtiz Food Products, of Chicago, Illinois."

"Oh. Right." Lucy had never heard of them but to her he certainly was not a Marks & Spencer, so it didn't count. Besides, if he was rich and all, why was he delivering pizzas so he could pay his Oxford fees? The girl must be wrong.

"Lucy!" Martha's voice had an edge to it. Lucy snapped to attention.

"Here, take my iPad and make notes when I talk. We're going to go room by room, so this will take some time."

Already bored, Lucy did as she was told, trailing from one overstuffed dark room to another overstuffed dark room, wondering why nobody had thought to bring light into the place. Even the kitchen, where a solitary chef who said he was from Tunisia stood at a gray marble counter slicing out-of-season bright yellow papaya and fresh figs into a perfectly beautiful turquoise bowl that Martha stopped to admire.

"Why, it must be antique," she said, stretching out her hand to touch its smooth, pale blue surface. "See how the light filters through it, I'll bet it's Limoges and rare, at that, because of the color."

"Mr. Ahmet likes to use his antiques," the man managed in deeply accented English, and Martha nodded; she had heard that before. It was a pity Ahmet's good taste did not extend to his furnishings, but she could take care of that. She glanced at her watch, wondering where Marco was, what he was doing, probably still on the track of the missing girl, though what he expected he could do about it was beyond her. Last time they'd spoken he'd been on his way to talk to the Brooklyn police.

Ahmet had left them alone to assess what he called "the damage," and because Martha did not know which of the many rooms he was in she now called him on his cell.

"I'll be right with you," he answered. And he was, and with him was Mehitabel, unsmiling, frozen into a kind of sartorial perfection Martha knew she could never hope to emulate. Feeling outdated in her tweed skirt and green, waxed, all-weather jacket, which was in fact far more suitable for a trip to the country than Mehitabel's obviously very expensive black cashmere dress that fit like a second skin on a body Lucy certainly envied, Martha said they had seen enough to be getting on with and she would be in touch with her suggestions and a proper presentation, with sketches and samples, and of course, alternatives for both since she knew how hard it was for inexperienced clients to make a decision.

"Anyhow, I'm here to help you with that," she said briskly, because she was suddenly in need of getting out of there, but then Lucy said first she had to go to the loo.

Mehitabel showed Lucy to the bathroom off the main hall and she disappeared inside, leaving Martha to make conversation with a woman who, for some reason, intimidated her. One way she had found to get out of these situations was to ask questions, and not answer any herself.

"So, Mehitabel," she said, with a cheerful smile, "how long have you worked for Mr. Ghulbian?"

Mehitabel eyed her coldly. "I do not 'work' for Mr. Ghulbian. I am his personal assistant. And you might say it's been a lifetime."

"Ohh. Right, well of course . . . I see . . ." Martha did not see at all. She turned her eyes from Mehitabel to the staircase with its patterned red carpet. "I wonder if you know then, since you are so close to Mr. Ghulbian, when we might be able to change that carpet, maybe get upstairs, take a look around. Obviously it will need some changes too."

Her smile faded as Mehitabel stared implacably back with not even an expression of interest. Her voice was chilly as she said, "Do not bother yourself with the upstairs. Your job is to take care of the main rooms down here. Mr. Ghulbian is no doubt paying you well and will expect the best results. If not," she shrugged, "trust me, everyone will know about it. This job can make or break you, Miss Patron. You had better be very careful."

Martha swore later to Lucy, she'd felt a chill crawl up her spine. "It was like I was on trial," she said angrily. "I was hired by Ahmet for *who* I am, *what* I do, *my* reputation, *my* taste, *my* experience, and this bitch is putting all that on the line. Warning me off. As though she owns him or something. And anyhow, why can't we look upstairs? What's she got hidden up there that's so special we can't see it?"

Lucy said, "She must be mad or something." She tried the pizza guy again. Again no reply. Shit.

34

Marco's next stop was a Brooklyn police precinct, but even there he did not trust enough to leave his bike outside. He carried it in and planted it on the floor beside him by the front desk, eyed by a female police officer, who, with her round face and pulled-back brown hair, in her blue uniform shirt and badge, looked all of sixteen. He thought either cops were getting younger or he was getting older. Interesting face, though; strong bones, probably Russian or East European descent. The artist in Marco always emerged; he never simply looked, he took it all in, that is until he realized she was eying him warily, then he apologized and told her his mission.

"I need to speak to the detective in charge of the Angela Morse case." He propped the bike against his hip and showed her his passport as proof of identity, so she wouldn't think he was simply another nut drifting in off the street seeking a bit of notoriety.

"And why would you need to do that, Mr. Mahoney?" She handed back the passport and looked him in the eye.

"Because I was there when she was killed," he said simply.

That got her attention, though she did fling him an under-the-lashes look as she tapped a name on her computer and awaited a reply. It came immediately.

"Detective Moreira will be out in a minute," she said, handing him several sheets of paper. "Just fill out these forms first."

Marco took a seat on a gray plastic chair, glanced at the sheaf of forms, and decided to ignore them. He was losing patience with bureaucracy; if they were interested in what he had to say, they could listen and make their own notes. His cell phone buzzed in his pocket. He grabbed it, saw it was Martha.

"Hey, hon," he said in a low voice. "Wazzup?"

He heard her laugh and was immediately cheered.

"You're even talking like them now," she said.

"Waddya' mean?" He laughed too. "Whatever," he said, "it gets the message across, though nobody seems to know anything at all about Angie Morse, other than she was a nice girl. Young woman," he added. "Have to be politically correct."

"You can call me a 'girl' any time you like. It's my sister who'd like to be a 'young woman,' because she's only seventeen."

"And you are . . . ?"

"Old enough to want to be a 'girl' again. But listen, Marco, are you still sure about this Angie? That you really saw what happened, that she didn't simply fall off the boat and drown?" She still doubted him.

His long silence spoke for him and Martha was sorry she'd even asked; it was just that he was obsessed with the redhead, the drowning, the Ahmet Ghulbian connection, and she felt it was better if he stayed away from the whole situation, let what was remain exactly that, no more questions asked.

"I met with Ghulbian again today," she said finally. "At his place on the marshes."

"Then you got to meet Mehitabel."

"I did. She's quite something. Gorgeous, in an odd way."

"Yeah, like the way a block of ice is gorgeous, all scintillating beauty outside and freezing horror in."

"Wow!" Martha said, impressed. "That's a perfect description. I bet you wanted to paint her, though."

Marco thought about that for a moment, then, "I couldn't do it. I don't know what's under her surface, that essence I usually perceive, the true person beneath the façade."

"But that's part of your talent."

Marco shrugged. "Anyhow, it's not her I'm to paint. It's the ever-affable, ever-charming Ahmet. Mr. Nice Guy personified."

"But he is nice. Anyway I thought so. He can't do enough for Lucy and me when we are there, serves us tea, of all things, proper tea with scones and strawberry jam with dollops of fresh cream and cucumber sandwiches. I haven't had tea like that since Mum would take us to Fortnum and Mason, for 'the works' as she called it, before we went back to school."

"Somehow, Martha, I don't think Angie got that kind of 'tea.' And I think Ahmet is involved and certainly that witch Mehitabel. Anyhow, I've agreed to do his portrait."

"But why? If you don't like him?"

"But I do like him. Obviously he has a history, but a self-made man is always interesting. Trust me, Martha, when he's shut up alone in a room for hours with me, I'll know more about him at the end of the day than his own mother might."

"Does he have a mother?"

"Not that I know of, but it might be interesting to find out. Get to know exactly who the real Ahmet Ghulbian is. Family circumstances usually explain that."

"But don't we already know?"

"All we know is the story Ghulbian told. About the family losing money, half Greek, half Egyptian, no names, no places, other than what the media have fished out, which, since he seems to have covered his tracks and planted info where needed, all comes out to mean exactly what he wants you to believe. I like Ahmet but I don't trust him, and there's the truth."

"Maybe I shouldn't have agreed to do his house, I mean, if you feel that strongly."

"Of course you must do the house. And I shall paint his portrait. Between us, we have the man covered. Trust me, by the time we finish no stone of his past will be unturned."

"Hmmm," Martha said, thinking worriedly about Ahmet and Marshmallows and the bleak location, and of the almost ravenous way he'd looked at Lucy when he'd thought Martha hadn't noticed. "I'll have to keep my eye on him," she said doubtfully. "Meanwhile, after I've completed the house—for which, by the way, I have a time-line of exactly five weeks—Mr. Ghulbian intends to throw a party. In fact, no mere 'party.' The man wants to have 'a ball' on the lines of Capote's black-and-white New York masterpiece."

"Then you'd better get yourself a new dress," Marco said.

"Black, I think. After all, I'm too old for white."

Marco was laughing as he closed the phone and went back to the police sergeant to inquire when the detective might possibly see him.

"Mr. Mahoney?"

The voice came from behind. Marco swung around, saw a stocky young man in his late twenties maybe, dark hair cropped to a stubble, goatee trimmed into a spike. He looked Latino despite having, as Marco would learn, a Portuguese name. He also had a long thin face, kind of Jesus-like, the way Marco remembered in Renaissance paintings, unsmiling and giving off the impression he'd been interrupted in something far more urgent and important than discussing Angie Morse's drowning with a guy coming in off the street.

He held a thin file and indicated the way to a small cubicle office where Marco sat opposite him, suddenly tongue-tied.

"So what do you know about Angie Morse that we don't know already?" Detective Moreira glanced through the half-dozen pages in the file, closed it, put it down on the small table between them.

"I know she was killed. I saw it happen."

The detective's face was unreadable as he sat back, legs spread, arms folded over his chest, looking silently at Marco. As though he could read his mind, Marco thought. Well if he could it would save him time and trouble, but if not he'd better tell him what he'd seen.

Detective Moreira listened without interruption. When Marco finally said that was it, he'd told him everything, the detective sat up straighter in his chair. "So where's the proof? The evidence, Mr. Mahoney? Did anybody else see this 'event'?"

"D'you mean did anybody else see Angie holding her head, fall off the boat, watch her drown, try to save her and fail? Unfortunately, no, sir, no one but myself."

Detective Moreira made no response, simply sat looking at Marco for a long moment. Finally he said, "I don't know why I believe you, Mr. Mahoney, but I do. And why do I? Because why the fuck would a man like you come in here with some cock-and-bull story, bringing trouble on yourself, taking on a responsibility and more angst than you've ever experienced, just to tell me about some young woman, unknown to you, that you saw, or believe you saw, killed. Unfortunately, this event allegedly took place in a foreign country. Out of our jurisdiction."

"But she was an American citizen—"

"And how do you know that, sir? Since you said you had never met her?"

"I found out who she was." Marco told him Angie's story, about the steak house, the shabby apartment, about reading the missing-girl article in the newspaper when he was in France. "I knew it was her, I knew I'd seen it," he said. "The only thing I don't know is who did it. And that's the truth. Sir," he added politely.

"In fact, what you are saying to me is that you were the last person to see Angie Morse alive. That no one else was there when she drowned. You were alone, Mr. Mahoney."

Marco stared at him. For a minute he wished he had not come here, that he had not gotten involved. But if he had not, a young woman would be dead with no person to remember her, no one to help. "What I saw was murder," he said coldly.

"Well, as I said, for some fuckin' stupid reason I'm inclined to believe you. We'll take care of it from now on, Mr. Mahoney. You can leave the matter with us."

Marco agreed, but as he made his way back on the orange bike, he knew he could not just let it go. He had to find her. He had to help her. Even if she was dead, he had to help her.

35

ANGIE

Time has no meaning. I am here, in this pleasant room with its two tall windows framed in bluish-gray shutters overlooking a treeless park, so green it reminds me of the watercress we used to grow on bits of flannel at school for our biology class. *School*. My laugh sounds harsh, too loud in the surrounding silence. School was another lifetime, a different *world* away from where I have ended up, because I have no doubt this is where I am to end up. Why this has not yet happened is what puzzles me. Why was I hauled out of the marsh that would so easily, so quickly, so silently have taken care of me without so much as a bubble left to indicate where I met my fate?

Why have I not yet met my fate? I can only think they have something even worse in mind for me. Some kind of torture perhaps, medieval-style racks and chains and sadistic practices that I know certainly Mehitabel would be capable of. Mehitabel must be an arch practitioner of S&M, it sparks in those evil eyes, in her steely body, in her, I am sure, unfeeling heart. I doubt she even has a heart. Which doesn't help me much now.

Mom, I thought, breaking down and crying again, though how I had tears left I did not know. "I tried, Mom," I whispered into the silence. "I really tried to get away, tried not to let you down. *Courage,* you always told me, you said that even when you were in pain, when you knew you were leaving me. And I tried to keep you, oh how I tried, I would have worked forever, anything, anywhere just to keep you alive, with me. You were the only person to ever love me, and that's the truth, Mom. All those guys, well maybe not so many as you might think, but anyhow the men in my life amounted to nothing, no one that I cared deeply for after Henry, the Southern college boy. I wonder what happened to him. Met some debutante with a Southern accent and married money, I'll bet. Odd, how you find out the truth about men too late. Maybe I'm just bitter, maybe I haven't yet met the right man, and now for sure I never will. I'll come and join you, Mom. We will see each other again, I feel sure of it, after all."

Footsteps clattered in the hall outside. I swung from the window, hand clutched over my heart, holding the edges of my dress over my breasts; I knew those footsteps.

The door opened. Mehitabel stood there, looking at me, taking in the dress and my nakedness underneath. A long time seemed to pass. Eons of time, a lifetime, before she spoke.

"Mr. Ghulbian will see you again," she said, coming closer, walking around me, inspecting me. "Think yourself lucky, my dear Angie. He's giving you a second chance."

She put her face close to mine, smiled that smile that curled only the outer corners of her red mouth, and added, "Something I would never give you. Remember that, why don't you."

* * *

Ahmet was sitting in his favorite red leather chair, fire blazing, the familiar scent of the logs mingling with the floral aroma from the bowls of hyacinths he had ordered delivered from London; they were out of season, of course, because Ahmet had to be different in everything he did. No white supermarket orchids, no too-tightly-budded red roses buried in swathes of fluffy phlox for him. The unusual, the rare, were what he preferred; the out-of-season bouquets of perfect white blossoms he sent his prey, his "girls" as he liked to think of them, wooing them with the eternal message that flowers meant love. As if he ever would, or perhaps could, love anyone other than himself. A narcissist he was and always would be, he admitted, as the door opened and he saw Angie standing there, pale, haggard, sunken-eyed, and most shocking, her shaved head.

What the fuck had happened to his Angie, the girl in the heels and tight skirt with the bold look in her eyes that made a promise she never intended to keep. Or rarely, anyhow, as he had personally found that night in the hotel, and subsequently, when they were in what he knew Angie had termed "a relationship."

"Angie," he said warmly now, "my dear, do come on in, you look so chilled standing out there in that flimsy dress. Why on earth has Mehitabel not found you something more suitable for this chilly evening?"

She made no response, stood, head hanging, not even looking at him. *Refusing* to look at him, he thought. So, okay, he could take care of that.

Ahmet knew how to play the gentleman even though he was not one. Now, he took off his own pale cashmere jacket, went and draped it over her shoulders. He stood in front of her, close enough to kiss, yet she did not lift her face to his, refused to acknowledge his presence in her own private world. He understood. Angie felt wounded by him, as well she might. And in fact, as she was very soon going to be wounded. He had no time for playing around anymore; he should have gotten rid of her when the opportunity presented itself, yet, thinking about it, perhaps not, because then he would have denied himself the pleasure of hurting her.

Mehitabel understood what he was about to do. She had disappeared, now she came back, carrying two long, narrow boxes. She opened the first and showed the whip to Ahmet. Opened the second, touched the rifle it contained with a soft finger, smiling at him. Their eyes met in mutual agreement.

Ahmet stood for a minute more, contemplating Angie, who from her drooped posture seemed to have removed herself to some other planet. He was about to bring her back from that place, back to him. He wanted to see her eyes, those eyes he had looked into when she was drowning, and this time he wanted to see them drowning in fear and in pain.

He took the whip from the first box, ran it through his fingers. It was an antique, of course, and from its history he knew it had been used in a turn-of-the-century gentlemen's club where such things as whipping were part of the favored sexual delights offered. Now, Angie was about to experience that delight, as he would himself, especially when she would look up at him, her face twisted in pain, and beg him to stop, her eyes imploring . . . those eyes . . . he wanted those eyes to beg him . . . only then would he be able to eradicate from his mind the memory of them when she had been drowning.

Mehitabel went to remove Angie's dress but he stopped her. "I want it this way," he said, taking a step back, surveying the helpless woman. "Helpless" was exactly what he believed all women should be. He was the strength, the power . . . and if not the glory then the one she would eventually worship. That was his intention. To subdue her strong will, eradicate her personality, turn her into his kind of woman: lost, submissive, beguiling, eager only to please. And then he would be done with her.

The whip did not crack as he snapped it back, yet it whistled as he brought it down, a thin noise like a snake's hiss, with a burning bite that notched her tender skin, left a raised red mark; as yet, no blood. Ahmet did not wish to draw blood, that was too amateur. He knew how to inflict pain in more ways than one, and pain was needed to tame Angie. Then and only then could he let her go.

She did not cry. She did not even call out, beg him to stop. She fell down and simply lay there, flat on the ground, untamed, unwilling to ask for his mercy.

After several minutes, Ahmet gave up. He nodded to Mehitabel to take care of her and stalked from the room, deeply upset. Angie had beaten him; he should be rid of her now, allow Mehitabel to take her away, never see her again. Yet he could not. He would not be beaten by any woman, and especially not this one.

Lucy came into his mind; chaste, simple, childlike Lucy. He knew he would never be beaten by her. Lucy would marry him one day, become mistress of Marshmallows, belle of the ball he would give to celebrate the house's grand opening. Lucy was a different woman from Angie, who he now hated with all the passion he had in the beginning put into wooing her, loving her. . . . Was it love? Had he just wanted to fuck Angie? He'd wanted to see that long red hair trailing across her white breasts as she lay next to him in that hotel bedroom, starry-eyed with his simple gift of the Cartier neck chain with its little panther ornament. One girl had seemed to promise sexual delight there for his taking; the other would be his virginal bride. And while he was thinking about it he thought he had better check on that, find out who Lucy was seeing, make sure nobody unlocked that chastity belt before he could. Lucy was important. Angie was expendable.

36

Martha, as well as having to get Ahmet's huge, unfriendly house together in a mere five weeks, now also found herself in charge of organizing the "ball" with which they would celebrate its transformation. She wasn't even sure she could get the place revamped in time, just getting workmen together in that outlandish marsh was an ordeal, to say nothing of accommodating them while they worked there. Why oh why, she asked herself after yet another fruitless phone conversation asking, *demanding* help. She was calling in all her markers, everyone she had ever done a favor for in business she was now telling they owed her. Fortunately, most were coming through.

She managed to find a construction company only twenty miles from Marshmallows that reluctantly agreed to help out though only when the money was doubled. She brought her own paint crew from London, grumbling all the way, suspicious of her promises that they would be put up at a very nice pub that also happened to serve hefty portions of food of the steak pie, haddock and chips variety, which suited them fine, along with free (on her) pints of lager to wash the dust down at the end of the day. She contracted private buses to get them all there and back. She laid on lunches of hot soup and sandwiches. She provided them with overalls and caps emblazoned with her newly designed Marshmallows logo: a chimney with a nest and a pair of wings on top. Try as she might, she'd been unable to come up with a "marshy" image; the bleak landscape simply did not lend itself to it.

Not only that, Ahmet had called her every day asking how it was going, when could he move in, what was taking so long? All in all, wearily, Martha sometimes wished she'd never met Ahmet, never taken the job. Marshmallows was so far from civilization she might have been in a different country. Plus, she had Mehitabel to contend with.

The mystery woman, as Lucy rightly called Mehitabel, was on top of every tiny detail; she showed up, notes in hand, comments prepared, always managing in an effortless way to make it appear that Martha and Lucy were getting behind, were not sure of what they were doing, questioning every single detail.

Still, by week three, the house Martha had envisaged began to emerge from the chaos and dreams into a reality. The tiled floors were gone, along with the red carpet on the stairs, the heavy furniture, the dark drapes, the too-solid-looking paneling, the many crystal chandeliers— only the walls now stripped to the bone awaited the softest of colors. Not white; she had decided that would be too harsh a contrast to the gray-green environment outside the windows. The drawing room was now pale Tuscan fawn, the floors an even paler scrubbed ash, the window frames an infinite blue that hinted of the Mediterranean and which seemed to bring the outdoors into the room. The windows themselves were hung with a creamy soft cotton lawn, weighted so they hung perfectly yet might still move in the breeze when the tall windows leading onto a paved terrace were open.

When she stood and looked out those windows, Martha thought the view was like looking into infinity: the soft rusty-gray paving stones punctuated with tall urns now full of clinging vines; then the long emerald "lawn" that led into the brownish green marsh that took the eye ever onward to the glint of the river and a low cloudy sky.

All the house needed now was the scatter of the antique Turkish rugs—chosen specially with Ahmet's background in mind—soft and pastel enough to blur into the background, with the grayish ash floors, the sofas and chairs in coordinating colors, though nothing matching; scattered with plump, luxurious cushions that invited you to sprawl.

Looking at her handiwork, envisioning the end result, Martha knew she had done a great job. There was only the delivery of some furniture and the antique pieces needed to complete the entire downstairs, and with time pressing and other work in hand, she felt she might safely leave that in Lucy's hopefully capable hands. If Lucy could get her mind off the cute blond pizza guy whose name Martha had now learned was Phillip, then she could. Anyhow, where was Lucy? Why did she always seem to be somewhere else when Martha needed her?

"Lucy," she yelled, striding back through the hall toward the kitchen, betting she would find her sister having a snack made by that nice Tunisian who seemed to be the only employee around here. She supposed Ahmet was waiting until his house was finished before he brought in a whole staff. "Lucy?" she called again, pushing open the green baize door leading into the kitchen. The green baize was an old-fashioned upstairs-downstairs touch she had thought amusing and hopefully so would Ahmet.

She did not find Lucy in the kitchen, though she did find

Mehitabel, standing by the sink, running what seemed to Martha to be a critical finger over its surface. The sink was old, a find Martha had foraged in a local sale. It was made of stone, which she'd had smoothed and polished and fitted with new drains and an electric garbage disposal, and a very smart, very tall chromium faucet that swiveled either way. Set in the pale gray granite counter, chosen by Ahmet himself, she'd thought it looked stunningly modernistic.

"This simply does not work." Mehitabel turned to look at her, that cold look Martha recognized.

Martha wondered if the woman ever warmed up, *ever* liked anything, ever, for fuck's sake, even smiled. Martha got on with most women, liked making new acquaintances, enjoyed her girlfriends, but Mehitabel was different though she could not quite put a finger on exactly why.

She put on her own smile and asked what was wrong.

"This faucet will have to go," Mehitabel said. "It's completely out of place. Mr. Ghulbian will not like it."

Martha walked across to the sink, stood next to Mehitabel, and inspected the fixture.

"Let me explain something," she said, coolly because she refused to be intimidated by this woman who was obviously out to do exactly that. "This is *my* job. Ahmet"— she threw in his name just to make Mehitabel understand that she and Ghulbian were friends—"approved every single fixture, every color, every granite, every floorboard. My job is to please my client. I trust you understand that? This house does not belong to me, neither does it belong to you. It is Ahmet's and he alone decides what works and what does not. Do I make myself clear? Mehitabel?"

Martha saw two bright spots of color flare in Mehitabel's cheeks, recognized the anger simmering beneath her cool surface. She had definitely not made a friend.

"I will speak to Mr. Ghulbian about it," Mehitabel said.

"Anyhow, I think you must wait and ask him yourself. I am expecting him here within the hour."

Martha picked up her iPad and her yellow legal pad with her drawings and notes, looped the ring holding the swatches of fabrics over her fingers, and offered Mehitabel another smile. "Too bad I have an appointment this evening. I won't be able to wait, but Ahmet can, of course, call me any time."

Mehitabel did not so much as acknowledge what she had said. An uneasy silence fell, broken suddenly by Lucy charging through the door, phone to her ear, sneakers squelching across the immaculate white-tiled floor, leaving muddy footprints.

"Oh, shoot," Lucy said. "Why can I never get him on the phone? He can't always be out delivering pizzas, can he, Marthie?" She stopped as a thought occurred to her. "You don't think he's out with another girl?" She looked suddenly stricken.

Before Martha could answer, Mehitabel said swiftly, "Well, of course, Martha, since you cannot wait for Mr. Ghulbian's return then your assistant must. She can take him round, show him what you suggest and what you have completed so far. Lucy can take notes and pass Mr. Ghulbian's personal thoughts on to you. Right?"

She was looking at Martha as though the matter was settled. No argument, Lucy would stay. But "No, no, of course not," Martha protested. "She has no car, she must drive back with me."

"You forget Mr. Ghulbian has a helicopter. Lucy might be home before you yourself, Ms. Patron."

She threw in the name as though an afterthought, something she scarcely had bothered to remember. Martha thought Mehitabel was quite a bitch in her own icy way. Anyway, she certainly did not want to leave Lucy here alone with her.

"Perhaps I can wait, after all," she said, knowing she sounded hesitant.

Mehitabel gave her another long look. "There's absolutely no need to worry, you know, Ms. Patron. Lucy will be perfectly safe here." She glanced at Lucy, who was eyeing the pie the Tunisian chef was making, a layering of eggplant and tomatoes and peppers and meat, topped with a lid of pastry, which he'd embellished with pretty cut-out pastry leaves.

Lucy was interested; perhaps she wasn't meant for interior design after all; she might try cooking school. Chefs earned a lot these days, she knew that from watching TV. She inspected her phone again; no message from him. She suddenly hated being seventeen. Older women knew how to deal with men who did not call, men who were, it seemed, not even interested. *Oh God, oh God, after what happened how could he do this?* She had practically given him her all the other night, and, despite a few previous "mishaps," it would have been the first time. Other girls she knew had succumbed even younger, or pretended to anyhow, smug knowing smiles and all, while she had said loftily she would hold out for her marriage bed. She'd been joking of course. Sometimes she'd hardly known how she'd kept her legs crossed, and she would certainly have unlocked those knees the other night with him, if she had allowed any more time to pass, in his embrace. There was an old-fashioned word for you. *Embrace.* Shit. She had been friggin' *entwined*! That's what she had been. And she wanted more "entwining." With him. She tried his number again, again without luck.

Getting off the phone and coming to her senses, she suddenly understood what Mehitabel was suggesting: that she wait here, discuss the decorations with Ahmet, be helicoptered back later.

"Why not?" Lucy said, feeling gloom settle over her

head like a cloud. "He" was never going to call, she might as well just stay here, take care of things for Martha.

"Don't worry," Mehitabel was saying to Martha as she took Lucy to sit at the kitchen table. "I'll make sure she's fed and watered. Just like a horse," she added with what Martha believed was humor of some sort.

"Well . . ." Martha was still uncertain.

"Oh do go *on,* Marthie," Lucy said, impatient to get back on her phone. "I'm your assistant, aren't I? This is what I do." And she planted her muddy sneakers on another chair and got back to her phone.

Martha gave her a quick kiss and departed, still worried she was doing the right thing, leaving her alone with Mehitabel, in that remote house, while Lucy surveyed the kitchen with hungry eyes. She was always hungry.

Mehitabel knew Ahmet had fallen for Lucy; she had observed the way he looked at her, his delight in her presence, in her youth, the way he mentioned her name, dropping it in the conversation as though by chance. Mehitabel recognized an obsessed man and jealousy dripped through her veins like ice water. In all the years they had been together Ahmet had never so much as expressed any feeling for a woman. Co-conspirators, they had known each other's secrets and secret wishes; understood each other, until now, when Lucy Patron had arrived to separate them, turn Mehitabel's perfect world upside down; make her future insecure and her innards churn with what she knew, for the first time in her life, was jealousy.

37

Martha's apartment in London's Chelsea was not far from Lucy's basement apartment. She drove there now, already late to meet her friend and coworker, Morris Sorris. Right from the moment she had met Morris, two years before, she'd told him she would never believe he had not made up his own name. He had not denied this but said everybody remembered it so what was the problem. And it was true, people did remember. "It's always on the tip of their tongue," Morris declared, smiling, and he'd never yet told Martha what his real name was.

"Not who I used to be," he corrected her when, devoured by curiosity, she'd asked him, saying how could anybody want to change their name to Morris Sorris.

"Easy. I'll never be forgotten" was his answer, and of course he never was, though Martha often shortened it to Morrie Sorrie, which offended him deeply.

He was short, very thin, with the haunted eyes of his Spanish ancestry, a thatch of black hair that went every which way and that he swore he could not control, though Martha had caught him several times looking in the mirror and giving it a fluff with his fingers to catch that casual just-out-of-bed look. Which there was no doubt Morrie had: girls flocked to him; the phone calls were endless; the texts; the waylaying outside the house, until Martha was forced to ask him please to control his personal life and keep it out of the way of his work.

Morrie lived in a done-over apartment in an old brick building in a newly gentrified part of Brixton, which used to be where nobody dared set foot after dark, or even during daytime, but had now been cleaned up, money had moved in, taken over. All was well, in Morrie's world, until his first encounter with Ahmet Ghulbian and the infamous Mehitabel.

They met at Marshmallows, where he had driven with Lucy, taking Martha's place while she took care of the everlasting arrangements for the ball.

"Just check that everything has arrived, finally," she told him. "You have the floor plans, you know where everything should go, you understand how the curtains should hang, that the lights are inset in the correct places, that the witch Mehitabel has not changed everything so she can blame the mess on me when Ahmet finally gets to approve it."

"Shit," Morrie said, bewildered. "I thought you were working with him. She's just the assistant, isn't she?"

"Trust me, she'll let you know exactly who she is, and exactly who you are on the scale of things. Don't take it to heart," she added with a laugh. "We've all been there. Mehitabel is a cow."

"Hmm, I could probably think of a better c-word, though I won't say it in your company."

"You might though, in hers."

Lucy was sitting next to him as they drove up to Marshmallows, between the avenue of stunted trees that looked, Morrie thought, taking a quick glance from side to side, like something from a Disney movie where the witch might be seen floating over the top. Mehitabel, in fact, he guessed.

"Well, so here we are at last," he said, climbing out, then grabbing his jacket from the backseat and slipping it on. He'd thought the Harris tweed appropriate for a country estate, but looking at this one he changed his mind; a top hat and tails, morning dress, might have been more appropriate.

"Do those birds always sit there, watching?" he asked Lucy, staring warily at the herons who had their claws wrapped around the curved edge of the roof tiles and were glaring menacingly at them.

"They just think we might be after their babies," Lucy said. "They're not dangerous. It's that woman we have to watch out for." But she laughed as she said it; very little upset Lucy.

To her surprise, the door was flung open by a manservant she'd never seen before they had even mounted the four stone steps that led to a pillared porch, so obviously an addition Lucy wondered what Martha was going to do about it. It would have to go, she was sure of that.

"Hi," she said, "we're the decorators." The man looked at her blankly. "From London," she added. "Patrons, that is. Mr. Sorris and I—Lucy Patron—have come to check work progress." Still he said nothing, made no move to let them in. "Mr. Ghulbian wanted us to check everything," she added, her voice faltering a bit; she had never before encountered such a silent reception.

"I must check that with Mr. Ghulbian," the man said abruptly, and shut the door in their faces.

"Shit!" Morrie said. "What the fuck's up with him, then?"

Lucy was already on her cell, calling her sister. "Buggie-wuggie, Marthie," she said when Martha answered, "they wouldn't let us in."

"Who wouldn't?"

"Some full-of-himself guy in a morning suit pretending to be a butler. My bet, though, is he's just out of prison."

She heard Martha laugh. "I'll call Mehitabel," she said.

"That cow," Lucy said.

"Don't worry, the cow will let you in, I'll make sure of that. And Lucy, while you're there, try and sneak upstairs, why don't you? It's like they have a yellow police tape at the bottom of that staircase, and God forbid you should try to get past it."

"Mmm, skeletons in the attic?"

"I surely hope not, but something's up. Anyway, you see what you can find out."

"The ex-jailbird in the morning suit is back," Lucy said. "Don't worry, big sister, I know this house like the back of my hand by now. Well, the kitchen quarters, anyhow. I'll demand to see upstairs."

"And I'm calling Ahmet to tell him you are going to do just that."

38

ANGIE

When I came around I was lying in a low tub. The water was cool and came up to my neck; only my head stuck out above. Instantly, I panicked. I was drowning again, going down into that bridesmaid's velvet blue, deeper into azure, darker into cobalt. . . .

"Sit up, for God's sake, why don't you," a voice snarled at me.

I felt Mehitabel's hand under the back of my bald head, gripping, viselike, to stop me I supposed from simply sliding back underwater again. I wished she would let go. Wished everyone would simply let go. I wanted to leave, didn't they know that by now, that I could take no more; that death was easier, softer, the gentler way out. Though out of what I had no idea, no concept, no inkling of what I was involved in.

My voice came back, throaty, raspy, yet my own, and I heard myself say: "What do you know about God, anyway. Just let go of my fuckin' head, you fuckin' bitch and I'll happily go away."

I never cursed, well, only when I was pissed off at female customers in the bar when they gave me the superior stare, the up-and-down, look-at-that-poor-bitch look, that made me want to throw their stupid cosmos in their faces and to hell with the job. But now I had no job, no drink to throw at anybody, no strength left anyway to so much as lift an arm to throw anything. Yet inside I burned with the new raw energy of hate.

Mehitabel tugged my neck harder, jerking me upward 'til I thought my spine must surely break. To my astonishment I realized I was still wearing the ragged silken dress I'd had on when Ahmet beat me. *Beat me to the ground.* How I'd hated myself for falling like that, allowing him to believe he had won, that I was simply another of his girls; girls I was certain now he'd tortured and murdered. How could I have ever become involved? How could I have ever believed a man like him, a billionaire, a man who had everything, who could have any woman, would want me, the lowly, ordinary hostess with the passable looks and the good legs. Thinking about legs, I realized there was a pain in my left leg, a deeper pain than anything I was feeling elsewhere, which was pretty much all over after the whipping I had endured. This was bone pain; the ankle, I thought, twitching it lightly, snatching back the scream as the extra jolt of pain seared through me. Dear God, could it be broken? And if it were, then how was I ever to escape? To run, you needed two legs.

"Shut up, cunt," Mehitabel said. She was soaping a sponge with a eucalyptus-scented oil which she proceeded to rub, so tenderly I thought she must have made a mistake, around my neck, over my breasts, softening the soapy sponge under my arms. She could go no further, because the rest of me was underwater, where, I had no doubt, clean though I might be from her ministrations, I would soon drown. I hated the thought of the soapy bubbles in my nose, in my head, in my throat. I would so much have preferred the clear clean azure of that Aegean Sea.

"Lift your left leg," she commanded.

I obeyed, flinching as she took the injured ankle in her hand and bent closer to inspect it. I thought I felt blood seeping, and she must have seen that because she tut-tutted and shook her head, Medusa curls bouncing as she dropped my leg back into the water, whereupon I yelled in pain.

"Oh, God," she said, sounding weary. "Will you never shut up?"

I turned my eyes on her, saw an iron-willed, beautiful woman, inflexible in her evil desires, a sadistic torturer, a cold-hearted killer, and yet now she was treating me with the tenderness of a mother with an injured child. Apart from her language, of course.

She twisted out the bath plug and sat back on her heels. We both listened silently to the water gurgling down the drain. When it was gone and I lay there, unable to move in the suddenly chilling empty tub, she got to her feet, came and stood behind me, put her arms under my shoulders and hefted me out so easily I was astounded. Of course I weighed very little by now, but even so I was a deadweight coming out of that tub. This woman had the strength of two men.

Now I remembered the sting of the lash, and every inch of my flesh where the whip had struck shivered with fresh pain. I wanted to cry with it but would not, I simply would not give her the pleasure. I found my courage from somewhere. If I were to die, it would be silently, I swore that, made a promise to myself, and my mom.

She pushed me onto a small padded stool, flung a towel over my emaciated body with a look on her face that told me she could not bear even to look at me, then told me to dry myself. My skin throbbed. Everywhere I patted, everywhere I rubbed, it stung, sometimes like a knife searing through me, and I had not yet even tried to put any weight on my ankle.

I glanced at Mehitabel, who was walking toward me carrying a small red box with a white cross on it and the words "First Aid." I thought how ridiculous it was, as though I'd fallen in the playground and grazed my knee. I had been flogged, beaten, almost drowned, and here was my sweet little lifesaver with her red first-aid kit.

She knelt in front of me, took my left ankle in both hands, turned it, inspecting it, causing me untold agony. I kept my mouth shut. I knew she enjoyed causing me pain and I was not about to give her further pleasure. Instead I said, "You should have used the rifle on me. It would have been quicker, served the same purpose."

She glanced up, surprised. Her eyes were glass-green, remarkable, quite beautiful in fact, rimmed with thick, dark lashes.

"But don't you understand yet, that 'pleasure' is to be taken slowly? Killing fast is a momentary thing, felt for a mere instant, before shock comes in. No, no, oh no, my dear beautiful Angie, the pleasure of pain is lengthy, extended, to be taken to the very final degree of time before the end comes. We have not yet reached that place with you."

She actually smiled at me, then "Later, we will, though," she said.

With weird bravado I heard myself reply, "Is that a promise?"

She eyed me for a long moment, my ankle clasped between her two hands. "Believe me, Angie, you will want me to keep that promise." And she gave the ankle a vicious twist that sent pain rocketing, and sweat beaded my bald head.

I was a wreck. I was a "non-woman." I was "nothing." With all that was left of me, of my heart, I wished I was dead.

It was not to be. The ankle was bound, something injected into my arm, and I drifted in another world.

39

Lucy was bored, sitting in the kitchen at Marshmallows. Morris was off somewhere in all that murky greenness inspecting the grounds, after which he would drive himself home, alone, while she was to go with Ahmet. She had made a few fruitless phone calls, unable to find the pizza guy, and was worried he'd dumped her, and that perhaps he thought she was a slut because after all she had gone that one step, or rather *hand,* too far, and that was the truth. Yet other girls did more, worse, and didn't consider themselves sluts, merely "mortal" with "feelings." Lucy had to admit she liked the feelings part but was finding it tough dealing with the rejection, which she had no doubt was what was happening to her right now.

"Oh, God, oh God," she moaned, staring at her useless phone, what good was a phone without a number for Phillip Kurtiz the Third, or "Junior" as his family called him in America. Shit, she could never go out with a "Junior," she'd rather die. Which she was afraid anyhow she might do, of a broken heart, of course.

And anyhow, what was she doing, all alone here in this

big creepy house in the middle of nowhere? Where was that woman, Mehitabel? Where was *Ahmet,* who was supposed to give her a lift back to town again? She had all the notes, safe on her iPad, and the samples stuffed into the worn green canvas messenger bag she wore slung across her body, the way they used to in World War I. She had seen that in old movies, terrifically sad, of course, but the uniforms with those Sam Browne wide polished belts and the bags like this were a terrific design. And now she was involved in the design business, she had become more aware of small details like that. Besides, it was handy for keeping all her stuff.

Water gurgled in the uncovered pipes over her head still awaiting their plaster casing. It sounded like a bathtub running out. She wondered who on earth could be taking a bath in this empty house. And then she heard footsteps.

Terrified, she was on her feet, bag in one hand, other hand clasped to her throat, when the door was flung open and Mehitabel strode in on spiky red heels that Lucy knew must have cost a fortune, though how she had time to evaluate that when she was half scared out of her wits she did not know.

"Shit," she said. "You frightened me."

Mehitabel looked her up and down as though she was taking in every scruffy detail, even though Lucy had on her favorite ripped jeans, her best gray sweatshirt with "ApplePie" written on it in red, and her new sneakers that were now covered in mud and had lost their "new sneaker" look.

Mehitabel did not apologize for startling her, merely lifted a shoulder and walked across to the sink where she proceeded to wash her hands.

Lucy watched silently. Mehitabel made her nervous. "So, when do you expect Ahmet back?" she finally said, sinking back into the chair and clasping the messenger bag protectively over her chest, as if she thought the woman might come at her with a knife or something.

Mehitabel still said nothing. Her back to Lucy, she ripped off two sheets of paper towel from the rack and dried her hands carefully. Next, she ran her hands through her hair, lifting her curls from her neck as though she were too warm, shaking her head so they fell into what Lucy thought was a perfect place. She envied that hair. Her own long blond locks were now damp and stringy with strands clinging persistently to her face. She wondered if there was a comb somewhere in the vast cavern of that messenger bag, where contents might be lost for weeks on end, which is why, she guessed, women carried small dainty little purses containing only a lipstick, a credit card, and a comb.

Mehitabel swung round. Leaning back against the sink, one ankle crossed over the other elegantly strapped ankle, she said, "So tell me, Lucy, since you are now a decorator, what do you think of Marshmallows?"

As always, honesty brought the truth from Lucy's mouth, without so much as an instant to think first.

"When we first came it was bad. I mean, it was pretty messed up, all gloomy and dark. Kinda creepy, in fact," she added with a giggle that filtered the reality of what she said. "Of course, Martha and I have still not seen upstairs yet, for all I know it may be filled with sweetness and light. Or bodies."

Mehitabel's mouth curved into what Lucy could have sworn was a smile and she smiled back, delighted to get some response.

"Filled with sweetness and light," Mehitabel said. "Sort of like yourself, Lucy. Isn't that what people say about you?"

"Certainly not, they don't! I'll bet nobody's ever said anything like that about me. More likely 'get a move on, Lucy, why don't you.'" She grinned, laughing at herself because she knew it was true: she wasn't lazy, exactly, she just liked to take her own time with things.

Mehitabel pushed herself off the sink. Looking at Lucy, she sauntered toward her on those spiky red heels, hands on her hips. Eyes narrowed, she seemed to take Lucy in, to delve into her brain, hypnotizing her into scared immobility.

Then, behind her, a door slammed and a voice said, "Well, well, there you are, my little Lucy. Thought I'd never get back in time. Marco's promised to be here too."

It was Ahmet. He checked his watch. "In ten minutes. We're going to pick out a location for my portrait." He stopped and took in Lucy, frozen into immobility at the table, at Mehitabel, halted mid-stride on her way from the sink. Knowing in an instant what must have happened, he took control immediately.

He said, "Mehitabel, please see that the drawing room is arranged, that drinks are available, whatever. Go do your job."

Without a word Mehitabel turned and left the room, though not before Lucy caught the hot red flush that rose to her cheeks, the flash of anger in her usually blank eyes.

"Oh, thank God it's you, Ahmet," Lucy said, her voice trembling just a little. "It was getting so late and kind of dark and no one else is here and I thought I heard noises and . . . well, well . . . I'm glad you are here."

"And I am glad too. No need to be afraid at Marshmallows, Lucy, my little one. This is my home, or at least it will be when you and your sister make it that way. Now, you look to me like a girl in need of a glass of champagne. Am I correct?" He turned as he heard the door open and Mehitabel came back in carrying a tray with a bottle in an ice bucket and two very tall, very slender, very fragile glasses. She put the tray on a side table and left immediately.

"Well, then, Lucy, my dear," Ahmet said, "why don't you and I have some of this and talk about progress on my interior design."

"I have to get back to London," Lucy said, still desperate.

"Of course, of course." Ahmet patted her knee as he handed her a glass, then lifted his own in a toast.

"To us. To Lucy, my lovely girl. To Marshmallows and the grand ball I shall give where you will be a star."

Ahmet saying she'd be "a star" reminded Lucy of why she had come here in the first place. "You mean in the film? The one you were going to show me the script of. Remember?"

Ahmet walked over to the wall of shelves immediately behind her, took a bound sheaf of papers from there, came back and handed them to her.

"The title is *Only the Best,*" he said. "And it's all yours, Lucy.

"Listen, sweetheart." He spoke softly, as though worried someone might overhear, though in fact Lucy saw no one about. "I have to fly to France in a few days, to check my yacht. I thought you might come with me, enjoy a quick trip. We can discuss all your plans on the plane," he added, catching her hesitation. "It will save time in the end."

Lucy said okay; after all, she was getting nowhere with the pizza delivery guy and there was nobody else on the horizon, and all in all she was pretty fed up with life at the moment. Nothing seemed to have gone right since she left drama school; no jobs, no career, no men. She knew she wasn't great-looking but, hey, she wasn't bad either, and she was sparky and people said she was fun, so what the hell was wrong? She decided she must have lost all her sex appeal since her "almost" foray into real sex, and now nobody wanted to know her anymore. Except Ahmet, who was old and boring but he was inviting her to his yacht, flying her in his private plane, talking about the script and about the ball he wanted to give and that she and Martha would plan. How bad could it be?

Later, she called Martha to tell her. Predictably, Martha went crazy.

"Don't you dare go with that man, Lucy Patron." She actually yelled, putting Lucy's back up.

"And why not?" she demanded, sounding, she thought, coolly dignified.

"I don't trust him," Martha said, quieter now but definitely worried.

"I thought you said he'd invited *you* to his yacht too? And Marco as well." Lucy seemed to remember Martha mentioning it.

"Yes, but we never confirmed anything."

"I guess he'll get round to it now." Lucy was suddenly tired of it all. "Can I come and stay with you tonight, Marthie? My place is such a mess."

"Oh, God, all right, of course you can. In fact it would be better if you came here, that way I can keep my eye on you."

Lucy had to laugh. "You can't suspect Ahmet of evil intentions. I mean, Marthie, he's too old for all that."

"And *you,* Lucy, are too young. Come on over, and bring Morrie with you, we can discuss the plans for the ball."

Lucy perked up immediately. "How wonderful. I can just imagine it now, all gilt and roses and . . . and a bunch of older people in long frocks twirling sedately to a waltz, or worse, doing a rhumba in a long line the way they do in old movies. . . ."

"Don't be ridiculous, and what you don't know is that Morrie is very well known as a party planner. He'll tell us exactly what to do, and how much it will cost."

"Do you really think Ahmet will care about that?"

"You'd be surprised the things Ahmet cares about, one of which is most certainly his money. How do you think billionaires get to be billionaires? Still, this is going to cost him a bomb."

"It will be wonderful," Lucy said, knowing that it would.

40

Marco was in bed with Martha when his phone rang. He groaned and put a hand over his eyes, not wanting to look, not wanting to admit anyone into the private place he and his lover, his woman, his lovely Martha were at. Her back was toward him, his body wrapped around hers, his leg across hers; a moment ago, the hand he now flung over his eyes in order not to check who the caller was had been cupping her breast: small, perfect, rounded, it fit as though it was made for him. Which he believed it was.

"Our Maker was good when he invented you," he whispered in Martha's ear. "But not when he invented the phone." Groaning, he tried to ignore it and thankfully, after a few more rings, it stopped. Then it started again.

"Someone is persistent," Martha murmured, taking his hand and moving it down her body. "But I'll bet no one's as persistent as I am when I know what I want."

He knew what she wanted, it was exactly what he wanted; they had both wanted it already for more than a couple of hours now. "I will always love you," he murmured, licking her ear.

"Oh, God." Martha sat up with a sudden jolt, sending Marco flying backward. "I forgot. Lucy will be on her way over here. I told her she could stay the night. Ahmet's invited her onto his yacht, of course I'll have to tell her she can't go alone. . . ."

"Then why don't we go with her? I have to talk to him about his portrait, I could use that as an excuse."

Martha smiled. "Perfect, Marco Mahoney. You are absolutely so freakin' perfect sometimes I can't believe you are that clever. You've just saved the whole situation."

"And I get to take care of my commission at the same time. I'm not looking forward to capturing our Mr. Ghulbian on canvas, but a promise is a promise, and he is interesting, in a strange sort of way."

Ahmet was not exactly thrilled with the news that Marco and Martha would accompany Lucy but he understood it was that, or no Lucy at all, and anyway, he was eager to get his portrait done.

He'd thought about it and decided on doing it on his yacht after all. He would be sitting in the captain's chair at the head of the table in the yacht's wood-paneled dining room that seated thirty. The paneling was ash, a color he was fond of—he hated the yellowness of traditional oak—and the captain's chair was an antique, rescued from a Boston whaler that had plied the Atlantic in the 1800s, and came complete with scars and rum stains and the aroma of old-time sailboats that really gave Ahmet a kick.

Sometimes he wondered about his conflicted personality, thinking about the good things he did: the young people he'd rescued from the streets; his support of them afterward; his generous gifts to charities; the true charity in his heart for the young and disenfranchised. Yet there was his other side, the one he hid from the world, from everyone, in fact, except Mehitabel. She knew his "other" soul, or lack of it; she knew how to protect him, act as his "beard" so no one would ever suspect the great man, the billionaire who had everything, of any wrongdoings. Certainly never of torture and murder.

"Murder" was a word Ahmet did not usually allow to penetrate the forefront of his mind. He was not a murderer. He was a fair man, a just man. His girls were chosen because basically they did not have real lives, they were hanging on to the threads of existence, prostituting themselves to buy drugs, living in squalor, or on the street, though there was also what he called his "higher-class" girl, like Angie, for instance. Now there was a young woman who could have been improved upon, had he had the wish. Which he had not. That other, darker side of his had taken over where Angie was concerned. Just thinking about her now, remembering how she refused even to wail, to cry, to scream when he beat her, excited him. Angie was too precious to set free, to lose into the darkness of "forever." He needed her as he had never needed another woman, and certainly never needed young Lucy, who was to be, he would make certain of it, his future.

Mehitabel had taken care of Angie for him. She'd moved her under cover of darkness, to the attic suite, way after anyone was around, though no servant ever slept at Marshmallows. Angie was safe with Mehitabel, who'd told him Angie was recovering, that she was eating a little soup, a crust of bread. Ahmet had smiled at the way Mehitabel had described it as a "crust of bread." She was nothing if not dramatic, but she was efficient. And loyal. But then how could she not be loyal. He owned her. She would never find employment anywhere else, he would make sure of that, should she ever make any attempt to leave, though he knew she would not; she was in too deep, and she was too dark in her own soul for any other life. Mehitabel needed what he had to offer, and she could consider herself very lucky they had met.

Meanwhile, Angie was here, in that room upstairs under the roof where the herons nested. Perhaps the tweeting of the young, the harsh cry of the birds, gave Angie some comfort in her pain and her sorrow, though he guessed by now sorrow had cut too deep. Angie knew her fate as surely as he himself. It would not be easy.

41

Martha was not surprised when, the day before they were to leave for France, Lucy called to say she couldn't make it, though she *was* stunned by the sheer outrageousness of it.

She gripped the phone hard; she even stamped her foot, she remembered later when she wondered why it hurt. "Don't be ridiculous, Lucy. You accepted. *We* accepted. We are all going and that's that. Even Morrie is coming along to help with the plans. Remember, this is a working trip, Lucy Patron, not simply a joyride."

"A joyride with an old man," Lucy grumbled, mid-bite, Martha could tell. It was breakfast time and she knew Lucy would be in the local Starbucks crunching down a toasted bagel with cream cheese and a double low-fat cappuccino with whipped cream. Lucy never got her calorific priorities straight. "Besides, I've got nothing to wear on a yacht," Lucy added.

"Then wear what you always wear. We can always go shopping in Nice, or Monte Carlo." Martha could tell by Lucy's silence that she was impressed with that idea.

"So, okay then. What time?" Lucy asked.

"Noon. And remember, Lucy Patron, this is a working trip. Bring your brains with you, please. If, in fact, you remember you have any."

Martha put down the phone, turned and met Marco's gaze.

"You think she's ever gonna grow up?" he said, shaking his head. Lucy was irresponsible and he thought she took advantage of Martha's sisterly concern.

"She's worried about Ahmet. And to tell you the truth, so am I, a little bit anyway. He's really coming on strong; you haven't seen the way he looks at her, practically eating her up with his eyes, when he thinks no one is looking."

Marco went over and took her in his arms again, naked body against naked body, cool now, fresh from loving, memories still entwining them as their bodies had earlier, holding them together, content.

"Don't underestimate your kid sister, Martha," he said. "She's a savvy seventeen-year-old, she knows where Ahmet is at and what he's after, and believe me, she's not going to give it to him."

"But what if he asks her to marry him?" Martha was frowning.

He said, "Well, that of course, would be a whole different ball game."

42

ANGIE

I should have known Mehitabel was not simply being kind, cleaning me up, bandaging my wounds, lotioning my bruises, rubbing oil so gently into my shorn head. I already knew Mehitabel was not a gentle woman, I was perfectly well aware that she was cruel, violent, sadistic, and very probably insane, and yet somehow I believed she was helping me, merely because I wanted it so badly to be the truth. I understand now that *wanting* to believe is halfway in the battle of *actually* believing; that, like anything, if you want it badly enough, you might actually imagine it to be so. Suddenly I believed Mehitabel cared, that she was here to help me. I didn't even stop to think there might be another reason. That's the way it is when you are desperate.

I tried to fill my head with reminders of how courage had gotten many people, ordinary people like myself, through tragic situations, through dangerous times, moments of terror and shame. Why then, could I not be like them, those brave members of the wartime French Resistance, the survivors of holocausts, of terror camps? I was in my own personal terror camp. There was no one here to help, only myself, my own reminders of my mother, of what she would expect, of people out there, free people walking the streets, heading to work, out on the town for a night like the ones who came into my restaurant, of how my life was then and might be again, if only I could find the courage to overcome my fear, my imprisonment, my sadistic treatment. If only I could keep my sanity.

Being locked up is a frightening thing in itself; being alone and locked up is a form of hell; not knowing who is going to unlock that door and what will happen next . . . was unthinkable. I simply could not go there, I must live for the moment, whatever moments might remain to me.

I've thought about the famous women who were imprisoned, left with their own thoughts, their fears for their future or their imminent demise, of Mary Stuart, Queen of Scots; of Anne Boleyn, the ill-fated Queen of England; of Joan of Arc, whose captors knew no mercy. And I also thought of the women who had struggled to keep their dignity while imprisoned in Nazi concentration camps, of their terrible circumstances, so much more harrowing than mine, degraded, humiliated, and in the end murdered. Some had survived though, which is how we know their tales; they had brought honor and glory to those who had not, and disgrace and the ultimate penalties on those who had inflicted this on them. There were no SS guards here, no soldiers with machine guns in turrets ready to shoot if you made a run for it. Then why did I not make another run for it? Why? I asked myself, over and over again. It came down to whether I was more afraid of staying and taking what they would do to me, or making a run for it and taking the consequences of either being caught and killed, caught and brought back and further tortured, or getting away with it. Free.

I thought of King Henry the VIII's doomed wives, alone

in their beautiful houses, of the famous women freedom
fighters in France in World War II; I racked my brains for
memories of school history lessons where I'd been told
about these women, how they had overcome their circumstances One way or another. It seemed to me that One Way
was okay, "Another" was not what I wanted even to think
about.

For me, there was only one way. I made up my mind.
Freedom would be mine, I knew it. And then Mehitabel
came back.

This time she was brisk, businesslike, cold as ever.
Again, she had brought clothes, which she thrust at me,
scarcely bothering to look.

"Get dressed," she said. "At once." And then she left.

It was a replay of what had happened not too long ago,
only the clothing was more comfortable. I eased the gray
sweatpants carefully over my lacerated limbs, pulled the
gray sweater over my shorn head—noting it was cashmere
as I did so, and therefore soft and did not hurt. There was a
pair of red flip-flops, too big but better than bare feet, although I did not know where I was going, a long journey
or short, a walk across gravel paths or grassy fields. I
knew nothing and that was the way I wanted it. I preferred
not to know my fate, that way I did not have to deal with it.
I simply accepted the situation, did as I was told, and bided
my time.

I sat quietly on the sofa, feet together in their flip-flops,
hands folded meekly in my lap, head downcast, lost in a
barrage of thoughts, the uncertainty, the fear. Then I heard
footsteps, the familiar clack of Mehitabel's heels on the
wooden floor as she came back. The key turned in the lock.
I lifted my head to look. At the vision that was Mehitabel.

She was in evening dress, long, dark green silky satin
cut close to her body, lightly draped across her hips, slit to
the thigh on the left. The bodice was perfectly plain, and

fit her small breasts as though it belonged, exposing a little cleavage, just enough to excite a man, I thought, though why I was thinking such a thing when my life was in jeopardy I have no idea. It's a woman thing, I suppose, being able to take in your captor, your rival, your enemy's appearance and assess it, even though your life is in her hands. Cunt, was what I thought as well. If ever there was a woman who fitted that indecent word, it was Mehitabel.

Her hair was piled up on top and fixed with sparkly diamond combs. A necklace—a simple strip of emeralds, if matched emeralds could be called "simple," sat perfectly on her slender neck. The color almost matched her eyes. I even took in her shoes, glimpsed under the hem of her slender skirt, delicately bejeweled cream silk with spiky heels that gave her an extra few inches of forbidding height. She wore a wide gold cuff on each arm, an emerald ring the size of a large gooseberry, and almost the same color, on the third finger of her left hand. Had she gotten engaged? To Ahmet? No, oh no, that could never happen. Ahmet would never marry, even I knew that.

"Get to your feet." She almost snarled the command at me and I obeyed quickly, slipping on my too-large flip-flops. I stood there while she looked me up and down, in my baggy gray sweatpants, the gray sweater that hung over my diminished breasts that had once been so pretty, had tempted men, had given them and me pleasure; at my pasty skin that had once been golden; at my sunken eyes that would no longer give a man a flirty look; at the face I never again wanted to see reflected in a mirror, so hideous I knew I had now become.

She stood assessing me, so completely in control I wanted suddenly to hit her. Rage made me tremble. Mehitabel, I knew, mistook my rage for fear. And I *was* afraid. Afraid I had nowhere to take that rage, no direction. I was helpless and she knew it.

She stepped closer, stood, relaxed, her face in mine, our eyes locked. A smile lifted the corners of that thin red mouth, then she took a step back, surveyed me again, held out both hands, palms up, showing me what she had. A collar. Made of leather. Encrusted with stones that to me looked like rubies and sapphires, a few diamonds marking the clasp. I looked at it, lifted my head, looked at her.

"Stand up straight," she commanded. I stood straighter. "Lift your chin higher." I lifted it.

And felt the chill of the leather collar as she wound it around my neck, the slight pull as she latched it, the softness of her hands as she patted it into place. I knew this was my final humiliation. Mehitabel had won. Ahmet had won. Though why I was so important when he could have had any girl, any woman, anyone at all, still bewildered me. Had I just happened to be the one handy for his sadistic sexual practices? The amenable girl with no background, no family, no one who cared? The woman who wanted to be loved and was glad to be with him. *The bastard.*

Mehitabel tightened the collar. She took another step back to admire her handiwork, then, before I knew it she had a leash in her hand, was clipping it to the collar, jerking my neck, tightening it.

I groaned in pain. In fear. In degradation. I was Mehitabel's bitch, on a leash, to be taken wherever she wished. Somehow, I knew it would be to Ahmet.

43

Morris Sorris made a habit of leaving his work behind him when his long day was over. It had often started at six A.M. in his car, heading out to some house in the boonies, or else to a freezing cold warehouse where unimaginable antique treasures might be found, if he got lucky, that is. Morrie figured that if he was getting out of bed for anyone before six A.M. he deserved to be lucky, and today he was. Of course the "warehouse" he was visiting that morning was no simple secondhand or "vintage" joint; it was an ex-garage in South London made over into a veritable fortress with the addition of spiked iron rails, crosshatched iron grills over the windows, and barbed-wire fences with a security guard day and night, protecting the valuable items stored there. Today, for instance, Morrie was to take a look at a set of ten dining room chairs, walnut with curved legs and lion's paw feet. Were they Sheraton? Morrie's trained eye, plus his instinct honed over the years for the false, would guide him on that decision.

He got lucky, the chairs he was certain, he later told Martha over the phone, were authentic though in a pretty bad state: the webbing, of course, was gone, there were chips in places though nothing that could not be fixed by an expert like himself, and they were still the original soft shade of good walnut, a wood which was becoming rare and costly. Morrie's father had been an expert carpenter, a worker in wood, and he'd trained his son well. There wasn't much Morrie could not do with wood, and for him, today was a bonanza. How often did a man get to work with the real thing, after all?

"I just wish they were not going to that house," he found himself saying to Martha, voicing a thought he had kept in his head for some time now.

"You mean Marshmallows? Why ever not?" Martha was surprised.

Morrie thought about why for a minute, then said, "I guess it's because they are so delicate, so beautifully made, it's rare to find a set like this, and that ugly house does not deserve them. I've seen Ahmet at home. They'll never be shown off to advantage in that massive bloody dining room with the captain's chair presiding over everything. And no doubt now, with the Captain himself, our Mr. Ahmet— probably soon to become Sir Ahmet if the rumors are to be believed—acting as the host with the most."

"I haven't heard those rumors, and Morrie, you'd better remember that Ahmet *is* 'the host with the most.' That's how he can pay us."

Morrie rang off and stared gloomily out the car window, his mind still on the Sheraton chairs he had just agreed to pay a king's ransom for on behalf of the billionaire "host with the most," who he despised for some reason he could not yet describe. As the saying went, he could not put a finger on it. The man was affable, reasonable, never arrogant as so many monied folks he had worked with had been. Money seemed like a second skin to Ahmet

Ghulbian; only a problem if something itched, got at his secrets. Morrie didn't quite know, either, why he suddenly thought that Ahmet was a man who kept his secrets well hidden behind that very pleasant face, the firm handshake, the I'm-one-of-you friendliness that rang so true. Or did it? And if it did, then why was Morrie so uneasy about him? It was, he guessed, because he was dealing with a secretive man. Ahmet kept his cards close to his chest, told you exactly what you wanted to hear. And Morrie knew that was dangerous. When you heard what you wanted to hear you felt safe, only you were not. You were in the power of the man telling you that.

He turned onto the motorway, heading back to Brixton and home; anxious suddenly for the simple reality of his own place, maybe for a pint in the pub with the lads to take his uneasy mind off Ahmet Ghulbian and Marshmallows. He decided against the Sheraton chairs. He would not even tell Ghulbian about them, would tell Martha they were fake after all. Marshmallows did not deserve the supreme quality, the craftsman detailing, the care and love that had gone into making them. He'd get Ghulbian some tricky Italian pieces with a little more flash, a touch more arresting, more of a talking point. After all, not too many would recognize an original Sheraton chair when they saw it, would they now?

His phone rang just as he was changing lanes. He moved into the slower lane before glancing down, saw it was Martha calling him back. He pressed Answer, twitched his earpiece into place, said "Hi."

"Morrie, I've got to have those chairs" was her opening line. It made him laugh.

"What are you, a mind reader?"

"No, just anxious. I already sent Ahmet the pics, told him how great they are, you can't tell me now they are not available, I'll never be able to explain it away. I mean, Morrie, this man is like the Bank of England, he'll pay whatever it costs, just make it right for him."

"Fuck him," Morrie said. And he meant it.

Martha's shocked gasp rattled in his ear. "Why? What's up with Ahmet?"

The answer to all Morrie's uneasiness about Ahmet came suddenly into his head. "I don't like the way he looks at Lucy," he said, recalling the man's eyes fixed on the seventeen-year-old; hot eyes, a predator's eyes.

Martha was silent for a minute, then she said, "Morrie, I know exactly what you mean, and I feel the same way. But we have to work with this man, he's planning the party on his yacht for next week, and the grand ball when the house is finished, hopefully three weeks from now. How can I tell him to fuck off? I promised him."

Morrie sighed too. "I know. And I have your plans for the yacht party, I love them, and also for the house. Two parties in three weeks, Martha, that makes it tough on you."

"Remember, I have my new assistant, Lucy, to help. She's actually getting her act together, beginning to come out of the stupor which, I have to tell you, was certainly not about Ahmet, who she calls a boring old man, but a pizza delivery guy, blond, blue-eyed, and Oxford-bound. I'm hoping the least it will do is give her enough spirit to go to college, learn something instead of lounging in that scruffy flat of hers."

"She's lazy, then?"

"Not lazy, exactly; more unmotivated, though now she tells me Ahmet has given her a script of some movie he wants her to star in. And trust me, Morrie, she believes him."

"Jesus. It's time she grew up, got a bit more worldly wise, I mean at seventeen these days, Martha, girls are on the ball, know how to handle themselves and men. Lucy's not daft, she's just delusional."

"Please tell her that, why don't you. I'd appreciate the input. Meanwhile, how's the lovely Marshmallows?"

"As lovely as can be expected. In truth though, Martha, it is getting better, you've worked quite a miracle on it, brought light into those somber rooms, though I'm still reluctant about the Sheraton walnut dining chairs."

"Me too. Now I think about it, I don't believe Ahmet deserves them, and anyhow he's much more the glossy, custom-Italian type. In fact, I'm heading out right now to that Italian decorator showroom and I'll bet I find exactly what I want."

"Or hopefully what you think he will want."

"You got it." Martha sounded happier now that it was resolved and she could get back to the parties. "See you on the yacht, Morrie, in a few days' time," she said as she rang off.

You bet she would, thought Morrie, if he could get his act together and chase up every supplier, every worker, the caterer, the electrician, the rental supplier of cushy cream sofas and chairs, all the workmen involved. It was, he decided, sighing again, though more happily this time, a hard life being a designer, decorator, dogsbody to the rich man who paid you well for it.

It was then he remembered he'd left his design portfolio on the stairs at Marshmallows, the same stairs he had never so far been allowed up, and neither had Martha or even little Lucy. Nobody was to be, in fact, until they had finished downstairs. That was what that witch Mehitabel had told them.

Morrie agonized for a minute but knew he had no choice but to go back and get it.

He swung off the motorway at the next exit, made a turn and got back on in the other direction. It was another half hour before he pulled again into the stunted-treed-driveway of Marshmallows.

Evening darkened the sky and the white birds hulked over their nests, silent for once. There was not a single sound to be heard, other than Morrie's own feet on the gravel as he strode toward the steps, then lifted the iron dragon's head that acted as a door knocker. It was heavy and, even from where he was standing, he could hear the sound booming through the house. He waited a minute but there was no answer. He took a step back, glanced at the house, there was no light in any window. Could no one be working there? Was no one looking after this large property, filled with valuables? There at least had to be a guard.

He lifted the heavy knocker again, rapped it this time, then again, harder; stood, hands in pockets, waiting for someone to answer. No one did. Shit. He was stuck. He had to have that folder, all his notes, all his contacts were in it; he could not work tomorrow without it. He grabbed the door handle and gave it a vicious twist. To his astonishment it turned easily.

He stood for a minute, wondering who might have left this house and all its valuables open to any passerby who, like him, might just try the door. Why did Ahmet not have guards? Why had Martha not arranged for that?

It was getting darker now as night approached. He opened the door, praying an alarm would not go off and leave him stranded, waiting for the police to arrive and arrest him. Of course he could talk his way out of that but all he wanted right now was to get back to Brixton, head for the pub and his mates and that oh so welcome pint, and fuck all this Marshmallows stuff. Fuck these marshes where tiny white lights now flickered, like ghost lanterns, on then off again, randomly, eerily.

This place was creepy by day; at night it could really get to you. He told himself he'd just get his file and get out of there, fuck the cops, and Ahmet and his Marshmallows. He could keep it. Well, not exactly, and he had to get his file so he could keep up with the work on the yacht, the party, the planned ball. All his freakin' life was in that file.

He stepped inside, walked quickly to the staircase. His file was not there. He stood for a moment, stunned. He had left it there, he was sure of it. Where else could he have put it? He had not so much as set foot upstairs; the only other place was the kitchen.

Reluctantly, he walked the length of the hallway to the very back, where the kitchen was located. He pushed open the door, and took a step inside before he saw her. Mehitabel. Lit by a single lightbulb over the counter.

Holding a tray with a bowl of soup, a crust of baguette, a linen napkin, utensils, and a glass of red wine. He might have thought she was going to have a simple supper alone except she was wearing a slinky long green satin evening dress and more jewels than he had ever seen on a woman before. She looked, he thought, absolutely stunning. Or at least she would have, had she not been staring so malevolently at him he actually felt frightened of her.

"Well?" she asked, stopping him dead in his tracks.

"Er, oh, well, I mean, it's me, Morrie, the decorator, I left my contact book, my notes. On the . . . well I thought on the stairs."

"They are on the table."

Her eyes moved to where they were. He followed her gaze, transfixed, went and retrieved them, turned abruptly, thanked her and quickly walked to the door. He felt her eyes on him all the way, boring into him. It was as though she were touching him, he thought with a shudder. He was glad to get out of Marshmallows, climb back in his car, swing round the driveway, gravel spitting from his tires as he took off. It was only when he glanced back that he noticed a light in the house. He thought it must be coming from the attic, right under where the herons nested. He didn't stop to think about it, but later, when he did, thought it must be Mehitabel's room. He just got the hell out of there before darkness settled over the marshes and life disappeared.

44

The next evening Ahmet was at Marshmallows again, alone in the room he called his library simply because two walls were lined with shelves containing a "bought-in" selection of leather-bound books of the "quick and easy kind" a cheap decorator might purchase for effect and certainly not for reading. In fact Ahmet's personal choice of reading matter, oddly, was Agatha Christie's mystery novels, which he kept in an old Vuitton trunk, used now as a side table topped with a squat dark-shaded bronze lamp. Ahmet liked his lighting dim; bright light hurt his eyes and whenever he was out or in overlit areas he wore the dark glasses that had become his signature.

Now, though, he lay back in his red leather wing chair, eyes uncovered but half closed, contemplating the future and what he was about to do to Angie, and what he wanted to do to Lucy, and how he might achieve both those goals without leaving a body to be found, and persuading a young woman to become his wife. His treasure. A jewel he might show off so they could say "lucky Ahmet, he's surely the man with everything . . . all the money in the world, a grand yacht, a mansion, the giver of sumptuous parties, everybody's friend—and now the possessor of a young and lovely wife." For Lucy would be lovely when he had finished with her. No, that was wrong, he was never going to "finish" with Lucy, he would marry her, they would be together forever; he'd see that she was dressed by the finest Paris couturiers; shoes would be made specially for her plump girly feet, her blond hair tamed by the best London stylist. And of course, any jewel she wanted would be hers.

He thought about all this, sitting there, the inevitable glass of good wine in front of him. A valuable Picasso plate that in any other collector's hands might have been displayed in pride of place on a wall, but here merely sat on the Vuitton trunk, contained the usual thin slivers of toast dabbed with the good pâté made by the eighty-year-old woman in Aix-en-Provence. Which reminded him, he must have a check sent to her; she would be needing help again by now; she was getting older and the farm where she lived was falling into rack and ruin, he'd get someone over there to take a look at it, fix it up for her. Poor old girl. He thought for a while of the old woman, living alone, thought how sad it was; still she had lived a good life, never married, devoted only to her animals and the quality of the product she so carefully sold to those who appreciated it. He had helped; gotten her into Harrods and Fortnum's, in a small way, of course, but that only made it more exclusive. She was able to live out her life in comfort, and he was glad because she had brought him pleasure. He always appreciated "pleasure."

There was a tap at the door, and he turned to look. It was Mehitabel. He said nothing, simply stared at her, taking in the elaborate evening dress, the emeralds, the diamond hair clips. Irritated though he was to see her when what he wanted was to be alone with his thoughts, he complimented her on her appearance, and asked, since she was so dressed up, where she was going.

"I'm here for you," was her reply. The satin skirt slid open over her thigh as she took a step toward him, revealing a pale, slender leg and a hint of what lay beyond where the skirt just closed together.

Mehitabel was not the woman Ahmet wanted but despite himself he felt aroused; she was sexy in her way, lovely for sure, if you only glimpsed her in passing; elegant, classy even, if of course you did not know her background. Mehitabel could pass in most situations these days, thanks to his help, and his teaching, and his money. But right now he did not know why she was here and what she wanted of him.

She came and stood at his elbow, reached across and filled up his glass.

"Please, take one yourself," he said, indicating a fresh glass on the tray. She poured a little of the red wine into it. As she leaned over he caught a glimpse of her exposed breasts, the dark, pointed nipples like shadows. It was obvious Mehitabel wore nothing under the green satin. Since Ahmet had never thought of her in any sexual way he wondered uneasily what was going on.

She stood in front of him, sipping the wine, a smile lifting the corners of her mouth. He knew enough to understand Mehitabel's smile meant either a secret, or trouble. "Okay, so let's have it," he said wearily; he was in no mood for game-playing, he had decisions to make, moves to make, earth-shaking moves. First, though, he had to figure out exactly what and how.

Mehitabel met his eyes. Her smile disappeared and she became all at once deadly serious. "I have something for you."

He was busy with his own thoughts, impatient. "Well, what is it then?"

"Let me show you."

Mehitabel strode back and opened the door. "Come in," she said, though not, Ahmet noticed, in a kindly way. She was giving an order.

He stared at the woman who came into the room, stumbling in oversize red flip-flops, drowning in too-big gray sweats, bent over as if in pain. Her shaved head gleamed naked in the lamplight and around her neck was a jeweled dog collar, attached to the lead which Mehitabel held raised high in the air so that it pulled the woman's neck, forcing her head up, so she would look at him.

"Dear God." Ahmet stared at the woman he knew as Angie; though how he'd recognized the former sexy girl with the come-on patter and the mass of wonderful hair and the eyes that promised a future, he did not know. This . . . *creature* . . . did not belong in his drawing room; she did not belong on earth, in the land of the living!

He turned to Mehitabel, said, "Why? *Why* did you do this to her?"

Stunned by Ahmet's reaction, Mehitabel took a step backward. Clutching a hand to her throat, she said, "But I thought only to please you, I wanted you to extract full pleasure from this—"

"From this S&M tawdriness? From dressing her up—then taking her down? Mehitabel, you do not know me. This is not what gives a man like me pleasure. *You* do not give me pleasure. You are here only to obey orders, to carry out my commands, not to think on your own, to decide what I like and what I don't like. Take this . . . person . . . away. Clean her up, dress her in her own clothing. No jewels. No bonds. Then bring her to me."

Still Mehitabel hesitated.

"Understand?" he barked, and Mehitabel turned at once, took Angie's arm, and led her out of the room.

Ahmet sank back into his chair. He took a great gulp

of the wine. He flung the beautiful Picasso plate into the hearth with its delicious toast and pâté made by the nice old lady in Aix-en-Provence. He lay back with his head against the soft red leather chair, put his hands to his face, covered his eyes. Tears trickled through his fingers. He was as alone as he had ever been in his life. And he had no idea what he wanted. The yacht party, the grand ball, the famous guests.

After a while he sat up, he took the handkerchief from his breast pocket, dabbed away the tears, took a few deep breaths, slowly, yoga style as he had been taught to do when meditating. He knew he could not go on like this, he must regain his control, put all thoughts of others aside, return to the man he had once been, the way he had started out, letting nothing, no one, stand in his way.

An Apple laptop sat on the desk under the window. He turned it on, waited a few seconds. Outside the window was only darkness. Appropriate, he thought, for what was about to happen. When the computer came to life he sent a message to France to immediately evict the old woman who made the pâté from her small farm in Aix-en-Provence, close it down, kill off the animals, demolish the buildings. Leave nothing standing, nothing alive, was his order.

He got to his feet, looked around at the lamplit luxury, the overstuffed sofas and the too-heavy curtains and too many Turkish rugs, too much of everything. Soon Martha would change all that. Everything would be gone. He would make a fresh start. There was only one thing to get rid of now.

He called Mehitabel to bring Angie to him. Again.

45

Marco, Martha, and Lucy, with Em tucked as always under Marco's arm where sometimes Martha thought she ought to be instead, though she told herself she seriously could not be jealous of a dog, took a flight to Antibes. Morrie remained in London, minding the shop, as he called it, and getting over what he'd told Martha was the scariest time of his life at Marshmallows, where he'd vowed never to return. That is until Martha told him he had to be practical, it was a job, he had work to do, and so did she; he should just get over it. Morrie guessed he would, but he would still not go back there alone.

Martha was a little surprised that Ahmet had not sent a car to meet them, but they took a taxi to Antibes and, after some discussion with the guard, were finally admitted onto the port where massive yachts and cruise vessels towered, some as high as fourteen stories, floating hotels for the famous, or merely the well-heeled. Their prows flaunted sharply into the sky making Marco think with longing of his lowly but beautiful wooden gulet, its prow painted with the face of a woman whose eyes showed the way across the sea. He felt an urge to be back on his small slip of land with his blue-shuttered one-room cottage with the stone terrace, the bottle of arak, and the sunset lighting everything with a rose-gold glow that lingered over the darkening sea. He felt Martha's eyes on him.

"I know what you're thinking," she said, squeezing his arm.

"Mind reader," he said again, as Em leaned over and gave Martha's face a lush lick. "That's exactly what I'd like to do," he added, stooping to kiss her ear, which was the nearest bit of her.

"Oh, give it up, you two." Lucy turned away in mock disgust. "Just look at that bloody great boat, why don't you?"

They did. The *Lady Marina* towered above them. They were ferried to the yacht on a speedboat by a sailor in white shorts, polo shirt, and sneakers, and greeted on board by the captain, also in his whites with his gold-trimmed cap and a firm handshake.

He told them that Mr. Ghulbian had left instructions they were to make themselves comfortable, that Martha should inspect the boat and get some ideas about what she might like to change, that anything they wanted was theirs, all they had to do was ask. Mr. Ghulbian would let them know later when he would be there.

Martha glanced at Marco, surprised at Ahmet's absence. He raised his brows at her, also surprised, as they followed a steward and Lucy, who was almost dancing with delight, along a spacious corridor to the suites that were to be theirs: one starboard and larger with a sitting area, wide windows, quilted silk walls and a blue-themed decor; the other port side with twin beds done out in a yellow-and-white stripe that made Martha wince.

"It's lost all that 'feel' of a boat," she said. "There's nothing the least bit 'nautical' about it. I can see I'll have

my work cut out if this was Ahmet's last foray into deco-
ration."

"No man decorated this," Lucy said, astonishing them
with her sudden perspicacity. "Not even a teenager would
want to stay in this cabin."

"Stateroom," Martha corrected her automatically, then
amended that. "No, you're right, it's only a cabin, there's
nothing grand and 'stateroomy' about this. We'll have our
work cut out, Lucy, I promise you that."

Lucy beamed. "Before or after we go shopping for
clothes?"

"After we've explored this boat," Martha said firmly,
and accompanied by Em, who sniffed every corner, searching, Marco thought, for her beloved gulet, as he himself
was, in his mind, instead of this pretentious over-gilded
rich man's toy boat. The sea glimmered, flat as a pond, as
though flattened by inertia and too much money.

It took Martha only ten minutes before she was on the
phone to Ahmet. He did not answer and she left a message that she was taking him at his word; she would be
stripping the entire boat and was getting to work right away
on a more appropriate seaworthy look for what was, after
all, under all that flossy decor, a quite lovely and certainly
very large boat. She promised it would be magnificent,
though in a more low-key way. She would complete it in
three weeks' time, which, as she closed her phone, she
crossed her fingers and prayed she would be able to do.

Now she must also turn her attention to Marshmallows,
where Morrie was helping, though he was still refusing to
go back there. Of course he would have to if he was to be
of any help at all, but Martha decided she would work that
out later.

Meanwhile, she took a shower in a stall that was all
beige marble and gilt fittings, and was anyhow too small,

and which Marco claimed was an impossible space for anyone over six feet, so she banged her elbows.

A sullen, older steward in what seemed to be the general uniform of white shorts and polo shirt unpacked and hung their things in a too-small closet space, and turned down the bed though it was still only early evening. Drinks were ready to be served on the afterdeck by another white-uniformed steward. Several bags of different kinds of dog food stood next to the glasses, though the steward informed Marco that of course, there was also chicken and steak if required. Em did "require," and when the steak was brought, she wolfed it in, Marco timed it, exactly one and a half minutes. Em was, he told Martha and the amazed Lucy, more used to a haunch of goat in Turkey and the occasional meat he added to her kibble at home. By then, the shops which closed in the heat of the afternoon were reopening and Martha and Lucy went off to get her something to wear, while Marco decided to take Em for a walk.

Antibes was a small town, sloping cobbled streets, a white church looming over all, still the fishermen's cottages, some with nets drying outside, chic shops with designer labels, and a sandal maker who was doing good business with tourists waiting outside; a couple of ice-cream stores with flavors like pistachio in a true faded green that made you know it was the real thing. Marco licked his cone as he walked, taking in the scenery, wandering the way visitors did with nowhere particular in mind. Marco decided it was a nice place to be, a good state of mind to be in. What he had to concentrate on now, though, was Ahmet's portrait. It must be completed before the ball, where it would be, Martha had informed him, "unveiled," a phrase Marco loathed but understood. "Just remind me not to be there for the unveiling," he warned Martha. "It's Ahmet's day, not mine."

The other matter lurking at the back of his mind was the red-haired girl. Angie Morse. "Missing, believed dead." Did he believe Angie was dead? For some reason, perhaps because she had disappeared so completely, he'd found himself drawing quick sketches of the way he imagined her; the sideways glance he felt sure was her practiced look for the guys who came into the bar, the kind of come-on look they expected, or at least hoped for, from their attractive hostess. The bar restaurant where Angie worked catered to guys on the loose, out for a good time, hoping to get lucky or at least look as though they were, impressing the other guys. Not that Marco would do that. He was his own man, whatever that might mean; he would bow down to no one, try to impress no one. He had no need, it was as simple as that.

Marco walked back to the port where the *Lady Marina* took up more space than any other yacht. As a large boat it had to anchor out at sea and ferry its guests back and forth in smart little Riva speedboats, plush with white leather and complementary white baseball caps to keep the wind out of the women's hair, with sailors standing hands-behind-backs, awaiting their return. The life of the super-rich was enviable in a way, yet remembering his own simple life, his gulet, his cottage, his evenings under the old olive tree with the glass of arak he'd often wished was a French chardonnay but really enjoyed anyway, Marco wondered why Ahmet needed all of it. *All this*.

He was alone, but for Em, when the captain came to inform him that Mr. Ghulbian was arriving in Antibes, that the helicopter had been sent to pick him up and that Mr. Ghulbian would be joining them for dinner later. Around nine if that was all right with Marco.

Sitting on the afterdeck, cold beer in hand, Em at his

feet, the unbeatable view of dozens of large yachts, sails
furled and men sluicing down the decks, the aroma of bar-
becued steak hovering in the air along with the faint tang
of jasmine blown on the breeze from land, Marco agreed
it was all right, though he very much wished he could be
alone with Martha. Well, and Lucy, of course. He thought
he'd better keep an eye on her; Martha was worried about
Ahmet's intentions. Then the two women came back
loaded with shopping bags, Lucy with a big grin on her
face.

"I've never been on a real shopping spree before," Lucy
said, thrilled. "Martha said it was because I was still at
school and who needed much there, I mean we sometimes
made our own stuff for a party, bought polyester in the local market and draped it around, it's amazing what you
can do with safety pins. Once, we were going to a party in
London, sneaking out and I had no tights and somebody
lent me stockings. I had nothing to hold them up so I tied
a piece of string around the tops. Worked a treat. Until they
started slipping down, that is. . . ."

"Lucy, for God's sake!" Martha was laughing, though.

"I'm going to put one of my new dresses on for dinner,"
Lucy said. "And please, *please,* could I have a glass of
wine? White and very cold," she added, giving them a mis-
chievous upward grin.

"It's yours," Marco called after her, "once I've approved
the dress. Nothing too short, now."

"Nothing *is* too short when you're seventeen," Martha
said, dropping a kiss on his cheek, scooping up Em and
sinking into the chair next to him, propping up her feet on
a cushion, accepting the chilled glass of wine from the
ever-attendant steward. "This must be what it's like to be
rich," she murmured, taking a sip.

Marco raised a brow. "Like it?"

"It's okay. For a change." Then she laughed. "Yeah,

I like it, but I also like to earn my money, and believe me, with this boat and the ghastly Marshmallows I *will* earn it. Morrie Sorrie is already coming up with more ideas, but he's scared to death of the place, swears it's haunted. And besides, he hates what he calls 'that woman.'"

"I'm guessing you mean 'this woman.'" Marco indicated the jetty with his bottle, and Mehitabel striding along it, rail-thin and looking, Martha thought, like the old Katharine Hepburn in a terrifying movie, wearing gray flannel slacks and a buttoned white silk shirt, her Medusa curls pinned severely back, the over-large sunglasses covering a good part of her face.

"What's she doing here?" She sat up, glass clutched tightly; the feeling of well-being had disappeared.

"That's for us to find out," Marco said.

46

ANGIE

I thought there was a certain honesty about Ahmet; it was apparent in his eyes when he believed you wouldn't notice; I might almost call it an "otherworldly" look, as though he was somewhere in a place he kept private from the world, and mostly, I suspected, even from himself. It would seem that the famous man did not want us to know the real man. I'll bet I'm one of the few ever to catch a glimpse of that side of him, much good it will do me now.

The scarecrow that used to be me stood before him, head unbowed, eyes fixed on his. You do not remain locked up, alone for who knows whatever length of time, without going crazy, and there is no doubt now, that "crazy" is what I am. More, it is *who* I am. Vanity still creeps in, though, but really it's not vanity, it's a matter of self-worth. I knew I was better than the figure I was presenting to Ahmet; the beaten-down woman, scarcely even female, a nothing person simply waiting for the end. Courage. My mother's remembered voice came back to me in a whisper that had grown fainter as I sank deeper into the sloth of acceptance of my fate. I had nothing left to fight with.

"You look terrible, Angie," Ahmet said, sitting back and taking off his dark glasses, the better to view me.

I made no answer.

"Come now, darling Angie, things are looking up." He glanced at Mehitabel standing behind me, the leash and collar she had taken off held in her hand with the gooseberry-size emerald ring. "I told you no bonds. Get that thing off her," he'd commanded and I heard the quick rustle of her green satin evening dress as she'd hurried to obey. Mehitabel was as much Ahmet's slave as I was.

I prayed he would not tell me to undress, though I had lost any modesty I might have had about being naked in front of people. I was a puppet; pull my strings and I moved; put clothes on me or take them off . . . I had no say in the matter. I knew my fate at Ahmet's hands and by now hoped it would come sooner rather than later, so as not to prolong the torture, because there was no doubt Ahmet was torturing me. Not in the way Mehitabel wanted, physically, sadistically. Ahmet was playing with my mind. He knew how much more terrible a game that was. Maybe, though, just *maybe,* I could play that game too.

"We are leaving here tonight." Ahmet checked his watch. "Now, in fact. Better not to be late for your own party, my dear."

I tried to keep my face expressionless but he caught the slightly raised brows, the question in my eyes.

"There is to be a grand party on the *Lady Marina,* a select group of guests, 'everybody' in fact who is 'anybody' in the south of France right now will be attending. Patrons is in charge of all the arrangements, my own Tunisian chef is in charge of the food, I told him it must be exotic, different, no smoked salmon rolls and dunking into tins of caviar; we shall nibble on quail eggs and lobster lollipops and the tiniest crisp lamb chops from the newest-born lambs that ever saw the hills of Provence. Murdered,

I should say, in my own personal honor, at my behest." He laughed when he saw my bewildered expression turn to one of horror. "What is it with you girls? Lucy Patron was just as shocked when I suggested that, yet I have no doubt you will enjoy them as much as the next guest, though of course they won't be told of the chops' background. I should hate to spoil anyone's enjoyment."

He put on his dark glasses, became once again the man in disguise, or was it the real Ahmet Ghulbian? I no longer knew.

"Mehitabel will dress you appropriately. We'll leave in half an hour. I shall fly the Cessna myself." He sat, looking at me, as though waiting to hear me ask where I was going. I didn't need to. He told me. "Back to my yacht, Angie, where it all began," he said, smiling.

47

ANGIE

I am surprised once again. Astonished, in fact. And scared
to death, or close to it anyway. I'm strapped into a seat on
the Cessna, next to Mehitabel, with Ahmet and a copilot
at the controls. Whether or not we are going to the yacht I
have no idea, because after the few minutes he'd spent
in his library, staring at my no doubt terrifying appearance, he'd said nothing. I was no longer the young woman
he'd seduced, made love to. Or had I seduced him? It had
not really mattered at the time and it didn't really matter
now. I had done what I had done, I had willingly walked
into this man's arms, into his clutches, and into a whirl-
wind of fear, of pain, of near death, which still lurked, a
shadow in my future. Or non-future. I want to say I did
not care, yet somehow through everything, the human
spirit takes control of the mind, sneaks in the back, whis-
pering to keep going, to keep trying, to keep your courage.
Never let go.

   I was warm in the gray sweats I'd put back on. Mehitabel had tied a soft chiffon scarf over my shorn head. I put
up a hand, remembering my earrings, felt them still there,

the twin small diamonds that had been an ill-afforded fourteenth birthday gift from my mother. I had worn them proudly every day since, changing them only for fashion when I needed those kinds of dangling chandeliers for work. Thinking about that, I could remember the person I used to be, though I still don't know the person I have become.

I heard the noise of the engine change slightly as the small plane began its descent. It was dark outside but I glimpsed a string of white lights along a coastline, the red and green riding lights on boats in a harbor, then suddenly a burst of stars and sprinkles in many colors as fireworks exploded from a long barge outlined against the horizon. A treat for the happy tourists, dining in seafront restaurants, lingering over late cups of espresso in the cafés in the normal world I no longer inhabited.

The Cessna bounced as it touched down then glided to a smooth stop. Mehitabel got to her feet, and stood looking down at me, elegant in her green satin evening dress. The jewels around her long neck glinted so beautifully I understood why women longed for them. They were money-no-object jewels and I knew Ahmet must have bought them for her, he probably chose them too because the slender strand was in excellent taste, nothing vulgar here. How the hell, I asked myself suddenly, was I able to think this clearly, when my mind had been destroyed? But had it? Could I still think, plot, plan? I told myself I was going to get out of here, out of this place, wherever they were taking me. I was alert, becoming myself again.

Ahmet was first off the plane, down the small flight of metal steps that dropped from the door, followed by the copilot, who did not look behind him to where Mehitabel and I sat. From the window I watched the pilot stride toward a small arrivals building, leaving Ahmet standing alone at the foot of those steps, waiting for us. Or, I suppose, for me. His prey, caught now, a bird in hand.

"Get up," Mehitabel said. They were the only words she had addressed to me on the journey of about an hour and a half. Of course, I got up. She reached into the overhead storage, took out a long knit jacket, thrust it at me, said to put it on. I put it on. She looked down at my feet in the red flip-flops, sighed and turned away. I guessed there was nothing she could do to change them. "Follow me," she said. I followed. I had no mind of my own. I was their puppet, a pawn, a nothing.

I breathed the fuel-scented air outside, walking behind Mehitabel, who carried the jeweled collar, which I guessed must be worth almost as much as Mehitabel's emeralds. She, so lovely in her green satin, her spiraling black curls standing out from her head as though wired with electricity, her heels clack-clacking along, and me, the scruffy woman anyone might take for a bonded servant.

A car waited, headlights dimmed. We got in, me first with Mehitabel giving me an urgent shove forward, then her, settling into the seat that smelled expensively of new leather; a short drive to the harbor. Mehitabel left, then a while later the driver brought me to a boat, a Riva manned by a man in a dark jacket, the prow of the yacht looming ahead. The name, the *Lady Marina*.

I was back in bondage then, on Ahmet's boat, lost to the world, a place where no one would ever find me. I had drowned once in the Aegean. Was I about to do it all over again?

48

Life at the beck and call of the very rich was not all bad, Martha said to Morrie while standing on the balcony of the hotel they'd relocated to while the party preparations were under way. Martha was sipping an early morning cup of very good coffee, and nibbling every now and then on a pastry picked from the basket of still-warm-from-the-oven goodies that were a calorific nightmare, but emotionally were a form of heaven.

"Why is it," she asked, "that we don't make croissants like this at home?"

"I heard it's the flour," Morrie said. "Or maybe it's the water. Whatever, this place beats Marshmallows hands down, no contest. Don't ever send me there again or I'll have to quit, okay?"

Martha laughed. "So okay." She threw him a sideways look. "Wimp."

"I'm telling you that place is haunted, stuck out there on those bleak marshes like something out of Dickens."

"You've read Dickens, then?"

Morrie gave a slight toss of his head. "Of course not. Nobody does, they just talk like they have."

"Marco has." Martha ventured this bit of information with another sideways look. Morrie looked sideways back.

"Well, Marco would, wouldn't he. I mean, he's got to talk to those sitters he paints, the well known, the well heeled, and of course the well read."

Martha laughed. "I hope we're not having a fight, because we have a lot of work to do. There's a party tonight, remember?"

"How could I forget." Morrie grabbed his iPad and began checking things off a long list. There were to be seventy guests.

"Better also check with Mehitabel," Martha said.

"Jesus. You mean I have to talk to that witch? She's nuts, Martha, friggin' crazy. I thought she wanted to kill me the other night, from the look in her eyes."

"Nobody is killing anybody, and she is Ahmet's right-hand man, so to speak. She deals with *him* for us. She is the last bastion against mistakes. Nobody can get past Mehitabel, not even me, and I'm the one making his party happen."

They both turned as the door opened and Lucy dragged in, her face childish with sleep, eyes half closed against the sunlight, clad only in a bath towel, her nail polish chipped, hair pillow-flat.

"Well," Martha said, "we have some work to do on you before you get to work. Shoot, Lucy, go take a shower, get yourself together. Remember you're working today."

Lucy drifted toward the basket of pastries, picked out a flaky croissant, poured more coffee into Martha's cup, added two sugars that came in paper twists, then sank into a lounge chair and took a sip. "I'm ready," she said.

Martha called downstairs, organized appointments at the beauty salon for both of them in a half hour's time, told

Lucy what she would be wearing that evening and don't even question it, got back on the phone checking innumerable details with the caterer and with Ahmet's Tunisian chef, who would be in charge, then she called Ahmet.

"My dear Martha," he said, sounding, she thought, as though he were smiling, "I know this will be wonderful, the best party ever seen in the south of France." Recalling the many amazing charity balls and Hollywood fantasy evenings, Martha doubted that, but said it would be pretty special and that he must not worry about a thing, she would see him later.

Clicking off her phone, she thought all that was needed now was good luck. And Marco. Where was he, anyhow? Of course, now she remembered, he would be on his way to see Ahmet; the famous portrait was to be painted, the one that Marco said would reveal the true man.

She never disturbed Marco when he was painting, knew he needed to be lost in his work, in his vision, his own world of color and line and senses. That's what made Marco's portraits so wonderful, somehow his own self, his own sensuality came through, though she thought Ahmet would be a hard man to capture. A man like that who kept his feelings locked behind a smile, a handshake, a kind word. It would be tough.

49

That evening, Ahmet stood at the head of the companion-
way waiting for his guests to arrive, elegant in a white
tussore silk rajah jacket, a style long out of fashion, but
because he was wearing it, would soon become fashion-
able again. Ahmet wore it because he liked the way it
looked, and the collarless jacket was cool on a summer
evening. Standing next to him, well, not quite next to, but
a step behind, was Martha, stunning in black silk with a
low V-neck, back and front, banded in sequined leopard.
It was daring for her but she'd been encouraged by Marco
to live up to the "flash" occasion and had succumbed when
shopping with Lucy. Who, she had to admit, looked a
dream in knee-length slate-gray chiffon that Martha had
thought too grown-up and too tight but now had to admit
was a winner. High at the neck, shoulder-baring, it clung
lovingly to Lucy's small breasts and narrow hips, ending
where a wisp of tulle peeked from under the narrow skirt,
showing off her nicely browned legs. Of course her heels
were too high, spindles to break her neck on, Martha had

warned to no avail, ankle-strapped, showing off her newly polished toenails. Black, of course. The choice had been that or purple. Martha's own toes were a nice turquoise, which went with her dangling earrings, a surprise gift from Marco, who'd arrived back at the hotel from the boat, where he'd again been speaking to Ahmet about the painting, allowing just enough time to get himself together for the party. Which meant a black tee instead of white, dark jeans instead of blue, and a soft-shouldered Armani jacket he'd had for years and vowed he'd never part with.

"It's my *only* jacket," he told Martha, inspecting himself in the mirror in their room at the hotel before they'd left. "I figure one is enough. It covers all occasions, from a presentation to the queen, to parties on grand yachts, and even weddings."

Martha thought how attractive he was, with his rumpled hair, his almost good-looking face, his complete unself-consciousness about his appearance—Marco wasn't even aware how cute his butt looked in those jeans. She was glad she was with him.

"We'll be the best-looking couple at that party," she said. "If not the most expensive."

"You're not a couple." Lucy stood by the door, ready to go. "We're *three,* remember?"

Marco quickly walked over and gave her a hug. "I'll never forget it, Lucy, baby," he said. "Though, in fact, we are a quartet; you forgot about Em."

Lucy rushed to pick up the dog from her basket and gave her a hug. "Will she be okay here, all alone?"

Martha said, "Don't worry, the babysitter will be here." Marco rarely left his dog behind and would certainly not leave her alone now, though her pleading eyes and piteous look followed them out.

* * *

The yacht looked wonderful, colorful flags and pennants fluttering in the breeze, white-jacketed waiters standing ready, and champagne—Taittinger, Ahmet's favorite—chilling in ice buckets. Martha had asked Ahmet his favorite color and been surprised when he'd told her orange; somehow she had expected it to be black. So now the tablecloths, napkins, flowers in rows of galvanized buckets were in every shade of tangerine and melon, and the scent of orange blossom, which Martha thought the true perfume of the south of France, was everywhere. The plates were hand-picked by her from Biot, a village near Vence, in a pale greenish glass typical of the area, as were the wineglasses, sturdy and outdoorish, instead of fancy and expensive. In fact, Martha bet Ahmet would be surprised when he got the bill for his party, which would be far less than he'd thought, yet the food was delicious, with spicy rice dishes, salads fashioned from leaves and herbs picked in the hills that morning, and filet mignon cooked simply in red wine. There was a bouillabaisse for the fish-eaters, made the true old-fashioned fishermen's way, with a mix of whatever they'd plucked from the sea that day, but always with the ugly red rascasse for flavor, and never with mussels. There was home-baked bread to dunk in the broth—well, almost home-baked, it came from the bakers along the harbor—and a lavender crème brûlée for after, or else sliced fresh peaches soaked in vermouth with, if wanted, a dollop of crème fraîche.

It had taken more hours to get together than Martha liked to think about. As she stood with Ahmet accepting compliments, her feet were killing her and she was wondering whether she could risk a second glass of champagne before her work was done. Marco came to her rescue. He slipped his arm beneath hers. Leaning into her, he said,

"You smell wonderful and look hungry. I'm taking you away from all this."

"You are? Where to?"

"See that table over there?" He pointed to the far end of the deck where a table for two awaited in the shadows; a candle flickered, a bunch of roses gleamed golden, the pale tangerine cloth draped to the floor, and two chairs tied with pale orange chiffon bows awaited. "Ours," he said.

"Can I take my shoes off?"

"Take off whatever you want."

She put her hand in his; it was the best feeling in the world. "Now I know why I love you."

"You mean you didn't before?"

"I don't know if I can just leave, I feel like I'm deserting my post, I have to keep an eye on everybody, make sure it's all right. I mean, this is my job."

Marco waved a hand, taking in the seventy happy guests at their tables, the champagne being poured, the quartet playing softly in the background. Lucy was dancing with a nice-looking young guy in an NYU T-shirt who Martha suspected was a gate-crasher, but her sister looked as though she was having a good time. Ahmet was presiding over a table of beautiful, expensive-looking younger women and important-looking older men. He caught her eye and lifted a hand in acknowledgment, mouthing a smiling thank-you. Morrie stood alone, propping up the boat's rail; he'd moved on from champagne and was knocking back a bottle of beer, relaxed. She went over and thanked him.

"Thank *you,* lovely Martha," he said. Then, "That woman is here."

Mehitabel, glamorous and frozen faced, was standing with other guests, emeralds gleaming at her neck, her gaze seeming to look inward as though she had other things than a party on her mind.

"There's no doubt she's a beautiful woman," Martha said to Marco.

"Sargent would have painted her exactly like that, the way he painted all those dead-eyed beauties," Marco said. "He saw what lay beneath."

Mehitabel caught their glance and walked toward them. Champagne glass in hand, she said, "Welcome aboard the *Lady Marina,* Marco, Miss Patron." She lifted her glass toward Martha. "I assume you chose these crude glasses for tonight's party? I should have thought you understood by now that Ahmet is used to only the best. You'll find the Tiffany flutes in the cupboard behind the bar. I suggest you change them. Our guests prefer the better things in life," she added, with that smile that lifted only the corners of her mouth and certainly never reached her eyes.

"Allow me to get one for you," Marco said, unsmiling. "I believe everyone else, including Ahmet, is very happy with the ones they already have, but of course, you are different."

Their eyes locked. "In what way am I different?"

Marco didn't understand why, only knew she was, and that in some way she was dangerous. It might be jealousy. Could she be jealous of Ahmet? It certainly was not jealousy of another woman, somehow he knew Mehitabel would not care about that; she would simply dismiss other women as of no account, mere hurdles in the stumbling block of the life of a woman on the make. He realized Mehitabel was ambitious, recognized she was ruthless and that he badly wanted to paint her portrait, capture all that lay behind that lovely face.

50

Of course, the party's finale was a fireworks display, bigger and better than the ones seen before, thirty minutes of glorious light and color and explosions, set off by the amplified music of Tchaikovsky's rowdy 1812 Overture, then, so gently, so perfectly when it was over, to Chopin piano études played on two white grand pianos on deck by a pair of music students to whom Ahmet had awarded scholarships; the girl lovely and composed in a long silvery dress, the young man intense and concentrated in black tie.

"The perfect ending," Marco said to Martha. "However did you dream it up?"

"But I didn't, it was Ahmet's idea. He's a surprising man under that powerful façade. Sometimes I could believe there's even a heart there."

Marco was still wondering if he would be able to capture all facets of Ahmet's personality, of his true being, on canvas. He knew he would have his work cut out for him because Ahmet was already calling the shots, about where he should pose, the chair he wanted to use, the jacket he would wear, even the lighting, something Marco considered his sole privilege to decide.

The next afternoon when Marco arrived for his appointment the yacht looked completely different; the flags and pennants were reduced to only what was necessary to identify the craft, and instead of expensively clad and bejeweled guests, a work crew was slung over the side sluicing down the ship. The lovely scent of orange blossom had been replaced by that of window cleaner and the buckets of flowers were massed in the stern ready to be sent to the local hospitals and old people's homes. The leftover food had already been donated to homeless shelters and the wines and champagnes returned to their air-cooled storage. Martha's work had not ended with the party; she was also the one who organized the cleanup. She was, Marco realized, very good at her job.

"Well, so there you are." Ahmet glanced impatiently at his watch.

Marco had not thought he was late or that there was any urgency about being spot on time, though mostly he was, because after all he was "the hired help"; he was being paid for what he did and he owed the buyer respect. Still, five minutes here or there could not be deemed "late." Irritated, he followed Ahmet into the long, light-filled salon where Ahmet had the chair arranged.

"I'll sit here," Ahmet told him, "with the light coming over my left shoulder from the window. I think it's best to have a full portrait of me seated rather than from only the waist up; it'll give people a better sense of who I am."

Marco raised his brow ever so slightly as he went to inspect the chair, a lovely mellow old piece in walnut, which he thought perfect. "A man of good taste," he said, softening toward Ahmet.

Ahmet agreed, immodestly, Marco thought as he set up his palette, then adjusted the already impatient Ahmet in his chair, the better to catch the light *he* saw, not Ahmet's choice, which made him even more testy and irritable, until Marco finally lost patience.

"Sir, we could replan this sitting if it would suit you better. Make it next week, next month perhaps, when you are less preoccupied."

"And what does my being 'preoccupied,' as you call it, matter to a painter? Can you not see the man I am, not what I'm thinking about?"

Marco eyed him steadily. "Usually, but this time, I'm not sure. I'm not certain I'm seeing what I'm looking for, only what you want to show me."

Ahmet looked silently back. Of course what Marco had said was true, not only of now, but always. "It's who I am," he said, giving Marco that genial smile. "As they say, what you see is what you get."

Marco busied himself setting up his palette of grays, sage-greens, browns, somber tones to be under-lit with soft white and ochre. Ahmet was a very masculine man, almost brutal deep inside somewhere, and he needed to capture that with his choices. It occurred to him he had no idea what color Ahmet's eyes were. He glanced up, realizing of course the reason he didn't know was because Ahmet always wore the dark glasses, wherever he was, day or night.

"I need to paint you without the glasses," he said.

"But why?" Ahmet was disturbed. "I've always worn them, they're a part of me by now. Everybody knows me with my glasses."

Marco stood in front, assessing him. "It's said, and I believe it to be true, that you know a man by his eyes. To me, seeing is the most important of the five senses. You know what you see, you understand the person into whose eyes you are looking. But of course, *you* know that." He laughed, lightening up the suddenly too-serious mood.

"We look into a woman's eyes and see ourselves reflected there, in her mind, or hopefully who we believe we are."

"And that's the man you're going to paint. The man I believe I am. Is that good enough for you, Mr. Mahoney?"

Marco raised his brows, he was back to being Mr. Mahoney; he knew he was in trouble. Whatever was upsetting Ahmet he needed to unleash it on someone, and Marco happened to be the only one there, until Mehitabel appeared.

Ahmet was sitting bolt upright in his chair like a man about to be interrogated, stiff and uneasy with the whole situation. He spun round when he heard the door, saw Mehitabel standing there in her newly acquired style of loose gray flannel slacks and white silk shirt, her hair scraped back with tortoise combs, wearing pink-tinted sunglasses, and obviously taken aback by Ahmet's fury.

"What the fuck are you doing here?" he demanded. "Can't you see I'm busy. And since when did you enter without permission? You'd better remember you work for me, Mehitabel, or very soon you won't."

Marco heard the underlying anger, saw that Mehitabel was afraid and knew he could not stay.

"If you'll excuse me," he said stiffly, "I'd rather reschedule."

Without a word, Ahmet got up and left and so did Mehitabel. Marco quickly packed his palette, his tubes of paint, his brushes and knives back into their bag, stacked the canvases against the wall, and made his exit.

The deck outside was empty, not a crew member in sight. The yacht was desolate-looking after the wonderful party the night before and it made Marco wonder suddenly if Ahmet had a true friend in the world. He seemed a man seriously alone, and with dangerous thoughts.

Seabirds circled overhead as he strode down the jetty, then stood for a moment, taking it all in, the blue-gray sky, the hovering clouds that foretold a storm, the expensive boats that cost more to run than most men made in a year, the casual easy gloss that money gave. He looked back at the yacht, thinking about its owner and how empty his life seemed, and thought how fortunate a man he himself was to have everything he wanted from his own life, the woman he loved, the job he loved, the little dog he adored. He was, he knew, a very lucky man.

He hurried down the jetty, jolting to a stop when he caught a sound, a cry of distress, a wail almost. He looked around, saw nothing, no one, only the seabirds wheeling overhead with their harsh cawing. That was all it was, the seabirds. Then why did he feel so uneasy? And why did he feel like he needed a shower and a drink?

51

Morrie had departed the sunny south of France and was back, alone, at Marshmallows, exactly where he'd sworn never to be again, measuring the deep architraves at the windows for curtains, a job that had been forgotten on his earlier visit. To say he was annoyed was an understatement; he was livid with fury. The job should have rightly been done by a minor helper, one of the young women who showed up to help out for free while learning from a famous designer so they could then put in their CVs their time spent working with Martha Patron, and the houses they had "worked" on, which meant a lot of the time fetching the coffee and buns, taxiing round to pick up forgotten stuff, and remembering to turn out the lights at the end of the day. And, dammit, measuring up for curtains, though they could not always be trusted to get that right.

Anyhow, this house gave Morrie the creeps. He'd sat for ten whole minutes in his bright blue Volkswagen Beetle, staring at the forbidding façade, with its odd mixture of gray wood and stone, the curved gray roof tiles and the spiky nest atop a chimney. No birds today though; he wondered if they had given up on the place too. God knows why Ghulbian wanted to live here, just the view from the windows was a nightmare, the flat watery meadows and sodden brown mud. Even the trees lining the drive were pathetic, stunted and struggling, their branches bare. Certainly no place for a bird's nest.

It was beginning to rain as he stepped out of the car, a thin sputter at first then it came down fast, turning the gravel driveway into mud puddles. Everything needed doing at this house, even the gravel needed replacing. Morrie decided he would take care of that first, fuck what Ghulbian said. If he expected workers to get to his house the man needed gravel or there'd be too many tow trucks showing up to haul folks out. He wondered why Martha had not thought of that, but guessed she had been there only on fine days and it might not have occurred to her.

He shrugged into his parka, put up the hood, and strode to the steps, knocked again on the door. He did not expect anyone to answer, nobody was supposed to be there, but after last time's scary fiasco with Mehitabel he was not taking any chances.

Of course no one answered. Martha had given him a key, a big old-fashioned iron one that, in fact, he thought suited the house better than brass Yale locks. This key let you into a mansion fit for a king; well, if not a king, then a rich man.

He started with the tall windows in the front hall, then went from room to room doing what he had to. He was an expert and he was fast. Every measurement, complete with description and photo, went on his iPad. He had not been contracted to do any upstairs work but anyhow he walked up to the landing and took a look at the splendid stained-glass window, which he was certain must be the work of Rossetti, the most famous artist in that medium, or at least have been done by a member of his team. There was a clarity to the glass, a gleam of pure color that lit the hall like a medieval castle.

It made him curious about what he might find farther up those stairs. Of course he'd been told not to go there, but that didn't mean he wouldn't. He didn't exactly pound up the stairs but he went quickly, nervous because he was doing something forbidden and because the whole place was menacing and he didn't know what he might find.

The stairs were carpeted in red, patterned in a sort of paisley motif that he knew must have almost brought Martha to tears it was so ugly, but the upper landing was of planked wood with here and there a Turkish-looking rug, again mainly in red. He stopped to take a few pictures on his cell; noted down a few measurements, justifying his presence in a place he was not supposed to be anyway. Then he walked along the upper hall where doors stood open onto bedrooms, mostly with huge dark four-posters plumped with plain white duvets, then on up the next flight to the attics. The steps were narrower here. There were just two doors. Right or left? Being right-handed he chose the one on the right.

A small bed was pushed up against the wall; a tossed-back blanket; a small pile of clothing on the floor; a flowered dress that looked as though it had been dragged through water; a comb thrown aside, a few strands of red hair still clinging to it. There was a small table and on it a tray with a bowl of what had once been soup, a molding crust of bread, and a glass of what looked to be red wine. The repast of a Parisian poet, a prisoner in his garret, Morrie thought. Except this was not Paris, it was Marshmallows and it was in the middle of nowhere and he was scared as hell.

He was out of that room and down those narrow stairs, galloping two at a time down the next flight, tripping on the goddamn awful red patterned carpet and out that fuckin' door, not even bothering to turn and slam it. He was out of there and this time he would never return.

He'd quit working for Martha if necessary. And he would warn her not to go to Marshmallows by herself. Something bad was going on, she should not be there alone. Somebody had been kept prisoner and he himself might have been the next.

He looked back before he turned out the gates, remembering the last time when he had seen the light in the attic window. Whoever that "prisoner" was had been alive then. Now he was sure that prisoner was not.

Brixton and the pub drew him like a magnet. He would watch the football on TV, have a pint, a sausage sandwich, be normal, goddammit. And that was final.

52

Ahmet could not bear the sight of Angie, skeletal, bald, seeming sunken into herself. He spent endless hours on deck thinking of her, kept in solitary confinement in a cabin below, which was surely far more luxurious an accommodation than she had ever been used to. He'd deliberately asked Mehitabel to give her the most important guest suite, the one Martha disliked so much with its quilted blue silk walls and golden window shades, which were sufficient, right now, to cut out daylight and also prevent anyone from seeing in. Ahmet was alone on board but for the crew member on duty-watch who kept discreetly out of his way, as did all the crew when their boss was around.

Angie was proving to be a bigger problem than he had anticipated and the reason, he admitted to himself now, was that he needed her. Angie had become his toy, to be played with any way he wanted. Mehitabel was the jailer, taking care of all her needs, telling the crew they had a sick guest on board who was here to rest and must not be disturbed. The crew were trained to be discreet, never to question, not to see what they were not supposed to see. It worked, when you were rich enough and they were paid enough.

Ahmet looked round at his yacht, at the length of gleaming rail that was polished every morning at dawn, at the pristine teak deck, the fresh white paint. Of course the yacht needed Martha's touch, which it would have soon, in a couple of days' time, which meant he'd have to get rid of Angie before then. *How* was the problem that now faced him.

He was not a man who liked bloodshed; he had learned in his brutalized youth there were better ways to achieve what you wanted than a knife to the throat, and anyway that was spectacularly messy, as he also remembered from his Cairo back-alley days when he'd seen a man killed right in front of him. Ahmet had gone to the souk to visit a shop specializing in knives, though what he wanted was simple, a small pearl-handled flick knife he might keep in a pocket, just in case. He never specified to himself what "in case" meant, only that situations existed in the place where he lived and the "boy" he was then had to be prepared if he were to survive to manhood; not a given in those days. Many died young, through violence or disease, or else simply "disappeared." As Angie must do now. And while he thought about it, the best place was of course the original location where he had almost done the deed but for some reason, pleasure mostly, he guessed, had not been able to finish.

Even the sea had not wanted Angie, despite all his efforts. He himself had brought her back from the Aegean, and from those marshes as if to prove his power over her, so she would know he was playing with her life and death. He'd enjoyed torturing her but now she was becoming a liability; people were inquiring after her, the media were onto it, the police were involved. It was dangerous to keep Angie around any longer and equally dangerous to try to dispose of her here. It would have to be Marshmallows.

Ahmet wondered why, for a man who had everything and who had been everywhere, his house on the bleak marshlands was his favorite, the one place in the world he could find peace of mind. Not always, but there were some nights, alone there, not a sound to be heard, not a footfall, no person, no animal, no ghost even to come back to haunt him, it was there he felt alive.

All the rest was just a façade: the glossy yacht soon to be transformed by Martha into something even more spectacular, more in keeping with his new stature in the society to which he was introducing himself and the new people who had come to his party and would attend the ball he was to give, people who would be glad finally to call themselves his friends. He also wanted to be known as a man who helped his friends, a charitable man, which in truth he was, though he preferred to keep that a secret, never wanted anyone to suspect his background might have been the same as the poor vagrants he helped from the dark alleys into new lives. Sometimes he failed, of course, some did not make it, but he gave them a shot at a new beginning, as he was now about to give himself. He was going to become Ahmet Ghulbian, friend to everyone that counted, host supreme, generous to a fault. And, in private, a killer. Which brought him back to Angie again.

Mehitabel kept her closeted in the guest cabin. "A prisoner of luxury," she told Ahmet with that slow smile that changed her eyes to stone. He admired Mehitabel, though she seemed to be getting a bit out of hand lately, a little "above herself," as the saying went. In truth, he no longer trusted Mehitabel, and he knew enough to believe the old adage credited to Mephistopheles, that if a man was only ninety-nine percent and not one-hundred percent with you, he was not your friend. Mehitabel had dropped to that ninety-ninth percentage; he could sense it in her body language, in the captured disdainful expression when she thought he was not looking, in the faint air of impertinence with which she turned and walked from a room. He had made Mehitabel, and he could break her. Without those emeralds around her neck she would be back to being a nobody. Or perhaps even, when he had used her for the final time, she would be nonexistent, the way Angie would.

What he needed now was to get back to Marshmallows, taking Angie and Mehitabel with him. The problem was that Marshmallows was still in the process of being renovated. The last report from Martha was that her assistant, a Mr. Sorris, was taking care of the final details, as was her sister Lucy.

Lucy! Dear God, he had not so much as considered Lucy in the scheme of the events he was planning. His little Lucy, who was to be the light of his life. Finally, he would have a reason for existence other than just the making of more money, of being the richest of the rich, the revered businessman admired by all and friend of none. He had not thought anything of her being alone at Marshmallows with one of Martha's male employees but now it bothered him enough to get Martha on the phone.

"Just to thank you again for the wonderful yacht party," he said, almost purring his gratitude, pleasing her.

"The first of many, I hope," Martha said, a little absently because she was facing ten different logistical problems of "how to" and "why not" and "where is it" and "what happened," and wondering if she was in over her head with this Ghulbian job anyhow. In fact Ahmet was the very last person she wanted to talk to right now, when all her plans seemed to be falling apart. Why was it people promised to fix, to alter, to make, to deliver by a certain date, then later told her it was impossible, and that was, as she reminded them fiercely, after she had paid a hefty deposit, the remainder of which money would not be forthcoming until she saw the end result. The "end result" usually came through after that, but not without some wrecked nerves on her part, which interfered with her relationship with Marco, who couldn't stand her when she was stressed out. He simply took himself off to paint and left her to it.

Martha did not blame him, but she did miss him. She had not seen Marco since the yacht party and the lovely time together in the hotel in Nice, just the two of them. Of course Lucy had been with them too and the dog. Martha thought it was a good thing the old family home was still standing because the numbers were growing; when you added together family and friends she was going to need all the space she could get. She also needed the commission from Ahmet to make enough money to redo Patrons the way it should be done, that is, to restore it to the way it was when her mother and father lived there. Martha wanted it to be exactly the same, only repaired, refinished, shiny with love and newness. "Home" would definitely be where her and Marco's hearts would be.

And now here was Ahmet Ghulbian on the phone demanding that his hideous place, Marshmallows, be finished even before the day of the party, which gave her less than a week. Of course much of the work had already been done. Morrie confirmed that it was looking good, apart, he said, from Mehitabel being there, and him telling Martha he would never go back because it was haunted. That was all she'd needed; it meant now she would have to go there alone to check on how work was going. She couldn't send Lucy, not after Ghulbian helicoptered her off with him like that, wining and dining her, coming on to her. Marco might have to remind Ghulbian that Lucy was only seventeen, that his behavior was not appropriate, that, in fact, he had better lay off. Meanwhile she would keep Lucy out of his way, take care of Marshmallows herself. In fact, she would go there today, check what was left to be done and see if what had been done was correct. She had time to get there and back to London before dinner.

She called Marco and left a message about where she was going and why, said she would meet him at their favorite Italian restaurant at nine, and that she loved him. Oh, and by the way, would he keep an eye on Lucy? She would take care of Ghulbian.

As she jogged through the rain and the puddles up the driveway with its scrubby trees and the hulking white birds that flew over the car, checking her out, then went and flew back and hulked under the eaves again, looking as miserable as she felt, she thought Marshmallows still did not give off a welcoming aura, no matter how she'd tried to change it. Of course new trees were to be planted, truckloads of them would be arriving, their roots encased in wooden crates. Mature trees, because Ahmet had neither the time nor the patience to wait for anything to grow. Instant gratification was his watchword, in more ways than one, Martha suspected. Anyhow, the trees would make a huge difference, as would the thousands of daffodil and tulip bulbs that had been planted, the many-colored variety with the shaggy petals that she adored, when spring finally came to this part of the gray world. *If* it ever did.

She parked in the semicircle of what was left of the gravel in front of the steps and got out, stretching her back. The house still looked gloomy and forbidding. No one was supposed to be there, but oddly there was a light on upstairs, in an attic, she guessed, though she had never been up there, never even so much as penetrated the bedroom floor. "Downstairs" was what she had been given to do and that was where she'd worked. She wondered who could be up there under the eaves near those birds, and if it was a guest why, in this vast house, had they not been given better accommodation.

Standing on the front steps, ringing the clanging great doorbell, hearing it echo through the empty house, Martha got the uneasy feeling that Morrie was right and the place *was* haunted. She heard footsteps crossing the hall, took a step back, ready to turn and run. The door was flung open and Ahmet stood there, with that smile on his face.

"Oh, thank God, it's you" was all she managed to say.

53

"My dear Martha! Had I known you were coming I would have organized a better welcome! Come in, please." Ahmet glanced anxiously at the now circling birds. "I hope they haven't bothered you; I promise to get rid of them before we finish the house."

"No, please don't, they've probably been here for generations, they're a part of the place."

Martha stopped to look back at them settling again in a row on the eaves; some held small twigs in their beaks, obviously in the process of rebuilding their nests. She thanked heaven there was something alive at Marshmallows after all. With its everlasting flat background of treeless marshland it was a hard place to love: in fact, Ahmet was probably the only man who could ever love it. She certainly could not call to mind at the moment any woman who'd want to settle here in the wilds with only the silence and the twenty-mile drive through the scrubland to find a village store with a carton of milk, a newspaper, another human being. She wouldn't bet the TV reception was decent either, which was something else she'd better check on since it obviously fell into her area of responsibility.

"Well, this looks great," she said to Ahmet, stepping into the hall, onto the newly finished floor, with the wide planks of chestnut she had specified, finished in the traditional way with square pegs and no visible nails. It looked spectacular, though she was not thrilled with the mahogany balustrade Ahmet had wanted to keep, and which did not look right with the chestnut. The red carpet was still there too, with the immense brass clips keeping it in place. She wondered why it had not been taken care of; she'd have to speak to Morrie about it, he had probably run out of there so scared he hadn't even thought about it again.

"This carpet will go, of course," she told Ahmet, standing at the foot of the steps next to him. "I'd prefer the wood to show, refinished to a more mellow tone, and with a narrow antique runner; pale, not this red that seems to be everywhere."

She saw Ahmet frown, saw he was concerned, and impulsively touched his arm, told him not to worry about a thing, she would get it right, *and* in time for the ball. "The plans are well under way," she added as she followed him into the library where, as always, a fire glowed in the hearth and the two red leather chairs awaited with a tea tray on the small table between them. She made a mental note to tell him to get rid of the huge Victorian silver set, the teapot was so clumsy she could barely lift it to pour, and the spoon handles so fancily embossed they looked to be museum quality, not everyday items of usefulness.

"We have to tone you down a bit, Ahmet," she said as he sat in stony silence while she poured and handed him his cup. She offered the milk jug, the sugar bowl, the plate of fig cookies. He accepted none of them, sat staring off into the flames, almost, Martha thought, as though she were not there.

"Ahmet," she said uneasily, putting her own cup back on the tray. "You are preoccupied, I can come back another time, there's no hurry, really. . . ."

He lifted his head, stared irritably at her. "What is this preoccupation you and Marco have with *my* 'preoccupation'? I have business matters on my mind. All I expect from you, Martha, is my house finished on time and looking exactly the way you told me it would, the way it did in the sketches, the plans. I expect the same from Marco—my portrait finished and presented on an easel in the hall. No more, no less than what I am paying you for."

Stung, Martha took a deep breath. "You will have everything you paid for, and probably more, exactly the way you did on the yacht." She got to her feet in one smooth move, snapped her bag shut, picked up the sketches, the metal ring with the fabric samples. She flung her green Burberry jacket over her shoulders and was walking out the door when he caught up to her.

He reached out and grabbed her arm. "I didn't mean to upset you, it's just that the young man who was here is saying my house is haunted, he heard things. None of this is true, but rumors are starting. It does my reputation no good. This place is my home, Martha, and I want it to feel that way. I want you to make it into exactly that. *A home.*"

Ahmet's expression was so earnest, he was so deeply concerned, Martha felt sorry for him, a man alone, a *lonely* man, rattling around in this too-big house in the middle of nowhere, with that unlit black hole of a space at the top of the steps where no one was allowed to set foot, and the fire always blazing in the library, the half-empty bottle of tequila, and the terrible silence all around them. Even the birds had stopped their cawing.

But looking into Ahmet's eyes, Martha felt nervous; she told herself there was no reason, he was her client, she knew him well by now; everybody knew his reputation as a businessman, a giver to charities. Yet no one wanted to really *know* him.

She thought about Lucy, of how she had been here, alone with Ahmet, and of Morrie racing out of the place, claiming it to be haunted. Unknown fear sent her own heart racing.

"I must get going." She headed for the door.

Ahmet was there before her, his back against the door, an expression on his face she had never seen before; eyes cold, mouth tight. An inner tension kept his body rigid.

"Not yet, Martha."

She glanced anxiously over her shoulder, thinking surely there must be a servant, a helper, somebody who took care of this rambling place, though she'd noticed there was no dust, the house was impeccable, cleaner than clean, with no people, no children, no animals, no jacket tossed casually over the back of the sofa, no umbrella in the hall stand, no collection of silly hats on the pegs by the kitchen door.

A sudden high-pitched wailing sound shattered the silence. Martha stared, shocked, at Ahmet, who took her arm and quickly walked her to the door. He led her out, closed it behind them, saw her into her car, shut her door, the polite gentleman to the end.

"I'll call you about the ball" were his final words as Martha sped away, the remains of the gravel spurting as it always did from her tires.

"Jesus," she said aloud, her heart still in her mouth, fear sending adrenaline pounding through her pulses. "I'll never come back here alone. In fact I'm not coming back until that bloody ball, and then it will be with Marco."

The crackle of Ahmet's helicopter overhead broke the silence, sending the big white birds into a frenzy. They winged so low over the car, Martha had to stop and allow them to regroup, then fly back to their nests. She thought if she were one of those birds she would be telling the others to get out while the going was good; there were better places to live than Marshmallows, whose frivolous name belied its dark secretiveness.

She noticed again, as she drove away, a light on upstairs. She wondered who might be up there, a maid perhaps, or Ahmet's valet? A human being, for God's sake. The house surely needed one.

54

The small Italian family restaurant Martha and Marco had been going to for dinner at least once a month ever since they'd met offered exactly what you would expect, which made it easier for their customers who had other things on their minds than to decide whether to try the new sauce, or order the same "old faithful" Alfredo, or even the "spag bol" as Lucy called the spaghetti Bolognese, which was spicier than most and left you with a small gasp and a need for another glass of red wine. You knew exactly what you were getting, down to the underdressed green salad and the "grandmother's recipe" chocolate mousse, which Marco could never resist.

"I swear you come here only for that," Martha said. She was sitting beside him at the small table, rather than across, because she was still freaked from the experience earlier at Marshmallows, and needed to be close.

"I come here to be with you," he said, scooping a spoonful of her untouched mousse, having already finished his own.

"Thank God," she said, with more feeling than usual.

Marco stopped eating to look at her. He put down his spoon. "So what's up?"

Martha wondered whether to tell him or not. Deciding that she should, anyway, she said, "It's that house. I feel there's something wrong there; it gives me the creeps. And today I heard this strange sound, oh, I can't explain it exactly except when I thought about it later . . . well, maybe it was a scream."

Marco saw traces of fear in her eyes. "Are you afraid of Ahmet?"

"Right *then,* I was afraid of him. It was something I caught, an expression. . . . I still can't say exactly what, just that I've never seen a look like that in anyone's eyes. It was as though he had switched off all feeling. God, Marco, right then I felt he was capable of anything. And that cry, a sort of . . . *scream.* He got me out of there fast, and believe me, I was glad to go, I would have run if I could."

Marco had not told her about the call he'd received from Morris, about the upstairs room with the discarded food and clothing. It was, Morris had said, as though somebody had been imprisoned there and had departed in a hurry. It was so bad Morrie would never go back, though he would also never tell Martha about it because he knew Ghulbian's was an important commission for her, and he would do nothing to jeopardize that.

"But I wanted to tell *you,*" he'd said to Marco. "I thought it important *you* know, because of Martha. After all, you're painting the man's portrait, you'll see enough of him to know the truth. But me, well I'm fucking scared of that place, and of him. I want nothing more to do with any of it."

The other call Marco was surprised to receive had been from Mehitabel.

He was alone in his studio, the light was fading and he was cleaning up, contemplating taking Em for a walk to

the café on the corner where he always had a ham sandwich, no mustard, which he shared with the dog. He wasn't
too happy to answer the phone call, especially when he
saw it was "caller unknown," but he did, and immediately
wished he had not.

"You remember me" was her opening gambit. "Mehitabel."

"The woman with only one name," he said. "And the
wonderful emeralds."

"Unfortunately the emeralds have gone back to Cartier.
I had them only for the night."

The mention of Cartier brought an image of the gold
panther necklace and Angie. "What can I do for you?" He
was curious despite his antipathy for Mehitabel, and besides he would still like to paint her. Like Ahmet, whose
sketches and Polaroids he'd pinned to the studio walls in
preparation for the portrait, she had an arresting quietude
that hid all emotion. What you saw in Mehitabel was
definitely not what you got. She was a cipher. An enigma.
A question mark.

"I need to see you," she said. "To talk to you. About
Ahmet. There are things you don't know."

55

Ahmet puzzled over Mehitabel's behavior; about the way she avoided his eyes, her sudden secretiveness. Entering his office unexpectedly, he'd caught her mid–phone call, which she had immediately cut off. When he questioned it, she'd told him it was a jeweler interested in lending her a necklace for the ball.

"Of course they're only after the publicity," Ahmet said. "We'll use Cartier, as usual, but get diamonds this time, not colored stones." He looked at her, standing nervously in the doorway, obviously dying to get out.

"Mehitabel, come back in here." It was not a request, it was an order and, as always, she obeyed.

She stood looking down at the papers arranged so neatly on his desk.

"I put everything about the ball there for you to approve," she said.

The slightly higher pitch of her voice told Ahmet his suspicions were valid. "Better tell me what you're up to," he said, very cool, very calm. "Before I find out for myself."

Mehitabel did not remove her eyes from the desk;

obviously wondering what to say, how to avoid his suspicions, how not to let on that she was planning her attack on him, not of course in the physical way a man like him might anticipate. Her strike would be emotional, and it was Lucy she planned to use as her weapon.

"I'm simply trying to protect you," she said. "You are my only concern, Ahmet. You look after me, I look out for you. I know where to find enemies, I know when you are being cheated on."

He glanced sharply at her. "What do you mean by that?"

"Cheated on? Why, by little Lucy, of course. And her pizza delivery boy, the one that comes over to her apartment after he's finished work, the one that stays the night with her. The one she's probably fucking, of course, Ahmet."

He was out of his chair, a powerful man, towering over her, his hands on her throat.

"Oh, God," she whispered, terrified. "God, Ahmet, allow me to finish . . . it's for your own good."

He flung her away from him. She fell back against the desk, a hand to her throat where his fingers had almost prised the life out of her. She hated him so much at that moment she could have killed him too, with the sharp paper knife he used to open envelopes and that he played with, constantly toying with it in his fingers while staring absently into space, as though remembering times past, when, Mehitabel had no doubt, he had used it. How many men, she wondered, had Ahmet killed, or caused to be killed? More women than men, she guessed now, seeing the bitter anger on his face, noting the tremor in his hands as he took a seat behind his expensive desk, in his expensive leather chair, straightening his expensive jacket. She could almost see him reminding himself who he was. His eyes, when he finally looked back at her, told her exactly who he thought she was. And that he could not do without her.

"We are comrades in arms, you and I, Mehitabel," he said. "You need me in order to exist, and I need you to take care of my very existence. To carry out my wishes, almost before I have thought of them myself."

She nodded, her hand still at her throat where she knew his fingerprints stained her neck.

"You will not touch Lucy," he said, in that cold, emotionless voice that held more threat than an angry shout ever could. "You will see that she is taken care of. You will become her friend, take her shopping for a dress to wear to the ball, make sure her hair is fixed properly, her makeup done professionally. I myself will choose the jewels she will wear. Please keep the dress simple, black, velvet, long sleeves; she is not to be made outrageous in any way. She will look like the well-brought-up young woman she is. The young woman," he added with a sharp glance at Mehitabel, "who I intend will become my wife."

"Hah!" Mehitabel threw back her head in a laugh. "And who is going to tell Lucy that she's going to become your wife? She's not one of your young sluts anxious for anything you throw their way. Believe me, Lucy Patron knows exactly who she is, and where she comes from, and even if she is thinking of fucking the pizza guy she's still the kind of proper girl who'll save herself for the marriage bed. And that bed will not be yours, Ahmet. How do I know that? Because Martha Patron will make sure it's not. If you doubt me, ask Marco. He will tell you the truth and I promise you won't like it."

A few days later, Ahmet was sitting uneasily on his yacht, in the chair he'd chosen for his portrait. The usual opening chitchat had been gotten out of the way and Marco was concentrating on his work, a slight frown between his brows because there was something different about Ahmet today; a tension that crackled around him, stiffened his neck, tightened the gaze he directed not at Marco but into some kind of space inhabited only by himself. There was no penetrating Ahmet's thoughts and no way Marco could work like this.

Sighing, he put down the knife he had been dragging over the ochre oil paint that was the background of the portrait; he couldn't even get that right, couldn't catch any magic anywhere today. Was it him? Or was it Ahmet? He glanced at the black rubber watch he always wore on his right wrist, then at Em, sprawled full length, legs straight out, front and back. She rolled an eye hopefully his way but knew better than to jump up and get excited. First, Marco had to give her the signal. When he did not she gave a noisy sigh and pushed her nose back into her paws.

Time crawled but it was finally five thirty. Marco was to meet Mehitabel at six. "Better wrap it up for today, sir," he told Ahmet, wondering again why he always fell into calling Ahmet "sir." It wasn't that he was showing undue respect; more like he did not want the intimacy of using the man's first name, and it was too late to be calling him Mr. Ghulbian.

Ahmet got to his feet. He straightened his jacket, came over to take a look at his picture, sketched out first in charcoal, now overlaid with touches of color. Getting the first impressions down, Marco called it. Truthfully, Ahmet did not think much of it. It wasn't strong enough, did not show him in the purposeful manner he'd expected. "I think perhaps more force," he said, putting a finger out to touch the still-wet canvas.

"Wait until the next stage, sir," Marco suggested, hiding his annoyance. He was not used to sitters getting up to offer suggestions on what he might do. "Oils will give more definition."

Ahmet threw him a disbelieving glance. "Let's hope so," he said, making no bones of the fact that he was not satisfied.

Ahmet was already on his phone as Marco left. Time certainly did not wait for Ahmet and neither did it for Marco. He was due to meet Mehitabel in ten minutes.

Em jumped up and down as he grabbed her lead, then led him triumphantly down the street. He stopped at a stall to buy a treat, gave Em half, then walked on. The café was a smart one; "posh" he would have called it, not a place he would normally have frequented, but he guessed for women like Mehitabel it was where they could show off their latest outfits, exchange the latest gossip. The bar was softly lit, the seating sumptuous, the martinis ice cold. He knew because Mehitabel was drinking one and the glass was still frosted white.

"Can I order you one?" she asked, not bothering to say 'hello, how are you?'

"Thanks, I'll have a Diet Coke." He was there on business, though he did not yet know what that business was, but he certainly wasn't about to drink with the enemy.

He sank into the softness of the chair, reminded himself to sit alertly upright, and leaned forward again, his hands between his knees, looking at her. She busied herself ordering the Coke, and did not look back at him. Soon, though, he knew she would be forced to, and then she would have to tell him what was so important that they had to meet without Ghulbian around.

With nothing left to fuss over she finally sat quietly, facing him.

"So," he said, "better let me have it, Mehitabel. What's so important you needed to see me right away? And alone?"

"It's about Ahmet."

"Of course."

"There are things you don't know about him." She put a hand to her throat, fiddling with the pearl choker, under which his observant painter's eyes noted the red blotches her makeup had failed to completely conceal. There had been violence. Shocked, he sat back, took a sip of his Diet Coke, waited for her to tell him what she obviously needed to tell him.

"Ahmet is a killer." Her voice was as calm as if she were talking about the weather. "He has killed many times, mostly women. He is a sadist. He does it to please himself."

She stopped and took a gulp of the chilled martini. Marco's blood ran cold. The dog's head rested, as always, on his foot. He felt glad of the reality of that when he listened to Mehitabel talking about Ahmet. He did not know whether she spoke the truth or was simply a woman out for revenge, out to destroy the man who had probably made her, who'd given her everything but himself. Mehitabel would never be Mrs. Ghulbian.

He held up his hand, stopped her. "How do I know this is true? Why are you telling me? What happens between you and Ghulbian is none of my business, I'm simply painting the man's portrait."

"Yes, and Martha is decorating his house, and *Lucy* is helping because he wants *Lucy* there, in his clutches, *Mr. Mahoney.*" She used Marco's full name with vicious emphasis and Lucy's with such venom, he was shocked. Mehitabel was not simply angry, she intended to have her revenge on whoever got in her way. Meaning whoever came between her and Ahmet.

"I know about the red-haired girl," she said, surprising him. "The one you sketch continuously. How do I know that?" She reached in her bag, pulled out a sheet of sketch paper folded into quarters, opened it up, showed Marco his own drawing of Angie Morse, one of the many he had done.

"Where did you get this?"

"Ahmet took it from your bag. When your back was turned, I suppose." She shrugged and gave him that tight smile of hers. "Mr. Ghulbian is not above a little petty larceny, Marco, you must know that. Of course he's rich, he can pay for anything he wants, including women, but that red-haired one did not come cheap."

Marco bent to fix the lead on Em's collar. The dog sat up, ready to go. "The red-haired young woman's name is Angie Morse," Marco said. Then added, "But why do I guess you already knew that? I also believe you know where she is."

Mehitabel said, "You mean if she is still alive, don't you?"

"I think I have to ask Ahmet about that."

Marco and the dog were already on their way out.

56

Mehitabel had three tasks. The first was to shop for a ball dress for herself, the second was one for Lucy, and third—outrageous, she thought, but she would do as Ahmet asked—for Angie. Angie who anyhow by now should be dead and gone and no longer a worry, though why Ahmet did not see this, did not envision the danger of keeping the woman alive—barely, by now—did not see he ran the risk of his losing everything, she could not comprehend. And all for a barmaid-hostess who'd never meant anything anyway, until Ahmet had made something of her. Women like Angie were the fluff in men's lives, not to be taken seriously, meant to be used then discarded, sometimes with an expensive goodbye gift, sometimes not even the "goodbye." And sometimes never to be seen again. Which one was Angie to be? Mehitabel wondered.

First, though, she called Lucy, tapping her nails impatiently against her phone as the number rang and rang without even a "sorry not here at the moment" message. Typical of Lucy, she thought, not a care in her head for the person calling, for anyone but herself. She remembered

Ahmet saying, "Well, after all, she is only seventeen," which, in legal terms was a definite danger mark.

Sex with an underage girl was not anything Ahmet would normally have worried about, but Mehitabel knew he would not step over the line with Lucy. The girl came from a well-known family, a family with connections, a background he did not possess. Any legal fight between the billionaire and an underage female of Lucy's background was sure to leave Ahmet the loser, not only monetarily, but morally. He would be destroyed. Which is exactly what Mehitabel wanted. How to achieve that was the question, and that question was still on her mind when she at last got Lucy on the line.

"Good morning, Lucy," she said in her best "nice girl" voice, though "sweet" was not something she could ever manage.

"Who is this?" Foggy with sleep, Lucy glanced at the bedside clock, a pretty little silver Tiffany that had belonged to her mother, with numerals so large she never had to open her eyes wide to catch the correct time, which suited her just fine. "It's only nine thirty, for God's sake."

Mehitabel said, "Not that I believe 'God' cares what the time is, but I do and you should. This is Mehitabel. Mr. Ghulbian has put me in charge of equipping you for the Marshmallows ball. He wants you to be even more beautiful than you already are. I'm quoting him on that. Besides, all the media will be there—TV, magazines, newspapers. Mr. Ghulbian would like to feature you in these publicity shots, he tells me it will prepare you for your future career."

Lucy lay back against the pillows, puzzling over exactly what her future career was supposed to be, other than working as Martha's helper, and anyhow she had a dress and did not want to go shopping, especially with a person she privately called "that woman." Martha did not like Mehitabel and neither did Lucy, in fact, "creepy" was the way Lucy thought of her, though why that was, she did not understand. Still, and she'd bet she was not the only one, somehow she did not think Mehitabel was the winner in the popularity stakes, though admittedly Marco did want to paint her.

"I have a perfectly fine dress I can wear," she said, thinking of the gray chiffon from the yacht party. "Martha will see I look all right, so no need for Mr. Ghulbian to worry."

"He asked me personally to take care of you." Mehitabel was insistent. "Especially since he has a piece of jewelry he wishes you to wear. So you see, Lucy, the dress has to go with the jewels."

"Funny." Lucy twisted a strand of blond hair absently in her fingers the way she did when she was bored or tired. "I always thought it was the other way round. Dress first. Then the bits and pieces, shoes, bracelets, tiaras," she laughed at that idea, "came last."

"These are important," Mehitabel said firmly. "They are usually kept in a vault at the bank but we shall get them out specially for you. I'll come round and pick you up in, say, half an hour?"

Lucy wondered why it was people were always wanting to come and pick her up in half an hour when the truth was she had only just gotten out of bed and had not yet so much as swallowed a cup of coffee. She glanced into the cubbyhole kitchen, saw the pot was still plugged in, found it still warm, poured what dregs were left into a mug which she first had to empty out. She didn't bother to rinse it under the tap, after all she wasn't about to get foot and mouth from whoever had drunk from it last. She smiled, thinking of Martha's face if she had seen what she had just done, and maybe Martha was right and she should straighten up her slovenly ways, get her act together, become a woman. Soon to be an eighteen-year-old woman.

So okay, maybe she would make a splash at the Marshmallows ball, maybe she would let Ghulbian get her a dress to go with his jewels so she could show him off. Or at least his money, she thought with sudden mind-numbing truth. Ahmet was okay but he was old and he was too rich and he was—her heart skipped a beat just thinking about this—dangerous.

Why she'd thought that, she was not quite sure, but there was something about him; his smiling, friendly, though not fatherly, behavior told her he was after her, and she didn't like it. Yet sometimes it gave her a thrill. Hey, a rich guy is after me, she could tell her friends. Old as Methuselah. Think I'm too young for him?

Remembering Mehitabel, she suddenly made up her mind. "Thanks, but no," she told her. "I have a perfectly nice dress I want to wear, and if Ahmet's jewels don't match, then let some other girl wear them. I'm sure he knows plenty of women. Thank you, Mehitabel," she said, ever polite, as she clicked off her phone. Then she called Martha.

Martha had not meant to go back alone to Marshmallows but, as always, there was a hitch in the plans. Morrie resolutely refused to accompany her, said she could fire him if she wanted but that was it. Of course she had not fired him, but remembering her last creepy visit to the house she'd needed someone to go with her. She got Marco on the phone.

"I'm scared of that place" was her opening line, which, of course, immediately got his interest, and his concern.

"You're talking about Marshmallows?"

"Damn right, and I have to go there to take care of details for the ball this weekend."

"I'm surprised anyone is going to the ball since Ahmet does not appear to have friends."

"He has now. Everyone I know was invited and most accepted out of straight curiosity. Besides, it promises to be the most extravagant bash of the year, it'll probably go down in history, at least it will if the media have their way, because every single one of the social correspondents is coming. I think I've bitten off more than I can chew, Marc, and I am really nervous now."

"So, what can I do?"

"Just be there with me. We have to make sure the driveway has been re-graveled, that new trees are planted, and the lanterns are arranged in those crappy little twisted things that pass for trees at that place, that the dance floor is waxed, the electricians are setting up for the microphones, that the platform for the band is finished, that the swimming pool has been covered where the rock group will play so people can dance; that the buffet tables are lined up along the route from kitchen to dining room, where small tables should be set with crisp white linen and fine china. And pray that none of the guests will run off with the solid silver cutlery Ahmet insists on using, though it's worth a friggin' fortune. Why oh why, Marco, does that man always have to show how rich he is? Why can't he just get over it and behave normally?"

"The truth is, Ahmet is not normal. Better get used to that idea, my love, because I can bet you will see both sides of that turbulent personality this weekend. If Ahmet does not get exactly what he wants, exactly what he paid for, there will be hell to pay."

Remembering Ahmet's angry words about getting exactly what he paid for, Martha felt her heart sink. She should never have taken on this job. And that cow Mehitabel was right, it could make or break her. Still, she had her team: four women and two men who worked with her, knew what she wanted almost before she asked for it. And who never minded either running out for coffee or joining her at the end of yet another shattering day for a glass of wine and a bit of a laugh, which certainly helped make her world go round. But most of all she wanted to be with Marco. She suddenly needed most desperately to see him, to feel his arms round her, rest her head in the crook of his shoulder, smell his own incense of lime and vanilla and sheer lovely sexy-man flesh.

She was calling him from her car, having run yet another errand, hot and sweaty, hair a limp wreck, nerves frazzled, her morning's makeup long gone, not even a touch of lip gloss. "I'm coming over right now," she warned him. "Just as I am, in sweatpants and furry slippers, in need of a shower and a hug and a kiss."

"Which do you want first, baby?" She heard him laughing as he rang off.

Oddly, what she said to him when she arrived was not the "I love you" Marco expected. Instead she said, "I'm really worried about Ahmet and Lucy. He had that woman call my sister to arrange to take her out and buy her a dress for the ball. A *dress*," Martha added, with a frown of anger, "that would go with the jewels he wants her to wear. No, wait a minute, that wasn't exactly what Mehitabel said. I believe it was the jewels Lucy *would* wear."

Marco's brows rose. "You mean, like it or lump it?"

"That's exactly what I mean, and that's why I'm worried about him."

Marco went to the fridge, took out a bottle of Chablis, found two glasses, poured the wine. He handed a glass to Martha, walked her over to the long sofa, with the old shawls and quilts he used in his work thrown over it, sat her down, adjusted a cushion at her back, removed her slippers, swung her legs up, then sat beside her and lifted her legs onto his lap.

"So, okay, tell me all about it, honey," he said.

Martha took a deep breath. "So, okay," she repeated his words, "I know I'm working for him. He's my boss. It's a major commission, the biggest I ever had. It's extremely important to me, not simply that I'll be making a great deal of money and Ahmet is a generous man where money is concerned, at least where Marshmallows is concerned, he is, but I can't stand him. Marco, something is wrong. I can't put my finger on it, I can't say exactly why or what, but I remember the bad vibes at that house, I can still hear that strange scream in my dreams. My skin crawls whenever I think of being alone there."

"Then you must never be alone there."

57

Martha was finally in the place she wanted to be, in bed with Marco. She had shed her old sweatpants and T-shirt, soaked herself in a long, hot bath, which Marco had drawn for her, making sure the temperature was perfect by putting his finger in the too-hot water and scalding it.

"It's okay, it's not my painting hand," he'd said with a grin though it hurt. Later Martha tenderly applied a pat of butter to the wound, her grandmother's remedy, she remembered. Marco didn't think much of it anyhow; he licked off the butter, said he needed toast to go with it, wrapped a grungy old paint rag around his finger and got back to the work he'd been doing, which was making love to the woman in his life. The love of his life.

"The thing is," Martha said, finally unraveling herself from his arms and sitting up. A frown scrunched her brow as she thought about what she wanted to say.

"The fact is, Ahmet believes this ball will be his social validation. It'll make him a member of a club he believes exists, but not for him. He hasn't been able to penetrate that other world, as he thinks of it, because he does not belong, he is a foreigner, an unknown—apart from his good works, that is—and there are many of those, I can attest to that. Ahmet certainly puts his money where his heart is, if of course we believe he has a heart. But I can tell you a lot of money has gone to help young men in trouble, and in a quiet way, so it's not self-seeking."

"In a way *it is* self-seeking. It's my belief Ahmet is making up for his own past, that once he was like them. Come on now, Martha, nobody could have such a squeaky clean background, emerging from obscurity the way Ahmet did. Have you—*we*, anyone we know, ever checked his background, that amazing life story of rich Greek Egyptian parents who lost it all in the crash and have never been heard of since? Though, according to him, they paid for a good education, got him on the road to success. Do you know who Ahmet's mother is? Do we even know her name? Is Ghulbian his *real* name, or just made up to prevent anyone getting at the truth? I tell you, I'm *painting* that man, I *see* the secrets hidden in his eyes, the face he keeps impassive by sheer strength of will—and a lot of practice, I'd bet on that. Ahmet has trained himself never to react, never to give his game away, never to let anyone know exactly what he is thinking. 'Spontaneous' is not a word we might ever use to describe your friend. He allows us to see only what he wants us to see. Even I, concentrating on the man's face, looking for his deepest emotions under the smile, the flat eyes, cannot find the truth about who he is."

"But we *know* who he is, everybody does, it's all been written about, we've seen him on TV, at events, at his wonderful party on the yacht. . . ."

"We saw what Ahmet wanted us to see. He's not like us, Martha. That man is riddled with secrets. He doesn't know the meaning of the word 'straightforward.' Ask him a simple question, how was your day, how are you doing, I guarantee he'll have three different answers ready."

Martha slithered out of bed, wrapping the sheet around her, suddenly chilled. "Oh, I don't know, I think he's okay under all that . . ."

"All that *what*?"

She sighed; she understood what Marco meant. "Oh, all that . . . niceness, I suppose. The generosity."

"Like, for instance, offering to buy Lucy a dress for the ball? When I say 'offering,' I get the feeling he was *insisting*. What kind of man does that, Martha?"

"A man in love?"

"A man *obsessed*. Lucy is on his mind and I wouldn't be surprised if he intended to marry her."

Martha jumped to her feet, the sheet still clutched around her nakedness. "Are you out of your mind? Lucy is underage, she still behaves like a child, for God's sake, she wouldn't even consider a man like that, my God, to *her* Ahmet is old. And that's the cardinal sin when you are seventeen."

Marco took her hand, drew her back onto the bed, waited for her to calm down. "Let's put it this way, sweetheart, he's not only old, he's dangerous. He has secrets, he has a past, he's ruthless and right now I get the feeling he's hiding something. And Mehitabel—"

"That cow."

"Mehitabel, the cow, is helping him. I'm willing to bet she knows everything that's going on and right now I also get the feeling she is a woman scorned. She knows Ahmet has another female on his mind."

58

ANGIE

There are times—sitting here on the hard little blue brocade sofa in my pretty little prison, a room I know inch by inch and could probably replicate in a drawing if I were asked to in a courtroom, though I understand of course there is no chance of that ever happening—still, there are times when I almost begin to like my small habitat, the way I imagine a snail must its shell. It fits snugly round me, eight feet by ten—I know the dimensions because I have paced it out, heel to toe, the old-fashioned way. It's certainly better than my original squalid cell under the roof where either the sun beat down with stifling heat, or rain poured with a sound like a railroad engine, slamming down with the weight of the world from a leaden sky I could hardly see.

When I was first moved from the attic and saw the small round porthole window, I believed myself to be back on board the *Lady Marina*. I'd welcomed the idea, thinking of the clean wind, the rushing of the sea against the hull, perhaps the sudden end that awaited me, once again, beneath the crystal clear Aegean. There seemed no purpose in continuing to live. For what? For whom? Surely Ahmet had tortured me enough. Every man must reach a point of satiety, where there is no more satisfaction to be gained from inflicting pain and torture on a victim. And what must he do then? Finally kill me off, of course.

But, here I am, hidden away again, though at least now I have a proper room, a proper bed though just a narrow cot, and a proper bathroom with a tub and a walk-in shower, all done out in beige marble like in a hotel. Could this be a hotel they had taken me to? I feel like Alice in Wonderland: I've fallen down the rabbit hole and discovered a whole new world. If I pull the chair over to the round window and climb on top of it, I can even glimpse a circle of wet-looking parkland with scrubby trees along a gravel drive and other new trees in wooden crates. There are people working out there, real people, men in shirt sleeves spading the new trees into a series of holes dug all the way along that drive. After they've done this, a whole other crew comes in behind, stringing up tiny fairy lights, as though for a party.

That was it! Of course, Ahmet was throwing a party to celebrate the "opening" of his new house. The "home" he had always wanted.

There was a noise outside my door, that clack-clacking I knew meant Mehitabel. She entered without knocking, just to catch me off guard I suppose, though what I might have been doing, imprisoned as I was without any means of escape, I don't know.

She flung open the door and stood there, looking at me. Over her arm she carried a plastic garment bag.

She walked into the room, threw the garment bag onto the chair, came over to me at the window, and stood with her face in mine, inspecting me.

"You look terrible, Angie," she said, finally.

Did I need her to tell me that? And why was she bothering anyway?

She went back out the door, reappeared moments later rolling a small suitcase.

I eyed her warily; I knew she was up to something.

"In the garment bag you will find the dress you are to wear tonight."

My eyes almost bugged out of my head. "Tonight?"

"Yes, Cinderella, you will go to the ball."

She laughed as she said it. I'd never heard Mehitabel laugh before, never so much as seen her smile, but there it was, a little tinkling laugh like a proper lady taking tea with friends, instead of confronting the woman she obviously considered her enemy and who anyhow was socially beneath her, the barmaid, hostess, club girl.

I had a quick flashback of that life, that normal, ordinary, functional kind of life lived by many young women. In a way it's women like myself who make the world go round, offering our drinks, our chat, our temporary companionship, attracting customers into our bars and sending them out again, a little happier, a little more attention paid to them, a smile on their faces. Nothing much maybe, but it still counts for something, to give another human being a small pleasure, that of being acknowledged, accepted, admired even. It was my talent, and I was proud of it. Now, though, I was nothing and I knew it.

Yet, here was Mehitabel, unzipping the garment bag, taking out the hanger with a beautiful dress, velvet, black as the dark side of the moon, long narrow sleeves, low V-neck, tightly corseted waist, spilling into a swirl of a skirt, the folds of which were cut so as to make a woman look slender yet feminine and which I knew would swish sexily around my knees as I walked. If I ever wore this dress, of course.

I made no comment, watching as Mehitabel took a pair of simple black suede heels from a box. I could see the number 8 on the side. My size. She upturned another bag, Victoria's Secret, spilling out a slew of lacy underwear, all in black.

Two bags were still unopened. She turned to look at me, slender as a knife blade in her gray silk shift, belted at the waist with a chain of gunmetal and silver. Sleeveless, it left her arms, with their long muscles, bare, skimming just above her knees, fitting her body like it had been made for her. Which, remembering having my short black work skirts tailored to fit closer, I guessed it had, and by a master couturier, I'd bet. There was nothing cheap about Mehitabel, except her brain perhaps. And probably her background. I was suddenly curious about that, I wanted to know who my jailer was, why she was.

"Mehitabel?" I suddenly found my voice and she glanced up, surprised.

"I was wondering," I said, managing a smile, which felt so alien I almost did not know what my face was doing, "I was wondering, Mehitabel, if you would at least talk to me."

She stood, arms folded across her chest, feet slightly apart, so totally in charge it scared me all over again. She looked capable of anything, but then what did I care? I had nowhere to go, only down.

"What I wanted to know, before . . . well, before anything else takes place, is actually who you are. Where you come from. Who your family is. I remember my mom so clearly, it's as though she's with me, even now. I wondered about your mother. I mean, she must have cared for you, raised you, picked you up from school, cooked pancakes for Sunday breakfast, told you bedtime stories. . . ."

Her face was inscrutable and I hesitated. "Oh, Mehitabel, we are just two women alone here, in this mess together. I don't know how or why I ended up here but you had a choice. You still have a choice. You can get out of this, Ahmet doesn't own you, he doesn't own me. Surely you know that?"

To my surprise, she lifted her chin higher, gave me a long, assessing look, almost a smile, just a hint of a change in her mouth, in her eyes. Then she said, "I know everything, Angie. Never forget that. And I will take care of it, in my own time. Remember that too. Meanwhile, you are to have your hair back, or a replica of it anyway."

She took a wig from the plastic bag, long, softly curling red hair that was so like my own used to be.

"Put it on," she said. "First the mesh cap, then the wig."

She handed them both to me and I did as she said. It was like being reunited with myself. The hair swept my bare shoulders, I patted it around my face, pulled tendrils forward. I had no mirror but it did not matter.

She said, "Now put on the dress."

I slithered into the black velvet. She came and stood behind me, tightened the corset laces, fluffed out the skirt. It felt silky, delicious, I knew I must be dreaming, and then she said, "Now, lift your hair up out of the way."

I did as she asked, lifting my neck as she clasped a golden necklace around it. Lacking a mirror I put up a hand to touch it, knew instantly it was another gold Cartier neck chain with the panther clasp. To replace the one I'd lost in the Aegean. And, again, my initials. *AM*.

Cinderella really was ready for the ball!

Mehitabel took my hand in her cold one and led me back to the chair.

"You will sit here, not move a muscle until I come and get you." She frowned, looking at me, tut-tutting. She had obviously forgotten something. She went to the other bag, brought out a box of makeup, then bent over me, applying a layer of powder, blush, gray eye shadow; no mascara though and no false eyelashes. A dab of lipstick that tasted of cherries.

"Well, well," she said, taking a step back and inspecting her handiwork. "Looks almost like the old Angie. Not that anyone will see, of course. At least, not at first."

She handed me a beautiful feather mask on a silver stick. "This is to be a masked ball. No one will know who anybody really is until the moment of unmasking is announced by Ahmet. And then we'll see what he'll have to say, won't we, Angie. I've brought you back from the dead, girl. I hope you appreciate that."

I did, but I wasn't sure Ahmet would.

59

Martha had done as much as she could to make Marsh-mallows the party house of the year, but no mellow light-ing, no arching rainbows in the sky, no white fairy lights seemed able to soften its harsh façade. Worried, she stood out on the front lawn—the only bit of grass that was real lawn, she thought, remembering she must post warnings: "Do not step on the grass" beyond the back terrace. "Wet-lands" she would call it. That would be enough to stop any woman putting her expensive new party shoes anywhere near it. They would stick to the terrace where the massive stone planters had been filled with sweet-scented stocks and fluffy cow parsley as well as the everlasting white roses Ahmet insisted on, as his "signature" flower. Why a man needed a signature flower beat Martha, but the cus-tomer was always right.

And in pride of place at the foot of the staircase where it could not be missed by all entering the house, on an ea-sel, stood Marco's completed portrait of Ahmet. A tough, very immediate image that looked almost slammed onto the canvas, it showed a hard man, a powerful man in his prime. It was there in the confrontational glare in his eyes—he had taken off the glasses at Marco's request, held them close to his chest as though about to put them back on. And although he was seated in the old captain's chair, he still looked like a "man on the move," ready for action.

Ahmet did not like his picture and told Marco so.

"I'd wanted more the classical banker setup, like everyone else in my business," he said.

Marco dismissed his complaints with a shrug. "You are not a classical banker. You don't like it, don't pay me. I'll keep it myself, show it here in my studio, perhaps send it on to a gallery I know."

Of course Ahmet could not accept that. He paid and, finally convinced it was a rare honor to be painted by Marco Mahoney, agreed to show it in his house.

Martha herself had found the time to change into the long, slippery, silver-sequined halter-neck dress she'd had for ages and felt comfortable in—and besides, she wasn't the "star" tonight so what she wore didn't matter so much. She was the greeter and helper-out.

She wondered where Lucy was, she was supposed to be here with the pizza boyfriend, but as yet there was no sign of her.

Garlands of laurel and bay were slung along the balustrades and over the doors and windows, also lending their more exotic scent. The windows had been left open and the creamy muslin curtains billowed in the breeze. Votives lined each side of every stairway leading into the garden, and fat amber and gold candles centered the tables, tied with a swath of ribbon. Martha had used the same glassware from Biot as on the yacht, and white plates printed with the repeated logo MARSHMALLOWS and the party date running around the edge; a souvenir of a grand evening for the guests.

A series of tents, rather than just the one massive one

Ahmet had wanted, dotted the front lawn, linked by trans-parent plastic passageways—in case of rain, Martha had warned Ahmet, because of course he also expected her to have control over the weather for his big night.

A dozen chefs manned the usually empty kitchen, with more outside working the barbecue. Dozens of waiters in white jackets, champagne jammed into huge ice buckets on tall stands, a display of terribly expensive red wine, a Bordeaux from a good year, as well as a lighter Beaujolais, and Sancerre and Chablis for those who preferred white. Perrier water, Badoit, Red Bull, Pepsi, every diet drink imaginable. Nothing was left to chance tonight; whatever any guest wanted Ahmet meant to supply it. Those were his orders to Martha. Who, in fact, was getting a bit fed up of "orders."

Standing at the top of the stone steps leading onto the terrace which led to the grass, where the "Wetlands" signs were now prominently displayed and also illuminated, Martha told Morrie she should never have taken on the job.

"But why not?" Morrie asked. He was there despite having said he would never return. He'd come for Martha because she needed him, not for Ghulbian.

"Because whatever I do, *have done,* I know Ahmet will not be satisfied. Men like him, with that kind of money, that power, like to wield it over you."

"Power makes men crazy." Morrie knew that. He'd met a few in his career. "Women too," he added, remembering Mehitabel.

Martha had worried about actually getting the guests to Marshmallows, out there in the wilds, but Ahmet had laid on a fleet of small private jets, helicopters, and limos, driving all the way, as Martha had done, though most were probably wondering what the hell they were doing so far out in the boonies. The party had better be good, Martha thought.

The band—an orchestra, really, a good old-fashioned set of musicians with saxophones and trumpets and violins, discreet in black dinner jackets—had taken their places near the newly installed dance floor. Outside, the rock group, a street-chic bunch of rather sweet guys who were more used to weekend gigs in suburbia and were thrilled Martha had given them a shot at this, were already strumming a few chords. The disco would be set up later. Things, Martha thought, with a rising heart, were looking up. Maybe it would be all right after all.

Her phone buzzed. It was Marco. "Where are you?"

"En route, stuck in a traffic jam caused I guess by Ahmet's party, more limos than I've ever seen even when royalty was present."

"No royalty here. Best we can hope for is rich."

Marco laughed. "That's the kind of people rich men know, other rich people. Anyway, girlfriend of mine, lover, sweetheart, I'm missing you. I'll be glad when all this is over and we can go back to being normal again."

"If 'normal' means searching out the lost redhead I think I'll just stay put."

Martha was weary of Marco's insistence on finding out what happened to the red-haired girl out in the Aegean. "And anyway," she added, "I still don't know what it has to do with Ahmet."

"What about Mehitabel?"

"That cow." She couldn't get her head around Mehitabel; the woman was a mystery.

"Well, I expect she'll be there tonight, no doubt taking charge, pushing you out of her way."

"I think I'll let her do that," Martha said. "In fact, my real work here is done. Everything's set, the music, the seating, the flowers, the wines, the food . . . all Ahmet needs is his guests to show up and he'll be a happy man."

"He'll never be that." Marco knew in his gut that was true.

"Well, here comes another private plane," Martha said. "I'd better get back to work as greeter, telling them where to go."

"Let Mehitabel tell them."

She laughed as she ended the call. Mehitabel would not be here to work, she'd be here to show off as Ahmet's woman, dressed to kill in—what else—red satin. On her, it did not look cheap, in fact it looked extremely expensive, simply cut to hug her body, narrow skirt, slit up the front so that when she walked her beautiful long legs were on perfect display, and which caught, as Martha noticed, the eye of many a man as she passed. And, here she came, on her way over to Martha again. What now?

"I need to talk to you about the food," Mehitabel said. "Obviously, canapés are being served for the next couple of hours. Then dinner, with assigned seating. I, of course, shall sit opposite Ahmet at the center table where I can keep an eye on things."

"You mean make sure everything's going well?"

Mehitabel gave her one of those withering sideways glances she was so expert at. "Of course that's what I mean. Don't forget I am the one in charge. I am personally responsible to Ahmet."

Martha wondered who that left her responsible to. Since Ahmet had employed her and was footing the bill and paying her, she had assumed it was her.

Waiters were lighting the tall white tapers in the antique silver candelabra, a dozen or more of them, preparing for dinner. Much later, after midnight, a full breakfast would be served for those exhausted from the dancing or who simply were still dying of hunger, with scrambled eggs, bacon, sausages, biscuits, pancakes, chicken hash . . . Martha had covered every possibility. Now all she had to do was greet the guests, shake their hands, and point them to where the music was playing and drinks were being served. Her spirits rose, she'd always loved a party. But anyway, where *was* Marco?

Standing outside on the only bit of lawn that was actually real grass and not marsh, Martha looked back at the massive house, remembering her hard work, thinking how good it now looked with its softened Syrie Maugham interior, pale and romantic, dotted with sumptuous Oriental rugs and Knoll sofas, the kind with tilted arms you could lean comfortably on, the fabrics all chosen to harmonize and blend, the antiques rounded up by her compatriots in France and Italy, as well as England. Every piece had a place, every piece was perfect. She had done a wonderful job, the best of her life, and she wanted Marco to see it before it got spoiled by the crowds of people, so you couldn't get a proper look.

Marco was sitting in his car behind a snorting eighteen-wheeler that had no reason to be on a one-lane country road anyway and should by rights have stuck to the motorway, except, he guessed, like himself, the driver had taken a chance and gotten off, hoping for better luck, trafficwise.

He knew he was close to Marshmallows because of the glow of arc lights on the horizon and the rainbow lights flashing through the sky, along with several beautiful small jet planes skimming the hedgerows on their way in to land. He sighed, engine idling, arms folded. He might as well be a hundred miles away in this lot.

It was then he noticed something different in the sky. A drift of gray across the tiled roof, where those bloody great birds nested. Could that be smoke? Probably it was; Martha had always lit log fires, "for effect," she would say, believing there was nothing worse than an empty grate.

She'd be showing off the new Italian limestone mantels she'd had made for the drawing room, if you could ever call any room in that pile a drawing room. It still looked like a mausoleum to Marco, fancy decor or no fancy decor.

He wasn't looking forward to this party, nor to seeing Ahmet displaying his portrait. There were times when he wished he'd never met the man. One of them was now.

60

At ten minutes before midnight, Mehitabel checked that the guests were all wearing their feather masks. She had to admit that thanks to Martha they had drawn an A-list crowd. Ahmet would be forever grateful to that superior bitch, or he would if Mehitabel did not do something about it. First, she had to find Lucy, who she knew was here somewhere. She had seen her arrive earlier on one of the chartered buses. She had been sitting next to—hand in hand with, in fact—a very attractive blond young man who Mehitabel had definitely not expected. No matter, she would take care of him. Meanwhile, she must get Lucy alone.

Ahmet, who was not wearing a mask at his own masked ball, stood by the door greeting the revelers, hidden behind their feathers and satin, eyes gleaming with pleasure as they saw the masses of flowers and the tubs of Taittinger and the amber candles softening the light and almost managing to make the big old house welcoming.

Mehitabel had to admit Martha had done an excellent job. Much good it would do her now. She thought of

Angie, locked upstairs, gauntly beautiful in her black velvet frock, the Cartier necklace at her throat, her red hair restored via the wig. And of Lucy, in the identical black velvet—how had Angie described it? "Black as the dark side of the moon." And she thought of how when he saw the two of them together, she would shock Ahmet out of his charming man-of-the-world image, what he might do. He might resort to violence and that would be the end of Ghulbian's social aspirations. No one would want to know him.

The crowd had thickened, small planes were still making their runs, bringing even more guests, and helicopters rattled overhead, spoiling the music for the guests, who wandered restlessly toward the food tents, wondering what was to come next.

ANGIE

I was alone, upstairs in the boudoir I had so suddenly been given, in the black velvet dress that might have been inspired by a Goya portrait of a Spanish maja, expensive and certainly fit for royalty. I crossed my legs and leaned on one elbow, inspecting my shoes. Black suede heels, not too high, simple, expensive of course, as was everything I was wearing, including the lacy underthings. It was a long way from Houlihan's Steak and Crab House, that was for sure. No use thinking about that now. It was gone for good.

There had to be a way out of here. This house was not the Bastille, it could not be escape-proof. I had to be the one who thought it out, discovered a way, something that would draw attention to this boudoir window, above which the herons nested, and beyond which the marshland glimmered, wet, sinister.

Music filtered up from the terraces, arc lights swept the

night sky, chattering voices, laughter, the wonderful smell of food, the kind I'd only dreamed about in this prison. I swept my hands over the black velvet, loving the silken feel of it, patted the wig into place, touched the gold necklace. This girl was ready for the ball. Only thing, I had to get out of here.

There was one sure way. In the bathroom was the perfumed candle Mehitabel had lit, and its soft jasmine scent filled the room. I went and got it. I was taking the biggest risk of my life, but I had no choice.

The curtains were a plain heavy silk. When I first put the candle to the hem it turned brown. The brown crept slowly upward, then quite suddenly flames crawled up the length. Smoke poured through the open window.

Terrified, I thought of jumping but saw it was too far. Unless someone noticed, came running to help, I was a dead woman.

"Oh, Mom," I whispered. "What have I done?"

61

Standing at the foot of the staircase of his newly refurbished home, Ahmet greeted his guests, his "friends" as he liked to think of them, because he knew once they had seen the splendor of his home, experienced his lavish lifestyle, and observed for themselves what a good man he was despite the reputation that preceded him, they would want to come again, return for more of the same. After all, the champagne was excellent, the food different, thanks to the Tunisian and his helpers in the vast kitchen, and the house looked superb with the tables set with his own "Marshmallows"-emblazoned china and the old silver cutlery. The wineglasses were the only thing that disturbed him, the inexpensive greenish Biot glassware when he would have preferred Tiffany crystal. But Martha had her say, and what she said was "enough is enough." Reality had to begin somewhere and for her it was with the glasses, and maybe with the straight-from-the-meadow cow parsley flower arrangements instead of only the expensive white roses Ahmet preferred and which flowers, anyhow, were not even, at least to his eye, properly arranged with a bunch of greenery, merely stuck in tall mason jars that might once have held jam.

"Give it a rest, Ahmet," Martha had said to him. "You can't be rich all the time."

Ahmet supposed not, but when you came from his background it was the only security, showing it off so no man, or woman, might ever think he had been poor. They'd believe that he was born into this, knew how to behave, just like them. Actually, women didn't seem to care much either way, only that he was rich, that he was generous, that, in fact, he was pleasant to be with. Most of the time. It was only later at night alone with him that women found he might become a little over-demanding. Not every woman was willing to feel the lash of the whip as well as the lash of his tongue as his anger against them spilled from his mouth. Ahmet was two men. He knew this was the truth and he liked it that way. He could be everyman. He could be his own man.

Music swelled from the drawing room that was big enough to have been called a ballroom, only Martha would not allow it. "Keep it small," she had warned, "or else they'll think you are showing off." Well, forgive him but he was showing off; he wanted them all, all these people he did not really know and who certainly had never invited him into their homes, to see who he was tonight. They shook hands and smiled into his eyes, said how lovely the house looked and wasn't Martha clever, while the orchestra played "Strangers in the Night" with a nice extra touch of violins that somehow made his house seem more intimate.

He glanced over his shoulder, searching for Mehitabel. She should have been there, she was his assistant, goddammit, she should be working, not cavorting off somewhere, acting like she owned the place. In that red dress that had cost him a fortune. As had the dress for Angie, the secret woman he could not bring himself to dispose of. Maybe later tonight after the party, when everyone had gone, the parking valets, the waiters, the cooks, the dishwashers who took care of all that expensive tableware by hand, the cleaners who vacuumed and wiped and tidied and cast out the wilting cow parsley. Then, he would deal with Angie. It was so convenient that the house stood on marshland.

And then there was Lucy. His own darling little Lucy, the innocence in his life. He had not yet dared buy a ring, he didn't want to rush her, but he had bought pearls, the real thing, a chest-length string of natural pearls clasped with a round eighteenth-century-old-cut diamond. No glitter for his young girl. Gentle was what she needed. And, anyhow, where was she?

He pushed back his cuff, checked his watch, glanced round for Martha. She was nowhere in sight either. Goddammit, where was everybody when he needed them? Didn't he pay enough for them to at least be at his side ready for his orders?

The house felt suddenly quiet: no one was coming through the door. He stood next to his portrait, which he was not the least bit satisfied with though everyone had remarked how like him it was. He didn't see it himself; thought he looked old, worn, hard even, when the truth was so different. He was kind, caring. When he was in the right mood, the right personality. He thought of Cairo, of his childhood, of his hated mother, and immediately wished he had not. This night was a celebration, not a wake. He had never mourned her, never would. He touched the pearls in his pocket, slipping them through his fingers, imagining fastening them round Lucy's slender young neck, how pleased she would be. The image made him smile.

As though he had summoned her, Lucy came through the door on the arm of a blond young man so good-looking he might have been her brother. Anger flashed in Ahmet's eyes as Lucy came up to him, holding the young man's hand. Ahmet put his arms round her possessively, felt her draw back, turn her cheek as he went to kiss her on the mouth, breathed in the scent of her before she got free.

She introduced the young man. "My pizza guy," she explained, her eyes laughing into the boy's with the sexual understanding, the togetherness Ahmet recognized. She might be fucking him, he wasn't sure, but still, right at that moment, he wanted to kill him.

"This is Phillip," Lucy said. The young man held out his hand then took a quick step back when he caught Ahmet's cold glance.

"Uh, great portrait, sir," the nervous boy said. "Good to meet you in person. You're famous, and all that. . . ." He retreated quickly, leaving Lucy still standing there, smiling uncertainly.

"You look beautiful," Ahmet said. And she did, so young and slender in her black velvet dress. "I have something for you."

He took the strand of pearls from his pocket, held them for her to see. "Now, bend your head."

Lucy did so. He lifted her hair, slipped the necklace on. She put up a hand to touch the pearls. "They're cold," she said. Then, "I know they're fake and all but still I can't accept them."

Ahmet laughed. "Why not, after all, they're only fake. And they look so good with that black dress."

Still uncertain, Lucy said thank you, as she reached back for the young man's hand, then turned and walked away wearing a fortune in pearls she couldn't even tell were real. But then, Ahmet thought, who could, except an

expert like the jeweler he'd bought them from, or he himself, because he had paid too much for them. It took a
seventeen-year-old girl to put him squarely in his place. It
made him smile, a regretful kind of smile, but after all,
she was still so young.

62

ANGIE

Burning silk has a particular odor, a frizzled almost metallic smell, like when you use the electric hair straightener too long, and your hair comes out all crisp. Smoke was already drifting from the window. Pieces of curtain broke off and flew after it, beacons of flame, attracting the attention of the visitors in the garden below.

"Fire!"

I heard the shout go up; help would soon be to hand. I hoped it wouldn't be too late. I had not wanted to drown, I did not want to burn. What would Ahmet do now, I asked myself, crouched near the window where the remains of the curtains fluttered, ragged black strips of what had once been fine blue silk. A gun was what sprang to mind; first water, then fire, then a bullet. That would be Ahmet's final move.

I'd started out as a personal sadism project for him, a sexual encounter, an unknowing messenger, carrying his illegal drug money. That finished, I had become merely a nuisance to be hidden away until I could be gotten rid of—silently—when the media had lost interest and were no longer asking whatever happened to that red-haired girl who disappeared. So many girls went missing every year. I wondered how many were ever found. And here I was, in my midnight-black velvet ball gown, the golden panther chain around my neck, wearing a wig as red as my own hair. Yet now, I saw a way out.

Sirens blared as fire trucks approached, blending with the shouts of terrified guests running from the house. I stuck my head out the window,

"Help!" I yelled. *"Help!"*

The firemen spotted me, a truck stopped beneath my window, a ladder was thrust upward, and climbing it came two men in yellow hard hats who, when they got to my too-small window and saw my terrified face, proceeded to hack out the glass and then the frame and haul me out through the gap.

"Good thing you're not a heavyweight," the one carrying me over his shoulder muttered as he descended the ladder and deposited me on the soggy ground. He looked at my smoke-blackened face, my wig tilted crazily to one side of my bald head, the golden jewelry, the black velvet gown, and the satin-and-feather mask I somehow still managed to clutch in one hand.

"Jesus," he said. "What was going on here anyway?"

I spotted Ahmet in the crowd and shrank back into the dark. "There's the owner, why not ask him what happened?"

"I have to see you're okay first; you've inhaled smoke, you might need hospitalizing."

I saw the emergency Red Cross station already set up, assured him I would go there immediately. Behind me the house was starting to burn room by room. Shadows and light danced across the wild, wet marshlands and rain clouds, even darker gray than the smoke, pressed down. The fumes choked us.

"Everybody out of here!" the fireman yelled, marching back to his crew as the sound of more sirens crashed across the night. "Out, everybody out!"

Men in tuxedoes ran to help haul precious antiques and women in sparkly evening dresses carried stuff onto the lawn until it looked like a valuable bric-a-brac sale. A rock group kept on playing like it was the sinking of the *Titanic*. Candelabra, with their white tapers still lit, made the disaster festive.

People in evening finery, seeking a way out, pushed one another out of the way, piling onto the chartered buses that had brought them, or into limos, searching the sky for helicopters that, of course, could not land, some begging lifts from strangers.

I looked for Mehitabel, I knew she had to be here. She hated Ahmet, even though he was the man she wanted. But Ahmet did not want her, and very possibly he wanted someone else.

I ran for one of the elegant chartered buses just as the door was about to slide shut.

"We're full, miss, overloaded already," the driver yelled at me.

"You can't just leave me here," I said, but he crashed through the gears and took off down the driveway with its old stunted trees and the new ones alive with white fairy lights, leading from the mansion behind me that was burning in hell.

63

Earlier, Lucy had managed to lose Ahmet in the crowd, and unaware of the beginning fire in the front, was sitting at the table in the kitchen at the back of Marshmallows, the only room she liked. She was chatting to the Tunisian chef she also liked in a mixture of English and his language, French, of which she had thankfully managed to absorb a few words at school, as well as on those long holidays on the French coast. That holiday language had mostly consisted of how much did chocolate lollipops cost at the wooden snack shed at the top of the beach, or why wasn't the outdoor shower working anyway because she had to get the sand off her feet before they would allow her into the car to go home. "Home" being the usual rented holiday villa, gradually being demolished under a pyramid of damp towels, wet bathing suits, grotty old sneakers, and single flip-flops for which never a match was to be found. Lucy had declared there was a flip-flop thief in the house and when they found him they would make him buy everybody new sandals, but no one ever owned up or got caught.

Now, she'd also lost Phillip, who'd probably had enough and decided to leave. Anyhow, kitchen tables were her favorite haunt; she could hitch up her black velvet, take off her smart new gold sandals, put her feet up on a chair, and sneak a taste of whatever the chef was bringing out next. Right now it was something called kofta, a tiny curried pastry which she loved. "I could eat the whole plate," she said, sneaking a second, or was it her third?

"You do that and I'll lose my job," the chef said. He stopped in his tracks, looking puzzled. "Did I leave an oven on?" he said, sniffing. "Something is burning."

And then they heard it, the shrill call, *"Fire!"*

Lucy grabbed her shoes. She stood for a minute, not knowing where to go. Then, "Oh my God, where's Martha?" And she slammed through the kitchen's swing door into a swirl of gray smoke.

"Come back, miss!" the chef yelled as his staff came running from the various pantries and workrooms. "Everybody out, call the police, the fire brigade, get everyone out." And he ran after Lucy.

He opened the door, stepped back. All he could see was smoke.

"Lucy?" he yelled. "Lucy, where are you?"

There was no answer. He stood for a few seconds, undecided whether to go after her. He'd heard her call her sister's name but had no idea where Martha might be, did not even know if she was still there.

He ran back into the kitchen, did his duty organizing his staff, getting them out, every last one, ran outside, found the fire captain, told him about Lucy. The fire captain swore, waved a couple of men after him, and headed in through the flames. The chef sank to his knees and prayed.

Lucy was outside, running through the wet grass, looking for her sister. The pearls swung to and fro, tangling together, choking her. She yanked at them but they would not break. She gave a mighty pull and they sprinkled onto the grass, catching the light of the flames and the moon as they lay there. She stood for a second, gazing at them. Finally realizing. A robber's fortune at her feet.

Ahmet sprang out of the darkness in front of her.

She screamed, stumbled backward, trying to get out of his way.

"Stop it, you stupid bitch," he said, in a voice so soft Lucy found herself obeying.

"But your house is burning down," she said.

"It was my home."

She ran from him, but the velvet folds caught between her legs and she stumbled. Still running, she plucked at the corset strings, ripping, tugging, felt it tear, struggled her arms free of the long sleeves, pulled the dress down over her chest, over her body, stepped out of it, left it lying there on the grass, an expensive black couture heap she hated but had finally agreed to wear under pressure from Mehitabel. And which left her in only the gray silk slip she'd worn underneath.

Barefoot, the slip plastered against her body by the rain, her long wet blond hair darkened, tears streaking down her face, she ran back to the house to look for Martha. She glanced round, saw Ahmet kneeling on the ground where she had left him, head bent, hands held out in front of him. She could have sworn he was holding the pearls.

She was behind the house, the grass felt like wet spinach under her bare feet, slippery, muddy . . . then she remembered. The marshes. She must be in them. Oh God.

She stood perfectly still. She was too far from the burning house for it to illuminate her way. In front was nothingness. Behind, not even a path to lead her back to Marshmallows.

She couldn't just stand there, she had to get away from Ahmet, find Martha and Marco. *Oh God, how she wanted to go home. . . .*

"Here, come with me."

She lifted her head, looked at the vision in front of her; the black velvet dress exactly like the one she'd been wearing, the beautiful long red hair, the feather mask.

"Come, I know the way. All you have to do is follow me."

Lucy thought it might be a ghost, yet ghosts costumed exactly the way she had been did not suddenly appear out of the night in the middle of the marshes, offering help. . . . But it had to be a ghost, an apparition, a forecast of what she herself would soon become, a dead presence left forever to haunt this place. Terrified, she screamed, but no sound came out.

The woman held out her hand. "My name is Angie. I was trying to get out of here when I saw you running."

The realization that the woman was real made Lucy's legs give way and she slumped to the ground. All remnants of her childhood security had left her. She was broken.

"It will be all right."

"I need to find my sister."

"We'll find her together."

Lucy suddenly needed the comfort of Marco, his masculine presence. She needed her family.

"Now come with me, you're so cold, we must get you home," Angie said.

"Home" to Lucy meant only Patrons, it meant her mother and father and her sisters, all the friends and cousins and the dogs and cats and ponies. . . . Suddenly, the desolation all around seemed even worse.

64

Stuck in the crawling traffic, Marco spotted a leafy path leading in the general direction of the house. It wasn't too far away, couldn't be more than five minutes, better than this fuckin' slow parade of sightseers all wanting a view of the fire. Ghouls, all of them, probably asking if anyone was in there . . . and God knows there would be, and it might be Martha, most certainly Lucy. . . .

Heart racing, he jolted off the narrow road onto the leafy lane and slammed his foot to the metal. The car leapt forward then shuddered to a stop. Shit! Oh God. What the fuck now!

Sitting next to him, her head stuck out the window, Em suddenly jumped up, slid through the gap, and took off in the direction of the house.

Marco yelled after her, but the dog was gone. He tried to get out of the car but the door was jammed on the driver's side. He slid over, tried the passenger door. Stuck. The sweat of fear trickled down his spine.

He climbed into the backseat, shoved at the door. It

opened immediately; he'd never locked it. He climbed out, stood looking toward the house.

"Em," he yelled. "Em, goddamn it, dog, get back here." Shit, he hadn't meant to call her a dog, she would never respond to that. "Em, you little bastard, get back here," he rephrased it, knowing she responded to "little bastard" as a term of affection.

He was in the only group of trees around, birches with pale silvery trunks, fragile leaves aflutter in the hot wind coming from the fire. The whole scene was unreal; Marshmallows looked like a movie set, a TV show, the backround music for the fire engines.

Traffic clogged access for the fire trucks, a helicopter battled the thick smoke; the shriek of the fire engines, the crunch of heavy hoses, then a great burst as water surged out of them. Oh God, he was too late, he was too late. . . . He ran in the same direction the dog had gone.

Out on the marsh, Angie had Lucy's hand grasped firmly in her own as they ran. She heard the girl's sobbing breath, knew Lucy was coming to the end of her strength, that fear and terror were robbing her of the will to go on. Lucy did not even know who it was, dragging her away from the inferno where she believed her loved ones were trapped.

Angie stopped. "Sit here for a minute. Rest, next to me." She pushed Lucy down onto the wet grass. It was cold, they might both die right there of exposure. She said, "Soon, though, we must go on. Your sister will be waiting for you."

She saw Lucy's blue eyes were blurred with tears. She was looking at a broken heart; she knew what it felt like. "I promise," she said, holding Lucy's hand more gently, "I promise you will be okay, but we first have to get out of here."

Angie crossed her fingers and held a hand over her heart. She wasn't sure if she could keep that promise, but if it was a lie, it was in a good cause. She had no idea where anyone was. Not only that, she was in the middle of the dangerous marsh. She had been through this before. She still didn't know how to put one foot safely in front of the other.

Martha did not know how it happened, just that suddenly there was fire all around. Smoke, thick as dust, choked her. Luckily she'd had emergency services on standby for the party. But where was Lucy? She stood for a moment, panicked, cell phone clutched in her hand. She'd call Marco, he'd know what to do. Of course there was now no phone reception, everything was chaotic, fire trucks, police, suddenly a dog darted past her. Em running straight into the flames. The dog must know somebody was in there, and ever faithful, had gone to rescue. Oh God, it must be Lucy.

Martha took a look at the burning house, measured the distance between the French doors where the glass had blown out and the front door that now swung crazily on its hinges, and knew she'd never make it. Besides, that's not where Lucy would have gone. She would have been in the kitchen. And of course, that's where the dog must have gone.

The kitchen was at the back of the house. Another fire truck screeched past her, men already tumbling off it, attaching hoses, running into the blaze. Martha froze where she was, realizing there was nothing she could do. Absolutely nothing.

Marco spotted her, lit by the flames, her shoulders drooping, her head bent. He knew she was crying, knew it must be about Lucy.

He caught up to her, turned her to him, held her, speechless, in his arms. There seemed nothing to say, no words of comfort or promise . . . yet he knew they must have hope. Hope was what life was about, the future they would have together.

Lucy had not questioned the woman holding her hand as they ran. All her trust was in her. She had only this person, her replica in the black velvet dress, her red hair blowing in the hot wind coming off the fire. She looked at her properly, finally taking her in, the cheekbones sharp as blades under the pale skin, rail-thin in the velvet dress that hung on her frame; her large eyes soft with compassion.

"Who are you?" she asked when they stopped to rest.

"A friend."

"You mean a friend of Ahmet."

"That man has no friends. I'm here because he trapped me, imprisoned me. I started this fire to try to escape. . . ."

Lucy tried to take in what she had just heard; surely nobody imprisoned women, nobody started fires deliberately, where people might be killed. She remembered her sister. "Oh my God, Martha!"

She tried to get up but Angie held her. "Stay here. Do not move an inch." She rose to her feet, smoothed out the folds of her dress, took off her shoes.

"But where are you going?" Terrified of being left alone, Lucy clutched at her.

"I'm going to get Martha for you," Angie said. "Trust me." And she was gone.

The night closed around Lucy. She could *feel* the darkness touching her, offset by the flames from the burning house, tamped down by the fire hoses. This woman with the red hair would get Martha back, she would get her and bring her here, and then Marco would surely come, and Em. Oh my God, the little dog.

65

Marco held Martha in his arms; she was quiet now but he felt her tremble. He wondered where Lucy might be and was afraid of the answer. The burning house sent off intense heat and he walked Martha away, out of range.

"Tell me what to do," she said. "I have to find Lucy."

"Of course we'll find her." He wished he was as sure of that as he sounded. He decided to leave Martha there and go back to the burning house, search around; Lucy might even be in the crowd of onlookers. Then he realized, of course she would not. Lucy would be looking for them, if she was still alive, that is. He wished he had not had that thought.

"I'm going back," he said to Martha. "Wait here, do not move an inch."

He jogged toward the house but was stopped by a couple of firemen. There were half a dozen trucks outside, plus several police cars. He went over to one, explained to the cop that he needed to get through, his young friend might be in there, but was told it was impossible.

"Can you help me?"

He turned his head. He was looking at the red-haired girl he had painted so often. The girl from Fethiye, whose drowning eyes remained in his memory. The girl he had been searching for ever since. Back from the dead.

"They tried to kill me on the boat. They kept me alive to torture me, they meant to kill me, make sure this time. They kept me prisoner here, and I started this fire to escape. I was afraid no one would believe me but now I'll tell it all to anyone who will listen. This man, this powerful billionaire, is evil and what I am now is testament to that."

She swept off the red wig and stood, humbly, before him. "It was all a game with them," she said.

Marco knew they had no time to waste, but first Angie insisted he round up the cops to help.

"The man is dangerous," Angie said. "He's angry, and he has a gun. And he has all this swamp in which to bury us without a trace. We need help."

Lucy lay shivering on the wetlands; she was so cold her teeth could not chatter because her jaw seemed frozen. She could not have moved a foot, not even a finger had she wished.

Ahmet loomed out of the darkness. The burned house cast a rosy glow over him as he stopped and looked at her.

"Well," he said, with something of the old power back in his voice. "Will you just look who we have here. The fine Miss Lucy. Paragon of virtue and fucker of pizza delivery guys. The girl who is too good for pearls. I guess diamonds are where you're really at. Girls like you, who think themselves better than other people, always really want diamonds. They expect a fair return for their sexual services, because for sure they don't get actual sexual gratification, that would be too demanding. Right, my little

Lucy? I mean, it's much more fun to fuck delivery guys and stable lads, that kind of thing, and hold yourself back, pretending virtue when a real man comes on to you, offers you the world."

He sank to his knees beside her, took off his jacket. She shrank away as he put it round her shoulders. "Can't say I'm not a gentleman." He touched her arm as he put the jacket round her, felt how cold she was, the icy chill that comes from exposure, and that he knew meant death if she stayed out here any longer. He stared at her, taking in her exhausted face, the slow tears oozing from beneath her swollen eyelids, the faint tremor that shook the hands he took in his. He could not bear it, he could not lose his Lucy.

He rose to his feet, scooped her in his arms. She weighed nothing, less than any of the precious oil drums that had made him wealthy. Holding her, shivering, close to his chest, he set off back across the swamp, not knowing where it was safe to walk, hoping he'd make it. He had to save Lucy.

The dog appeared out of nowhere. A shrill bark, a quick flash as it ran past then circled back again. It leaped up at Lucy, licked her dangling arm, sniffed, yelped some more. Ahmet knew this was Marco's dog. Marco was here. He would help Lucy.

Standing there holding her, Ahmet waited until he heard their voices. When he saw their approaching figures silhouetted against the red glow, he took a long last look at his beloved. Then he laid her on the ground, wrapped his jacket over her again, saw that the dog had run off toward the voices. The dog would bring them to her, they would find his girl. He would be gone. And there would be nothing they could do about it. All they'd have would be a story from a strange, crazy red-haired woman who nobody would ever believe. Lucy would not even remember. If she lived, that is.

He remembered the Beretta, removed it from his jacket pocket. He stood for a moment more. He did not kiss Lucy. He never had. He turned, and strode off into the night. He knew where he was heading.

It was Marco who found her, of course. And who glimpsed the man walking away. He knew who it was.

66

Ahmet was back on the MV *Lady Marina,* off the coast of Fethiye, alone on deck gazing out at the deep cobalt sea, lit every now and then by a flicker of phosphorescence. Nature was magical, he thought, and more powerful than man. No one knew that better than he, who had survived storms in the Mediterranean, typhoons off the coast of Japan, and hurricanes in the Pacific. One thing he had no control over was the weather, a fact which, complete narcissist that Ahmet was, annoyed him. He would have paid his fortune, well, a part of it, to any scientist who could give him that power. Meanwhile, what he did have power over was people. "Human beings," as they liked to be called, though "human," to him, was a relative term and he himself was of course above all that. He had power; he did what he pleased; took care of life and death any way he chose. Tonight it was Mehitabel's turn.

He sat for a while longer, contemplating the fact that he had lost out on Angie, that she of all people had been the one to have beaten him, come out the winner in their stupid battle. A battle which should never have started and would not have, if he had only used his fuckin' head and not become entranced with her.

Was he entranced with Angie? Yes. But he was also entranced with Lucy. There was a difference, though. One was a woman of the world, the other a girl who needed to be taught the ways of the world.

He closed his eyes, sitting there on the deck of his yacht, recalling the feel of Lucy's warm young neck as he'd clasped the pearls around it, breathing in the scent of her, the heat, the new sweat that layered her skin and a French perfume he knew but could not identify, and which she had sprayed on too lavishly, leaving a drift of it behind wherever she walked. It was a young girl's mistake, no real woman would have been so unsubtle. Except maybe Angie, but that would have been for a different reason, which was because Angie didn't know any better; she had not been to the same school of life as Lucy. Angie was from the streets. Like himself. That's why he liked her. And why, like Mehitabel, she was a danger to him, and also like Mehitabel, had to die.

It had been so easy. He had been sitting here, just like he was now, when he'd heard the rustle of silk behind his chair, the soft tap-tap of Mehitabel's heels. He turned his head, glanced up at her.

"Are you here to apologize for the disaster?"

"I don't believe apologies are necessary. We are one, you and I, Ahmet. You know that. Whatever you do or say, I accept. And expect the same from you."

She'd taken the chair next to him, silk rustling as she sat down. He'd taken her in, seeing the beauty, and the shallowness, her personal pain and her lack of feeling for others. She was right about the two of them being the same, of course.

He stood, reached out a hand, pulled her to her feet again.

"Where are we going?" she asked as he marched her onto the top deck where the white helicopter waited.

"To the airport to pick up my plane. It's time to go home, Mehitabel."

She stared, surprised, back at him; they both knew he had no "home" anymore. Marshmallows was gone.

"We'll go check it out," he explained, guiding her into the helicopter. "Talk about rebuilding. I know you'll have some good thoughts on that, I can always trust you to come up with an answer."

Momentarily pleased, Mehitabel fastened her seat belt. In a short while they were at the small airport, boarding the Cessna. Ahmet took the controls himself. He was a homing pigeon, heading for Marshmallows.

Viewed from the air, through the everlasting mist, the ruined house was merely a collection of broken walls, blackened stone, dangling steel girders. Not a tree. Not a flower. No sign people had ever lived here, partied here, imagined a future here. All there was were the marsh lights and the unexpected caw of a white heron, frightened from its new nest by the roar of the small plane's engine.

Ahmet dropped into a landing, trundling slowly over the bumpy strip of grass, pulling up at the very end where grass became the deeper green of marsh. He leaned over and unbuckled Mehitabel's seat belt, then got out and walked around to her side, opened the door, indicated she should also descend. When she did so, he took her hand, looked at her for a long moment, then held it to his lips. She stared back at him, nervous.

"Now, Mehitabel," he said, "it's time for a walk." He took a step back, pulled the gun from his belt, the small Beretta. It fit his palm as though made for it. "Or do you prefer a bullet?"

Mehitabel froze. She had seen death many times, been the cause of it, the instrument. She had never expected it to face her.

"You must have known one day it would end like this," Ahmet said. "People like us, you and I, we don't live ordinary lives. And we die by extraordinary means. Now, I suggest you go for a walk. Take off your shoes, you'll be more comfortable, and the marsh grass will be cool against your bare feet."

Mehitabel slipped off her shoes. She stood barefoot, terrified, waiting.

"Please be so good as to walk away from me, my dear," he said. "I would hate it to be any other way. And you're a woman who knows, anyhow, when you're beat."

Mehitabel did. Turning, she began to walk very slowly away. The grass was cool. Wet. The mud clung to her ankles, sucked at her calves, until it was a struggle to move forward. It was very dark ahead of her. The darkness of forever.

She was to die in the swamp but Ahmet put a single bullet into her just to make sure. Then he stood for a long while, waiting, watching as the marshes took her over, and the river rose and then, the great wall of rushing tidal river. No one would ever find Mehitabel. Only her shoes had remained, forgotten where she had stepped out of them, such a short while ago.

67

A few days later, Ahmet was sitting in his favorite captain's chair, on the deck of the *Lady Marina,* the one used for his portrait, waiting for Marco. He had called Marco, asked the favor of his company, said he had something important to tell him. He'd also said that Marco was the only one he wanted to know about this, and that he trusted his discretion completely.

"I like you," he'd said, and then, in his usual less than tactful way, "Better than I like your portrait of me."

"Well, that should take care of that, then, sir" was Marco's response. "It's my version of you. You must look at it that way, or else you paint your own picture. One way or another."

"I'll take it this way. I'm no artist, and whatever I think I know, one day it'll hang in the National Gallery next to the Rembrandts and Picassos."

Marco smiled. "Well, perhaps not next to the Rembrandts." Still he had accepted Ahmet's invitation, a command really, more out of curiosity than anything. He wanted to know what the bastard was up to this time.

Lucy was out of the picture, safe with Martha. Marshmallows was gone and would never rise from its ashes. Angie was safe in a rehab facility found and paid for by Marco. Mehitabel was no longer around, which caused Marco to think the worst, but even then he couldn't believe Ahmet would simply have gotten rid of her. Not in that way, anyhow. He'd probably simply fired her, sent her out into the real world to fend for herself. It was the kind of thing the man would do. "Cruel" was too soft a word to describe Ahmet.

The MV *Lady Marina* was moored in the Aegean Sea, just off the Turkish coast. The lights of the port of Fethiye glimmered in the distance and the air was so clear that through the darkness Ahmet could see his small plane, bearing Marco, coming in to land.

He sighed, as he raised a hand to summon a servant, a man in the *Lady Marina* uniform of white shirt, white shorts, and white deck shoes. There would be no scratches on his boat from idiots wearing loafers and heels; you came here barefoot, or in boat shoes, that was it. His signal alerted the two men standing behind him, awaiting his wishes.

"Tequila." He gave the order in a loud, clear voice.

They obeyed instantly, and in minutes were back with a galleried silver tray holding two bottles of tequila from which to choose: Patron Silver, or a pure agave. Ahmet indicated the Patron, accepted the highball glass they filled halfway, topped off with ice and a twist of lime.

He settled back in his chair and took a long drink, savoring it while at the same time keeping an eye on the plane, which had now landed. The jolly little golf cart with the red-tasseled canopy was waiting as Marco stepped out and stood, looking around.

Picking up his binoculars, Ahmet kept Marco in his sights as he got into the golf cart with the two bodyguards and drove rapidly to the water's edge where the Riva awaited. Ahmet put away the binoculars and took the Beretta from his belt. It would be so easy simply to take care of Marco right now. One clean shot and he would be gone. A nuisance no more. No more prying, poking his nose into affairs that did not concern him. Minding other people's business was, Ahmet knew from experience, not a good thing.

He wondered exactly how much Marco did know about his business. Quite a lot, he suspected; perhaps he was even onto his money laundering activities, global in scale, with connections from here practically to eternity. By now, he'd probably have guessed about the drug running, though he would certainly have no way to prove that. And of course he knew about his play for Lucy. Marco had removed Lucy from his clutches. And Angie.

Ahmet understood Lucy was with Martha. But where was Angie? Gone to the dark side of the moon. With all Ahmet's contacts, his friends in wrong places, he had failed to find her, and Angie was the one person who could destroy him. She knew everything, her story would be sensational. Angie Morse could still ruin him.

He sipped his tequila, watching the Riva get closer, the wake spraying behind. The Beretta was in the right pocket of his white linen jacket. He knew how to use it. The only question was would he.

The Riva pulled up alongside. He drained his glass, then got to his feet, and strode to where the steps had been lowered into the water.

Marco caught his eye as he clambered from the boat, until finally they stood on deck, face to face.

"Well, Ahmet, here I am," Marco said. "It had better be worth it."

"Unlike your portrait, this time it will be."

Marco smiled. Ahmet was the eternal rich kid, never satisfied with what he'd got.

"Come, let's sit over here." Ahmet waved him to the stern where cushioned banquettes in a blue-green that matched the color of the sea awaited, next to small tables, candlelit of course, with one of the white-jacketed waiters, ready to serve.

"Tequila all right with you?" Ahmet lifted his glass to show Marco. "It's what I'm drinking."

Marco refused; he thought he'd better keep his head. He had no idea why he'd been invited here. Martha had not wanted him to go. Ahmet was unpredictable, he was a dangerous man who had lost what he had been searching for all his life. *Acceptance.* He had also lost his home. And he had lost Lucy, who, in fact, he'd never had. He had even lost Angie, the girl he'd lusted after, and God only knew what had happened to Mehitabel, who had simply disappeared. As, Marco was sure, had many others who'd had the misfortune to have dealings with Ahmet Ghulbian, who he realized had lost everything, except his money. He understood now why he was here; he needed to know the truth.

He took a seat on the blue-green cushions and asked for a bottle of Heineken, though he would not drink it.

"So, sir," he said, looking into Ahmet's eyes, still covered by the goddamn dark glasses.

Of course Ahmet noticed. He took them off. "That's better, now we can see each other clearly. See what each is thinking, even." He laughed. "I always find that useful, but tonight it will be more useful for you. First, I want to tell you about my project."

With a flick of a finger, he summoned the servant, who was there in an instant, refilling his glass, adding fresh ice. The night was very dark, no moon, only the distant lights of Fethiye twinkling along the coast, then suddenly there was the slap of water against the hull as the big yacht began to move smoothly through the sea. Marco had not expected this, he looked with alarm at Ahmet, who smiled back, as though enjoying a joke.

"No need to worry, it's simply a whim of mine, I so enjoy being on the water at night. I thought, a trip around the harbor and back, that's the way the pleasure boats describe it at seaside resorts. That's all, Marco. I can assure you, no harm will come to you." He kept his hand on the Beretta in his pocket while he smiled.

"I have a question," Marco said. "What did the red-haired girl mean to you? What was so important about her?"

"Important? Angie? Well, yes, in a way I suppose you are right, she was important, simply because I could not break her. No matter what I did, no matter what happened, that girl came through. Water, marshes, fire, imprisonment . . . she came out of it all. Now, you have to admire a girl like that, right, Marco?"

Marco remained silent.

"And then there was Mehitabel, who I did manage to take care of in a slightly more permanent way. It's not good business to have a woman that close to you, knowing your every move, wanting what you've got. Envy is one of the great sins, Marco, as I'm sure you also know. And by the way, do not bother about a second portrait of me, I'm leaving this one to the National Gallery, where I'm sure it will be treasured for years."

"You're not leaving anything to anyone yet," Marco said.

Ahmet sighed as he took another swig of the tequila, motioned again for a refill.

"What would you say if I told you that I've never had an emotional relationship?"

Marco thought the question did not demand an answer. He took a sip of the beer. It was ice cold. His hand was freezing just from holding it.

"Because of that," Ahmet went on, "I have decided to leave my fortune, such as it is, to my newly created project. It's called the New Souls Foundation and every penny will go to support it. Its work will be to help young people, especially young men, the lost souls we see on the streets of the world, to attain a better, more meaningful life."

Marco did not believe what he was saying and was wondering what exactly he was up to; what he wanted to gain from it. Again, he said nothing.

"So, there you have it." Ahmet got to his feet. He stood over Marco, staring down at him. "You have no idea how I envy you," he said.

He put the glass of tequila he had been clutching on the small table, turned and looked up at the sky, moonless, cloudless, an infinity of sky.

Marco watched as he walked to the stern, stood staring down into the blue-black sea that seemed to be part of the night, and the cool froth of the white wake, at the endless sameness of it all. And then Ahmet stepped off the deck into the water.

"My God!" Marco yelled out.

The guards came running, the yacht slowed down, swung around, returned to the spot where he had jumped. They circled for hours, joined by the coast guard helicopters, uniformed men in powerful boats, a diving crew. Nothing.

It was as though Ahmet had never lived. He had certainly never belonged.

68

Six months later, Lucy was sitting on an uncomfortable little faux-wicker chair in a corner café in Paris's St. Germain, sipping, not so delicately because after all she was still Lucy, a large café crème piled with whipped cream while at the same time devouring a pretty pastel-colored macaron that tasted of raspberries.

Martha sat opposite, with a more sedate espresso into which, unable to resist temptation, she dipped a macaron. Em slumped under the table, having already devoured her own macaron, "for being a good dog," Lucy, who had given it to her, explained. Truth to tell, Martha could not quite believe all this was real. They had almost lost Lucy, had gone through the hell of fire and devastation, and, before he died, the attacks of the expensive lawyers sent by Ahmet Ghulbian, denying any connection to the events of that night at Marshmallows, or anything else that might have been said to have taken place.

There was, after all, no evidence linking him with Angie Morse. And Mehitabel, the woman who might have been able to tell the truth of the matter, had disappeared, without, as the police said, a trace. It was assumed she had perished in the flames as Marshmallows burned, though no remains were ever found.

Looking at her sister, sitting opposite, so fair, so young, so . . . unwounded by all that had happened, Martha thanked heaven Lucy was so basically strong, and thanked the parents who had made her that way.

She and Marco were living together in Paris now, and Lucy had come to stay before beginning a chef's course. Miraculously, considering all that had happened and Lucy's talent for escaping responsibility, she had suddenly found a way in life. It was what she needed, and "chef" loomed as a possibility on the horizon. The Tunisian had become a friend who also gave her lessons on the side while he was working.

Marco had a new Paris studio. He had moved on from portraits into what he called his own heart, a new direction of creativity. A freedom, he called it.

And Martha was working on a house in the south of France, near Villefranche-sur-Mer, an old farm she had been commissioned to refurbish. She was in love with it, and in love with life, and grateful for everything because she had come so close to having it all taken away from her. But life had moved on. They were free now, and always would be.

69

ANGIE

Sometimes, though not as often now as time passes and the memories recede, I ask myself, Why me? Why was I picked out to be Ahmet's victim? I am sure there were others, though nothing has been said, formally, and no investigations made, because of course a "disappearance" does not constitute a crime; you need a body for that and fortunately I did not become "a body" as I'd feared when I was pushed off that yacht into the deep cobalt and azure Aegean Sea. It's then I wonder what happened to Mehitabel, what Ahmet did to her, how he got rid of her. Her shoes were found, of course, by the side of the tidal river, and it was thought she might have been trapped.

I'm changing my thoughts now, my behavior, my life. I'm on my way to becoming that person my mother wanted me to be. In a coffee shop, I still haven't gone up in the world, yet, anyway, working sometimes 'til midnight, but this time it is to earn money for college, which hopefully looms in my future.

I thank God I have a future. I even have an apartment on a nice quiet street in Greenwich Village, owned by a friend of Marco's, but which I have permanent designs on for myself.

Once I finish college, of course, and eventually become a teacher. Not little kids, it's the big ones I want, the tough teens in the tough neighborhoods. I reckon I can teach them a thing or two, with my experience.

I ask myself how can a woman like me have such aspirations? No background, no money, but now I have a sense of myself I never had before.

Am I wounded by it? Of course I am. Can I put it in the past? Sometimes. Do I think about it often? Not as much anymore. After all, it's not the kind of memory you want to keep for those long nights alone in bed with only your thoughts for company.

Maybe that will change too, soon. There is someone on my horizon, a teacher, a few years older, a whole lot wiser.

And now I have my friends: Marco, my savior; Martha, my angel in disguise; Lucy, who is so silly sometimes and so lovable, and under it all far cleverer than we suspect, who comes over to practice her cooking on me whenever she is in town.

I envied Marco his dog, so much I even got one of my own. Small, whippet thin, skinny little legs, russet color, alert eyes, and an underbite that exposes his bottom teeth in a permanent smile. A joke of a dog.

I found it, as Marco had found his, outside a café. It did not ask for food, it simply sat there waiting. Trusting. When I got up and walked away, it followed. I said goodbye, but it persisted. And I knew it—she, Rusty—belonged.

I have my life. I have friends, a dog. I have a future. One way or another, what more can a girl want?

Read on for an excerpt from
Elizabeth Adler's next novel

THE CHARMERS

Coming soon from Minotaur Books

PROLOGUE

———

THE PAINTING
WALTER MATTHEWS
April 14, 1912

Walter "Iron Man" Matthews was propping up the first-class bar on the new luxury liner, the RMS *Titanic,* as it plowed steadily through the Atlantic. There were no waves, no wind. The ocean was flat as a board. A faint haze hung over it, under a sky so glittering with stars it outshone the great ship's own lights.

He was downing a double Macallan whiskey, his preferred pre-dinner tipple wherever he was in the world, be it on a boat or in a London drawing room, in a Manhattan penthouse or a canoe floating down the Amazon, because, of course, in places like the jungle one must always take one's own supplies. It was the only civilized way, even though in the jungle one's boots might be attacked by fire ants, and in the drawing room one's soul attacked by someone's unlovely daughter "tinkling the ivories" as they called it, without a speck of emotion.

He placed the painting on the bar. It was a river scene by the artist J. M. W. Turner. He had fallen in love with its misty colors.

It was professionally wrapped in waterproof covering.

"Just in case, sir," the art dealer had said with a faint smile. "One can never trust the ocean."

Quite right, Walt thought now as he became aware of a grinding noise and a sideways lurch that sent his glass sliding half the length of the mahogany bar and almost into the lap of another fellow. He waved an apologetic hand even as he slid from his seat because there was no more traction to hold him in place. Gravity had shifted and with it the enormous, new unsinkable ship.

He was one of the first on deck. It was bitterly cold. A white cliff loomed beside them. They had struck an iceberg, formed by the cold waves of the Labrador Current mixing with the warm waters of the Gulf Stream.

Ever the gentleman, he helped the ladies into the constantly moving lifeboats that lifted and dropped with the movement of the ship. He never let go of his painting though, kept it tucked inside his dinner jacket. He had been about to go down for dinner and of course had dressed appropriately for his position in first-class. He kind of regretted the dinner; it would have been good, solid fare, a bit Frenchified perhaps as they often were on the big ships, but he enjoyed that. And he regretted the Macallan, which had spilled all over the place, including on his hand-tailored Soames and Whitby jacket, even staining his pristine white shirt cuffs that were linked with circles of gold and sapphire, matching the studs in his starched white shirtfront.

The situation was disastrous, he knew it; recognized what fate had in store for all of them; heard the screams of the terrified women on the lower decks, the wails of children and infants, the cursing of the seamen attempting to get the insufficient lifeboats lowered from the constantly shifting ship.

Now, the ship slipped even lower, tilted, stern up. The lifeboats already in the water pulled away, afraid to be caught in the whirling downward current as the liner quickly began to sink.

"Mr. Matthews, sir, come this way." An officer grabbed his arm, tugged him toward the ladder over the side, leading into a small dinghy. But Walt stepped back when a young woman ran toward them, screams dying in her throat, fear written across her face.

Here," he said, grabbing her arm, "now jump." And he gave her an almighty shove that sent her dropping feetfirst into the orange dinghy.

"Jump yourself, sir," the officer beckoned him from the dinghy.

But Walt could see it was already overloaded and, holding the painting over his head with one hand, he jumped into the icy depths. The winter temperature was minus two degrees. He might last, at most, fifteen minutes. He grabbed onto the dinghy's rope with his free hand, splashing his already-numb feet in his good crawl stroke, wondering if this was, in fact, the end. How ironic, he told himself. And how much he would have enjoyed that dinner.

He knew he could last no more than ten minutes. But then, quite suddenly, from one moment to the next, the water grew substantially warmer, certainly now above freezing.

The warm Gulf Stream current was what saved him. He was picked up several hours later, along with the few other survivors and taken aboard a passing cruiser, the *Carpathia*, where he was revived with brandy and hot blankets, after which he took to his bed—a small lower bunk in a lower cabin—and, with the painting stashed under his pillow, slept the sleep of the saved. He was one of the few.

The painting would some years later end up in the rose-silken boudoir of his mistress and love of his life, the wonderful, beautiful, well, almost beautiful, if you looked at her the right way—the glorious Jerusha.

Part One

THE PRESENT

1

Antibes, South of France

The Boss, as he was called by everyone, even those that did not work for him and merely knew his reputation, strode purposefully past the seafront terrace bars until he came to the one he favored, where he pulled a chair from a table in the third row back, closest to the building. He always liked to face the street, the crowds, the other customers, keep his back against the wall, so to speak. Backs were vulnerable, his particularly so.

Despite the heat he was comfortable in white linen pants and a blue-and-white-print shirt, sleeves rolled up over his muscular forearms. His watch was neither gold nor flashy, though it was certainly expensive.

The chairs were small for a man his size, big, built like a wrestler. Most chairs were, except of course for the ones specifically crafted for his many homes. He was a man who liked his comforts, and coming from his background, who could blame him? Though you could blame him for the way he'd gone about getting them.

The waiter recognized him. Smiling, obsequious, linen

napkin draped over an arm, and tray in hand, he inquired what his pleasure might be.

Lemonade was the answer. The Boss did not drink liquor, not even wine in this wine-growing country. The estates around St. Tropez in particular produced a benign, gently flavored rosé that slid down comfortably with a good lunch of lobster salad, or with the crisp and very fresh vegetables served raw with a house-made mayonnaise dip. They crunched between the teeth and had the added benefit of making the eater feel virtuous at not having had the hearty sandwich on the delicious locally baked bread many others were tucking into.

The lemonade came immediately, along with a bowl of ice and a spoon so he might help himself, decide how cold he wanted it, how diluted. He took a sip, and nodded to the waiter, who asked if there would be anything else. The waiter was told that there was not, but that he was expecting someone. He should be shown immediately to the table.

The Boss's original Russian name was Boris Boronovsky, which he had changed some time ago to a more satisfactorily acceptable European Bruce Bergen, though he looked nothing like a "Bruce." He had a massive build, exactly, he had been told, like that of a Cossack from the Steppes: mighty on a horse, saber in hand, ready to take on the enemy. Yet his face was lean, with craggy cheekbones and deep-set eyes, lined from a lifetime of scouting for danger, which was all around. In his world it was anyway. And now at the international property level where land was fought over for the millions it would bring, that danger was ever-present. He knew always to look over his shoulder.

The Boss certainly took on the enemy, though not in an overtly aggressive fashion. He was more discreet, more subtle, more specific in his methods. He had always known, even as a child growing up—or more like existing—in the cold cabin outside the town of Minsk in Belarus, that he was destined for better things. No forest cabin for him, no logging trees, risking life and limb with a power saw; no dragging great lumps of wood still oozing sap onto a tractor so old it no longer functioned and was pulled instead by two donkeys with long faces like biblical animals in Renaissance frescoes. There was just something about those donkeys that made Boris think that, like in the paintings, they should have golden halos over their heads. Sometimes there was an unexpected tenderness in him, odd in such a brutal man.

The donkeys worked hard, were obedient to his commands, alert when he gave them food, drank from the stone trough when he permitted them to stop, thin sides shivering, ribs sticking out. Until one day they were not pulling hard anymore, their heads drooped with weariness, too weak to go on. He shot them where they stood, butchered them, sold the meat door-to-door in the town as fresh venison. Nobody knew the difference, or if they did they never said because Boris was intimidating, with his height, his massive build, his intense dark stare.

It wasn't long before he realized the power that stare and his very presence brought to any scene, whether it was the local market or the city streets. He was from a poor family who'd given him a brief education and strived to elevate him in society. He would certainly have become moderately successful, a big fish in a small pond, but the one element in Boris's character that no one perceived but himself was that he was capable of doing anything. Anything at all to further his ascent into the larger world he knew existed and that he wanted to be part of. More than part of; he wanted to own it. As he wanted to own the women in his life. Besides, he enjoyed intimidating women, liked to see fear in their eyes. It pleased him.

There was only one way to leave, and it was not out the front door.

It had taken several years existing in a number of Ukrainian towns, then on through Poland, Hungary, Croatia, and ultimately France, before he achieved his goals. And the place where he was most comfortable, of all the homes he owned, was the sprawling villa overlooking the Mediterranean in the hills in the South of France. Which is where he was now, in Antibes, at the café, sipping lemonade iced just sufficiently to his taste, awaiting the arrival of the man known merely as "the Russian."

Everybody in the Boss's world had a name that was not the one they were given by their parents at birth. Those were long forgotten, buried like their enemies, or their victims, long ago. The Boss had given up carrying out any such distasteful tasks himself. Now, he employed men like the Russian to do them for him.

But the Russian was late. The Boss tapped his fingers impatiently on the table and the waiter popped up immediately next to him. He waved him off as he saw the Russian wending his way through the tables to where he was sitting. He was a plain man, undistinguished in any way, which was crucial to his job. Nobody ever recognized him, nobody so much as remembered him. Medium height, medium hair, maybe receding a bit, glasses sometimes with wire rims, sometimes horn-rims, sometimes no rims at all. Often a Panama hat, open-neck shirt, never a tie unless it was a city job. Inexpensive jacket but not too obviously cheap, after all he made good money doing what he did. Didn't like to flaunt it on the job, was all.

He took a seat opposite the Boss, offered his hand, which the Boss did not shake. Stung, the Russian called over the waiter, ordered a dirty martini, two olives. It was barely eleven-thirty A.M. and the Boss did not like it. A man who drank could be a dangerous man. He waved the waiter back, canceled the order, said to bring a double espresso and be sharp about it.

The Russian made no complaint, he knew better. He sat quietly, listening, as the Boss told him what he wanted done. "There is a house in the hills nearby. In fact you can see it from here." He pointed across the arc of the bay to the greenery beyond, and a glimpse of a pink stucco villa. "In that house is a painting. Small. The artist's name is Turner. The woman who owned the house died recently."

The Russian nodded. He knew about Jolly Matthews's death.

"I immediately made an offer to buy the whole property, the hectares of land adjoining it, plus the contents, including artworks, most of which in my mind are worthless, but that the old woman enjoyed all her life. She was a social acquaintance, known to all as Aunt Jolly though her real name was Juliet Matthews. When she passed, I made contact with the legal representatives of the heir, a woman by the name of Mirabella Matthews. A writer of some kind of entertaining novels."

The Boss was a snob about both art and literature, though he scarcely read anything other than the local newspaper, the *Nice-Matin*, and *The Wall Street Journal*.

"The heir, through her representative, has refused to sell. I wish to build a fourteen-story condo on that property. I increased my offer considerably. Meanwhile, through subtle means, I found out the details of the contents, and that the one piece of real value is that painting. I want it for my collection. I cannot get it by legal means. Therefore, I am asking you to take care of this task for me."

The Russian nodded. It was the kind of work he did. None of it was legal, none of it could be mentioned, most of it was lucrative. He had removed jewels from vaults, pearls from necks, cars from underground garages. Everything had a value and there was always somebody willing to pay.

"I'll get you the painting," he said.

The Boss named a price. The Russian shook his head. "It's not the value of the painting," he said, then added, "sir," as compensation for what he was about to say. "It's what it's worth to you."

"It is worth everything," the Boss said. And it was. He wanted that land and the painting the bitch, Jolly Matthews, had denied him in her lifetime. He would have both now that she was dead. Of course the police were looking into her death, and rightly so, because obviously, with a knife in her back, she had been murdered.

Perhaps a robbery, the police were speculating. Maybe the house was turned over, that sort of thing. They'd never traced that knife, though. There were millions like it and the Russian knew every source. Jolly Matthews had gotten in the Boss's way, triumphed over him in life but not in death. All he had to do now was get his hands on her property.

Architectural plans were already drawn up, documents were ready to be submitted for planning permission, already promised and paid for, of course. Millions would be made by everybody, though the green hillside would disappear under a plague of small villas, most of which would be bought by people who intended them to be rented out and everybody knew that in a couple of years rental properties often became shabby and neglected, and would downgrade the area.

The Boss did not care about the future. He would make money from each part of the deal: the sale of the land, the construction of the buildings, the sale of those properties, the infrastructure—roads, water, electricity. And to top it all would be the fourteen-story apartment building, the max allowed even to him in the restricted area, and the top three floors, which would become for a few years his new home. His would be a magnificent view down to the sea, of the yachts, the palm trees, a view better than most everyone's. Not all though, because this was a rich man's playground, yet certainly better than many of his soon-to-be neighbors.

And to highlight it, he wanted the Turner. Of course he could buy any painting he desired, and had. His walls were already adorned with a couple of Picassos, maybe not the best because they were, even for him, hard to come by and usually went through private, almost secretive sales. He had a few Impressionists, as well as some Italians: a Raphael, a Caravaggio, whatever his advisors recommended. None of them impressed him but they were expected of a man in his position. This Turner painting had become an obsession and he was a man who got what he wanted.

Right now, the thing he liked best of all that he owned was the fifty-foot Riva he sailed himself, at top speed the length of the coast from Marseille to Menton, leaving other boats awash in the great surge of its wake. There'd been a few insurance claims as a result but of course he'd settled quietly, out of court. In that sense, he was a man of his word, and held respect for his fellow sailors.

He was aware, though, of how impressive he looked to those in the passing boats, with his great height, his white captain's cap with the gold braid and navy-blue anchor, his sun-browned chest, shaved-off hair so he did not quite resemble a bear, which is what some woman had told him, mocking him, while he ran his heavy hands over her own lithe body.

Actually, he had liked the comparison; he'd chuckled over it, looking at himself in the mirror over the bed, a great bear, full of power. That was him.

And he wanted his condos on that land, and the painting, the Turner, on his wall. Everything Jolly Matthews had denied him in life would be his now that she was dead. And if that meant removing Mirabella Matthews from the scene, so be it.